Nora Magnessen awoke feeling happy.

It was not hard to be happy in the warmth of her husband's love. Viktor and she had much to be thankful for. They'd been accepted in Cana, and their children had grown up in the security of the town.

Even her son Paul, who was not Viktor's child, was now married to a local girl and working to build her ranch into a kind of Sun Valley resort. Their daughter Alice was on her own and doing well. Even young Mitch was discovering himself. Nora just wished Janet would stop her rebellion, but that would come too, she felt certain . . .

But nothing in life is certain, Nora!
At this moment, in his bedroom, the
new owner of the lumber mill has awakened.
David Rosenzweig has seen Viktor Magnesson at a
party and thinks, perhaps, he has seen him before—
when that shock of white hair was blond
and when people were gathered together.
but not for a party . . .

Other Books
by Frances Casey Kerns

A Cold, Wild Wind
The Stinsons
*The Winter Heart**
*This Land Is Mine**

*available from WARNER BOOKS

ATTENTION: SCHOOLS AND CORPORATIONS

WARNER books are available at quantity discounts with bulk purchase for educational, business, or sales promotional use. For information, please write to: SPECIAL SALES DEPARTMENT, WARNER BOOKS, 75 ROCKEFELLER PLAZA, NEW YORK, N.Y. 10019

**ARE THERE WARNER BOOKS
YOU WANT BUT CANNOT FIND IN YOUR LOCAL STORES?**

You can get any WARNER BOOKS title in print. Simply send title and retail price, plus 50¢ per order and 10¢ per copy to cover mailing and handling costs for each book desired. New York State and California residents add applicable sales tax. Enclose check or money order only, no cash please, to: WARNER BOOKS, P.O. BOX 690, NEW YORK, N.Y. 10019

Cana and Wine

Frances Casey Kerns

WARNER BOOKS

A Warner Communications Company

WARNER BOOKS EDITION

Copyright © 1979 by Frances Casey Kerns
All rights reserved.

ISBN 0-446-82951-X

Cover art by Elaine Duillo

Warner Books, Inc., 75 Rockefeller Plaza, New York, N.Y. 10019

A Warner Communications Company

Printed in the United States of America

Not associated with Warner Press, Inc., of Anderson, Indiana

First Printing: June, 1979

10 9 8 7 6 5 4 3 2 1

*For my sisters
Audrey and Lucille
and
For Minnie Kerns*

1

Nora Magnessen woke five minutes before the alarm clock rang. Daylight was coming, but it was still dark enough in the bedroom to make the clock's luminescent dial worthwhile. She stretched, pushing the button so the alarm wouldn't ring, and then lay still a few minutes. This was one of her little luxuries. Unlike Viktor, she was not a person who could come full-awake and be out of bed all in a single motion —unless, of course, there was something startling, demanding her immediate attention, a child's crying or the ringing of the telephone.

Viktor was not beside her now, but he often got up first. He loved the early morning, winter or summer. Nora, on the other hand, tended to feel more pleased with the day, almost any day, when it got to be a little past eight, or on toward nine.

She lay there listening to the birds who had all seemed to come awake at once in a burst of enthusiasm, singing, flitting noisily about from tree to shrub to roof. The light was brightening by the minute now and the little breeze through the window gave promise of a hot day, though it was still cool enough in the bedroom that the sheet and bedspread felt good. She could smell roses on the breeze. They were in the glory of their bloom now.

If she got up right now, she could watch the sun come up over the eastern ridge of mountains far across the hills and farmlands of the Alder Valley. Nora smiled a little, lying still. She was a comfortable woman who, on occasion, chided herself for being perhaps just a little too complacent, but she was thinking lazily that she had seen many sunrises and that there would be opportunities for seeing many more.

A truck was coming along Tamarack Road, their road, stopping with the motor idling, then moving on. That would be Joe Withers, the milkman. Nora had heard that in most larger towns and cities home delivery of milk was a thing of the past, but she hoped Joe would last forever. If Viktor was in the house, which he probably wasn't, and the coffee was ready, which it probably was, he and Joe might have a cup together while Joe's old truck idled erratically in the drive. But no, Nora thought she heard voices around at the back of the house—Viktor would be in the garden—and Joe came back soon to move his old truck on down to the Adams house. Except for the fading sound of the truck and the increasing, energetic clamor of the birds, it was quiet again. Nora thought she'd probably better get up, but there was not much conviction in the thought, and she lay a little longer.

Probably the difference in her and Viktor's sleeping and waking habits, she mused lazily, was a result of childhood training and habit. Viktor had grown up on a farm, his grandfather's farm in Denmark, and she, Nora Mitchell then, had always lived in town. Granted, Fox Falls, Iowa, had been no larger than Cana, Idaho, on whose outskirts she now lay musing, but when Nora had been a little girl, even a growing-up adolescent, her father had been one of the wealthiest men in Fox Falls, the owner of a small plant that made farm machinery parts, and there had been no reason for Jim Mitchell's only child to get up before the sun. In those days there had been a maid and all manner of luxuries—that is, they were luxuries so far as Fox Falls was concerned.

But the plant had been lost. Nora's father had suffered a long, painful, and terribly expensive illness before his death in 1940. Nora had been fifteen then, when the plant had to be sold, and Ken Jorgensen, who bought it for less than it was worth, had made a good-sized fortune from war work. Nora and her mother were left with nothing but the big old house on Jefferson Street, but Mama, Alice Malloy Mitchell, had never been one to give up. She turned the place into a fine boardinghouse. No maids now; no sleeping until the last possible minute before schooltime. Just Alice and Nora to cook and clean and do all the rest of the work, and Alice determined that Nora *would* finish high school. Nora had finished. By that time, war was raging, and there was a long list of people eager and waiting to be tenants at Mrs. Mitchell's.

Nora threw off the covers now, a little impatient with herself. What was all this going back to girlhood? She was fifty-one years old, mother, grandmother, wife of a man who had done every bit as well as her father in business and was a kinder, gentler, more overtly loving man than Jim Mitchell had ever been.

She slipped into a robe, went to the bathroom, and stood brushing her slightly wavy brown hair, hardly thinking to notice the growing streaks of gray. I'm going back in my mind, she thought with a little wry smile, because Viktor Magnessen is a partner of Alder Valley Lumber and Hardware; he is almost sixty-six years old; he has worked so very hard all his life and he still won't sleep past sunup on a Saturday morning or any other day. I remember Daddy worked hard too, but he did know how to relax, sometimes. But what in the world would happen to us, both of us, if Viktor decided to retire? Well, thank goodness, in Cana there were very few places that insisted on a mandatory retirement age, and certainly it couldn't happen to Viktor in his own business—his own half-business.

Nora had heard that they were thinking of being unionized over at the Holland Mill, taking on all those rules like mandatory retirement. It was not the Holland Mill now, of course, had not been for more than two years, but it would take a long time for Cana to begin calling it anything else. The mill was owned now by a man named Rosenzweig, a rather strange man, an "outsider," whom no one could seem to get to know, or maybe they just didn't try, Cana could be that way. Still, it had been the Holland Mill for three generations, and Holland was much easier to say.

Nora put her feet into the fluffy slippers Patty had given her for Christmas. They would be too warm soon, but just now the floors were too cold for walking around barefoot.

She heard the newspaper hit the front screen and looked out in time to wave to the Hendrix boy pedaling away on his bicycle, dark hair glowing with the new sun. He seemed too young for the paper route, especially when it was winter, but she supposed he must be thirteen or fourteen. Mitch had had a route at that age, and before him, young Viktor. Always, when she thought of their dead son, Nora had to control an impulse to rush to Patty's room, or to wherever Patty might be, just to look at her, to make sure she was all right. Instead, now, she stood on at the window for just a moment and looked out to the south and east across Cana from the eminence of the gradual hill up which Tamarack Road climbed as it ran northwest away from the town. Cana was a nice town, something like twenty-five hundred people. About all that was visible to Nora among the full-leafed, late-June trees were the mill's smokestack and a few church steeples. Several vehicles were moving now a few blocks down the hill on the highway. She could catch a glint of sun on each as it passed the intersection. There would be extra tourists and old-timers in town this week. The following weekend was Fourth of July, the country's true Bicentennial day, and all next week, beginning tomorrow, had been declared Cana Centennial Week to celebrate the hundredth anniversary of the little town's founding.

Unconsciously, Nora ticked things off on her

fingers. Alice home on vacation. Faye Holland due back in town any day now. The party at the country club tonight, which Paul insisted they attend, then that big get-together he and Sharon were having up at Cloud Valley in a few days ... one of the busiest weeks in a long time, officially beginning tomorrow, but Nora had a lot to do today. She left the bedroom feeling good, eager for the day, the week, the summer, but not in any great useless rush about any of it. That was the kind of person Nora Magnessen was.

On her way to the stairs, she tapped softly at Mitch's door. It wouldn't do any good, of course. Mitch wouldn't be wakened by the trumpets on Judgment Day, but it seemed the polite thing to do now that he was a grown man, nineteen, her baby.

She opened the door and called him. No movement. Mitch was as tall as his father, and broader, with Viktor's blond hair, tousled now with the covers half over his head.

"Mitch!" She shook his shoulder. It wasn't easy.

"Huh? Wha . . ." He opened one deep blue eye and let it fall closed again.

"You said to wake you so you could go to the store with Dad."

"Oh. . . . Oh, yeah ... okay."

"I'm going to fix breakfast."

"Okay, Mom, I'll be down."

He burrowed his deeply tanned face into the pillow, and Nora left him. Maybe he would get up, maybe not. She rather hoped he would sleep a while. He only got home about once a month now and he had been out late last night. Viktor always liked to be at the store around eight, though they didn't open until nine. People sometimes kidded him about sweeping out, but it was no joke. He often did it.

Theirs was a good old house, well-built and sturdy, with a comfortable, friendly personality all its own. Twenty-three years ago when they'd bought it, it had already been more than thirty years old. Except for normal upkeep and a few redecorations, they had made few changes. Nora stepped over the creaky board at the top of the stairs—the one the kids tried to avoid for their own various reasons late at night. She thought, as she had been thinking for the past year or so, that the downstairs hall and the kitchen ought to be repainted. Well, all things in their season.

Yes. Viktor was out there in the vegetable garden beyond the backyard. He turned toward the house as she watched and she mouthed that the coffee was ready. Good grief! He was cutting corn! Now she'd have to get it ready for the freezer with all the other things there were to be done today.

Mixing biscuit batter, Nora could still see through the big kitchen window out across the back part of their property. It was a pretty piece of land, a good big lawn with trees and shrubs and flower beds, the vegetable garden and a number of fruit trees and, at the very back, little Tamarack Creek, just emerging from its miniature sandy canyon, where the children—theirs and the whole neighborhood's—had had accidents, fights, and such years of fun.

Viktor's hair shone in the sun as he came up

toward the house with two great basketsful of corn. His once light ash-blond hair was white now, not gray or yellowish, but a beautiful, thick, slightly curly white. There was no stoop to his tall, broad-shouldered body, and he walked quickly and easily. Nora knew there would be pleasure in his squarish, blue-eyed face; he loved the corn because he had helped it grow, he loved the morning, he loved living. He left the corn on the back porch and carried in the milk, eggs, and butter Joe Withers had left.

"I knew you wouldn't want to freeze the corn tomorrow, it being Sunday," he said a little apologetically, kissing her cheek, "and by Monday, it would not have been at its best."

"I'll get it done," said Nora, unruffled, returning his kiss. She had never really quite gotten used to Viktor's accent, to the pleasure of hearing his deep, calm voice. It was not much of an accent now; he had been in America almost thirty years, but she loved it and had never quite come to take it for granted.

"I didn't bring in the paper yet," she said.

"I'll get it." He was pouring cups of coffee for both of them.

"You know, Viktor, we really ought to paint this kitchen, and the hall."

"When we can get to it."

"Well, I sort of wish we'd got it done. I mean it would be nice to have it new for the Centennial and everything. I don't know *why* I didn't get it done. I thought sure I'd do it before school was out, but time just passed...."

"You needn't do things like that, Nora," he said. "I'll do it, maybe next weekend."

"Next weekend's Fourth of July and all the special celebrating."

"Yes, well, I'm not interested much in those things. Maybe—"

"Daddy!" It was Alice, hurrying into the kitchen. Alice usually hurried and her voice was often a little imperious, though overlaid by tones of love and patience. "By next weekend—after next weekend—all the big celebrating will be over for Cana."

"We're not having much of it here," he pointed out calmly, bending for her kiss on his cheek.

Alice had arrived home only yesterday on vacation, but already one could feel the house and household beginning to tighten up a little as things tried to fall into place for Alice. Well, Nora thought, she was named for my mother, and my mother was a manager and an organizer, all right, but I can't remember Mama being as *busy* about other people as our Alice.

"What I'm trying to say," Alice was saying as she gave her mother a quick hug, "is that you should have had the painting done, and a lot of other things all along. I mean *had* them done. My word! It's not as if you're poor. When on earth are you going to start taking things easy?"

"Maybe not on earth," Viktor said dryly.

"But Daddy, you've both always worked *so* hard! When have you ever, *ever* taken Mama on a real vacation?"

Viktor thought about it. "We were in Moscow for your college graduation and your sister's. We stayed two nights in a very nice motel both times."

"Oh!" spluttered Alice, laughing a little in spite of herself. Nora, sliding the biscuits into the oven, smiled to herself.

"You talk as if it had been Moscow, *Russia*," Alice tried to reason.

"And—what was it, Nora? Three years ago?—we went to Denver."

"To a hardware convention," scoffed Alice, losing patience. "Why won't you, after this Centennial fuss is over, come to San Francisco for a nice long visit and let me show you around? And you could go on to Hawaii. . . . Why don't you *retire*, Daddy? It's time."

"I think I'll retire to the front porch and see what's in the paper," he said and left them.

Alice sighed.

"You should have stayed in bed, hon," Nora said. "No need for you to be up so early."

Alice was looking out the back window. "Oh, no! Mama, are you going to have to put that corn up today? I thought you wanted to come with Sharon and me to see about the decorations and things at the country club."

"No, I don't know anything about getting ready for fancy country-club parties. I'll stay home with Patty and Jamie, and, yes, I'll get the corn in the freezer. Besides, I have a feeling your Aunt Faye may get back today and I wouldn't want to miss her. And then there's—"

"Shall I fry the bacon?"

"Well, yes, all right."

Alice often burned bacon, or didn't give it time to get done enough, but she always had to be doing something. She was a tall girl, and graceful when she was not feeling too rushed. She had Nora's brown hair, which she kept very stylishly, and Nora's roundish face, which Alice did not think was very well suited to her own character, and her eyes were brown like her mother's, but more intense, less likely to smile.

"I know why Daddy won't go away this summer," she said worriedly.

She was having trouble separating the bacon strips because she was trying to do it too fast. Nora wanted to offer help, at least advice, but controlled herself and began beating up scrambled eggs.

Alice said bitterly, "It's Janet, isn't it? and that creep. Somebody ought to paddle her bottom."

"We are worried about Janet," Nora admitted slowly, then more brightly, "but we couldn't just start traipsing around, Alice. There's all this special stuff this year and we're finally beginning to feel like old citizens of Cana. There are the things Paul particularly wants us to be here for. And then, before we know it, school will be starting and Patty—"

"Mother, of course you love Patty. We all love Patty, but you've raised your family. You shouldn't feel you have to be tied down by another generation. She could stay with Paul and Sharon."

"Well, I don't know," Nora hedged. "Your dad and Wes are talking about expanding the store again, but we'll talk it over some more when there's time."

"Look at Aunt Faye," Alice urged. (She had the skillet too hot.) "She's been traveling around almost ever since they sold the mill and—"

"She keeps writing she can't wait to get back here and settle down." Nora couldn't help sounding a little triumphant.

17

"Well, you ought to give some things a try. Daddy, at least, is getting on, and you haven't been anywhere."

"Alice, your dad's been all over Europe. He speaks, or he used to speak, four languages besides English. He doesn't want to go back to any of those places, and I'm not interested either. When we moved to Cana, he'd been roaming around for years, except for those five years in Fox Falls after we were married. He said then he hoped we'd never move again and so did I."

"I'm not necessarily talking about moving, Mama, just traveling, *seeing* things while you still both have your health. Why, where have you been? From Iowa to Idaho! What kind of travel is that?"

"Don't you think that's done now?" Nora asked apprehensively, proffering a paper-towel-covered platter. "Here, I'll do the next batch and you relax a minute. You're supposed to be on vacation."

Alice relinquished the fork and perched on a kitchen stool. Her face softened as she looked out the window again. "You know, what really woke me was the birds. I can sleep through traffic and all kinds of city noises, but I'm not used to birds like this anymore. It's nice."

Pipes clanked as the shower was turned on upstairs.

"I guess Mitch did get up after all," said Nora, taking proper care of the bacon.

Alice said dreamily, "Remember when Vik and I used to take Janet and Mitch down to the creek when they were just learning to walk and let them wade? Do we have any pictures like that?"

"Oh, I think we must. There are boxes and boxes of pictures and newspaper clippings and things in the attic."

"Maybe I could go through them, make a kind of family scrapbook or books while I'm home this time. We ought to have things like that."

"Yes, we should. It would be lovely to have all those things put into some kind of order, but you're going to be awfully busy with the Cloud Valley thing and all the rest of it."

"Oh, I'll have to do whatever I can to help. Sharon doesn't really bolster Paul, back him the way she ought to. You remember how Paul used to say he was going to be a millionaire by the time he was thirty? Well, he's thirty-two now, but he'll certainly make it before he's forty if this Cloud Valley thing works out, and I can't see a reason in the world why it shouldn't, except —Sharon."

"That ranch was Sharon's home, Alice. You have to think of that. Her grandfather homesteaded up there. He and Jeff Holland and old Charlie Bonner's father were just about the first white men in this whole valley."

"I know all that, Mama, and I do understand about sentiment and things, but progress is the thing that counts. You move with the times these days, roll with the punches, or you're left behind, wondering what you've done with your life. . . . Even though we're only half-brother and -sister, I think Paul and I may be more alike, understand each other better than any other two people in this family."

"That may very well be true," said Nora gently, pouring the scrambled eggs into the skillet.

19

"Was Paul's father a go-getter sort of person?"

"I thought so once," Nora said quietly. "Of course, I was eighteen then. I knew *that* Paul less than a month, married him, lived with him four months; then he was sent overseas and killed in France." She looked thoughtfully out the window. "I just really can't imagine what I'd think of him now. . . . But what about you, honey? I know you're a go-getter sort of person, but you've hardly said anything about your job since you got home."

"You know I like the job and I love San Francisco. I wrote you a couple of months ago that I've been made office manager. That's a little unusual for a girl who's just twenty-six. Now I wait and watch for an opportunity for the next step up the ladder. Yes, I'm a kind of driving person, but I envy Paul his certainty and daring, the sparkle and verve he has with people. I'll bet he could still sell someone the Brooklyn Bridge. I feel— awkward, self-conscious with strangers. He never seems to."

"But you never know," Nora said thoughtfully, looking into the oven. "It's hardly ever possible to know, with someone else, how much is real and how much is acting, for the sake of whatever they're trying to accomplish."

"Hi, Grandma; hi, Aunt Alice," said Patty, yawning in the doorway.

"Why, honey," said Nora, "you didn't have to get up."

"Yes, I did too. Mitch is in the shower. You know how he splutters and squishes around in there, and he even sings. That's the worst of all. Besides, if Carolyn Adams' mom will let her, we want to spend the day together. At the tree house. Is it okay with you, Granny? Can I drink my juice now? I'm thirsty."

"Drink your juice. You and Carolyn can play in the tree house some of the time, but Jamie's going to be here part of the day and I was hoping you'd help me look after him."

"Sure, we can do that."

"You ought to comb your hair first thing when you get out of bed, Patty," said Alice.

"I'll do it before anybody sees but family," she said blithely. "I'll take Grandpa's juice to him too."

Patty was seven now. Her parents, young Viktor and Anne Dixon from Alder Falls, had married in their first year of college. When Patty was two and spending a night with her grandparents, her parents were killed when a log truck crashed into their car. Patty was very much like her father and grandfather, already showing signs of more than average height for her age, the strong regular features, but there was a hint of red in her light hair as there had been in her mother's, and her eyes were brown. Nora fretted over Patty more than she had over any one of her own children. Why was she ten minutes late from school? Suppose she fell from the tree house? Was the cold really only a cold? Nora tried to squelch the fears and worries by telling herself it was her own age, plus the horror of the parents' accident, and she wanted, more than almost anything, a happy, normal childhood for Patty.

Mitch came in as they were sitting down around the table.

"Well," said Alice, half-teasing, "I'm very surprised to see you up, considering the time you came home last night."

"Were you still awake?" he asked, feigning concern.

"No, I was wakened. You and your friends don't show much concern for other people at three in the morning."

"Alice, you're going to be just a perfect old maid."

"I just wish he wouldn't sing and squiggle so much in the shower," said Patty fervently.

"Pass the butter, please," said Mitch, unperturbed.

"Who were you out with?" asked his sister, then, softening her tone, "Anyone I know?"

"It's really none of your business, but I was with Shane and then some others." He chewed thoughtfully and swallowed. "You know what, Alie, you'd be damn lucky if you could get Shane to marry you."

"Shane *Bonner?*"

"Sure. Do we know any other Shanes? And the only other Bonner is old Charlie. I guess you wouldn't want him."

"When I marry, *if* I marry," Alice said primly, "I want some idea of the stock my husband comes from, some notion of what my children may turn out to be."

"Mmm, yes, quite," said Mitch in straight-faced mock agreement. "Now I suppose you want to know where we went. Well, first we went to see Paul."

They all looked at him now, except Patty, who was planning her own day.

"People in Blackbuck and above there—some

of them—are going to fight this project of Paul's in Cloud Valley."

"Oh, for heaven's sake!" cried Alice. "Environmental reasons, I suppose. And what are you doing, getting mixed up in it? You don't live up there. You don't have any interests. This could make Paul's whole life and you're his brother. Why are you running around with Shane anyway? He's years older than you."

"I work for him, remember, or rather for Charlie. Old Charlie's ready to go take a shotgun to anybody comes up there even looks like a skier or a condominium buyer, but Shane and some others are trying to convince him to work through the system."

"That'll be the day!" spluttered Alice, "if Charlie Bonner tries to turn environmentalist after all the clear-cutting he's done. What on earth do those people think ought to be *done* with that land?"

"It could be left a ranch," Mitch said. "That seems to be what Sharon wants, if anyone ever asked her, or it could be incorporated into the national forest."

"What an absolute *waste!*"

"Please," Mitch said, rubbing his head, "we already got all that from Paul."

"Did you keep him up arguing nonsense until three in the morning?"

"No, he—uh—sort of threw us out, so we fooled around a while at Mack's and places."

"Mitch, when are you going to *do* something with yourself?" she cried in consternation. "You've been out of school well over a year and you're just—frittering."

He grinned. "Maybe I like to fritter. Anyway, you'd think it amounted to a little more than that if you were bucking logs for old C. Bonner."

"That's just seasonal work. What are you doing with your winters?"

"Last winter he went to Arizona," put in Patty. "I'll bet Grandma wrote you a letter about it, Aunt Alice. He worked in a mine and he hated it."

"Aren't you going to college?" pursued Alice.

"Maybe someday," said Mitch carelessly around a mouthful of food. "I can't decide what I'd study. Forestry, maybe."

"Why? Are you hero-worshiping Shane Bonner or something? Isn't it a forest degree he's got? And what's he doing with it? Cutting and hauling logs."

"His degree's in wildlife management," Mitch said, looking at her sharply. "What have you got against Shane all of a sudden? He was Vik's best friend and he's always been around here a lot, ever since they moved down so he could go to high school. I used to think you were sweet on him. So did everybody. Are you jealous or something because—"

"I am not! I just think you'd be better off with people nearer your own age, and—better people."

"Shane is a fine boy, Alice," Viktor said quietly. "You've been away several years. Maybe you've forgotten—"

"No, she hasn't," Mitch said angrily. "She's just turned into a goddamn bossy snob."

"Mitch, I don't want you talking like that," said Nora mildly.

"You see!" cried Alice triumphantly. "It's all this associating with those—loggers...."

"Now, Alie," said her brother, beginning to grin.

"And if you call me Alie again, I'll slap your face."

Viktor said calmly, "Anyone could guess that at least part of the family is home again. Both of you stop behaving like small children."

"I know why Mitch is going to work with Grandpa today," announced Patty into a little silence. "It's so he gets to see Peggy Lou Collins. She's working at the store till she goes to college."

Mitch said, "You know a lot of things, don't you, Miss Blabbymouth?"

She giggled. "I know Peggy Lou's mother doesn't want you to go on dates, even if Mr. Collins and Grandpa are partners."

"You see," said Alice, pouncing. "It's probably because of the kind of people you've been running around with."

"It's because," Mitch said angrily, "Doreen Collins is a—" He stopped at a warning look from his father and took another biscuit.

"Well, if you can't make up your mind about school just yet, why can't you go into the business the way Bruce Collins has?"

"Because I don't want to, for one thing; because there's not room for another partner's son, for another. When I decide what to do with my life, I don't want to start out as son of anybody. Dad understands that. He didn't do it. Wes Collins inherited his interest in Alder Valley Lumber and Hardware from his father. Now Bruce will inherit someday. When it's like that, how can you ever know if you could have made it on your own?"

"So you're going to make it on your own with a chain saw?"

Viktor said, "Are they really going to make up this petition you're talking about? The Blackbuck people?"

"Yes. Gary Hunt said he'd draw it up."

Viktor frowned and stood up. "I'm going to wash up a bit, change my shirt. You'll be ready?"

"Yes, sir. Dad, I—"

"Never mind."

"Patty," Nora said, "run up and get me a needle and thread. That pocket's going to fall off your shirt."

After a little silence, Alice said, mystified, "Who . . . ? Oh, Gary Hunt! That's the one Janet..."

"Your father would rather not have him mentioned, Mitch, and you know it," said Nora.

"I am sorry, Mom. It just came out. He's the only one interested right now that's had any law training. He didn't finish law school, but—"

"I don't know of anything he *has* finished," snapped Nora. "I hope old Charlie and Shane and those other people aren't pinning any hopes on him because he'll lose interest in that just the way he does in everything else."

Mitch grimaced. "Except his great philosophical tome. He's been working on that for at least a month now."

"I'm going to see Janet," said Alice sternly, "when we're up at Cloud Valley. I'll straighten that little twirp out on a few things. Did you see Daddy's eyes? She's breaking his heart."

"Alice, I'd rather you wouldn't," said Nora sadly. "Janet's of age. She'll have to make her own decisions. Mitch, have you seen her lately?"

"Yes, last Wednesday. She's all right, Mom."

"Why is Gary willing to help with this petition thing? The few times we've seen him, he's been nearly foaming at the mouth about the rottenness of the system."

"I guess it's just something to do," Mitch said a little lamely, "some trouble to help stir up. Nobody's counting on him much, but we can't afford to hire anybody yet."

"What are they *doing* up there?" cried Alice with scorn. "Living off the land! Back to nature! If they were sixteen or seventeen you might understand it for a little while, but Janet's twenty-two and he's—what? Twenty-eight or something? I never heard such a bunch of flagrant nonsense. If they have to act like such idiots, they could at least get married or go and do their *living* somewhere else. They could do that much for the family if they don't care anything about themselves. This must be the juiciest piece of scandal Alder County's had in years."

"I thought you were a liberated woman, Alice," said her brother. "Marriage is a big nothing to our generation, remember?"

"Mitch!" said Nora. Her eyes had suddenly filled with tears.

"Oh, I'm sorry, Mom," he said with deep contrition. "I've got such a big mouth. I don't really believe that and I wasn't talking about Janet. It's just that every time Alice comes home, she gets us all squared away for two or three weeks. I swear I don't know how we manage the rest of the year." He turned to his sister. "You were ready to call me a male chauvinist pig a while ago for suggesting people you might marry instead of falling on the floor in admiration of your career. You think *you're* a big-deal liberated woman, but you talk about Janet like she's not fit to be stepped on. Mom and Dad are willing to let things work themselves out. I think Dad left like that because he knew you'd start in. Just leave Janet alone, do you hear? I don't care if you yammer at me for three weeks, but leave her alone."

"Who do you think you are—" began Alice fiercely, but Nora said,

"What is it, Mitch? I mean, is there something we don't know about?"

Mitch shrugged. "Nothing new, Mom. She's working weekends at the Blackbuck Cafe so they can afford to live off the land, that's all. She said to tell you they're doing fine. Charlie wanted her to come over and cook for the camp, but Gary said that would be too confining, too establishmentarian, so she's working three or four days a week for Ruby McCrarie. Charlie sent us up there on Wednesday night to see if she'd cook and to ask about the petition."

"Us?" Nora asked.

"Shane and me. Only he wouldn't get out of the jeep. Gary really is a creep, but, you know, you can sort of take him for a little while, with several grains of salt, only Shane hates his guts. Janet went out and talked to him and he wouldn't even come in then. He wouldn't have gone at all except Charlie didn't want me driving his dented-up old jeep after dark...."

"But what will they do when winter comes?" said Nora almost pleadingly.

"Other people have stayed the winter up around there, Mom, lots of them, and they are getting the cabin fixed up pretty good."

28

"I used to think," said Alice tautly, "that Janet was a pretty smart, sensible kid. But here she is, a registered nurse, working as a part-time waitress and living ... I just can't imagine what's happened to her."

"Well," said Mitch, standing up as he heard his father's step on the stairs, "I think she used to think it was love."

"Used to," began Nora, half hopefully. "Do you mean you think she may—"

"Who says love?" cried Patty, flinging herself at Mitch from the doorway.

Mitch scooped her into his arms and brushed the ceiling with her hair. "*I* say love."

"For Peggy Lou?"

"No, for you."

"Would you marry me instead of her if I was older?"

"Nope."

"Why not?"

"Can't."

"Why not, poor little Uncle Mitch?" she asked, looking down from her great elevation.

"Because I am your uncle and the sheriff would come and take me away."

"Sheriff Terry? He's nice. Why would he take you away?"

"Because it is not allowed for uncles and nieces to marry with one another."

"Why not?"

"Do you know you're a pain? Now shut up and let go. Grandpa's waiting for me."

"When you come back you'll tell me?"

"When I come back, I will tell you everything."

He was doing a very bad W. C. Fields, and

29

Patty, returned to the floor, was almost collapsing with giggles.

"More than you tell Peggy Lou?"

"More than I have ever told anyone in the entire world, my dear, but for the nonce, if you do not get out of my way, I shall have to kick your behind."

"What's a nonce?" cried Patty, but he had escaped into the hall.

"Mitch," called Nora, "is Shane still in town?"

"He's staying till tomorrow," called Mitch.

"Is Charlie down too?"

"No."

Viktor was honking the horn of the pickup.

"Tell Shane to come for supper," Nora said, "and there's plenty of room if he wants to stay the night here."

"I'll tell him," yelled Mitch from the front door, "if Alie can promise to behave, show a proper restraint, and—"

"*I'll* be at the country club, you little snot!" yelled Alice. Then, discomfited by what seemed to her an utterly childish outburst, she began energetically to gather up the dishes.

2 ∽

"Well," said Viktor as he and Nora drove home, "I think things are going as Paul hoped they would. Everyone seemed to be having a good time."

They had dropped in only briefly at the

country club, of which they were not members, to have a look at Paul's party. There had been a dinner first, to which they were not invited, a dinner for twenty-four people whom Paul considered most potentially interested in his project, and now there was a private dance for a much larger group, with a small orchestra imported from Boise. A few guests, Paul's parents, some high-school classmates in town for their fifteenth reunion and other celebrations of Cana Week, had been invited out of propriety, friendship, sentiment even, but most of the guests were people whom Paul was hoping to interest in his Cloud Valley development.

"I never feel right at things like that," said Nora, relaxing in her seat. "I feel frumpy and old and I'm never sure what to say to people. Have you noticed how young everyone has gotten to be lately?"

Viktor smiled. "You're not frumpy. You don't look nearly as ancient as you really are, and there have been very few times when I've seen you at a loss for words. Think how old *I* am."

After a moment, she said thoughtfully, "You know, maybe Alice—and Paul—are right. I don't often think of how old either of us is, but maybe we ought to do something...."

"Do what?"

"Well, I don't know. Take a trip now and then or something. People are supposed to do— different things as they get older."

"Where would you like to go?"

"Oh, Viktor, *I* don't know. Nowhere, really. It just seems, if you really stop and think about it..."

"When children grow up, some of them want to reverse roles," he said calmly. "They seem to get the idea it's time they started looking after their parents. If you and I want to take trips or do such things, we will. Meanwhile, don't be convinced by your children that you're not capable of making up your own mind. Maybe it's a kind of getting even for them, a refund on all the decisions we forced on them when they were little."

She thought about it for a moment, smiling a little with memories, and said, "Well, I guess they can't really be blamed for that." Then, sobering, "Alice seemed to be dancing quite a lot with Bill Goodwin. Did you notice?"

"No."

"I really do wish she'd marry. I suppose I go along with a lot of these liberation things, in a way, but I just can't help believing that a woman —and a man, too—need real companionship, a lifelong kind, to have a chance of being really happy. Marrying the right man wouldn't have to stop Alice from having her career. It wouldn't be Bill Goodwin, of course, but some man she knows in San Francisco. I wonder if she dates much."

"Haven't you asked her?"

"Well, no. To tell you the truth, I hesitate to ask Alice much of anything like that."

"I haven't noticed Alice hesitating," he said dryly.

"Yes, but I wouldn't want her to think I'm prying or trying to be too bossy."

They had come down off the long hill called East Ridge and were driving beside the Alder River, most of the lights of Cana coming up on them from the north and across the stream. This was the state highway that came up from the interstate, passed through Alder Falls, and followed on up the river valley to Blackbuck.

"Sharon doesn't look well," said Nora with concern. "I suppose it's just that she's tired, but..."

"I don't see why she had to spend the day working on this party," Viktor said. "I thought it was supposed to be catered and handled by the club."

"Oh, you know what a perfectionist Paul is. He was afraid they wouldn't get everything just right, and of course he didn't have time to see to it himself. But then she'll have to go up to Cloud Valley and get everything ready for that thing he's doing up there, a dozen people or so. Patty and I may go along if you don't mind—I mean, so I can help with the cleaning and cooking and things. I told Sharon I might. She's taking one of the Martinez girls, but it's going to be an awful job with no one having used the old house for so long. Will you be going? for the picnic or any of it?"

"No. All the Collins family has been invited, and someone has to stay with the store."

"Paul *did* ask you—didn't he?"

"Yes, but it was only out of courtesy, I think. We don't need to be shown around the ranch and told about his plans. We already know. He wants people up there who might be interested in investing."

"Are we going to? Invest, I mean."

"I don't know, Nora. We'll have to talk about it some time. To tell you truly, I don't like the idea. It would mean growth for the county, jobs, additional taxes, all the things Paul points out, but..."

"Sharon doesn't like it either," said Nora. "I think that's mostly what's wrong with her. She's just plain miserable."

"Still," said Viktor, "Paul is right when he says someone will do this sort of thing sooner or later. I suppose, if it looks as if the thing is going to get off the ground, we might put in some money, just a token sum, because it's Paul."

"Viktor," she said gently, "you've always been such a good father to Paul. Sometimes he can be more trying than any two of the others put together, but you've never shown any difference—favoritism or..."

"I never think of his not being my son, Nora. He was just four when we married. I've never understood why you keep bringing it up."

"Well, because he *can* be trying, I mean more trying to the patience at times. He's always been so cocksure and set on having his own way."

"So can they all be. Look at the way Alice works so hard to get us all organized in two or three weeks' time to last the whole year. Think of Mitch, the way he's so complacent about not making up his mind about anything. Remember the way Vik worried us by marrying so early, and..."

"Janet," she said quietly.

"Yes."

There was a silence before Nora, speaking a little awkwardly, said, "Sharon said Janet may come too, to help get things ready up at the ranch. Viktor, I ought to talk to her. She—"

"No, Nora, don't. Let's just let her—them—work it through."

"He's such a—creepy boy!" She shuddered. "Janet could have had all kinds of choices. I'm afraid for her."

"I know," he said tiredly, "but she knows we're here and I think that's about the most we can do for now."

They came to the intersection where another state highway ran east across the valley, turned west on the main road, and crossed the river into town. Nora peered down River Street, trying to see if there might be any lights at the old Holland House, but the lights from the mill beside it made it impossible to tell.

"I thought we would have heard from Faye by now," she said wistfully.

"Maybe she wants to stay away until Cana Week is over."

"Oh, no, I don't think so. You know Faye loves celebrations, or just about anything else."

The center of town was busy, the theater's first feature just having ended. People, mostly very young ones, strolled along the sidewalks or drove, honking, waving, and yelling to one another around the square.

Nora said slowly, "What you said about my mentioning Paul's not being your natural son . . . I forget it too, most of the time. When I do remember or bring it up, it's usually because I'm so—grateful."

"Nora, my darling girl," he said gently, almost with reproof.

"I'm glad of having Paul," she went on, speaking a little faster than usual, "but I've al-

35

ways—ever since his father was killed—been a little—ashamed about that marriage. I was such a child then, and so was the first Paul. I doubt it would have lasted if he'd lived. We hardly knew each other and both of us had so much growing up still to do. Even before I got the word he was dead, I couldn't remember what he'd been like or—anything. I'd look at his picture when I read his letters, to try to remember. Mama told me when I said we were going to get married that I just had an overdose of patriotism, but who ever listens to their mother when they're eighteen? . . . But it's sad, you know. Before he was sent overseas, I was already beginning to know we didn't really love each other, and then he died . . . You know, I don't mean I think of him often or—or —it's just that I feel sorry about him sometimes, and that our Paul was born before there was real love between two parents."

"I suppose," Viktor said quietly, "that no human being ever lived who didn't have things to be sorry about. But the past is over—irrevocable. It can be made up for a little perhaps, in some ways. I hope you haven't been punishing yourself all these years, when you think of it, for something you did when you were hardly more than a baby. Probably it was a kindness, a good thing, for him to remember. You could never do anything but good. . . . It could have been bad, perhaps, if there had been anything calculated about it; anything . . ."

He stopped lamely, and something in his tone—unhappiness? bitterness?—made her try to see his face clearly, but they had passed through the bright section of town and were continuing north along the highway. After a time she said, feeling, somehow a need for lightness, "I wonder if David Rosenzweig is really interested in this venture of Paul's?"

"I think he may be. He seems to have a good deal of money to play with."

"Well, Paul surely must think so or he surely wouldn't be inviting him to all these things. He seems such a sour, grumpy man and there's something about him that just gives me the willies, Viktor, it really does."

"What is it, do you think?"

"I don't know. It's a little as if he thinks he's —God or something, looking down on mortals and chalking up their shortcomings, their weak points in his mind. Haven't you ever noticed him staring at you?"

"As a matter of fact, I have, but that could well be because I have more shortcomings and weak points."

"I'm serious," she said a little urgently. "Has he ever said anything? I mean, he looks as if he's trying to place you or..."

"He did ask me once, a year or so ago, if we'd met somewhere besides Cana. I never knew him."

"Well, he's got an—an evil eye. It's obvious as anything that he has nothing but disdain for Cana and everything and everyone here. And so does *she*—Gloria. She was already almost falling-down drunk when we left and it was only ten-thirty. I've heard she's on the verge of being an alcoholic."

"Who told you that? Old Mrs. Adams?"

"She did, yes, but so have a lot of other people. And there's that look in her eyes, so superior and sulky and dissatisfied. She gives me the willies too."

"This is really no place for either of them, I think. They've always been used to a city. I think it won't be long before he turns the mill over entirely to a manager and goes away."

"But I wonder why he didn't just do that in the first place."

"Perhaps he wanted to bring his wife away from the city, try another kind of life."

"She *is* a lot younger," mused Nora.

"I doubt there's as much difference in their ages as in yours and mine."

She grunted. "The difference is that I'm not always waiting and on the lookout for somebody to jump in bed with. Probably that's the most of what's wrong with David Rosenzweig."

"Granny Adams thinks this too?"

"Do you think I have to get all my ideas from Belle Adams? There's a—a something about Gloria that lets you know she's like that. I'm a woman and I can feel it. I thought men were supposed to be able to pick up those kinds of— vibrations a mile away."

"Maybe she's lonely."

"Well, of course she's lonely, living with that creepy man and having almost nothing to do with anyone else, but—"

He swung the car left onto Tamarack Road, saying, "Maybe she's lonely for the company of other women too. It's especially hard in a little town like Cana to get started with making real friends. Remember how it was when we first came? We were outsiders for years, still are to some people."

"I *do* remember," she said with vehemence. "I got pregnant with Janet right away and it seemed to take forever to begin really getting to know a soul. They were all bright and friendly and curious if we met on the street or at something that was going on at school, but then they just seemed to forget I was alive. Except for when you called, our phone wouldn't ring for months, until I got to know Faye. If I'd had a sister, I know she couldn't have been as good a friend as Faye Holland. She had little children of her own, worked at the mill, Dan got sick and died, then she had old Jeff to take care of all those years, but Faye is a person who just seems able to *make* time. She always—oh, Viktor, look! Could that be her new car in the driveway?"

3

"You see," Paul Magnessen was saying eagerly as he and Howard Compton studied a map he had tacked up on the den wall, "this would be the area for the summer home colony, maybe fifty or so, eventually, nice little secluded cabins, good-sized lots with the woods and all left in between, what they'd call a green belt near a city. Here would be the condominium area—we've thought thirty or forty to start with—eight per building, with various restrictions, like one building for adults only. The rolling meadow here, with the woods and stream, could make a perfect golf course—maybe a small dam here. There's always something about even a little lake that attracts people. We might renovate the old ranch house as a club, but I don't know, it'll probably be torn down. Tennis courts over here and . . . Sharon, can't we have some of that coffee? Or would you like a drink, Howard? Betty?"

Sharon moved in a kind of daze to the kitchen. The coffee had not finished perking and she sat down, hoping fervently that Betty Compton wouldn't follow. Sharon had been up since six on Saturday and it was now past three on Sunday morning. Those things Paul was saying, she could recite them by rote, in her sleep, and she hated all of it. His words went on in her mind and she could see him, standing excitedly before his map, his sleek black hair, sparkling hazel eyes, his average-height, sturdily muscled figure straight and erect and good-looking in the new suit.

Howard Compton had been in Paul's class at Cana High—a sugar-beet farmer's son—but Paul had forgotten his existence until a few weeks ago when he, or rather Sharon, in helping to arrange the fifteenth class reunion festivities, had found that Howard was an architect in Denver. Naturally, then, Howard and his wife had been invited to the Magnessens' very select dinner and private party at the country club. Howard, it seemed, was doing nicely in his father-in-law's architectural firm. Speaking for himself, and tentatively for the firm, he found Paul's Cloud Valley project very interesting, so interesting he had dragged poor, rocky Betty to the East Ridge house to hear and see more. Betty was not going to follow to the kitchen. She was half-conscious on the den couch, whether from liquor or boredom it would have been hard to say.

If she had followed me, Sharon thought, too tired to have any feelings about the thoughts, I'd say, "Did Howard marry you because you were the boss's daughter?" And then I'd say, "Oh, don't get upset about it, honey. Paul married me for my dowry. You see, my grandfather homesteaded up in Cloud Valley way back in the 1880s. There were quite a lot of McGoverns once, but then they dwindled away, to Boise, Idaho Falls, Portland, I don't know where else, and my dad was left with the ranch. They only had me —my parents—and my mother died when I was seven. Dad wanted a boy; I've always been a disappointment to somebody. He loved me—I guess. Only the best boarding schools for Sharon, a nice, elderly governess-type lady for vacations. Daddy died when I was seventeen. He'd had his will made for a long time, since whenever it was he decided I was all there was going to be.

"My daddy was the granddaddy of male chauvinists, Betty. He left the ranch in trust for me, to be handled by the Alder Valley National Bank—that's old man Homer Grundy—*but*, Betty, my sister woman, when I married, Cloud Valley went to my husband. If I did not marry, the ranch was to remain in trust with the bank until I died, heirless, of course, and always well provided-for during my lifetime—I could even live up there—but then the place would go to the federal government, to become part of the Stafford National Forest, which you will note from the map already surrounds it on three sides.

"So I got the word about the will and everyone else up and down the valley got the word. Maybe Paul Magnessen got it a little later than some because he was away in his last year at college. But Paul knew how things were going to be, and you know what, Betty? So did I. He was four years older than me, but I'd known him as long as I could remember. His family used to spend time in the summer at the Holland place on Blackbuck Creek and they'd visit with us and at old Charlie Bonner's. We went riding a lot, Judy and Barbara Holland, Paul and Vik and Alice and Janet Magnessen, Shane Bonner, maybe some others, and me. . . . Anyway, I knew him, and a year after Daddy's will was made public, we were engaged. No, I am not crying. I get sniffles when I'm very tired, that's all.

"We didn't get married until 1970 because Paul had to do a hitch in the Army. He was a pilot. Now he's a member of the American Legion, VFW, Rotary, Lions, JC's, Alder Valley Improvement Association, real-estate board. Ah, sorry; one gets carried away.

"But we *did* get married, yes, in 1970. I married Paul Magnessen and he married Cloud Valley, or Cloud Valley as it *will* be. He's told me that sometimes, flying missions from Bangkok over Vietnam, he'd picture it in his mind, the summer homes, the condos, golf course, all of it. Not Sharon.

"When we'd been married about two and a half years, Paul decided—all things in their season—it was time we produced a child. So we did and I wish to God Jamie was upstairs now instead of at his grandparents'; I'd go and hide in his room and watch him sleep. . . . So I thought, well, okay, I'll have lots of kids and expend my talents and love on them. Paul says there ought to be at least three years between children. Jamie's three now and there's no indication of another on the way. I'm not at all sure I can have more and I'm afraid of finding out. I don't think it would matter to Paul and I know he'd never go for adoption. He's always felt left out or something because Viktor Magnessen's not his natural father. I've never been able to understand why he seems to feel so conscious of it. They're a wonderful family and the only difference they make in their children is due to the fact that each one is a different person. But it bothers Paul somehow. I think it's part of the reason he's such a driving, *do*ing person, because he feels he has to prove something, but I don't know what.

"I love kids, Betty. I'd like to have six or eight of them, live on the ranch, *run* the ranch. ... And, Betty, I still love him—sometimes.

"He's in there now, while you sleep the sleep of the just, pointing out to good old Howard where the ski runs would be, and the lodge. That's national forest land, that high up, he's saying, but arrangements can be made—"

"Sharon? What are you doing?"

She started. He was standing in the doorway.

"Waiting for the coffee."

"Well, it's done. Can't you see the light's on? Listen, I know you're bushed, but fix us some breakfast, will you? Betty's passed out and we're going to get her up to the guest room, but Howard's really hooked. We want to talk some more. Just some bacon and eggs and things and then you can get to bed. It's going to be a big week, *really* big!"

Sharon stumbled to her feet, her slight figure seeming unconscionably heavy and unwieldy. She pushed her dark hair back, rubbed at her scratchy, watery brown eyes, and began breakfast.

Her thoughts went on, no pretense of telling them to Betty Compton now; the string had just begun to unwind, tangling and snarling. He would have had the project well under way by now, in honor of the Bicentennial, Cana Centennial, and Paul Magnessen, except that the time was not right. After all, he's only been really established in real estate for a little over five years. It's *his* land up there, except what would have to be leased from the government, that part up on Cloud Chief Mountain where he wants the ski runs, but he needs a lot of capital for the development and he had to prove himself first by getting to be the hottest real-estate man in Alder County. It's a hick county, but he's done it and that's saying a lot because there are plenty of realtors around these days, with Blackbuck Reservoir just six years old and so many city people wanting to live in the country or at least to have summer homes. Now, Paul James Magnessen can kick off his dream in conjunction with Cana Week and keep saying, "One day Cloud Valley will be more popular than *Sun* Valley."

Sharon's thoughts were brought up short as she found herself standing distractedly in front of an open cupboard rather than the refrigerator, looking for eggs.

Last night—no, Friday night—Mitch and Shane were here and they looked at Paul's map. He didn't give them the verbal tour. They knew the ranch as well as he did and they had no investment capital, no interest in a membership in the Cloud Valley Club. After a few minutes,

Mitch got down on the floor and helped Jamie stack blocks, but Shane just stood there, not moving anything but his eyes, looking at the map. Shane had gray eyes, like still water on a cloudy day, and his hair was bronze, a dark bronze shade that Sharon had never seen before anywhere. If it was a woman's hair, you'd know it was dyed. He was about Paul's height but looked taller because he was thin and wiry. Paul began to talk a little. He was uncomfortable. Shane could make anyone uneasy by just being still for a long time the way he could be. Sharon thought he must have developed that ability as a counterbalance to his grandfather. Old Charlie was always hopping around and gesturing and yelling. But finally Shane turned away from the map.

Paul was saying, "Sit down. What will you have to drink?" He didn't ask Mitch because he could never think of Mitch as anything but a kid brother, and he wouldn't have asked Shane except for the vague uneasiness that was making him more than a little angry. He said, "How is it in the woods this year?"

"Things are all right," Shane said, lighting a cigarette. "The pine beetles are bad. There aren't going to be any lodge poles left up there in a few years."

"Well, I guess old Charlie's doing his best to get to them first." Paul smiled.

Looking up from the floor, Mitch said, "Shane's mostly hauling again. Charlie can't keep truck drivers."

Shane said mildly, "It's only because he wants a load delivered to the mill and the truck back at the show in two hours. To him, that seems the most reasonable thing in the world, since the round trip's only about eighty miles, and half of it's over decent roads."

"And," added Mitch, "the truck he's driving —it's that old red one Charlie's had forever— hasn't got brakes worth a damn."

Shane had a nice, slow smile that warmed his gray eyes. People said it was exactly like his father's and some distrusted him for it. "That helps the time pass faster," he said, but then he sobered and shook his head slightly at Paul's gesture toward the bar.

"Thanks, no, Paul, and I don't think I'll sit down because you're going to be asking me to leave in about two minutes. Old Charlie sent me down here, Charlie and some other Blackbuck people. I won't give you what he said verbatim because there was a lot of it, but he—we—don't want your development. They said to say nobody's got any intentions of doing things behind your back, but it'll have to be fought however we can. There are enough, more than enough, summer people, fishermen, hunters, half-assed prospectors, and the rest in the upper valleys now. We're not looking for any more progress."

Paul's face had flushed slightly. This was no surprise, but he had not expected it to come quite like this.

"You can go back and tell Charlie and the rest of those old goats—"

"I know." Shane nodded. "And they know. They just told me to deliver the message. Nobody expected it would change your mind about anything."

He moved toward the door, and Mitch got up to follow.

46

"Mitch?" Paul said, "what's your part in this? Do Dad and Mother know about it?"

"My part is that I go along with the others up there. I can't stand to think about that country being ruined, overrun by a bunch of dudes. Mom and Dad don't know anything about it yet, so far as I know. Anyway, they don't know I'm here."

"Well, if you plan to try to help those old sticks-in-the-mud stir up trouble, don't bother coming back here."

"He didn't mean that," Sharon said, going with them to the door.

"Sure he did," said Mitch, grinning. "It doesn't much matter to me. It's a pretty rough life being kid brother to Paul and Alice both. I can see you and Jamie at the folks' and other places. You're coming up to the ranch next week?"

"Yes. Big party for interested capitalists."

"Ride over and see us," Shane said. "We're cutting just the other side of Jamison Saddle."

"I'll have to stay and clean up afterward," she said. "Maybe I can find time. I hate to think how long it's been since I've been on a horse, and it's been ages since I've seen old Charlie."

Sharon could hear Paul and Howard now, coming back downstairs after getting Betty to the guest room. She buttered toast.

Charlie Bonner was seventy-six. He liked to say he'd started with the century, born in January 1900. For as long as Sharon could remember, he'd been called "old" Charlie by everyone, including, sometimes, himself. He was a kind of county "character," who could outswear, outdrink, outwork, and generally outdo any two ordinary men. This was not necessarily old Char-

47

lie's claim—he was not much given to boasting about himself—but it was affirmed by most ordinary men who had tried to swear or drink or work with him. And when old Charlie set his mind to something ...

"You know, Betty," Sharon's thoughts ran, "my unaware, newfound, bosom friend, as you lie asleep, I could transmit to you the thought that a lawyer, a much-respected young man here in Cana, one whom Paul considers his best friend, but who shall remain nameless because he keeps asking me to sleep with him, told me I could have contested that will and probably would have won. I didn't even think of doing it at the time. I wanted Paul."

She poured tomato juice. Paul liked a Bloody Mary after a night like this. Her inner conversation switched to Charlie Bonner.

"I tell you what, old Charlie. You fight progress and development in Cloud Valley, you and Shane and whoever else, and I'll be a kind of secret underground of one, here in the fashionable East Ridge section of Cana, and we'll see what's to be done. If he *can't* do the Cloud Valley thing, if he simply *has* to give it up, let it stay a ranch or go back to forest, maybe he'll notice me, want me—a little."

"Good!" said Paul jovially, "it's ready. Sit down, Howard, sit down. The kitchen's better than the dining room this time of morning. Say, to get away from business for a little while, do you remember, in our junior year, that football game with Alder Falls when ..."

4

Janet woke early, just as lambent daylight came with soft increase through the trees around the cabin. She lay still for a moment, getting straight in her mind what day it was—Tuesday, the last Tuesday in June—and what she would do with this day. Then she got out of bed, shivering in the chill morning. Gary lay very still, snoring softly, his hair and beard very black against the pillow and blanket.

Janet opened the old range as quietly as she could. Just as she had supposed, there was not a spark or an ember to be seen. They had not yet been able to master the banking of a fire so that it would last through the night. Wrapped in an old robe, her feet still bare and shrinking a little from the cold, splintery floorboards, she took out some ashes, put in newspaper and kindling, and started a fire. There was a bucket of water. She dipped out what she needed for the coffee pot and set the bucket on the stove too, to heat. She slipped her feet into Gary's boots—they sat there, handy, and her own slippers had holes in them—took the other water bucket, and went outside.

The sun was just coming up over Mount Stafford above her. She could see the sun just touching the rugged peak of Blackbuck Mountain up to the northwest and, to the northeast, the brightness was advanced farther down the smoother sides of Cloud Chief Mountain. Birds sang, squirrels and chipmunks chattered, all of them busy with their own morning duties. The air was completely still, utterly clear. Later it would be fragrant with the smell drawn from the evergreens by the sun's heat, but now there was no scent to it, just a dampness left from the night that felt good in the breathing. The smoke from her fire was going straight up and in a moment would be touched by the edge of the advancing sunlight.

Janet left her bucket for the moment and went up the path to the point. The point had no name; there were too many similar to it in this mountain country, but for a long, long time, it had been *her* point. Almost directly below was old Charlie Bonner's ranch, down in the valley of Blackbuck Creek. Nothing of it could be seen from here except smoke rising from the chimney as the light increased. It was several miles away by trail, a few hundred feet lower in altitude. Charlie spent little time there now, but his father had homesteaded the place. It was leased this year to some people running sheep. But in Janet's childhood, Charlie and Shane had lived there most of the time. Shane had attended the community grade school in Blackbuck, before the community was moved, and they had used the ranch as headquarters for logging operations in season. When Shane was ready for high school, old Charlie had bought the little house on the edge of Cana, and now, most years, their cutting operations were too far away for the ranch to be convenient. Charlie had always been far more interested in logging than ranching, but he liked having the old place kept in the family, even if other people did live there.

Looking to her left, Janet could see, beyond the lower south flank of Mount Stafford, to where the V of the meeting of Blackbuck and Cloud Creeks had once formed the beginning of the Alder River. Now it was the headwaters of Blackbuck Reservoir. The lake lay hidden from her now, the valley still in mist, waiting for the sun. The community of Blackbuck had stood once just at the head of the river, but when the dam was built, its few citizens were moved ten miles down the valley to near the dam site. Some simply took pay for their land and went away. Ruby and Bill McCrary had exchanged their "one-horse ranch," now inundated by the lake, for a good piece of commercial land near the dam. Ruby would be up now, trying to take care of the Blackbuck Cafe and Cabins, trying to tongue-lash Bill and the kids into helping. Janet was working now for Ruby, Friday through Monday, when things were busy. She was glad she didn't have to go down today. Almost, she wished, she never had to go anywhere. Ruby was good in her way and it *was* a good thing to see other people sometimes, but she had always loved this place so much.

Today she must go over to Cloud Valley Ranch to help Sharon. Probably her mother and Alice would be there, maybe Aunt Faye. Janet felt no guilt about what she and Gary were doing, but she dreaded the attempts to explain it, which most people seemed compelled to try to force from her. She was sorry about her parents. They were worried, puzzled. How could it hurt, their eyes kept asking, to go along with convention just a little? But they tried to show their acceptance of her as an adult, which was more than many parents would have done in this sort of situation, and to let things alone. Alice would be another matter. Janet dreaded seeing her sister.

When the sunlight touched the lake, she turned and looked back down toward old Charlie's place. The very faintest of sounds came up to her; someone chopping wood down there maybe. She was cold, but the sun was about to reach her and she went on crouching on the rock, the very top of her point.

It was not her point, they had said, Paul, Vik, Alice, Sharon, Shane, Judy and Barbara Holland, with tolerance or scorn, as suited their dispositions. She had not "discovered" it. All those years, she had been the youngest of them allowed to go on their summer rides, only because she rode so well and mostly didn't bother them. By the time Mitch had grown up enough to be the accepted youngest, Janet had felt very grown-up indeed.

The Hollands had a house, a summer place, on Blackbuck Creek just above where the two big creeks met, and when Aunt Faye came up she always liked other people to come too. If you took the road from her house to the northwest, it was about five miles to the Bonner place. If you went northeast, it was about seven miles to the McGoverns', but you could cross over, on foot or horseback, by a trail around behind Mount Stafford where it was only six miles between the ranches.

Janet had always liked going off by herself on those rides they'd had. At first, they were always yelling and looking for her because she'd been so little when she'd started riding with the older kids, but eventually they left her more or less alone, and one day she had found her point.

She tied her horse to a tree and just stayed there, quiet, happy.

After a while, the others had come up in a body. Vik said they had tracked her. She knew it was Shane who could follow a trail and so did the others, but they had been such close friends, Vik and Shane, that it seemed whatever one did was also done by the other.

"Don't get too close to the edge of that rock," Alice had said when they were still so far away she almost had to shout.

But it was a big rock, maybe twenty feet across and thirty feet long, nearly flat in its rough-surfaced way. Janet had pointed that out.

"It's probably undercut," Paul had said in his know-it-all way. That must have been the last summer he had spent much time in the mountains or with the "kids."

Vik had got off his horse, gone out to the edge of the rock, lain down, and peered over. "It's only undercut a foot or two."

"Well, this is as good a place as any to have our picnic," Barbara Holland had decided.

"But back down there under the trees," Alice had said. "Not out on that old hot rock. Mitch, you stay where I can see you. I don't want you falling down that mine shaft."

Janet had been lying on the rock, hardly paying any attention to them. It was hot but she liked it. She was half dazed by heat and lethargy and contentment. She lifted her head and said, not nastily, but only matter-of-factly, "It's my rock, my point. You can have your picnic here if you want to, though."

Then the scoffing had begun: *"Your* rock!"

"Do you think nobody else ever set foot here?" "What about Indians and hunters?" "What about that crazy old miner that built the cabin down there?" "Besides, this is national forest land; it belongs to everybody."

But Shane had said, "It can be her point if she wants it to. What difference does it make? Everybody likes to have a place."

And Judy Holland said, "You better get off there, Vik. It's Janet's rock and she didn't give you permission to crawl out and see if it's undercut."

Sharon slid off her horse and unstrapped a canteen. "May I?" she asked Janet ceremoniously.

Janet, still lying raised on an elbow, nodded uncertainly.

Spilling a few drops of water from the canteen, Sharon said solemnly, "I christen thee 'Janet's Rock.'"

"Okay," said Vik with an overdone sigh of relief. "Now can we, for Pete's sake, eat?"

Janet huddled happily now in the first rays of the sun. There was no real warmth yet, but the brightness gave an illusion.

So when Gary had grown so restless through the winter in Spokane, talking about back to nature, living off the land, how he could work on his book so much better away from cities and people, Janet had known where they should come.

She had got her nursing degree a year ago and had been able to go right to work in a large hospital. Spokane, for Janet, was a very big city and, though she could always make friends easily, she had been lonely. In the late fall, near Thanksgiving of last year, she had met Gary. He was a law student just then, but he dropped out at the end of that semester. It had required all she earned to afford living in Spokane. Gary worked sometimes, but never for more than a few days at a stretch. However, when they had decided to live at the cabin, he had written his mother asking for money, and she sent a small check each month. With what Janet could earn working at McCrarys', if they could save any of it, they might be all right through the winter.

There had still been a lot of snow in mid-April when they had come, but they had had warm sleeping bags and enough other things to make living just possible until they could begin getting the old miner's cabin back in shape. The cabin had been well built to begin with, but it had been completely neglected for years.

The Forest Service had blocked up the old mine shaft to keep someone from being injured or killed. The prospector—no one seemed able to remember his name—had called his mine Lucky Streak. He had dug his life away in the shaft and tunnel and, so far as anyone knew, had never made a cent from it. But he believed, Janet thought fiercely; it's believing that counts....

If only the people she cared for could understand about Gary, just a little; how his mother was now in the process of divorcing her fourth husband, how his life had been spent being shuffled from one school to another, with his mother telling people he was her nephew; how there had never been any love or stability in his life; how he earnestly espoused so many causes and movements and still could, with reason, be so anti-people; how he could be so interesting, different, such fun to be with when he felt safe enough to let down his guard of bitterness a little; what real intelligence he had when he wasn't spending all his energies on trying to antagonize someone.

Janet turned to her right and looked at good old Blackbuck Peak, all of it in sunlight now. Unwillingly, she stood up. "Thank you for this day," she whispered, to no one, nothing in particular. "Thank you for my baby."

She went back down past the cabin, Gary's too-big boots scuffing on the rocky path. Filling her bucket at the spring, picking up an armload of wood, she went back inside. She made more noise than she intended because the wood slipped as she was putting it down. Gary groaned and opened his eyes.

"My God, it's hardly sunup. Do you have to get up in the middle of the night?"

She set the new bucket of water on the stove and went over to kiss him. "It's beautiful today. The coffee's ready."

"I don't want any coffee, Janet. Don't you know how late I was up last night, working?"

His thick black beard tickled her face. His long hair was a conformity to nonconformity, still looked on askance by many people in Alder County, but only Janet knew that the chief purpose of the beard's cultivation was to hide a very bad, belated case of acne. She liked the beard, and the secret of its real reason for being made her feel warm and tender toward him.

"I'm sorry," she said. "Go back to sleep now. I'll probably be gone when you wake up, but I'll try to be back around six."

"Gone where?" He yawned. "You don't go to Blackbuck today."

She poured herself a cup of coffee and began

to make as good a job as she could of a bath from the half-bucket of water that was hot.

"No, but I told you, remember? That I'd go and help Sharon and the others get ready for that house-party thing."

"Christ, I don't want you contributing to that crap. Do you want a lot of people up here, fouling everything?"

"I'm only helping Sharon, not having the people. Anyway, they'll be there twenty-four hours or something, not here at all."

"You dopey kid! Can't you look any farther ahead than that? Suppose big papa Paul *builds* his dream resort? You'll have been a contributor."

"I don't want it to happen. I don't think it's going to, but I suppose if it does, it just—will."

He sighed, closing his eyes. "*Qué sera, sera,*" he said, mockingly. "That's the only philosophy you've got, isn't it? You say the same thing about Bonner's operation destroying the forest."

"They're *not* destroying, Gary, not really now. So much of the lodge pole is being killed by pine beetles, and that's almost all they're cutting this year. Anyway, why always pick on Bonner's? Holland's people are cutting in Stafford, and other independents besides old Charlie."

"All right! This year, this year. What about last year and the years before that and all the years to come? You can only think in the present tense, can't you?"

She had stripped off the robe and was washing herself with absorption. She wanted to tell him about the baby, had wanted to tell him for weeks. If he looked at her now, he would have to know. She smiled secretively. No, he wouldn't know from looking, not quite yet. It only *seemed* as if it should be obvious. . . . Gary would not be happy about it. She was convinced she could bring him to being happy, but it would take time. She'd keep it her secret a bit longer.

Janet's hair was very long, thick, dark ash-blond, straight. Her eyes were the deep, clear blue of the Magnessens and she was a little above average height for a woman, though fine-boned and slender. Her face was neither squarish Magnessen nor roundish Mitchell. It was an English face, an elongated heart-shape, the fair skin liberally sprinkled with freckles. Her father said she looked like his mother, who had been English, who had died when he was ten, and for whom Janet had been named. That other Janet had been a Cobleigh before she was a Magnessen. Karl, Viktor's father, had gone to school in England and had done his apprenticeship in carpentry with that other Janet's father in the Yorkshire Dales. There was a song about a Cobleigh, and this Janet, drying herself on a piece of blanket, sang part of it softly. "Tam Pierce, Tam Pierce, lend me your gray mare. All along, out along, down along, lea. Us wants to go to Whitticombe Fair, With Bill Brewer, Dan'l Whittan, Peter Gantry, Peter Guerney, Dan'l Stewart, 'Arry 'Awkes, Old Uncle Tom Cobleigh and all, Old Uncle Tom Cobleigh and all."

"Are you clean?" Gary's voice startled her a little. She had thought he was asleep again.

"Cleanest thing you ever saw," she said, turning to meet his meaningful smile. "Except my hair. I haven't done that yet."

"And pure?"

"Oh, yes, indeed."

"Then come here before you get your hair wet." ...

When she got up again, Janet said softly, "Shall I fix some breakfast?"

"No, I'm going back to sleep, but you know something? It is a kind of beautiful day. Listen, Janet, I think I'll have to go to Cana, or probably Alder Falls today. It's a hell of a shame to have to go down the valley on a day like this, but I've got to try to look up some things for my own work and for that petition they want drawn up. Forget about Cloud Valley and come with me. We might as well stock up on groceries if we have to go down. Surely dear Mother's check will be at the post office today."

"I told Sharon I'd come, Gary," she said apologetically, vigorously rubbing her lathered hair.

"Who's more important?"

"You know the answer to that, but Alice will probably be there, and Mama and Aunt Faye. I told Sharon I'd come. I want to see them, and you never like going near the family—"

"Damn right I don't," he said petulantly, turning away, settling the covers around him. "Well, don't take the bus. I'll need it if I have to get the goddamn groceries."

"Okay, I'll ride the cycle," she said placidly.

Her hair still lathered and piled on top of her head, she was slipping into jeans and a worn shirt.

"You know this family stuff is a bunch of shit," Gary was muttering. "I think you're fixated or something, always babbling about your father, mother, sister, brother—God!"

She took up her hair brush and the old piece of blanket. "I'll be going in a little while. Get some more sleep and I'll see you about six."

"Maybe I won't *be* here at six," he said truculently. "I ought to go to their picnic and give them a lecture. How come we're not invited if it's such a goddamn big family affair?"

"The family affair," said Janet with equanimity, "is the preparation. The house-party thing is for Paul's big investors."

"Bunch of fucking capitalists! Anyway, you just don't want to go down in the valley where it's hot and crawling with people. If you cared a fart about my book, you'd go and do the research and get the lousy groceries so I could stay here and get some work done."

"I'll do it tomorrow if you want to wait," she said and closed the door softly behind her.

Janet, to her family and friends, had never been known for her docility or meekness. She was an arguer, a scrapper—"feisty," old Charlie called her. But with Gary it was different because Gary was different. In those first months, she had gone along with everything he suggested, because she loved him, she cared about his work and how he felt about things; she was afraid of losing him. She came to realize, though, that the more pliant she was, the moodier he got, the more suspicious of her motives, the more dependent. Recently, with as much calm as she could muster, she had begun, a little, to live her own life again. Today, to her surprise, she actually felt angry with him. He was selfish, childish, frightened. But—poor Gary.

She went down again to the spring. A deer had been there since she got her water. She spread the blanket on the mossy ground and, lying on her back, let her head hang into the pool, reaching up and back to rinse the shampoo from her hair. When it was done, she climbed up to Janet's Rock, spread the blanket, and lay down on her stomach so the sun could get at her hair.

"What is so rare as a day in June? Then, if ever, come perfect days; When Heaven tries Earth if it be in tune, And over it gently her warm ear lays."

It was hot on her rock now, though it couldn't be much past eight o'clock. Janet was glad of the heat. The spring water had been so icy, her scalp still tingled. She sat up, brushed her hair, and lay down again. I'm going to fall asleep here. But if I do, it's all right. It won't be for long; it's too hot. . . . I wonder if Daddy will be coming up for Paul's thing? If I don't see him soon, I'll just go down and make a point of seeing him—at the store, maybe. I want him to forgive me—no, not forgive, because he isn't holding any grudges or being scandalized. I want him to stop being hurt by worrying over me. I wish I could tell him about the baby. I think I'd rather tell Daddy than almost anyone. . . . I can't, of course, that would only make him worry more. . . . Suppose Gary doesn't ever get used to the idea of it? . . . Suppose he does and thinks we ought to get married? . . . Oh, it's so lovely here today. . . . "Old Uncle Tom Cobleigh and all, Old Uncle . . ."

5

"All right, now, Nora, *tell* me things," said Faye Holland peremptorily. "We haven't had half a chance to talk and there's a lot to make up for."

On Saturday night, Faye had spent only a scant half hour at the Magnessens'. She just couldn't wait to get home, she said, home being the old Holland house down by the mill. On Sunday, there had been an old settlers' gathering at the city park. Faye was not an old settler, nor even the blood relative of one. She had come to Cana as Dan Holland's bride twenty-eight years ago. Dan had been the only one—the youngest of three brothers—who had cared to go on in the lumber-mill business his grandfather had started. Jeff Holland, Dan's father, had accepted Faye almost immediately so that she was much more readily acceptable to Cana and the county in general. Faye and Dan had had two daughters, but Faye was always in and out of the mill office or working on the mill's books at home in the big old house Jeff had had built back in the twenties during a particularly good year.

Dan had lived only eight years after their marriage and Faye and the little girls had grown more and more indispensable to old Jeff. His other sons and their families lived far away, cared nothing for the business. Jeff and Faye ran the mill and there was never a mill manager outside the family until 1969, when it finally became apparent, even to Jeff, that he was too feeble and the job was too much for Faye to carry almost alone. They hired Bert Adams, a long-time mill foreman as manager, but Faye was still always there, and every evening she spent time with Jeff, even after he had to be hospitalized, telling him how things were going and he still teased her about her "middle Atlantic" accent.

When Jeff died in 1973, his two remaining sons wanted to sell their shares in the mill. Faye had been left a one-third interest in the business, Holland House, and the property up on Blackbuck Creek, the summer place. With two-thirds of the business up for sale, Faye threw in her share too. She was forty-five and tired.

Still, going to the old settlers' picnic had been an obligation for her as far as Cana was concerned. She was the only one with the Holland name left now.

On Monday, she had had to go to Boise to take care of some business. She and Nora had talked several times by phone, and today they had driven up to Cloud Valley with Alice and Patty, to help with preparations for Paul's house party. Patty and Jamie were playing outdoors now; Sharon, Miguela Martinez, who did cleaning work for some of the East Ridge people, Alice and Janet, were cleaning the house, making beds. Faye and Nora were in the big creaky old kitchen, Nora making barbecue sauce, Faye potato salad.

"I think you'd better talk," said Nora, smiling. "You're the world traveler."

Faye shook her head vehemently. "Not any more I'm not. Oh, Nora, I've come to stay and I can't even begin to tell you how good it feels."

"You *look* so good, Faye, as if you've lost

63

ten years somewhere. I was worried about you when Jeff died, and after. You looked so worn out and sick sometimes."

Faye's hair was dark brown, with streaks of gray she didn't try to hide. Her eyes were a golden brown, incisive and penetrating. She was rather an average-looking woman except for the warmth, interest, and vitality that seemed to radiate from her.

"It took poor old Jeff a long time to die," she said sadly, "and I was all there was of family for him to talk lumber with. Barbara and Judy weren't any particular trouble growing up, but they needed me too. Sometimes I used to wake up in the morning just sure I couldn't take on another day, then that damn mill whistle would blow and I'd turn into a fire horse again. . . . You know, this looks like enough potato salad for a regiment? . . . But I'm rested now, Nora, and I'm back to stay.

"I've been everywhere I thought I might like to go, or ought to go. Nothing's the way I remembered it back in New Jersey, of course. I've been pretty much all over Europe and I don't think much of most of it, not even of Paris, where Barbara and her husband feel so lucky to be. I'll tell you this: That young man will never get far in the diplomatic corps. He's about as diplomatic as I am. But he's a junior assistant to a junior something, and they think it was the luckiest day of the world for them when he was assigned to Paris. The two little boys are darlings, but what grandmother doesn't think that?

"And it didn't take me long to get full up to here of Southern California. Do you know, Judy wanted me to look into some of those retirement communities they have all over the place there? My lord, I'm only forty-eight and most of them won't take anyone under fifty-five, but she thought maybe I ought to get my name on a list."

"What about the cruise?" asked Nora. "All we ever heard was three or four words, scrawled on picture postcards."

"Well, some of that was nice. I always have liked ships and the ocean, and some of the places were beautiful or interesting, but it was all so *organized*, and most of the people were *old*. I'll never *be* old like that, Nora. I'd rather be dead than spend my time in conversations about laxatives and be moved around by a tour director and a clock.

"I never really thought I cared much for Alder County, but, as all that time kept passing, it kept looking better and better, so I finally thought, Faye, get the hell home and start *doing* something."

Nora laughed. "So what are you going to do?"

"Well, I don't know. There's no need for me to get in any awful hurry about anything. I may sell Holland House, or let it be turned into something. I love the old place, but it's too big, too full of memories, too near the mill. Maybe I'll get Paul to sell me one of those lots up on East Ridge and have something small and nice built. Then maybe I'll start a business, just a little one, a dress shop, antique place, bawdy house, book shop. I really still don't know what middle-aged ladies on the loose do. I guess that's what I've been trying to find out for the past couple of years."

"You ought to marry again."

"I knew you'd say that. You're about the

fourteenth person who's said it since I got back. Old Charlie Bonner even propositioned me at the picnic on Sunday."

They giggled and Faye said, "If it had been Shane now..."

"Faye!"

Still smiling thoughtfully, she said, "He's too good-looking for his own good, that boy. Haven't you heard about how vain and silly widows my age get? Believe me, I've seen some dillies. But seriously, Nora, he's terrifically handsome and he's a fine person. Why hasn't he married somebody?"

"I would have thought you'd ask him."

"Oh, I did. Shane just grinned and old Charlie said he couldn't let him take the time for any such foolishness. But I wonder . . . does he brood about his parents?"

"I don't see how he could help it sometimes, Faye, do you? I mean, Steve died in prison—if Steve *was* his father—and no one knows a thing about the mother."

Faye said, "You know, Dan and I talked to Charlie about adopting him when he first brought him home, but that old man was like a she-bear with one cub. He'd hardly speak to us for a year."

"He and Vik were so close," said Nora. "After Charlie finally gave up and moved to town winters, I sometimes thought we *had* adopted him, and Charlie too."

"Well, for their sakes, Shane's and Charlie's, I guess I'm glad he wouldn't let the boy go. It's a kind of wonderful thing for that crotchety old man to have the young one to lean on and love him and be proud of. Charlie's had a hard life, losing his wife so young, Steve turning out the way he did."

"What kind of proposition did he make you?" asked Nora, smiling.

"It seems they can't keep a cook at their camp. He said if I'd come and do the cooking, he'd see I stayed an honest woman." She laughed. "But what I'm going to do for now is this: I'm going to see Cana Week and the Bicentennial business on the Fourth, then I'm going to close up Holland House again and spend most of the summer at the place over on Blackbuck. Any friends who think I'm worth seeing will have to come up there. I'm just going to be quiet and..."

"Demure?" suggested Nora.

"Oh, yes, demure as hell. I'm going to think and decide things and then go to work this fall. Don't let the girls know we're done with these things. Let's take some coffee out on the porch. You haven't told *me* a thing yet."

They sat there in the cool, still air, the noises of the creek, the children's play and the activities inside the house coming to them faintly. Nora talked about her children and other people they both knew.

"I hear Doreen Collins' uncle, Floyd Sheppard, the state senator, will be making us a speech on the Fourth," said Faye when they had got around to that. "Doreen and her folks were at the picnic Sunday, but I didn't see Wes. How is he?"

"I think he got there for the end of it. Maybe you'd already left. He and Viktor had to take both pickups and go down below Alder Falls to get some things. The truck that was bringing them broke down and they wanted the stuff in the store on Monday morning."

"Is Mitch serious about Peggy Lou? Forty people must have told me they're practically engaged."

"Yes, I think he is pretty serious, but they're not engaged, and I hope they won't be, for a long time, if ever."

"I don't suppose Doreen would be too pleased."

"No, and I don't think they'd be as serious as they are if she'd stop making such a fuss about it. You know how kids that age have to dig in their heels if they think parents are getting too bossy."

"Doreen will never forget that, according to her and the Sheppard family, she married beneath her. She surely wouldn't want that to happen to Peggy Lou. Peggy's gotten so pretty while I was away and she seems a sweet girl. It's Bruce who's like their mother. If you ask me, the Sheppards were lucky to get Doreen off their hands—beneath, above, or sideways. She's led Wes a hell of a life."

Nora nodded soberly. "He's a good, kind man, Wes. I wouldn't have another soul in Cana know it, but, for the past year or so, lots of nights he's slept at the office at the store. He's told Viktor he'd just rather not go home sometimes. That's all. No complaining or telling his troubles."

Nora was looking away down the valley and she said, after a little silence, "Faye, if Janet was one of your girls, what would you do about this thing she's doing?"

"Why, Nora, I don't see how I could do anything. She's of age. Young people do that these days—live together without benefit of clergy—old ones, too, for the matter of that. What's the boy like?"

"I guess that's the worst part of it, really. He's as bitter as gall and I just can't understand our Janet caring for him. She's always been such a happy, loving, optimistic person. . . . Gary's several years older than she is, long hair and a beard. One of these world reformers, only I don't think we'll have to worry about any big, serious changes if it's left up to him. He's all talk —hot air, more like. He's writing a book. . . . I know people live together, but Gary's such an —objectionable person. People—Belle Adams and a lot of others—are always saying to me, 'Don't you wish they'd get married? make some gesture at decency?' But the truth is, I'm glad they haven't. I can't imagine Janet staying with him much longer, and what worries me most is that there'll be a baby. I *know* Janet and I can't think why she's stayed with him this long—it's been since some time last fall—but I can't stand to think of her being hurt and stuck with a child by a man like that."

Alice came out then and, finding the two older women unoccupied, suggested they make sandwiches for the lunch of the work crew and the children.

Back in the kitchen, Faye said, "Tell me about the Rosenzweigs."

"You must have heard more than I know."

"I've heard a lot of guesswork and rumors."

"Well, I don't know much more than that. He's cranky and high-handed and not popular at the mill. I've heard Bert Adams say he's a hard man to work for, and you know Bert's the kind who can usually get along with almost anybody. They don't have any more to do with Cana or the county than they have to. They've had that really nice house with a swimming pool and everything built down the river a way. Sometimes, they seem to have people in to visit from somewhere else and they go away pretty often. I don't know, really, why they live here at all. Viktor sort of says the old man's trying to keep his young wife out of trouble."

"What's she like? I never have seen her, you know."

"I've heard she was a night-club singer when he married her. I've also heard she's his second wife. She must have been a very pretty girl, in a—full sort of way, if you know what I mean. I'd guess she's in her mid-thirties, but I think she'd still be awfully nice-looking if she didn't layer on the makeup and spend so much time with mirrors and with trying to be sure every passing man notices her."

Faye sighed. "I know the mill people aren't happy. I think I've heard about it from every worker and most of their wives. I can't help feeling I've let them down."

"What could you have done with just a one-third interest? Most people are still at least glad the mill didn't go to Pacific Slope Lumber. They've gobbled up every independent mill of any size in this part of the state except Holland's."

"I don't know what I could have done with a one-third interest, but probably something. That mill and those people took up a good part of my life. I still care."

"Well, Sharon said the Rosenzweigs will be

here for the barbecue tonight. Paul's surprised and awfully pleased that he agreed to come. Talk to them. You can probably find out more in one evening than the rest of us have in two years."

"Probably," said Faye complacently, and they laughed.

6

David and Gloria Rosenzweig rode in silent splendor into Cana from their new home two miles down the river. The afternoon was hot, but the big car was comfortably air conditioned, its windows tightly closed against exhaust fumes and the scent of roses, against traffic noise and the sounds of children laughing at play.

"I have to stop at the mill," said David, leaning to the intercom. Through the glass, they could see the wizened old Negro chauffeur nod politely. "Just for a few moments," David said apologetically to Gloria. "We've had some invoices missing and I want to see if they've been found."

She sighed restlessly. "I think this whole trip is a bunch of crap. Any time I have to go farther *up* this godforsaken valley, it's a bunch of crap. I don't know why we have to go stay at some scroungy old ranch house and look at *land*."

"Maybe you'll enjoy it a little, darling," he said, trying to be cheerful. "We haven't been up in these mountains before. They say the scenery is very nice."

71

"If you want to show me some *nice* scenery, then let's go to New York, or at least San Francisco. If I hear Cana Week or even Bicentennial again, David, I swear I'll throw up. You promised we'd go to Europe this year."

"The year is not quite half over yet, my love," he pointed out with an awkward attempt at teasing.

She looked at him with contemplation and contempt. He was forty-two and looked sixty, almost bald, his remaining thin iron-gray hair carefully combed, his face deeply lined, the dark, deep-set eyes flicking uneasily.

David Rosenzweig had been a child during World War II, had been in a prison camp for years, had seen members of his family, one after another, simply disappear. But when they could find and claim him, there had been wealthy relatives in the United States. Young David had attended the best schools and then had done well for himself, very rapidly, in his uncle's pulp and paper business.

There had been what his family considered a good marriage, but David and his wife did not feel it was so, almost from the first, and they separated after five years and two children. David had been thirty-two then and he had begun to have a true belief in fate and that for him it was all to be ill.

But on a business trip to New York in 1971, he had met Gloria Daly, and suddenly he became convinced that if he could have her, his whole life would be changed. He could find things to laugh about again, see, perhaps, irony rather than galling bitterness in so much that happened to him, perhaps have other children—Esther, his former wife, was doing all she could to turn his two small daughters against him. He was all that remained now of his branch of the family, and every man wanted a son, a son and a beautiful wife.

Gloria was beautiful when they met, a dark, lusciously voluptuous woman in the very ripeness of her prime, but she was frightened, even then. She had been modestly successful as a singer in small clubs, but this modest success had had its beginnings years before and it remained only modest. She had just become thirty when she met David, and what—the question would not be stopped from creeping into her mind sometimes at four or five in the morning—what happened to modestly successful night-club singers after they were thirty? thirty-five? forty?

He kept coming back to the club night after night, taking her out, taking her home, pleading with her to marry. Well, why not? she had decided when she woke unexpectedly at eleven o'clock one morning, a ghastly hour. She had heard that Atlanta, where he now lived, was not so bad. He had shown her, in black and white, his financial situation, eagerly, like a little boy bringing home a kindergarten drawing. She didn't like him at all well, but you couldn't have everything. He agreed to take her to Monte Carlo and then on a Mediterranean cruise as a honeymoon and they were quietly married. Gloria had a beautifully expensive wedding dress. After all, a wedding, any wedding, didn't happen to a girl every day.

Before the honeymoon ended, both of them were all too well aware of incorrect estimations. David found that Gloria was always going to be flirtatious with almost any man, perhaps more than flirtatious; he knew she was not the change he had hoped for so fervently in his life, but only another complication; that it would be wise, if he wanted her for himself, to take her away to a desert island. He heard of the proposed sale of the Holland mill and felt that that was about as near to a desert island as he would be able to coax Gloria.

Gloria learned that the "security" of marriage was not nearly all it was cracked up to be —David's concepts were more like bondage than security. He wanted a son, for God's sake, and he got huffy if she even looked at anything else male. She found he was not much good in bed, but then she herself had never been really much turned on by bed itself; her thrills came from seeing men get turned on about it. She learned his money was not all it had shown promise of being, not the way it was invested; then, to her absolute horror, she found he was considering buying a lumber mill in Idaho.

"Where?" she had cried in anguished indignation when he had told her he was having his attorney go over the papers.

"And I've found a very nice little piece of property for sale just south of Cana and about fifteen miles from Alder Falls, the county seat. We can have any kind of house you like built there."

"Between what and what?" She had been shrieking by then. "My God, David! I don't even know where *Idaho* is!"

But he went ahead with it, and Gloria came with him. She was afraid of trying to break back into her business and there was nothing else she could do. It had been hard enough getting started when she was twenty-one and had first changed her name from Dalowitz to Daly. Now she couldn't bear the thought of agents, managers, and patrons saying again, "Gloria who?"

So she went with David and she barely tolerated his pathetic attempts at humor and love, his fussy supervision. She didn't care that he chose the servants and tried to make sure that he, or at least they, knew where she was and with whom at all times. She had the house pretty much as she wanted it, this beautiful car, the furs and jewels, trips as often as she could force or cajole him into them—and he *would* take her to Europe this year.

David had begun to worry a little about money, not that it was a serious fear, or likely to become one. Gloria wanted so much. There were the alimony and child-support payments. His financial statements did not look nearly so pleasing as they had a few years ago, though he could still well afford a few additional good investments. Buying the mill had been a heavy drain, and the mill had not done so well in the past two years as it had in several years immediately prior to his purchase of it. Gloria's constant discontent was an irritation at times, but he was still obsessed with her, though he was not sure why, unless it was that he felt he had never really won at anything and was determined, somehow, to prove himself with her.

They had reached the mill, and the parking space in front of the offices was full. Someone had even taken his own reserved space. "Drive around, George," instructed David irritably. "You can wait at the back. I'll only be a few minutes."

To Gloria he said, "Would you like to come in?"

"Are you kidding?" she said icily.

As soon as David had gone inside, she said to George, "We'll go around to a liquor store while we're waiting. This fancy little bar's almost empty."

They were back in ten minutes. A log truck had pulled in while they were gone and sat, idling roughly, waiting to be unloaded. It was an ancient, battered red truck with "C Bonner" slapped on in black paint.

"Go in and see if Mr. Rosenzweig's been looking for us," Gloria said to George. "For Christsake, don't shut off the motor, you old fool! Do you think I want to roast to death?"

She was mixing herself a gin and tonic, and one for David. He was always at her about drinking too much, but then he was always at her about everything. If she had to go on this overnight camping trip, she was going to need a lot of fortification. David had assured her there'd be a house, a room, a bed to sleep in, that only those who cared to would be camping out, but Gloria was dubious. Gloria thought she had something that was the opposite of claustrophobia—she couldn't remember the name of it—a fear of open spaces. And that's what the West was to her, despite the god-awful mountains with their highly overrated scenery. From Chicago to the West Coast, all that Gloria thought of as a vast frightening emptiness, no civilization, no luxuries. She was still a little surprised to find even the bare necessities, like concrete runways at the Boise airport, capable of accommodating medium-sized jetliners. Sometimes, when they were coming back from somewhere and she had not got too drunk on the plane, trying to drown her sorrow about coming back, she half-expected to look down and see a cow pasture instead of a reasonably modern airstrip.

She sat back, sipping her drink, the car shutting out some but not nearly enough of the mill's horrendous noise. George came back.

"Mr. Rosenzweig's on the phone, ma'am. He said to say he's sorry it's taking longer than he thought, but he should be right out."

In looking at George, Gloria's eye had been caught by the driver of the old red log truck. He had opened the door and slid to the ground, lighting a cigarette as he leaned wearily against the shady side of the truck. He took off sunglasses and a cap, wiping his sweating face with the cap, then holding it in his free hand to let the hot little breeze blow over his hair.

"My God!" breathed Gloria and leaned closer to the tinted glass. Bronze hair, dark and burnished, lying in waves all over the neatly shaped head, a rather narrow face with every feature absolutely perfectly proportioned to every other, not a big man, rather slightly built, but strong and muscular-looking. There were imperfections, of course. He was dirty and tired-looking, and the skin of his face, which was almost too fair, looked as if it had been burning in the sun all summer. Somehow, the sunburn gave her a feeling of tenderness toward him. It made him look younger than he probably was. Could it be he was a virgin, something that looked like that?

Somebody from the mill's unloading crew, an old, bald man, came over and they talked. Gloria could not hear, but they were obviously discussing getting the old truck unloaded. The young man looked harriedly at his watch, indicating he was in a hurry; the old geezer shrugged, shook his head, as if there might be a wait, he was sorry but couldn't help it. He went away and the young man slumped against the truck, dragging on his cigarette.

Gloria glanced into her compact mirror and hesitated only a moment more before getting out of the car. "Hi," she said. "Hotter than hell, isn't it?"

He looked at her face—gray eyes he had, cool and dark with beautiful long dark lashes—and nodded, smiling a little.

"I'm waiting for my husband," she said, holding the monogrammed glass in her hand a little more obviously. "There's an extra gin and tonic in the car here, and air conditioning."

He glanced down at his torn shirt, dirty overalls, and boots, looking a little shy. "Thanks, but I'm driving."

She smiled disdainfully. "You certainly are. That truck must be a hundred years old. Come on, it'll do you good to relax. . . . I'm Gloria Rosenzweig."

He should be impressed. He should have *been* impressed, with the car and all. He was looking at her now, not just at her face, but the way she liked a man to look at her, but all he said, softly, was, "Yes, I know."

That irritated her. She turned sharply and went back to the car, perfectly conscious of how she looked, walking away, and that he was watching. Once inside, she stretched like a cat, luxuriating in the coolness and comfort, sipped her drink, and peeked into the mirror in her bag. Then, impulsively, she leaned forward and found a cheap plastic cup, mixed a very strong drink, and said to George, "Take this to that man over there. He's a kind of friend of Mr. Rosenzweig's and they've got no business making him wait in this heat."

When David returned, she was drinking his drink and mixing a fresh one for him. The old log truck had been taken away.

"I'm sorry to have been so long, darling," said David. "Oh, gin and tonic? Where did this come from? Well, it is good in the heat. Now, George, I told you the way to go, didn't I? All right, let's get going. It should be cooler up there, Gloria. It's almost two thousand feet higher, you know."

"Mmm," she said, meaning nothing.

As they passed swiftly and smoothly through Cana, David said, "I really am sorry it took so long, darling. I had to call Boise about those invoices and then Viktor Magnessen came in with a very nice order—the lumber yard, you know. This property we're going to look at belongs to his son."

Gloria remembered Paul Magnessen quite well. She had been strongly aware that he was attracted to her at that country-club dance the other night. Quite a handsome, sexy type too, in a dark, masterful sort of way. She preferred thinking about the other one just now. She had never seen a shade exactly the color of his hair, and those luscious thick dark lashes in the sunburned face...

David sipped his drink and said thoughtfully, more to himself than to Gloria, "I wish I could think of who it is that man reminds me of. I swear I know Viktor Magnessen from somewhere, or someone *so* like him. There's something different now, the age, the hair—"

"David, you've been going on like that about that damned man forever. I'm sick of hearing about it."

The road followed up the Alder River, through irrigated farmland, with ranches farther back, on and among the hills. From certain places, all three points of the elongated triangle formed by Stafford, Cloud Chief, and Blackbuck mountains could be seen. Only a few summer-white clouds briefly altered the hot, bright sky.

"Fix me a drink, will you?" said Gloria, suddenly impatient with the long silence. She loathed auto trips.

David looked at her with what might have been suspicion, then at the contents of the gin bottle, but began making drinks for both of them.

"He has some very good ideas, I think, Paul Magnessen. This valley could certainly use some progress and expansion. He claims, and so do others, that this place we're going to see has all the potential of another Sun Valley."

"It's *not* Sun Valley," she said shortly. "If we have to go someplace and stay within this damned state, why can't we *go* to Sun Valley?"

"Because we live here and I think it's time we took an interest. If this place has half the potential that's claimed, there'll be money to be made. You wouldn't mind that, I suppose?"

"How? There's nothing there but an old ranch."

"Development, Gloria. We might, for instance, invest in some acreage at, say, five hundred dollars an acre. In a few years, as the place is built up, we might subdivide and sell for two thousand an acre. Or I might invest in the corporation young Magnessen is planning to form and take some overall profit. That would take longer, but it might amount to a good deal more."

They passed swiftly through Blackbuck, scarcely aware of the little scatter of buildings. The lake was beside them now, blue and only vaguely restless in a faint breeze.

"Do you remember those people we met once in Boise named Cramer? He's a vice-president of PSL."

Gloria yawned. "No. What's PSL?"

"Pacific Slope Lumber," he said patiently, "*the* competitor with no competition around here except my mill. Anyway, the Cramers have a summer home on the other side of this lake somewhere. It's really rather pretty, isn't it? And this Cloud Valley where we're going is still higher in elevation, so it should be even cooler. Nicer in summer, more snow for skiing in winter. There's no lake there, of course, but Magnessen plans a small one."

"How about another drink?" she said.

"I think I've had enough, thank you," he answered meaningfully.

She sighed and leaned forward impatiently to pour it herself. He put his arm behind her so that she was encircled by it when she leaned back. She let it go, feeling more relaxed now, almost limp with the drinks, less unhappy.

The road was only graveled now, but the heavy car moved smoothly past a sign that read, "Entering Stafford National Forest."

"I really have been thinking we must take more interest in the community, the county, a project like this one."

"I'm only interested in getting out of here," she said, leaning her head against his shoulder. "David, you don't really plan to stay on in this nothing place, do you? You can't be *that* crazy."

"Yes, I do plan to," he said. "Can't you see the advantages of being a big duck in a little puddle?"

"Yuk!"

"It's not a pretty expression," he said soberly, "but it's what we are here, you know, and we ought to take advantage of the advantage."

His hand caressed her breast. She sipped her drink.

"I've been asked to join some things, the Rotary and such, and some of the ladies have called on you."

"If you think I want to be part of a sewing circle or something . . . They don't want anything to do with us, except to snoop."

"We're not the only Jews in town and we're certainly not Orthodox. I don't think we'd have any problem getting into the country club, for instance. The Epsteins are members, I know. They're the ones who own several mercantile stores around the valley and they seem a nice family."

"I know *her*. She's an old frump. She looks like a big fat hen that never can get its feathers unruffled."

He laughed and said, still smiling, "I've even thought we might attend one of the churches."

She had just sipped and she spluttered with gin and laughter. "Good God! Now I know you're kidding."

"Only about half, darling."

"But *why*, David?"

"As I said, to make us more a part of the community, so we'll be more content here, and—for the future."

She pulled away from him sharply. "Now listen, don't start that crap about a son. I swear I'll scream if I hear it again. If you want another brat so bad, get yourself a handmaiden or whatever they called them, like some of those old farts in the Old Testament."

There was a silence. They had reached the upper end of the lake now and turned east. They crossed a bridge with a sign, "Blackbuck Creek," passed for a mile or so beside towering, tree-covered Mount Stafford, which seemed in places to overhang the road, then another bridge, "Cloud Creek." They turned northeast, following up this stream on a much less used road.

"How much farther?" demanded Gloria sulkily.

"Five or six miles," he said quietly, wearily.

She opened her bag and looked into the mirror, straightening the shining black coils of her hair, renewing her lipstick. I don't know why I bother, she thought peevishly, for a crumby barbecue with a bunch of hicks. The very nerve of him, keeping at me to get pregnant! I don't look thirty-five, but I am, and having a kid, Christ! . . . Maybe I ought to start playing a little golf or something, though. I've put on five pounds this past year, just from sheer boredom. Then she remembered him again.

"David, who is C Bonner?"

"What?"

"C Bonner. I saw it on a log truck while I was waiting for you at the mill."

"Just a gyppo logger."

"What's that?"

"Well, it means he's independent, has his own operation, doesn't work for PSL or us or anyone. The gyppos supply us with the logs we don't cut ourselves; in fact, they supply about half our logs."

"You mean a man has a saw and a truck and..."

He smiled tolerantly. "It takes a little more than that, darling. C Bonner—old Charlie, they call him—has three trucks, I think. He has quite an operation. I believe he's working up this way this year, as a matter of fact, ten miles or so from where we're going."

"This was an old red truck," she said, studying her face in the mirror. "Looked like it ought to be in a junkyard."

He nodded, puzzled, but vaguely glad of her interest. "Yes, I know the one you mean. People have told me, though I don't think it's true, that that's the first log truck the old man ever had and he won't junk it. They say his grandson drives it most of the time. Either he's the only one with the nerve, or the only one the old man will trust his antique with."

David, usually so reticent, became almost expansive, and there was not a little of wistfulness in his tone. "They're a special breed, loggers. I've visited some of their camps. The gyppos are—wilder than most, not being union or anything, and their truck drivers are the wildest of all, always pushing and striving to make time. They have a pretty good safety record, really," he smiled his wan smile, "but then, who's going to get in their way? They drive these back roads as if they were superhighways and they the only vehicle on them, always pushing to get one more load to the mill."

Gloria, of course, was not listening, bored, distracted with her own fretful thoughts, until he broke off to say, "Why, look, there's one of Bonner's trucks now."

This was a green one. It flashed past on the downgrade, leaving the big sleek car in a cloud of dust.

"Does the grandson have really wonderful red hair?"

He looked at her sharply. She was smiling faintly at herself in the mirror. He looked away. "I really haven't the faintest idea," he said coldly.

Gloria's smile widened a little. She had beautiful teeth, small, sharp, and white in her lovely olive face.

7

"You look tired, Janet," said Ruby McCrary. "This is the first chance I've had to take a good look at you." She had noticed the red marks on the girl's face earlier, glanced at them again now, but refrained from asking anything.

Janet had just arrived in Blackbuck in time for Ruby's six-thirty opening of the cafe, and there had been breakfast—not many customers—then the cabins to work on, getting ready for the weekend, this being a Friday. The truth was, she had had almost no sleep the night before, and she had to stifle a yawn as she and Ruby took a short coffee break.

"Well," Ruby went on to explain the answer to her own comment, "ever'body around here in the tourist or ranching or logging business gets to looking tired by the middle of July. It's like the ants and the grasshoppers—you know, in the Bible. We're the ants and we got to make hay while the sun shines. I just hope to God Bill stays up there in the woods and works for old Charlie the rest of the summer. I did tell you Charlie sent down to see about finding a couple of hands and a cook, didn't I? One of his men got hurt, first of the week, and another one quit. They say they haven't had a decent cook all season. Bill can be a good one when it suits him." She laughed. "Bill's tried workin' in the woods for Charlie before but it never lasted long. He thinks *I'm* a slave driver, but maybe cookin' won't be so bad. It's good money up there, while the season lasts. This place just barely pays for itself, and what Bill mostly does around here is ring up sales and talk to people. Some men are like that—just not natural-born workers—women, too, but it seems to show up more in men. How's that book of—uh—Gary's comin' along?"

"Pretty well," said Janet, trying not to let her voice sound dull. "I think he's about ready to have some of the first chapters retyped." She sipped her coffee. "Ruby, if there's room, can I stay down here tonight? I told Gary I might. There's something wrong with the bus and it won't go uphill very well."

"Why, sure," said the older woman warmly. "If all the cabins should happen to get rented, you can stay at the house with us. Have Cindy's bed if you want to. She's goin' down to Alder Falls to see about work and stay overnight with a girl friend." She sighed. "My lord, you get 'em up old enough to be some help around the place and they run off someplace else to look for a job."

Janet stood up. "I guess I'd better go and finish with the beds and things before lunchtime."

"If you can catch Billy or Micky, send 'em in here. They can help with salad and stuff for lunch."

The Blackbuck cabins were rustic log, drafty, and ill-furnished. They stood in a picturesque scatter among the trees near the river not far below the dam. To Janet, the linen cart seemed very heavy today as she moved it along the stony paths.

She had told Gary last night, or rather, he had finally figured it out for himself. They had been making love, and as he ran his caressing hands over her, he had become abruptly aware of the new swelling of her lower abdomen.

"My God! Why didn't you take those fucking pills!" he shouted, his voice going shrill with anger.

"I did, Gary," she said, her own voice rough and uncertain from fighting tears. "They're not guaranteed. They—"

"You're lying!" He flung off the covers, turned up the oil lamp, and threw a stick of wood into the stove. "You did this deliberately, you little bitch. I told you I never wanted any kids. This lousy, stinking world doesn't need more people."

She turned away from the light, slipping back into her pajamas, biting her lips together to try to stop their trembling.

"Mother Janet!" he cried mockingly, "barefoot and pregnant. Just about fits you, doesn't it? Just about your level of mentality. How long is it? —how far along?—whatever the hell it is they say."

87

"About three months," she said quietly, trying to muster some of her own former enthusiasm to communicate to him. "It should be an Aquarius baby, Gary. I thought we could—"

"Screw Aquarius! Now I suppose you think we'll line up a preacher and all that other establishment crap."

"No."

"Well, it won't work. I've told you everything from the very beginning—no ties. That's why you've done this, isn't it?"

"Honestly, Gary, I *took* the pills. You've picked them up at the drugstore yourself a couple of times. It's just that—"

"Sure, sure!" he sneered, "but not for a long time, now that I come to think of it, and how do I know you weren't throwing them down the toilet or something? Wasting money along with the rest of this shit?"

"I *took* them," she said angrily. "For some people—a few—they just don't work. I can't help that."

"Women have been saying things like that since the beginning of time. It won't work, you know. I don't feel even the tiniest pinch of compulsion to watch over you, help you build a nest and all that crap. You got yourself into this."

She said nothing. He stalked around the room, slammed a book on the table, threw another stick of wood into the range. Then he came back to the bed and began getting into his clothes. "I *was* going to work on the book tonight, but you've managed to screw that up too."

"Shall I make some coffee?" she offered. "We could talk—"

"Talk about what, for God's sake?"

She tried to make her voice sound brave, matter-of-fact, a little enthusiastic. "Well, for one thing, I've been thinking—I'm a nurse and there are lots of books. We could deliver the baby right here—it'll be the middle of winter—or wherever we are. Lots of people are doing home deliveries these days."

Gary went greenish around the edges of his beard. "Do you want to make me puke along with everything else? Christ! Do you think I'd want anything to do with a filthy mess like that? Besides, what makes you think that 'wherever we are' will be the same place? You know how I feel about traps and ties."

She was putting on the coffee pot and kept silent.

"I don't want any damned coffee. What you'll do is get rid of it."

"What!"

"You're a nurse, so get it out of there."

She gulped. "Gary, I won't do that. I don't really know how, or have any—instruments, and even if I did, I—couldn't."

"Don't you feel filthy?" he cried. "Think what's inside you, a slimy, little fishy-looking thing, a parasite, living off you. How could you let me make love to you all this time, after you knew?" He shuddered. "Christ! *I* feel filthy, just by association."

"You *were* an accessory." Janet had not meant to sound so bitter and angry, but she had never believed it would be quite this bad, even at the beginning.

"I'd rather masturbate than be mixed up with a thing like that. I'll never screw with you again until you've got it out—if then."

He had gone on and on until finally Janet pulled one of the rolled-up sleeping bags from under the bed.

"It's a nice night," she said. "I'm going to sleep out."

"Do you think I give a fuck?"

"Tomorrow's Friday." She gathered some clothes and the alarm clock. "Ruby's expecting a busy weekend. Maybe I'll stay overnight in Blackbuck tomorrow."

"Stay all year. Run home to your precious family. I'm not enough for you. That's always been it, hasn't it?"

"No, it's not."

"You promised to start helping with the shitty typing next week, but I suppose you'll be having morning sickness and all that fakey crap women have dreamed up over the centuries."

"I've had it. It's mostly over now. I'll do the typing and whatever else is needed. I'll have the kid while I'm working in the fields and never miss a weed or a cotton boll or whatever." She let the door slam.

The night was fairly bright, with a half moon and no clouds to speak of. Janet climbed up to her rock and spread her things. Zipped into her sleeping bag, she checked that her clock was wound and set. It was already past midnight.

The light was still on in the cabin. She turned away from it, determined to sleep, and she must have dozed, for suddenly Gary was beside her, groping at her face. The moon was temporarily clouded.

"Janet, you've always said you love me." His voice was low, breaking a little with pleading and hurt. "Nobody ever *did* love me. You know what a bitch my mother is. Since I was about twelve, the few times I've been anywhere near her for a day or two, she's made me pretend to be her nephew. Her last two husbands never dreamed she had a kid. That's how I can keep getting money out of her—blackmail, I suppose—but, goddam her, she owes me *something!*"

"I know, Gary," she said gently and tentatively took his hand.

"But *you*'ve said you love me."

"Yes. . . . I knew you'd be upset about the baby, Gary. Truly, I didn't mean it to happen, but it's a fact now. Don't you think you could—after a while, I mean—come not to mind so very much? It won't interfere with us and—and maybe we can make up, a little, with this baby, for some of the things you've never had."

"Make up, hell!" He was furious again. "Why should I try to make up to anyone for anything? *I*'m the one who's been cheated all my life. . . . If you love me, you'll get an abortion."

"Gary, it's too late," she said pleadingly. "Three months is—"

"Some places, they do it as late as twenty weeks, don't they? I don't remember where, but I read that someplace. I'll telegraph good old Emily for the money. You go and get it taken care of. My God! I can't bear the thought of you swelling and getting grotesque and ugly and shameful-looking. Then a brat, squalling and squirming—Christ!"

"Gary, I want my baby," she said softly, adamantly. "I still do care about you, but I won't have this baby killed. Somehow, it was meant to be. We tried not to let it happen, but it did. I was awfully upset when I first began to suspect, but now I'm glad. If you can just give yourself a little time, maybe it won't seem so terrible to you. I wish you were not so hurt, but honestly—"

He snatched his hand away from hers and slapped her as hard as he could. After a moment, she could hear that he was crying. Something inside her seemed suddenly to have turned cold and hard and—indifferent?

"You're just like all the rest of the world. I should have known better than even to begin thinking I could trust you. I sat down to write after you came up here, and there was just—nothing. You can't have any idea what that's like. You've ruined my book, you whore, you and your belly."

After a moment of silence except for his erratic sobs, she felt she must say something, even a little kind. Her voice was dull with multiple pain. "You've been getting on so well with your book. You'll be able to go on tomorrow or the next day. Everyone has times—"

"It's the thought of that—*thing* ... I'm going to take the cycle and go somewhere for a while. I don't know where, or when or *if* I'll be back."

"All right. What will I do about the bus?"

"How the hell should I know? You've managed to ruin everything else."

She waited; he was still beside her. "You'd better think about this thing good while I'm gone, Janet. Maybe get your folks to take care of the abortion. That would be faster than sending to Emily, and they hate me enough to spend the money. I will have to come back, for my books and my things, and you'd better be rid of it, or on your way to have it done."

Silence.

"Do you hear me?" The voice broke in a furious shout that echoed among the rocks and trees.

"I won't kill my baby."

"What's all this *my* baby stuff, for Christsake? Don't *I* have anything to say about it?? I have no doubt I'd be expected to provide support for the brat—if it really is mine. Maybe—"

"I didn't think you wanted to have anything to say about it, except—"

"I say *I don't want it!* If you make some sense and get rid of it, see it doesn't happen again, *maybe* we can talk about trying to get back to where we were, *if* it seems worth it after this."

He left her. In a short time, the motorcycle roared up. It took a long time fading off down the mountain.

Janet had all the beds in the cabins made now, and the bathrooms stocked. She went in by the cafe's back door, slipped into her uniform, rewound her braids more tightly around her head, and went into the kitchen.

"Two families and one of old Charlie's truck drivers," reported Ruby, "and it's not even quite noon. I already got the order from the logger and the folks by the door."

The truck driver was not Shane. Of course he was not, Janet told herself impatiently. Ruby would have said it was Shane if it had been. Why did she feel like crying because it wasn't Shane? Because she wanted so desperately to see some of her family just now—not to tell them anything, only to see them, hear them, maybe touch them for a moment—and Shane was the same as family. She took the orders, served the customers automatically.

Gary would be all right, or at least better.

He'd have to be. Surely he'd have to be. But if he wasn't—well, then he could leave. It was her place up there, Lucky Streak, the cabin, all of it. The back-to-nature thing was only a passing fancy for Gary. She was the one who really cared. If he decided to try to go on with their life together, then she would try to be pregnant as unobtrusively as possible. That made her smile ironically as she set plates before an elderly couple. If he did not want things to go on—well, she was not going home to be a burden and a shame to her family. She could go on working at something—almost anything, for a while, of course—and there were places for unwed mothers in the cities. And when the baby was born, with or without Gary, she could love it enough for two. She remembered her shifts in the nursery of the Spokane hospital, the soft inner warmth that had come each time she took the small weight of an infant in her arms.

Shortly after one, Faye Holland came into the cafe. She did not sit down, but went straight back to the kitchen where Ruby was cooking and Janet was making a cold ham sandwich.

"Looks like you two have got plenty of business."

"Why, Faye! How are you?" cried Ruby. "Sometimes Fridays or Mondays are like that, with so many people taking three-day weekends these days. All that stuff going on in Cana two and three weeks ago kept some folks away from up here."

"Well, I've been at the place up on Blackbuck Creek for two weeks now, all by myself, but I decided I'd better get back to civilization for a while or it could get to be a habit, just staying up there. Your mother called last night, Janet. She and Patty are driving Alice to Boise to get her plane for San Francisco. They'll be staying overnight, so I thought I'd go along for the ride, maybe do a little shopping. Nora asked if I'd seen you. How are you?"

"I'm fine, Aunt Faye."

Faye came a little closer, studying her face. "You look a little peaked to me. How's Gary?"

"He's all right."

"Working on his book?"

"Most of the time, yes."

"What can we give you to eat?" asked Ruby.

"Those chicken fries look good. One of those, mashed potatoes, Thousand Island dressing." She moved to the door but turned back. "Well, now, Ruby, Blackbuck is coming up in the world. You've got yourself some distinguished customers."

"Who?" wondered Ruby, trying to peer past her shoulder.

"Paul Magnessen—but you've had Magnessens before—*and* the Rosenzweigs."

"My lord! those new people at the mill?" Ruby went to the window and rubbed a clear spot in its steam to look at the parking lot. "Look at that car! It's a block long, and a colored driver. What'll we do with him? I don't think we've ever had a Negro eat here before."

"Feed him," said Faye succinctly and left them.

"Faye!" Paul greeted her warmly. "Here, sit with us. You know David and Gloria Rosenzweig, of course."

Faye shook hands with David, who had risen,

and returned Gloria's slight, frosty inclination of the head with a nod and a thoughtful look.

"You've been hiding," Paul accused her. "Nobody's seen you since Fourth of July."

"I was up at old Charlie's camp a week ago," she said. "Otherwise, I have been keeping pretty much to myself. What are you folks doing up here? Something to do with Cloud Valley?"

"No, as a matter of fact, David and Gloria are thinking of renting the Cullen place."

"Where's that?"

"You know that land up near the head of the lake on the Cloud Creek side that used to belong to Jim Everett? Some people from California named Cullen bought some of it and had a really nice summer place built. When we had that get-together at Cloud Valley, the Rosenzweigs mentioned that they might like to rent a place up here for the summer. I didn't know of a thing then, but I got a letter from Jay Cullen a couple of days ago saying they weren't going to be able to make it this year and that the place could be rented if I could find the right tenants. . . . Oh, hello, Janet."

"Mr. and Mrs. Rosenzweig," said Faye smoothly, "this is Paul's sister Janet."

Janet acknowledged their greetings, but her smile was because of Aunt Faye. Paul, she felt almost certain, would not have introduced her as his sister in her waitress's uniform, but it was so typical of Aunt Faye, who tended, usually without malice, to be a little deflating to people like Paul. Faye was a down-to-earth, all-your-cards-on-the-table sort of person, and Janet loved her. She wondered about talking things over with her.

Well, maybe sometime, when she knew more about what needed talking about. Aunt Faye could probably be more objective than most of the people she cared about.

"Maybe you'll show me where the little girls' room is," said Gloria to Janet. "I don't see any sign—and can we get a cocktail?"

Something about Gloria Rosenzweig tempted Janet to direct her out back to the privy that still stood there. Aunt Faye might have done it, but there was the good name and civilization of the McCrarys and Blackbuck to be upheld.

"It's a lovely house," Paul was going on enthusiastically to David and Faye. "The Cullens', I mean; very nicely furnished. And what about you, Faye? I thought you were going to look at some lots on East Ridge."

"Yes, well, I plan to. I'm going to see Matt Erikson if I have time while I'm in town and find out what kind of a house I want. Then I'll look at land."

"I thought one looked at land and then fitted the house to it," said David with a smile.

"Not this lady," replied Paul with a tolerant laugh. "She's apt to do anything backward."

"Well, she certainly did all right running the mill," said David warmly, "backward or forward."

Faye was strongly tempted to start asking him about board feet, the new planer, freight charges, the union, but she determinedly put down the urge.

"I've been thinking, Paul, that I'll turn Holland House over to the city, or maybe the county."

"What?"

"Yes, it could be turned into a library, museum, general club meeting place, I don't know exactly what."

He was dismayed. "That's a very valuable piece of industrial property."

"But there aren't any industries."

"We need some, though, at least one other sizable one besides the mill. It would stabilize Cana's economy nicely and that property would be an enticement if you're ready to sell. With the house torn down—"

"I don't want the house torn down, Paul."

Janet brought their drinks, and Gloria returned.

"No hot water in the damn john," she muttered to David. "Is this all there is up here in the way of a restaurant?"

"It would seem so, my dear," he said softly as Paul and Faye went on talking. "It was your idea to look for a summer place, remember, though I think you're absolutely right. It really is several degrees cooler here than in Cana, much quieter, nice scenery."

"Well, the place better have hot water and a lot of other things. If we take it, I want to ask Ben and Velda Schwartz up right away—that is, if they'll leave their kids someplace. You know what boating nuts they are, and Paul says there's a boat with the place."

David was jealous of athletic young Ben Schwartz, and he frowned. "I thought you wanted to be far from the madding crowd."

"Well, for Christsake, I don't want to just sit up there and petrify."

"Shall I take your orders?" asked Janet.

"I've already ordered," said Faye as they seemed to wait for her.

Gloria, after casting the Ben Schwartz barb at David, now turned to Paul. "Will you order for me, please? I have a terrible time making decisions."

At Ruby's insistence, Janet went to the McCrary house in midafternoon and slept for a couple of hours when things were not busy. She felt much better then, and thought that now people who knew her would not keep questioning the state of her health.

The evening was busy, with people up for the weekend or summer people from around the lake having an evening out. Ruby's food was simple, but she gave lavish helpings and the cafe was a friendly place with its adjoining bar. By nine o'clock, everyone was gone from the tables except for a young couple who was taking the last vacant cabin.

"We'll close up soon," Ruby said. "Ray'll keep the bar going, but nobody'll want food. If they do, they'll be out of luck."

The couple had gone and both women were working on clean-up when a truck drew up with a heavy hiss of air brakes. "Why, there's Shane and your brother," said Ruby. "I better heat the griddle up again."

Janet met them at the door and hugged them, an arm around each.

Shane grinned. "We ought to stop in here more often."

"What are you doing taking logs down at this time of night?"

"One of the dozers needs a part," Mitch said.

"So, since somebody had to go to town, Charlie made us wait to get a load on."

"How did he let two of you get away?"

"Shane's already been down with two loads today, and Charlie was afraid he'd go to sleep. I thought I'd go see Dad. Mom's gone to Boise with Alice, I guess."

"Shane, you just look awful," Ruby was saying fussily. "That old granddaddy of yours'll have you wore out before you're thirty."

"I haven't got long to go then," he said, "but Charlie does more work than anybody and he figures everybody ought to thrive on it. A steak would be awful good, Ruby, if it's not too late."

"Course it's not too late. Sit down, both of you. Do you want some coffee?"

Mitch said, "I think I'll get a beer, see what's going on on Ray's side of the building."

"I'll have my coffee in a bowl," Shane said wearily, "one of those big crocks you've got back there."

Janet brought him a cup. "I can bring them two at a time," she offered.

"This will do for a minute. We brought your puppy."

"What?"

"Remember when we were first moving the show in up there and you came to visit and saw the ranger's dog Dixie? You asked Bud if you could have one of her next pups? Well, they're about six weeks old now and getting underfoot up at Cloud Chief Station, so he's out there. You did say a male?"

"Oh, I'll go and see him when I've brought your food. Will he be afraid out there alone in the dark, do you think?"

"I don't think so. We've got him in a box. He was asleep. Bud said to tell you he's the pick of the litter, and Charlie said to ask if—Gary's drawn up the petition."

"He's been working on it. I think it's almost done."

Mitch came back through the connecting door with his beer, and Janet refilled Shane's cup.

"You just sit down and talk to them," Ruby instructed when she went to the kitchen. "I'll bring things. Don't you want somethin'? You didn't hardly have any supper."

"I'll fix their salads, Ruby, thanks. Maybe I'll have a glass of milk or something."

When she returned to the dining room, Shane had brought in the puppy in its box. It looked up at Janet with great, sleepy dark eyes, yawning prodigiously.

"Oh, he's just beautiful!" she picked him up tenderly and held him against her cheek.

"He's going to be big," Shane said. "Look at those feet."

"Shane picked him out for you," Mitch said. "He said this pup reminded him of you. I guess it must have been the feet."

"No," Shane said, "more like the ears."

"Here, hold him," she said. "I really may as well bring the coffee pot."

When she came back and took the puppy on her lap, she said, grinning, "I guess I couldn't expect you to take Bud Stallings a kiss?"

They laughed and Shane said, not meeting her eyes, "I'd give it to Dixie, though."

"Now what's this?" demanded Ruby, coming in with the steaks.

"It's a Seeing Eye dog, Ruby," Mitch explained quickly. "See how he's looking around, seeing everything?"

"You just see he's out of here before somebody from the Board of Health comes."

"How long's Gary plan to be in the wilderness?" asked Mitch, cutting into his meat.

"I—I didn't know you knew he'd gone in."

"He came through camp this morning and left his cycle. I didn't see him. Joe Butler said he said he was going to hike in for a while."

Janet looked at Shane to see if he had known Gary was gone when he asked about the petition. He had.

"He said just a few days," she extemporized, looking down at the puppy. "He's gotten stuck on something about his book, so he ... What will I name you?" she asked the little dog, who was licking her hands frantically and, somehow, making her want to cry.

"We've called him Wrecks," said Mitch, "you know, with a Wr."

"Well, you're not to call him a dumb thing like that again," she said. Then, "You're coming back tomorrow?"

"After we get the logs unloaded and the dozer part," said Shane.

"There's something wrong with the bus," she said. "Dewey, over at the station, doesn't have them—the new points he thinks it needs—but I could get them in Cana, couldn't I?"

"Sure," said Mitch, and Shane said, "Do you want to come with us? We have to try to be back at our show by noon."

"Well, it's Saturday and Ruby..."

"What's this?" asked Ruby, coming to take the fourth chair at the table. And when she had heard, she said warmly, "You go on, Janet. You never see your folks. I can manage just fine in the morning. It won't be the first time, that's for sure. How's my Bill gettin' on with cookin' up there in the woods, boys?"

8

Viktor got up as early as usual that Saturday morning. He dressed, went downstairs, put on the coffee and then went out to pick some peaches. It was good, knowing the house behind him was not empty. He did not mind staying alone, of course; occasionally, it was very pleasant, but last night, as he had sat reading and smoking his pipe, he had suddenly remembered that five years ago on this night, young Vik and Anne had died, their small car crumpled in a collision with a log truck. He shivered and hoped Nora would not take note of the date....

How proud he had been when that little boy was born!—awed. There was Paul, just turned five, whom Viktor had considered his child from the time he and Nora were married, but there was something very special, ineffably good, about a man's first son. When Nora had told him, so early in their marriage, that she thought she was pregnant, he had been uneasy, a little dismayed, though he had tried hard not to let it show. She was so happy and excited. Viktor had felt that there were still so many things to be sorted out in his mind, so many things that needed the perspective of passing time. Was he ready for new fatherhood? Did he have the right after . . . ?

Once he had begun to know Nora Mitchell, there had been little question of his marrying her, whether or not he had the right. She and her kind, incisive, businesslike mother had been balm, the medicine he needed after the horrors of war and the uncertain, half-lost years that followed. And, once they were married, there had been no question of Nora's being put off about that first pregnancy. She loved children; wanted a houseful of them.

"It'll be a boy," old Alice Mitchell had predicted, almost from the beginning. "And he'll be named for you," Nora had said contentedly to her husband.

Viktor had not been pleased about that. Somehow, he did not want anyone else to bear the name Karl Viktor Magnessen; it had been through enough—too much. But Nora was adamant. "Of course that'll be his name. He'll be the fourth generation. Or is it the fifth? There's something special and nice about carrying a name on like that. Next time, if we have a girl, I'd like to name her for Mama, but this is little Viktor."

Sitting there alone in his living room last night, Viktor could not help wondering if there might be a curse on the name. His grandfather had been all right, a fine, strong man who lived to an old age and never had any serious problems, physical or emotional, that Viktor knew of, but his father, who had been called Karl, had been somehow badly marred by the First World War. Viktor, born in 1910, could not remember his father prior to the war, though he was told that Karl had once been a laughing, carefree young man. Afterward, where his own memories began, his father had been a big, brooding man, almost a shadow who, when he did speak, was usually in opposition to something. Peter, the older brother, and Christiana, the little sister, had seemed acceptable to the father, when he happened to notice them, but he and the second son, Viktor, had rarely found common ground or agreed about anything. When his wife, Janet, died in 1920, Karl had become ever more withdrawn. He was a fine carpenter, a master builder, and his work was all he seemed to care to think of. The grandparents had raised his children on their dairy farm near Copenhagen. Peter's ambition, almost from infancy, had been to run the farm. Perhaps Karl had assumed that Viktor would follow him in carpentry, though Karl had never said so openly. So far as Viktor's life work was concerned, Karl had never said anything more than, "No, I do not want you going away to school."

The grandparents had smoothed that out somehow, so that Viktor had been able to study in London, Paris, Vienna. Probably they had offered to pay for it and Karl had shrugged sourly and forgotten. The grandparents had paid initially, but then Viktor had begun working at anything he could find and had managed to make most of his own way. His brother Peter, he learned years later, had resented his going away, all that education, the way their grandmother had boasted.

Grandmother Rachel, and her stories—always stories! She knew the myths and fairy tales of three countries, in addition to some Greek ones, and when those palled on her imagination, Viktor suspected, she changed them to suit herself or made up new ones. She had had a lot of stories about curses being placed on a name or a family, and almost Viktor's first thought when they had received the call about young Vik and Anne was the memory of such a story. Anne had just announced to them that day that she was pregnant with a second child—another Karl Viktor Magnessen? ...

But if such a phenomenon existed, such a curse, he, this Viktor, sitting in the living room of the comfortable old house on Tamarack Road, Cana, Idaho, was responsible. All those years in Germany ...

Sometimes, after he had come to know Nora, and as the passing years slowly salved his inner wounds, there might be entire weeks, then months at a time, when the memories did not come into his conscious mind. Nora, comfortable, self-assured, complacent Nora, who almost never doubted, had been his salvation, Nora and the children and, in those first years, Nora's good mother.

When they knew that Vik and Anne were dead, after the first numbing shock, when Nora had begun to look for reasons, she had said through her tears, "Somehow, it was God's will. We're just not meant to understand everything." For Nora, to find a reason, even such an ephemeral one, made things a little more acceptable, a little more bearable. As a young man, Viktor had believed there were many things in life that had no reason, that life, being, was something like chess pieces flung helter-skelter on a board and then a game attempted. But when Nora had sobbed those words, he had asked himself, is it a punishment? If there is a God, a Something, does He—

It?—have such a long, cruel memory, such an ability for holding grudges against someone so insignificant as I, that he would take my son instead of me?

Later, when the pain of loss was dulling slightly, he had tried to convince himself it was a foolish idea, that he was steeping himself in guilt and self-pity, becoming brooding and morose as he remembered his own father's being, making Nora bear most of the burden alone....

She would be with Patty and Faye now, in a Boise motel. Alice's flight would have left more than two hours ago. Alice herself would be getting back to her San Francisco apartment by now. Nora and Faye would probably stay up most of the night, talking like a couple of young girls, and tomorrow they would shop, and Nora would enjoy touring the stores far more than little Patty did.

Nora had a capacity for getting something good, something enjoyable out of almost everything. She was the most wonderful, tenacious lover of life he had ever known. They were right, Alice and Paul and the others. He was about to be sixty-six and he ought to do more things with Nora, spend more time with her, be suffused in his own pleasure because of that which radiated vicariously from her.... But once they had found Cana, bought the house and his share of the lumber and hardware business, one of the things Viktor had enjoyed and appreciated most was the resting—not a nonworking kind of rest, but of having found a Place, his place, where he could stay, could be quiet, more and more rarely tormented; for the most part, at peace.

He tried, smiling faintly, to communicate with his wife over the miles between Cana and

Boise: "I love you so dearly. You have always been the best thing in my life, the very best. No questions, no probings, because you are so honest, so open and forthright that it scarcely enters your mind that everyone else may not be as you are. You gave up Fox Falls for me, the place where you were born and your parents were born, to come to a place where we were both strangers because I could not stop being restless. You have always simply accepted me for what I am—what you have believed me to be. I ought to try more often and in more ways to show my love for you; how very much I love you. You made me want to be alive again, with the things a healthily living man wants—a priceless wife, fine children, a home, a business."

He had stood up abruptly from his chair. While she's away, I'll paint the kitchen and hall. He smiled with the anticipated joy of her surprise and pleasure. It's not too late to call Wes now and tell him I may not be coming in until late tomorrow. Then I'll go down to the store and get the paint. We've got just the colors she wants. I can get an early start in the morning. They aren't likely to be back until around suppertime. By then, even most of the smell will be gone in this weather.

He made the call and the trip to the hardware store, but when he was back, he was restless. He could start the painting tonight, it was what he would have liked to do, but it seemed a little silly. He smiled. If he kept the house lighted up all night, old Belle Adams down the road, knowing Nora was away, would speculate to anyone who would listen about what had been going on. And if he started the job now, he would finish it. He was too tired for that. The restlessness was the memories, the whole long train of them, started by the recollection that five years ago tonight his son had died.

Viktor started, shivering, at the sound of the engine of a heavy truck as it whined up the hill, air brakes hissing in front of his house. But it was a truck of Charlie Bonner's, he could see by the outside light—not the old red anachronism, but a newer, blue truck. Shane! Not only Shane, but also Mitch and—and Janet. Had they, or one of them somehow sensed how much he needed not to be alone on this particular night? Or was he simply getting as superstitious as his good old grandmother?

They were tired, the three young people, and Viktor was tired; now he could give in to it. There were things for sandwiches in the refrigerator, but Mitch was the only one with an interest in food. Viktor had a beer with his son. Shane found the bourbon and Janet asked for some in her Coke. They sat around the kitchen table, talking rather desultorily for a while, then went to bed. Janet made up the couch in the little downstairs room, which was a place of many purposes, so that she would not have to come down to take her puppy outside.

Viktor had still been awake to hear the loud old clock downstairs strike one, but then he had slept deeply, and now, as the sun rose over the high ridges to the east of the valley, he was placing furry peaches gently in a basket, moving about slowly and with pleasure through the dew-wet grass.

Janet came up silently behind him and put her arms around his waist. "Guess who."

Viktor turned and kissed her. "One of my favorite daughters. How are you? It's going to be another hot day."

"Can I have that peach?"

"Why do you think I picked it? You shouldn't be up so early."

"The puppy woke me. Isn't he a darling, Daddy? I don't know what to call him."

Viktor looked down at the fat, fluffy black pup, making his awkward way through the grass to Janet's still-bare feet.

"You ought to wash that peach, you know," he said.

"It's all right," she said round a mouthful. "Shane's up, drinking your coffee. I came out to ask if I can borrow the pickup. Then he can leave the log truck to be unloaded and we can see about the dozer part and the points for my bus. After that, I'll come back and cook breakfast for all of us."

When they had been gone about a half hour, Viktor went into the house with his peaches and began mixing pancake batter. Mitch came downstairs, rubbing his eyes. Viktor had begun to fry sausages when the others returned.

"Walt Roberts hasn't got the part we need," Shane said harriedly. "He called Boise and they're sending it up on the bus, but the bus won't be in till noon."

"Jesus!" Mitch said. "Old Charlie'll have both our asses."

"That's no way to talk in front of a lady," Janet said primly. "Here, Daddy, let me do that; exactly what I was going to fix, pancakes and sausages."

"We stopped at our house," Shane said, "and

I found some clean clothes. I'll have a shower before breakfast if there's time."

"Charlie really is rough on him," Mitch said angrily when Shane had gone upstairs. "Sometimes it seems like he takes everything out on him, and Charlie can always find something to take out. Shane's doing all the book work, payroll and everything this year, hauling most of the time, cutting when he can, trying to pacify the crew. I wouldn't take half the guff he does from that old man."

"Oh, you know Charlie's mostly bark," Janet said, "at least to family. Shane knows it, for sure."

"You always have got along with old Charlie better than I have," Mitch said. "What I mostly try to do is keep out of his sight. I guess it's because, deep down, I've always been a little afraid of the old buzzard."

"That will probably pass, little brother, as you grow older."

"Yeah, but seriously, I've always wondered, Dad, is that the way the old man treated Shane's dad? I mean, it would be enough to make anybody go wrong, or however it is they put it."

"I can't say for sure, Mitch. All that happened before we came here. I suspect it is, though. Charlie expects a lot from himself and as much from other people, especially family. They say Steve didn't work for him much after he was grown. He was in the Army and they say he just—bummed around a lot, an early hippie-type, beatnik, whatever they were called then... But I think Shane and the old man have a very special relationship. It's love, but of a rather unique kind. Shane can let Charlie's rough tongue pass most of

111

the time, but, now and then, he can be just as stubborn as the old man.

"I remember once here at our house when they got into an argument about college. Vik and Anne were home, I remember; it was the Christmas of their first year in college. Charlie was going on about higher education being a waste of time and money for most people, and Shane said he intended to begin college the next fall, when he had finished high school. Charlie raved about that. He said twelve years of school was more than enough for a logger and a lot more.

"I went outside and started splitting wood for the fireplace and Shane came out to help. In a little while, Charlie followed and went right on about the college idea, saying the boy wouldn't have a cent from him for such crazy notions. Finally, Shane sunk his ax into a big log and just turned around and looked at the old man until Charlie ran down. Then Shane said, 'I've been paying my way since I was about ten. I can do it at college, too, and if you don't like it, you can go to hell.' Then he walked away. Charlie's face turned red, but after I'd split a few more logs, he pulled out the ax Shane had been using—and it wasn't easy for him—and he said, 'That's some boy, Viktor, and he'll do it too. He don't git stubborn and contrary about a thing very often, but when he sets his head, hell, high water nor nothin'll stop him.' And he was smiling. Charlie brags about Shane all the time, but not in his hearing. Still, I think they understand each other."

"His dad really did kill somebody?" Mitch asked.

"Oh, yes. It was in a fight in a bar in Alder

Falls. There were several witnesses. He was sentenced for second-degree murder."

"And his mother?" Janet said softly. "I can remember kids saying his father was a convict and his mother a whore."

Viktor frowned, nodding sadly. "Shane has had to fight that all his life. He used to fight it with his fists, and Vik would fight the other boys too. When I think back to when they were in high school, it seems to me Shane always had at least one black eye. Then—I don't know if the others just got tired of saying things, or if he just stopped fighting that way. He was good on the football team and a lot of other things and I guess the others just had to let it go."

"He didn't want to be on the football team," Janet said, and they both looked at her sharply. "Remember in his senior year, the game with Alder Falls, almost the last of the season, when he got that broken rib? Mother and I went to see him at the hospital. Mama was fussing around, changing the water in some flowers someone had sent and he told me he was glad it happened. He said he had always hated football anyway. At that time, it seemed to me that any high-school boy's dearest ambition in life would *have* to be being first-string quarterback, which was what he was, but I asked him, if he didn't want to play, why was he doing it? And he said, 'I got so tired of fighting. I don't know if it's harder to live up to being old Charlie's grandson or to live down being Steve's and whoever else's bastard.' Then he blushed and said he shouldn't have said that to me. It was years before I really understood."

There was a sympathetic silence before Viktor said, "I don't know about the mother. A few people say she was married to Steve, but I doubt it. From other things I've heard, I think Steve wouldn't marry. They say she came to old Charlie after the sentencing and said there was going to be a baby. After Steve was dead, it must have been a year or so later, the way Bill and Ruby McCrary tell it—they had their ranch then, on the river—Charlie came driving up in an old pickup and he had a baby lying on the seat, maybe six months old. He wanted to buy some milk and he asked Ruby for a little advice about babies. That's the first the valley knew of Shane."

"But what about her?" Janet asked intently. "Did she die, or did Charlie have some way of making her give up the baby, or what?"

"Nobody knows for sure. You know how good people around here are at finding out things, but old Charlie never would talk about it. Once, after Vik and Shane had come to be such good friends, Vik told me Shane didn't know any more about it than anyone else, except the old man."

"How awful for him!" Janet said softly. "I guess I've always taken him for granted, like another brother, but it must still hurt him, thinking about his parents, wondering. . . . It's especially awful the way kids can be, calling someone a bastard and things, hurting..."

"It's not the children who are cruel," said her father almost harshly, looking out at the sun sparkling on drying grass and leaves. "Most of such things they wouldn't know about unless they heard them from their parents." Then he spoke more gently, "But Shane is strong and sound of mind. He certainly still thinks and wonders at times, but it's not left him bitter or warped. He's seemed for years like another son to your mother and me and we're as proud of him as we are of the rest of you."

"He's turned off the water," observed Janet, getting up. "I'll cook his pancakes."

As Shane ate his breakfast, Viktor asked him what he would be doing for the winter.

"The Forest Service and the Bureau of Wildlife want some studies done, animal movements and migrations, food supplies, populations, snow depths, things like that up on the edge of the wilderness area. I could get some hours of credit toward my master's degree, and stay at High Lonesome Lookout up on Blackbuck."

Janet shivered. "That's right at timberline. What a place to spend the winter!"

"You're going to be at Lucky Streak, aren't you?" For just an instant, there seemed something sullen in his eyes.

"Well, yes, I think so, but that's not nearly so high or—lonesome."

"What about Charlie?" asked Viktor.

"He's talking about staying at the ranch again, maybe renting the house here in Cana. I wish he wouldn't. There won't be any neighbors up there, come winter, but he says he's had enough of living in town. I'll have a snowmobile for getting in supplies and I could come and check on him, but it's pretty far from anyone."

"I could watch out for his smoke," said Janet. "You can always see smoke from the ranch from my rock." Turning to Mitch, she said, "And what will you be doing?"

"Now just a minute! I thought Alice went back to San Francisco."

"Really, though, Mitch, are you just going to be a logger all your life?"

"Don't say *just*," he said righteously. "If a job needs doing, it's a worthwhile job, right, Dad?"

"That's so."

"Well, I didn't mean there's anything *wrong* with it," she said a little lamely. "It just seems as if . . ."

"When I was in high school, I thought for a while I might be a civil engineer, the way Vik was going to be, but now I think that was mostly because I—well, wanted to try to make up, a little, for his being dead, and that's no way to plan a life."

Shane sat back and lit a cigarette and Janet said, "Why don't you join the unhooked generation? Those things can kill you."

"So can a lot of other things. I'm too old and set in my ways for the unhooked generation."

"Baloney," she said, brushing his still-wet hair with her fingertips as she went to the sink.

"Well," Mitch said nonchalantly, "since Dad's staying home and we can't leave until noon, I guess I could go down and help at the store for a while."

Viktor smiled. "Peggy Lou's not there. She and Bruce and their mother went to some big Sheppard function in Alder Falls, or rather they will be going. It's a luncheon honoring Floyd for something."

"Oh, well, then . . ." Mitch said uncertainly.

"Well, then," said his sister decisively, "you can help Daddy with the painting. I was going to, but he's got nearly a bushel of peaches on the back porch. I'm going to fix those for the freezer so Mama won't have to do them when she gets home."

She sat by the kitchen table, peeling and slicing the peaches, while Mitch and their father began with the yellow paint. Shane was working in the hall with the beige.

"Mom is just going to love that yellow," Janet laughed. "It's so bright and awful." After a little silence, she said, "Daddy, Aunt Faye stopped in at Ruby's yesterday on her way down and it made me start wondering. We couldn't possibly have a better aunt if she were a blood relation, but what relatives *do* we have?"

"Well, I really don't know, Janet. Your mother had an old Aunt Mary in a home in Wisconsin. She used to write her sometimes, but the old lady died years ago. Nora's father died when she was a girl, you know, and her mother shortly after your sister Alice was born. I wish all of you could have known and remembered your Grandmother Alice. She was a marvelous woman. Your mother is very much like her.

"By the time she died, she and Nora had built that boardinghouse into a thriving little residential hotel. She left it to us, and the money it brought made it possible for us to come here to Cana."

"Why Cana?" asked Janet.

"Because that's where the water was turned to wine, remember?" said Mitch.

"That's true," said their father. "Besides, we had taken a vacation a year or two before and we both liked this country. My grandfather was Norwegian. His family moved to Denmark when he was a boy—that's more than a hundred years

117

ago now—but he had a great love for mountains. Denmark is a gentler country, not so hard to make a living in, and he loved his dairy farm, but I've heard him say so many times that he missed the mountains, seeing them, *feeling* them there. I suppose I must have inherited some sort of atavistic feeling like that about mountains. Then, in Bavaria, in the South of Germany, where I once lived, it was very beautiful...

"Cana seemed a nice-sized town to us; we didn't want a city. It is not so high that the winters are severe, yet there are the mountains nearby. Your mother liked the name. She said, for one thing if we came here, there might be another miracle and I'd stop being so restless."

"You did roam around a lot, didn't you? But really, I meant *your* relatives. Didn't you have a sister and brother?"

"Yes. When the Germans invaded Denmark, Peter and Christiana got away to Sweden. Peter ended by fighting in the English Army, and Christiana later married a Norwegian who had also fought for England. We wrote each other a few times, long ago, but somehow it stopped. I don't know. Families drift apart—some do. When we were children we were very close. Our grandparents saw to that. Our mother died when I was ten. Our father was always busy with his carpentry business. He was a true craftsman and there was always more demand for his work than he could fill. He was not at home often.

"Our grandmother's name was Rachel. *Her* mother had been an Orthodox Jew who came from the area of Kiev in Russia as a young girl, to Denmark. You've heard this all before."

"Tell us again," they both said eagerly.

"Well, we all worked hard on the farm and we went to school. Always, we got up before dawn for the chores and we had others when we came home. Our grandmother was always cooking and cooking. She was a woman who worried if you didn't take at least two helpings of everything. And she told us stories, working in the kitchen or dairy, sitting by the fire in the evening with her mending basket—stories and stories, and songs.

"She died while I was away at school, and our grandfather died just at the beginning of the war. When I got back to the farm after the war, Peter had everything almost as I remembered, but it was a very different and sad place to me without our grandparents."

"You roamed around a long time, didn't you?" Mitch asked. "Before the war, I mean."

"Oh, yes, England, France, Austria, Switzerland, Italy—then Germany."

"Dad, you've always said it wasn't such a bad prison camp where you were put when you were interned, but you—you always look as if it was bad."

"Many others were much worse. Ours was a small one, some factories and—and a hospital." Viktor was concentrating hard on the cupboard he was painting.

"No ovens?" pursued Mitch, "or—or crematories?"

"No, not there."

"Did it have anything to do with—what was it? your great-great-grandmother's being Jewish —that you were interned?"

"She was my great-grandmother," he said quietly, "but I was a foreigner, and the Germans were interning all foreigners at that time."

"Why didn't you get out before they nabbed you?"

Viktor was silent for a moment. "Stupidity, I suppose. I was working near Munich. I liked the work I was doing. When you hear of terrible things like accidents or bombings or internments, you sometimes only half-believe them, half-listen, or you feel sure they only happen to someone else."

"And you were there four years?"

"Yes."

"Tell us about the escape."

"I don't like talking about it, Mitch, not any of it. It was nothing spectacular. Believe me, there is nothing spectacular about a garbage truck. . . .

"I spent the last months of the war in France. When I could, I got back to Denmark. My father had died during the war. Peter and his wife were afraid I wanted a share of the farm, though I didn't. After a short while, I went to England and visited some cousins of my mother's in Yorkshire. I couldn't seem to settle down there either. Then someone remembered a distant relative who had a farm in Iowa. He wrote and said he would sponsor me, give me work, and I thought America might be an interesting place to visit.

This old cousin, Silas Cobleigh, was a sour, stingy old man, and he watched over my farmwork as if I were a boy of twelve. After a few months I left him and went to Fox Falls to another job and I soon met your mother."

"So really," Janet said thoughtfully, "we don't

really have any relatives anywhere, not that we know anything about."

"No, but we have each other," said her father gently.

"And Cana watching over you," added Shane, coming in from the hall. "Could I get a cup of coffee? Anyone else?"

"That's a bad habit you have too," said Janet, "drinking all that coffee."

"I think Alice really did leave you a little haunted or something, peachface. Are you eating more of those than you put in the pan?"

"They're healthier than coffee and cigarettes," she said pertly and then looked around. "Mitch, you're dripping paint on the floor. For Heaven's sake, what's the matter?"

He was standing utterly still, a look of awed concentration on his face. "I've just had a thought, a—a kind of—calling. Don't any of you dare laugh. It really was like that. All of a sudden I know. I want to be a doctor."

No one even smiled. The boy was altogether too shaken, too wonderstruck. Shane put down his coffee cup, took the brush from Mitch's hand, and got a cloth to wipe up the paint drops. Viktor, facing away from all of them, murmured something in Danish, perhaps German. Shane was the only one who noticed and he did not understand, but he had a glimpse of Viktor's face; it seemed stricken too, but with sorrow, not wonder.

"That would be great, Mitch," Janet said softly. "Here, sit down a minute. A person can't take too many revelations like that. You should have seen what you looked like."

"It's the damnedest thing," he marveled.

"It's like I've known all the time but—didn't know.

"You ought to start applying to schools right away," she said. "It's probably already too late to get in anywhere before January."

"Yes. Yeah, I guess I better."

Shane said, "You did have me worried for a minute there. I thought you were getting a vocation or something."

Mitch still could not smile. "But it is. Not the priesthood, but . . ."

"Sorry. I was teasing. Here, have some coffee."

"And you could treat all the family free," Janet said happily.

"And you could be my nurse."

"And Shane could be a patient."

"No way," he said, stepping back a little.

The three of them were laughing now, but Viktor, his back to them, said abruptly, "Give it more thought, son. Give it a lot of thought. Being a doctor, a profession like that, ought to be a lifetime commitment. I wouldn't like to see you take it on too lightly."

9

"Shall I drive?" Sharon asked tentatively as they walked away from the others calling good nights. Paul felt a prickle of irritation. She was probably saying, tacitly, that he had had too much drink. He almost never did that, but he was tired. He handed her the keys he had already taken from his pocket and settled back in the passenger's seat.

"Do you want the top up?" he asked belatedly.

"No, I like it this way." She took a heavy sweater from the back seat and pulled it on over her beige evening dress.

"Not a bad evening," Paul said speculatively as they came out of the drive from the Cullen place onto the lake road. There were still a few lights showing, seeming extra bright among the trees on either side of the lake. "The Rosenzweigs seem to like the place up here, all right, and they seem to be changing—or he does—his ideas about the county. That was kind of a mixed group they had."

"Yes," Sharon said a little absently. She was tired, too, and had not found much enjoyment in the evening, but then she was not much of a party girl. Her private idea of a good, enjoyable evening was having one or two couples for cards and talk; visiting Paul's parents, which they did less and less often these days; or simply staying home together, she and Paul and Jamie, which happened even less frequently. However, she was, now, enjoying being alone with Paul, talking together, just the two of them. That seemed to happen more rarely than any of the other things.

She said casually, "Where did you go with Mrs.—with Gloria?"

"Just over to that two-acre piece of land Bud Werner may be wanting to sell. She thought a little boat ride might be nice by moonlight."

"And was it?"

"The boat and the moon were all right."

"Didn't you even try to seduce each other?"

"Well, if we did, nothing came of it. . . . She's an odd kind of woman. I can't help thinking she's actually pretty neurotic. Her motto seems to be lead a man to bed, but don't let him fuck."

"You seem to have found out some pretty pertinent things for a simple little boat ride."

"For God's sake, Sharon, you aren't going to start the jealous-wife bit! Whatever Gloria is, she's not the woods-nymph type—might muss her hair or something."

"Well, did she like the land?"

"Hell, she wouldn't know a good piece of property from a manhole cover. I only took her over because she asked me to. She seems to concentrate a lot on doing whatever she can to make the old man jealous. It seems to be about all there is to her life."

"Then that doesn't seem like a very good way to get him for a client."

"I think it may be, though," he said thoughtfully. "I think being jealous of her, trying to keep up with her, believing he's got something every other man in the world wants, gives him some kind of perverse pleasure, a feeling of superiority, maybe."

After a moment, he went on, "He seems to be thinking of quite a sizable investment—Rosenzweig, I mean—and those house guests they have from back East seem interested too. It seems that once the mill owner gets interested, a lot of locals with some money decide to break loose. Morris Epstein is definitely wanting a piece of the action now, and maybe Dr. Taylor. Did I tell you Ted's almost finished with drawing up the incorporation papers? . . . And then there's Howard Compton's father-in-law from Denver. Howard called today. They'd like to come back and look things over in a week or ten days, get some fishing in while they're here. Can you go up there so they can stay at the ranch? I'll be there all the time I can."

"I was thinking of going sooner than that, Paul. Maybe Sunday. It would be good for Jamie."

"Just the two of you?"

"I'd thought of seeing if Patty wants to come."

"I don't understand how you can seem to *want* to isolate yourself like that, with just a kid or two."

"It's not as if we'd be going into the wilderness. The Quarles aren't a half-mile away in the foreman's house. Would you try to get up then and spend some time with us—before the others come?"

"I doubt that I can next week," he said with what sounded like reproof. "You know I'm trying to get a lot of other things wound up so I can spend more time on the project. I want to get some surveying and things done up there before winter. . . . I know you're tired, Sharon, so am I. Maybe, say in January or February, we can have a real vacation—Mexico, Hawaii. How would that be?"

"I'd like it." And it would be good to go away with him somewhere, but she knew that even if he chose Katmandu, Paul would still be selling real estate, chiefly the Cloud Valley thing, but generally boosting Alder County. He could never stop working. Just recently, she had reread *Babbitt* and it had made her cry. There *were* other things about Paul. If only she could *know* him, know rather than suspect—hope.

She said, "You could hire another salesman right now. Why don't you?"

"No need, so long as things can be handled as they are. I've been thinking we might send Jamie to that new nursery school in the fall, and you could come into the office and handle some of the secretarial work. Then maybe you'd understand more about the business, how interesting and exciting it can be at times."

She already knew more than she wanted to, but refrained from mentioning the fact. Instead she said, "Anyway, I think Jamie and I will be spending some time at the ranch soon. It's already almost the end of July. He loves it up there so much and—so do I. Maybe we'll go over and spent part of a day at old Charlie's camp. Jamie's old enough now to be interested in most kinds of machinery and work. Anyway, I want him to remember as much as he can about the ranch before..."

"Sharon, I know you're not happy about the project. I wish to God you'd try to share just a little of my enthusiasm. We never seem to share anything. Can't you see what a financial position this thing would put us in if it goes? Can't you understand and accept that nothing stands still? That old place, converted as it will be, will be something the whole state can boast about.... What is it now?"

Tears had sprung to her eyes. "It's—it's home. That's all."

"What about the house on East Ridge?" he demanded angrily. "You have never seemed to give a damn about it. Nobody in the county has a better place. Some are bigger, granted, but nothing is more modern. We do lack a swimming pool, but we could have that. . . . I wish to God you'd stop mooning and *do* something with yourself. If you don't want to go to work, why can't you take more interest in some of the women's groups? the country club? things like that. You can shoot a game of golf that would shame almost anybody. Why don't you—"

"I want another baby."

"Oh, for Christsake!"

"You promised—"

"Look, I'm not a fairy godfather. I've been doing my best with wand-waving at the right times, but a pregnancy just seems to be one thing that won't come into being exactly when you want it scheduled."

"Paul," she said slowly—this was not the right time, but there never would be a right time—"a year ago, when you caught mumps from Jamie, do you think . . ."

"Good lord! isn't it humiliating enough that I *had* the damned disease at my age without your making a stupid suggestion like that? If you think I'm going for a sperm test or something like that, you're really crazy. How long do you think it would take word like *that* to get all over the county?"

"I really don't care about the county. It's our business and no one else's. . . . But you could go to Boise."

"Just have a little patience, that's all. How many kids would you have if it was left up to you? Eight or ten, I'd imagine. God!"

"Don't you care about Jamie?"

"Of course I *care* about Jamie, but that doesn't mean I want a new one squalling the house down every year. You know there's not a decent place around here to entertain clients besides a man's home. I don't want you tied hand and foot with pregnancy or a new baby all the time. Where's your liberated spirit, woman?"

"I guess I missed out on that, too," she said bleakly. "I'm not at all the right wife for you."

"Oh, good God! . . . Even if it were true, you can't bury it in a houseful of kids. Now let's not have any more of that kind of talk."

He leaned over and kissed her cheek, patted her hand on the wheel briefly, but she knew he was already thinking of other things.

"Did Aunt Faye say anything to you about the lot she's buying?"

"Yes, she's having a ball with plans and she likes the lot. Matt Erikson seems to have put off his jobs for other people and is going to start building for her right away. She's having a landscaper up from Boise."

Paul smiled. "There's a lady who gets things moving when she sets her mind to it. I thought she'd want a place on the other side of the ridge, away from town, but she said, 'No, I guess I'd better be where I can see the mill.' So she is, but she also overlooks the golf course. Before she paid for the property, she went up there early one morning, and again in the evening, to make sure she could hear the damn mill whistle." He sighed. "I wish somebody could get her to change her mind about Holland House. It's going to be such a waste if she does what she's thinking of. She came to the City Council meeting Monday night, and she's going to talk to the county commissioners. She wants to lease the place to either the city or county for a dollar a year, with the provision that the house not be torn down as long as she lives. Then the property would come to the city or county."

"That seems reasonable enough."

"Yes, but it's the best piece of industrial property in Cana. The house is in the way."

"It's a lovely old house," Sharon said. "What does she want done with it?"

"Oh, you know Faye. She's got a hundred ideas. She thinks the first floor might be made into a really nice restaurant which, God knows, Cana needs—but right next to the mill? Probably all the customers would turn out to be millhands and, knowing Faye, she'd want them fed free. She thinks some of the rooms might be used as a county museum, which we certainly need to have, and the rest for office space. She wants the grounds kept as a park, called Holland Park, and she'd pay for the upkeep of that."

"Is she coming into the Cloud Valley thing?"

He shrugged irritably. "I haven't got a clue. If I ask her directly, she just says she still has to think about it. Even if she invested just a token amount, it would be great publicity. People around here will follow a Holland into anything."

"What about the petition, Paul?" she asked tentatively. "Somebody said they have it ready to take to the county commissioners and then wherever they have to go from there."

"Let them," he said negligently. "We can't stop them, but they can't stop us either. It may end up being one of those long, drawn-out things, maybe with an environmental-impact study and a lot of crap like that, state and federal agencies trying to get into the act all over the place, but that won't stop our selling stock and going ahead with surveying, beginning to build, and such. It could hold up the skiing part of the thing because that will be federal land, but Ted Carpenter's done quite a bit of checking. The ranch itself is private property, no restrictions. So long as we provide approved, adequate drinking water, sewage disposal, and such—which we'll do—we can probably go right ahead with most of it. The damn petition is going to make some things difficult, drag it out as long as they can, I suppose, just for the hell of it, and the publicity, but it will all go eventually. This is one of the poorest counties in this part of the state and it badly needs any additional residents and revenue it can get. The half down around Alder Falls isn't in such bad shape, good farmland. But from a little way north of Cana, lumbering's been about the only business we've had till Blackbuck dam went in. You know how many people we have on unemployment all winter. There'd be plenty of jobs while the building was going on, then some could get jobs at the ski lodge, or as caretakers for the summer places, things like that. New tourist places could go in around the lake, and the county could damn well make use of the additional property taxes. Floyd Sheppard certainly goes along with the project and he can help us in the legislature. The petition's a damned nuisance and not much else. These people up here around Blackbuck will not realize that just letting us go ahead, not trying to make waves, will be the making of them and this whole end of the county."

There was a rather long silence before Sharon

said, sounding tired, "Aunt Faye said something about a store."

"Oh, she's looking at business properties, something fairly small that she can run herself. Faye can't be satisfied for long unless she's trying to manage six or eight things at a time. She doesn't know just what she wants yet. She told me she's wavering between a bookshop and a whorehouse, but thinks one might be too placid and the other too exciting, so she's trying to come up with a compromise."

"Which is the exciting and which the placid?"

They laughed and he said, still chuckling, "Speaking of compromises, did you read the paper today?"

"Yes, but if anyone was compromised, I missed it."

"You were supposed to miss it, but everybody in the county will know before the week's over. You read old Fred Petrie's resigning as magistrate?"

"Yes, ill health."

"Health, hell!" Paul laughed. "The old fool went down to Alder Falls and spent some time at Fannie's place, and he paid—with a check!"

"Oh, Paul, he didn't!" She was almost choking with incredulous laughter.

Fannie Fontaine's was a club in Alder Falls, but everyone in the county who had reached the age of accountability knew it was also the only recognized brothel.

"The old fart's gone senile," said Paul. "I've suspected it for a long time. Yep, a check in the amount of a hundred and ten dollars to the Club Fontaine. He must have had himself quite a night. When his check came back to the Cana bank, someone took it straight to Homer Grundy, and things started heating up. You know what a hypocritical goody Homer is. A group of city fathers went to old Fred and asked him if he had been feeling as well as might be lately, then hinted about the check. They asked Ted Carpenter, but he's too busy and doing too well with his own law practice."

"Poor old Fred," said Sharon with another giggle.

"Well, I've heard Fannie takes food stamps in an emergency, so I guess anything goes."

After a silence, she said, "Do you know if your mother and dad were invited to the Rosenzweigs? Wes and Doreen were there, so I wondered..."

"Doreen's uncle is our state senator, remember? And her dad owns a quarter of the lower valley, plus half interest in the food-processing plant at Alder Falls. They're more in the Rosenzweigs' class. By the way, did I mention that both Floyd and Carter are coming in on Cloud Valley? ... As a matter of fact, though, I think they were invited, Mom and Viktor, but you know how they both are about big parties. Something urgent probably came up, like the lawn needed cutting or Patty wanted to have a friend stay overnight."

"I've noticed," she said slowly, "that you call your dad 'Viktor' more and more often lately. Why is that?"

"Oh, I don't know," he said carelessly. "People just do that sometimes as they get older. One thing, I guess, is that we don't have much in common anymore. He seems more like somebody I just—know, a little."

"But you don't call Mom 'Nora.'"

"He isn't my natural father, you know."

"You were such a little boy when they married, Paul. Surely no one could have been a better father."

After a moment, he said quietly, "Vik was his boy. I can remember when Vik was born. Ever since then, I've wondered a lot about my own dad."

"I can't believe Viktor ever meant you to feel that way."

"How?"

She touched his hand. "Well—left out or anything—resentful."

He laughed without much mirth. "I'm a big boy now and I'm fond of him, of Viktor, and of Mom, of course. I wish they weren't such sticks-in-the-mud, but they're not likely to change. . . . I suppose the main thing is I've never really felt comfortable talking for long with him, with—Dad. We never did have many common interests. I remember when I was really little, I used to want him to tell me about the war because my real father had died in it, but he'd never talk about it. He and Vik and Mitch always found plenty of things to do and talk about together. . . . Anyway, I've got my own life now—we have. I'm glad Mitch has settled on being a doctor, on being anything respectable, but he's so excited about it, I'm afraid it may turn out to be just a flash in the pan, coming up all of a sudden the way it has. I've offered to let him come in with me, but he won't talk about it.

"Sharon . . . I'm going to have to do something about Janet. She's making fools of all of us in front of the whole county. I stopped in Mack's bar the other night and a couple of men I didn't

133

know were saying some pretty nasty things about the cute little hippie girl working at McCrarys' in Blackbuck and how she is living up in the woods with some hairy kid."

"I don't know what can be done," Sharon said. "It seems to me the thing will just have to work itself out. You shouldn't waste energy worrying and getting angry about it. A lot of people are doing that kind of thing now—"

"Not in Alder County, they're not. Do you think they're on dope?"

"Why, no, Paul, I don't think so."

"Well, I've been thinking of going up there, to the Lucky Streak cabin, and telling them to get out, maybe of offering them some money to go."

"But why? I mean, I didn't know you were *that* upset about it."

"Because her name's Magnessen and so is mine. One of the major reasons is that I've been asked to run for county commissioner this fall and I'm giving it some very serious consideration. This crappy scandal connected with my name could put me in as bad a position as old Fred Petrie." He was not smiling now.

"When were you asked?" she said, surprised, unable to stop a sweep of regret. So much, probably, for the winter vacation he had mentioned earlier and for other nights in each month that he might possibly have spent at home.

"A few weeks ago," he said with pride. "I wanted to have my mind pretty well made up before I mentioned it to you."

10

David and Gloria Rosenzweig were getting ready for bed. In their house down the valley and normally in this house, they did not often share a bedroom, but two out-of-town couples were spending the weekend, and this house was not large enough for separate bedrooms.

"Did you have a nice evening, Gloria?" asked David. He was taking off his shoes. To Gloria, there had always been something faintly disgusting about a man removing his shoes.

"Oh, I suppose it could have been worse," she answered languidly, surveying her face in the mirror as she prepared to remove her makeup. "I *do* wish this place had a decent dressing room."

"Do you want to stay on here through August, or go back to the valley house?"

"I think stay," she said absently, smoothing on the cleansing cream with a firm upward motion that was purported to prevent sagging and wrinkles.

"If you like, we could buy a site and have our own summer place built next year."

She smiled faintly into the mirror. "Yes, that's where Paul and I went in the boat tonight. He was talking about some land that's for sale and I thought it might be fun to see it by moonlight."

David had not failed to notice their absence and, to him, it had seemed a long one. She had, up to now, refused to go out in the boat with him.

"I can tell you this," said said peevishly, gently patting away the cleansing cream, "I can't see that we've met anyone in this godforsaken place—despite your valiant efforts—except maybe Paul Magnessen that might be worth knowing. Those Sheppards that think they're such big cheeses! What a bunch of hicks! Especially the daughter, what's her name? Doreen Collins? You see, I'm even learning some of their stupid names in spite of myself. . . . What a bitch she is. I'll bet she hasn't been to bed with a man in at least fifteen years. I feel sorry for her husband, though he probably doesn't deserve it."

David stepped out of his trousers and folded them carefully over a chair, then hung his jacket and shirt over them. Gloria's clothes lay scattered around the room for Bessie to take care of in the morning.

"What about Mrs. Holland? She seems an interesting woman."

"I have never known a woman who was the least bit interesting to me." She stood up and let her light robe fall to the floor, revealing a filmy pink nightgown. "David, you're getting a paunch," she observed in passing, "and I wish you'd give up your silly scruples and buy a toupee. How old are you?"

"Why, I'm forty-three, Gloria," he said. His birthday, ten days ago, had completey slipped her mind. She seemed to find nothing about him worth remembering.

"Well, you look a lot older. Honestly, one of these days, someone is going to come up and compliment you on your lovely daughter. What has aged you so, I wonder, my sweet?"

"The war, I suppose," he said drearily. "I was only a child, but the prison camp—seeing my family taken away . . . I've always felt older and—"

"Oh, let's not go into all that again," she said shortly. She was turning slowly, surveying herself carefully in the mirror of the closet door.

"Is there a pencil around?"

"What?"

"A pencil. Yes, there's one on the nightstand. Hand it to me, will you?"

She took the pencil, placed it snugly under her right breast, straightened her shoulders, and the pencil dropped to the floor.

"That's the test," she said exultantly, "and I pass with flying colors. I just read it in a magazine. If a woman's breasts don't sag enough to hold a pencil like that, then she doesn't need to wear a bra."

She tested the other breast and was, for a moment, completely happy.

David came and took her in his arms, the hardness of him rising up against her thigh.

"When are we going to Europe?"

"Late in the autumn, my love, when the busiest part of the working season here is done."

"And you're still determined to go on living here in this crappy county?"

"Yes. I'm rather coming to like it, Gloria, and I think you might too, if you gave it and yourself a chance. Come to bed now."

"In a minute."

She disengaged herself unceremoniously and went to the window. Pulling back a drape, she stood there in the chill night air, her nipples rising up ripely.

"One good thing about this place is that you can run around naked and only the people you want to see you will. You know, David, I'll bet you could sleep with Faye Holland. She loves *every*thing about that goddam mill so much."

"I don't think I'll try."

Gloria smiled. "That's one thing we could do to liven things up around good old Cana, start a wife-swapping club for the cold winter nights."

"I think I'll keep the one I have. Come to bed. You're going to freeze."

"Can you get me warmed up?" Her little smile was meant to be teasing, tantalizing, but there was something dubious, cynical in her tone. "I'll bet she's sleeping with somebody."

"Who?"

"Faye Holland. You hardly ever see a woman looking so sleek and smug unless she's being laid pretty often."

"Come along then, so you can be sleek and smug."

She moved slowly toward the bed, watching his puffy dark eyes glow with desire. Gloria was rarely interested in having sex, but she was always very pleased by that look in a man's eyes—any man's.

"David," she murmured, slipping into bed, "the next time we go to a real city, promise me you'll go to a really good place and get a toupee."

"I'd feel so silly," he whispered, hungrily caressing the soft curves of her.

"No, you wouldn't. You'd get used to it and like it, and *I'd* like it."

"Well, all right, we'll see."

"And for my present, I'll need a new coat."

"Yes, love."

"You know, I feel sorry for Paul Magnessen, too, with that mousy little wife of his. Isn't it ridiculous the mess so many men make of their lives, just by marrying women who are wrong for them?"

Afterward, Gloria spent a long time in the bathroom, douching, lovingly rubbing night cream into her skin.

"Have you noticed my nice tan?" she asked, finally returning to bed.

"Of course. It's very becoming."

The lamp on his side of the bed had been switched on, and David held a timber-trade magazine.

"But this is enough," she said complacently, engrossed in a careful study of her skin coloring. "I mustn't get one bit tanner."

"You're very beautiful."

"Am I, David?"

"The most beautiful woman in the world."

She stroked his cheek once. "Why don't you go and fix us a couple of drinks? We could start planning the trip to Europe."

"We've both had quite a lot to drink tonight, dear, and there really are a few things I should read. I've been asked to speak at a Rotary luncheon in a few days."

"Oh, big deal!" she flared in sudden anger. "That's a man for you. As soon as you've had your screw, it's back to the old Rotary meeting. Haven't you read any books about the importance of foreplay and then of concentrating on your wife a little afterward?"

He let the magazine drop to the floor and reached for her, but she said "Don't! You're ruining my hair."

"You were in the bathroom so long," he said apologetically, "and you usually say you're sleepy afterward."

"Well, I *am* sleepy, but I just thought we might talk a little, something besides logs."

She opened a door in the lower part of her nightstand and took out a whiskey bottle and glass.

"I suppose you don't want any. If you do, you'll have to find yourself a glass or drink out of the bottle."

"Thank you; I don't want any."

She stiffened and shuddered. "What the hell was that?"

"Only an owl."

"God, the noises here! Creepy!"

"Did you like the land Paul Magnessen showed you?"

"I didn't see much of it," she said without interest. "There's a little beach, two acres I think he said, trees all over the place. He asked if you wanted to go, but you were busy with Epstein and some others. . . . He really is quite good-looking, isn't he? and have you ever noticed? He doesn't look much like the rest of his family, not the ones I've seen, anyway. That sister of his seems to be causing quite a scandal, living in sin up here in the woods someplace. People certainly get desperate for things to be scandalized over around here."

She poured a little more whiskey into her glass. "Do have some of this."

"No, darling, I really shouldn't drink as much as I do."

"You're telling *me I* shouldn't drink as much; isn't that it?"

"I haven't wanted to bother you with it, Gloria, but I've been seeing Dr. Taylor. He's fairly sure I have an ulcer. He thought I should go for some tests, but if it's there, it's there; if it's not, it's not. I don't have time or patience for a hospital."

"Oh, God!" she groaned. "What a romantic subject *that* is. Now I suppose he wants you on a diet of milk-toast, and tea."

"No. I just thought I should see what he had to say. It won't interfere with our lives."

There was a brief silence, then she said lightly, "I forgot to tell you, but I suppose your good spies, George and Bessie have, about a young man who came by one day last week on a motorcycle. Did they tell you?"

"George mentioned that someone had stopped to borrow a little gasoline."

"I don't like them watching me, David. I feel like a child. There's never anything real for them to report. I'm surprised you haven't bought me a chastity belt."

She propped herself so that her bosom showed to better advantage. "It was funny, really. I was out on the deck, sunbathing. I'd given those two niggers strict orders to keep away. I was on a blanket, doing my front, and all of a sudden, I saw this man walking down the drive. I rolled up in the blanket, but I know he'd seen me. You can tell about a thing like that. I asked what he wanted and he said ... well," she giggled, "I won't tell you what he first said, but then he said his motorcycle had run out of gas. I sent him around back to find George and when he came back, I'd got my shorts and halter on. He looked hot and tired and sort of pissed off, so I offered him a drink. He had this long black hair and a beard, so I couldn't really tell much about what he looked like, but I suppose he was in his late twenties. His eyes sort of burned, you know, like in those old pictures of prophets.

"It turns out he hates everything about Alder County too. His name was Jerry or Gary, something like that. And guess what? He's the one living with Paul Magnessen's sister, only I got the idea that's not going to last much longer. He's trying to write a book and seems to have decided he needs to go to New York or somewhere, and I don't think he has it in mind to take the girl.

"I thought he looked like he could use some money, shabby clothes, not very clean, so I told him George could use some help with the lawnwork for a few days, but he said he wasn't a gardener and left."

She sloshed a bit more whiskey into the glass. "I wonder what it would be like."

"What?"

"Oh, being completely off in the woods away from everything, sleeping with a man like that, and all the rest of it. We saw the girl one day, remember? At that scroungy little cafe: long, blond braids, freckles, not much of a figure."

David got up, searched his jacket pocket, and tried, unobtrusively, to swallow a pill.

"Is that for your little tummy?" she asked scornfully.

"Yes," he admitted.

"Christ!" she sighed. "I suppose you'll be gulping them in restaurants and all sorts of public places. Does screwing me give you a bellyache?"

"Gloria—"

"Harry and Cynthia have asked us to come for a cruise on their yacht in September, you know. It would be a change. They're going to some little place on the West Coast of Mexico where they say Americans get real royal treatment."

"We can't go."

"I don't see why in hell not."

"Because I need to be here. It's just about the busiest time of year."

"Then *I'll* go."

"No, darling, I don't want you to."

"You don't want me to do anything." Her voice rose. "I'm more than half a prisoner in this stinking place and you're always frowning at me like I'm a naughty little girl. I *will* go if I want to."

"All right," he said mildly, "but you'll have no money to spend, no credit cards, and if you borrow from Harry and Cynthia, I won't repay them."

She was furious, gulping her drink. Ordinarily, almost always, he could be handled, manipulated, but occasionally he got stubborn and, as yet, she had found nothing to combat it. It seemed to be happening more often, too.

"You asshole, bastard sonofabitch!"

"You can probably do even better than that," he said calmly. "But go to sleep now. We'll have the trip to Europe and we'll spend some time in New York this winter. That will have to be enough."

She had turned her back and was arranging the covers viciously. David took up his magazine again until she said sullenly.

"How do you expect me to sleep with that goddam light on?"

Almost immediately, he dropped the magazine, turned off the lamp, and prepared himself for sleep.

Gloria, despite the burning anger, was becoming deliciously drowsy. Though they were not touching, she could feel that David was lying tensely awake. She smiled maliciously. Maybe she would have to miss the yacht cruise, but she would make him pay for it. She made her breathing deep, slow, and even for a few moments; then, as in sleep, she moved voluptuously toward him until her thigh touched his. "Paul!" she murmured. "Oh, Paul!"

David started, his whole body stiffening, and it was a long struggle for Gloria to keep laughter from breaking her slow, even breaths.

11 ◯

Shane woke early. He had slept little, but more was out of the question. During the working season, holiday or not, it was not enough for old Charlie to get up at daylight; he arose "with the mornin' star" so that breakfast could be over and, when they were in the woods, the men could be ready to begin work with daylight. This was Labor Day, the first time old Charlie had been to town since Fourth of July. Since his cutters were paid by the board feet they cut, they could take a day or two off now and then if they wanted to, but the old man never seemed to rest. He was up now, and not quiet about it. He was banging around in the kitchen, making enough noise for a bear, cursing and whistling off key by turns.

The little old house in Cana had not been in very good shape when Charlie bought it thirteen years ago, and its condition had been improved only when absolutely necessary. Charlie would, with pride and joy, spend thousands of dollars on machinery, but repairs to a building cut him to the quick. The house was almost the only residence left now in its neighborhood, near the highway intersection. It was set at a little distance behind Vince Kucharski's service station and, on either side of that, was Mack's Bar and Walt Roberts' Supply. Walt carried or could order most of the things Charlie's business needed. As an added attraction, Walt's place had a big, almost empty back lot where Charlie could keep some of his machinery over the winter, free.

Shane's room was small and he cared little more for "fancy housing" than Charlie. The walls and ceiling were unpainted plywood. The linoleum had been scrubbed and walked on for so many years that there was no discernible pattern left; it was only a slightly variegated, depressing brown. He had a single bed in order to have more room, but the mattress was new and comfortable, though paint was peeling from the old iron bedstead. Beside the bed was a strip of Navajo rug, and the bed's spread was an Indian blanket. The rug's colors were dark and brooding; the blanket's were bright, almost garish. Shane liked studying them, the way the colors intertwined and blended, showing him different patterns and scenes, depending on his mood and the light.

The room also contained a mismatched old bureau and wardrobe, a night table that was an unadorned orange crate, and one solid wall of bookshelves, completely filled. It was the books and the Indian art pieces that made the place home.

Very occasionally, when Shane was angry,

depressed, or more usually totally exhausted from the work in the woods, he would say to Charlie, "I won't be back for a few days," and, not waiting to hear more of the old man's tirade than he could help, would come here and lock himself in. Sometimes he would go down the highway a block or so to Effie's truck stop for a meal; sometimes he didn't bother. It was not a quiet neighborhood, not with the banging from the service station and Roberts' place, not with revelers leaving Mack's late at night, not with the highway traffic, but he, Shane, could be quiet. He would sleep and read, sometimes sitting or lying utterly still for minutes, perhaps hours, staring at nothing, thinking, or, now and then, not thinking.

By the second day of his absence from camp, Charlie started telling the truck drivers to stop at the house and tell him to haul his ass back to the woods, but Shane kept the curtains closed and the doors locked and made no response to their knocking and yelling. He went back when he was ready.

He got up, yawning now, and went into the cramped little bathroom. Hot water was a good thing to have. If anyone got any at camp, he had to carry it and heat it himself on the kitchen range. He disliked the face that frowned back at him from the steamy mirror as he tried to make his hair lie down in a more acceptable way. There were big dark circles under his eyes and his too-fair skin looked almost raw, the way it always did during the logging season, from sun and wind. It would not tan; just burn and peel and burn again. He ought to grow a beard, moustache, sideburns, he thought, never shave again, but that reminded him of Gary Hunt. His straight, dark brows drew into a bunchier frown, the razor dug into his chin, and blood welled from the cut.

He was tired, achingly tired, even first thing in the morning, but it was always like that when they were working a show. This had been a bad summer, not the work, he was used to that—the rest of it, and it was not over, might never be over. "You're the closest thing to a big brother she's got now," Ruby had told him sternly. "It won't do for Paul to find out till he has to, and Mitch is too young to be much help."

Charlie's piercing blue eyes checked him out in quick glances as he came into the kitchen. It was hard to tell, lately, what kind of mood the boy was going to be in. He said mildly, "Looks to me like you ought to be old enough to learn to shave without needin' stitches."

Shane said nothing, just threw the Band-Aid wrapper into the wastebasket and stuck the plaster on crooked.

"I liked to a' never found the coffee pot," Charlie grumbled. "I wish that ole lady Shelton would just clean the place up like she's supposed to do an' quit her everlastin' rearrangements. You want some ham and eggs?"

"No, not now." He poured coffee. It was bitterly strong but they liked it that way.

"Three days a' good weather wasted," Charlie lamented, cooking his own breakfast. "This holiday stuff's a bunch a' goddam shit. We'll likely be snowed out of up there by the first of October an' them big he-men loggers'll be settin' on their backsides at Mack's, cryin' 'cause it's winter. By the way, you seen my falsies anywhere?"

"They're in the soap dish in the shower."

"Now how the hell'd they git there?"

Shane had no idea, so he made no answer. He looked at the old man's back, straight and sturdy. Both of them were of little more than average height, but Charlie had a stocky, big-boned frame, which made his grandson look almost delicate beside him. Charlie was not wasting and thinning the way some people did with aging, nor was he growing fat. His big hands were hard and strong as hammers. Muscles bulged strongly beneath his overalls and undershirt. A few streaks of black still hung on stubbornly in his iron-gray hair. All the rest of the crew had left the camp on Friday night, but Charlie and Shane had stayed until late on Sunday, keeping an eye on dying slash fires and repairing the loader. Charlie thrived on work, any kind of work in the woods, and he had always been determined that it would be the same for his boy.

"You're not going to *eat* those eggs like that!" Shane said, shuddering as Charlie thumped his plate on the table opposite him.

"I am. Like what?"

"You just warmed them up a little. They're not cooked."

"Well, if you wanted 'em done some other way, the skillet was there. This here's called sunny side up."

"I can't look at them."

"Well, hell, nobody's forcin' you. Git up off your rear an' make some toast. I forgot that. Why don't you git married?"

Shane started a little at the abruptness of the question.

"You're twenty-six," Charlie told him. "I don't know of you hardly ever havin' a date or anything."

"I don't know of my hardly ever having time."

"You've got plenty of time in the winter, now that you're through with that college business. Thank God you didn't bring home one a' them women that's too educated to wear a brassiere or use a broom. Pick out some girl that's a halfway decent cook. Then we'll have a cook up at the show an' not always have to be huntin' one."

"I'll put an ad in the paper," Shane said dryly, then, turning, "My God! You *are* eating them."

"You don't want an egg cooked to death. It don't put no lead in your pencil that way," said Charlie placidly, dabbing at his yellowing chin.

"*You* get married," Shane said, turning away quickly. "Marry Mrs. Shelton. She wouldn't let you eat eggs that way, while they're still—alive."

Charlie chuckled. "I don't need no ole widder woman bossin' me around."

The "old widder woman" was at least twenty years younger than he. He said,

"You ever go to Fannie's?"

"I have."

"How often?"

"Not for a long time, but it's none of your business."

"Well, *I* go. I guess you heard about old Fred Petrie an' his check."

"Only about twenty times."

Charlie laughed, choking a little on some toast. "Blamed ole fool!" He sobered. "Your grandma was a fine woman, Shane, finest God ever made. When she died, I knew I couldn' find nobody else'd be half the woman she was. I knew I never would want to marry agin, but a man needs a woman sometimes, just for a while. . . . God, it's been near fifty years since Georgia died."

Shane had poured more coffee for both of them and sat down again. Charlie looked up and found the sober gray eyes on him, still and steady, in that way that could make him feel so itchy.

"Are you ever going to tell me about them?" Shane asked softly.

"Who's that?"

"You know, Charlie. My parents."

"Why, there ain't nothin' to tell, boy. You've heard the story."

"Not really. Not from you, straight through. Just a bit or a piece now and then. You used to say when I was older. What's the excuse now?"

Charlie moved uneasily under those direct eyes. "The past is over an' done with, that's all. A young feller like you ought to be lookin' ahead to the future."

"Grandma's part of the past. You talk about her."

"She was a wonderful woman."

"And they weren't wonderful. I know that much, but I've got a right to know more, all I can. I never have been at all sure who I am."

Charlie sighed, blowing on his coffee. "Honest to god, Shane, there ain't that much to tell. Course you know who you are. Sayin' a thing like that don't make no sense at all. . . . But sometime in the winter, or up in the woods, maybe, if you still want to talk about it . . . I don't like this place, ought to sell it. . . . You goin' to the parade?"

"No."

"What *are* you gonna do with yourself today? Looks to me like you ought to git some more sleep. You're lookin' downright puny at times lately, but be ready to leave for the show around four."

"I told you I'm going to see that man in Boise tomorrow about the High Lonesome job—"

"Now, Shane, that's a bunch of damn foolishness, shuttin' yourself in up there all winter."

"It's something I want to do. Some of the work will give me credit toward my master's degree."

"Now ain't that a purty come-off! What about the business? Don't you give a hoot in hell about somethin' I've worked all my life to build? An' my daddy before me."

"When I was getting the bachelor's degree, I didn't miss much of any season. I'll be around, but to be really honest with you, Charlie, and I'm sorry about it, I don't want the business. I don't much like logging. I thought you might have caught on to that by now. I've tried—most of my life. . . . I'll be back at camp sometime tomorrow night and I'll work for you all I can through the seasons as long as you're working, but—"

"Just waitin' around for me to die?" the old man shot at him bitterly.

Shane lit a cigarette and went on quietly, "But after this year, I won't do any more hauling. I'll buck logs, I'll be a cat skinner, anything but drive those trucks."

"You're the best driver I've had," Charlie cried incredulously. "You can git in four trips to most anybody else's three. You been haulin' since you was sixteen, you—"

"I've been doing it because you want me to, because drivers are hard to get and keep. I've always let you push me too hard with hauling, and it scares hell out of me."

"What! That ain't no way for a man to talk."

"Sometimes, on that hill down from Jamison Saddle, roads like that, I count the tons I've got pushing me. On those single-lane roads with almost no turnouts, where you can't see any distance ahead, I think about the way Vik's car was just crumpled up to almost nothing. On the highways, I wonder if this is the day I'll have to hit the brakes and jackknife, or maybe there won't be any brakes—"

"Quit that! You're talkin' like a yellow-bellied dude. I hauled near sixty years and never had nothin' serious happen. I'd still be doin' it if we could git decent crews like we used to have that didn't need wet-nursin' to keep 'em at work."

"I know all that, but I'm not you. I can't count the things I've done in my life to see if I could, because I didn't want to, or was afraid of them. If I haven't proved to myself by now whatever it is I've been trying to prove, it's just not going to happen. So I mean to stop trying and try to find the things I want to do."

Charlie sat staring at him for a moment, puzzlement, disappointment in his eyes, then turned to the window that overlooked Roberts' back lot.

Finally Shane said gently, "I'll be going out in a little while and I'll try to be back in camp by suppertime tomorrow. You won't be leaving at four, will you? I thought you were going to have supper at Magnessens'."

"I forgot," Charlie said. His voice did not sound angry now, or sullen or outraged. It sounded small, hurt, and—old. Shane tried to wash the lump out of his throat with the last of his now cold coffee.

Charlie said dully, "They asked you, too."

"I told them I have to go to Boise. My appointment's at nine in the morning. Charlie, listen, I . . . well, I'll see you tomorrow."

12

The day was partly cloudy, cool when the sun was covered. Still, Janet, wearing an old sweater, was sitting on her rock, trying to dry her hair. It was not that the cabin had become unpleasant for her, but simply that she preferred being outdoors and the rock was the best place of all, even though Gary had come so near to ruining it for her.

The black pup Shane had brought her, now grown from a furry, big-eyed teddy bear to an awkward, leggy three-month-old, sniffed about busily, making playful pounces at sticks, at shadows, at Janet, nipping her, snuggling deep into her hair. In the midst of his play, she heard the car far down the mountain, and tears sprang to her eyes in the midst of her laughter at the pup. Stop it! she told herself fiercely, you will not start any nonsense.

She knew it would be Shane and he knew she would not be in the cabin. He did not even go to the door, but came straight up to the point. The puppy barked and ran at him.

"Shut up," he said in a friendly tone and reached down to scratch the little dog's ears. "Hi," he said and sat beside her.

"Hello, Shane."

"You're nuts, sitting out here with wet hair."

"The sun will be out again in a minute. How did you know I wasn't working?"

"Ruby told me last night you'd come home for the rest of the weekend."

"And how are they managing? She and Bill and the kids?"

"Things looked pretty busy as I came through Blackbuck, but it's all right, I guess."

"I should have stayed. This is one of their biggest weekends, but they kept quarreling so, Bill and Ruby. It never used to bother me much. All of a sudden, I just felt like I had to be by myself."

"Do you want me to go?"

"No." There was more intensity in the word than she had expected.

They sat silent for a long while. The sun came out again and she began, without thinking about it, to brush her hair slowly, looking down and away toward the lake. Shane looked north, to the rugged peak of Blackbuck Mountain. The puppy came dashing up and tried to take the brush from Janet. They both smiled as he worried gently at her hand, growling.

"Does he have a name?"

"His name is Loki. Do you remember all Daddy's stories about those Norse gods? And we used to call you Loki the Red because of your hair? Well, he was also called Loki the Bad and the Good and that's what this little monster is, aren't you?"

The pup ambled off to the shade of a small nearby spruce, flopped down, and was immediately asleep. Another long silence and she said tentatively,

"What did Ruby tell you?"

He picked up a strand of her hair and held it out at full length, watching it sparkle and lighten as it dried in the sun. "Quite a lot."

"Tell me."

They did not look at each other.

"She said you're pregnant and Gary has gone away." His voice was husky and he cleared his throat and kept his eyes turned away.

"But I didn't tell her, not anything. I even bought a girdle to wear and I need it now. I wanted to go on working for Ruby through hunting season. I have to work somewhere, but I didn't want anyone to know about the baby—not yet. It's not that I'm ashamed about it, but I ought to be the one to tell Mama and Daddy and Mitch and—"

"Some women like Ruby don't have to be told things like that. She probably knew it before you did."

She tried to see his eyes but he wouldn't let her. From his profile, she was afraid he was angry, or was it hurt?

"Is she telling everybody?"

"Ruby's not like that, Janet. Charlie and I stopped there for supper last night on our way into town and she told me in the kitchen. She says Faye's the only other person she's mentioned it to. Faye will be coming up to see you soon."

"For what?"

"I don't know. I would hope to try to persuade you to move somewhere closer to people for one thing. You don't need to be isolated like this with just that goddam motorcycle to use. Ruby said you'd be welcome to one of their cabins if you want it."

"But why didn't she talk to *me*? Why did she have to mix you up in it?"

She turned to him and her eyes, again, without warning, filled with tears. "It doesn't mean anything," she sniffled impatiently, wiping at the tears with her hair. "It's a thing some pregnant women go through, crying every time they turn around."

"Ruby thought a big-brother figure might be the easiest one for you to talk to just now, since you didn't seem to want to talk to any woman. She said you wouldn't likely want to tell Paul, and Mitch is too young."

"Poor Mitch," she said, barely audibly.

"Mitch will be all right. I've never thought of him as a bigot."

"Yes, but people his age are usually so idealistic and so—so vulnerable."

She went back to the slow brushing of her hair. "It's not fair, Shane, for you..."

"When did Gary leave?"

"Well, in the middle of July, when I first told him, he went up into the wilderness area for almost a week; you know about that. He hated me and the baby and everything. Abortion was all he'd talk about.... I couldn't, Shane."

"I know."

"Can I have a cigarette?"

"I thought you were part of the unhooked generation."

"Damn it! Will you give me one or not?" She was half-crying again, trying to smile.

He cupped a match away from the breeze and lit one for himself as well. Then, gently, he put his arm around her slender shoulders, brushing her hair out to cover it with his free hand. That was better, for both of them, because now they did not have to try to look or not look at each other, and the light pressure of his arm was warm and strong, bringing her near to tears again.

"He made it like a choice," she said dully, after two slow draws at the cigarette. "I had to choose him or the baby, and after he was gone—no, before he left—I knew there wasn't any choice.... Shane," her voice was small and awed now, "this morning it moved. I had just waked up and was lying in bed and—I felt it. It was like a—miracle."

After a little, she went on soberly, "When Gary came back, he was pathetic—and scary. Really, he's had such a lousy life. He said I never had loved him, that nobody ever had. We were up here, on the rock, and he—he threatened to jump, but I just couldn't promise about the abortion."

"I doubt that he meant it," Shane said harshly after a moment. "I think he only wanted to make you do what he wanted, and to ruin the place for you, the way he wanted to ruin the baby and..."

She nodded against his shoulder. "I finally figured out that that must have been mostly it, too, when I'd got calmed down enough to think straight. Only—I'm afraid he really will do it one day, kill himself. He's the kind—"

"He's old enough to be responsible for himself, Janet," he said roughly. "I hope you're not going to worry too much over him for the rest of your life."

After a moment, she went on dully, "Finally, he went to the cabin and started throwing things in the bus, almost everything—and then he left. I couldn't stop shaking for a long time, but I finally went down to the cabin. He'd left the petition against the Cloud Valley thing. It was almost done, so I finished it to get my mind on some-

157

thing else. For a while, I was scared to death he'd come back, but then it began to be *my* place again, mine and Loki's and—the baby's."

"So now what?" he asked gently.

"Well, I can make enough for groceries working for Ruby until the end of October, if she'll have me. I wish my folks wouldn't have to know until then.... After that, I'll go to Boise, to one of those unwed mothers' places, I guess. When I come back someday, I suppose I can say, for Cana's benefit, that Gary and I went away and got married. Maybe I wouldn't come back at all for a year or two. Then it will have mostly blown over. I can get a nursing job almost anywhere, pay our bills and all. Mama and Daddy—the others, too, I hope—will love the baby, once it's born. Maybe they won't hate me for very long."

"They won't hate you at all, Janet. Nobody ever has, and your folks won't want you going away someplace alone to have the baby."

She frowned thoughtfully. "Maybe I'd better go right away then. I could just stop a few minutes at the house and say Gary and I are going away somewhere. Then I could write them later that we got married, and about the baby. The only thing is—I wanted to stay here at Lucky Streak as long as I can. I love it so much."

"Have you seen a doctor?"

She laughed shakily. "Are you completely crazy? I'd have to go at least as far as Boise to be even half sure of not running into someone I know."

"You're a nurse. Don't you know how important prenatal care is?"

"I know how healthy I am."

"But can you take your blood pressure and all those other things they do?"

"How do you know all that stuff?"

"I don't know. From some book, I suppose. I'm going to Boise tonight because I have to see a man about the wildlife-management job tomorrow. Come with me and see a doctor, all right?"

After a long moment, she said almost inaudibly, "Separate rooms?"

He stiffened. "What do you think I am?"

"It's the other way round, Shane. I don't quite know what you think *I* am."

"I think you're—Janet, the one I've always known, and I think you're cold and we ought to go down and build up a fire."

She said, "Please don't say anything to stop me. I have to tell you, maybe more than anyone else, that there wasn't anyone before Gary. I mean I . . . the thing I feel really lousy about is the way I was about Gary, for months and months. I've made such a fool of myself and only made everything worse for him. Now, when he's been gone only a little over a month, I just can't remember why I ever thought I loved him."

"Don't try to remember." There was pain in his voice but she was too caught up in her own meditations and questionings to notice at that moment. "Maybe you can mostly forget all of it eventually."

"Shane," she said slowly, "we've always been honest with each other, sometimes almost to the point of brutality. If I ask you something, will you tell me the truth?"

"If I know it."

"Did you—a long time ago, when I was still

159

in high school, before Vik died, some time in there—did you love me? Not like a brother?"

"Yes."

"I wish you'd told me."

"You'd probably have laughed."

"No, I—well, maybe I would have. I guess I used to laugh at a lot of things that weren't funny. Remember the song about 'only yesterday, when the world was young'?"

"It will be again."

"I wish I could ask you, or somebody, to make that a promise."

"Come down now. It's going to rain. We leave for Boise whenever you're ready."

"Could we—wait until it starts getting dark? So people won't see us together? I'm sorry. I don't mean that the way it sounds."

"I know. We'll wait."

"I've got a chicken I can fry for us."

13

On a Saturday in September, Faye Holland held an afternoon open house at her not-quite-finished new home and, afterward, a buffet supper for a number of invited guests. She had hired two girls to help, but Nora, too, had been there all day. The supper guests included the Magnessens, Collinses, Rosenzweigs, Epsteins, the Drews, who owned Cana Drug, Bert and Betty Adams—Bert was manager at the mill—Tom and Lou Edwards, editors and publishers of the *Cana Chronicle*, Mr. and Mrs. Carter Sheppard, Dr. and Mrs.

Taylor, Dr. and Mrs. Striker, Sheriff Rex Terry and his wife, Amy, and some others, including Charlie Bonner.

"How in the world did you get him out of the hills?" Nora asked.

"I told him I'd have his order canceled at the mill," said Faye with a small, grim smile. "He said he could probably get a bigger order from the PSL mill at Alder, so I just told Shane to make him come."

"Odd-lookin' place," was Charlie's terse comment upon entering. "What kind of design do you call this?"

"Middle-aged Faye Holland," she said and kissed him on his grizzled cheek, which made him grin foolishly and feel a little glad he had come.

The house was rather an odd combination of things. The architect, whom Faye had rushed unmercifully, had rather cringed at some of his work. It was a half-timbered English cottage—she would have had a thatched roof if there had been a thatcher to be found. On the main floor were a spacious living room, a small dining room, and one that Faye simply called "my room," a combination of small, intimate parlor, library, and office. Above, under eaves and gables, were two large bedrooms. Below, in a semibasement, were kitchen, laundry room, maid's room, and a den, done in various—the decorator said clashing—shades of red.

"There's a stereo and lots of records downstairs," Faye said to the supper party. "Anybody who wants to, go on down and dance, watch TV, whatever. I think most of the county must have passed through here this afternoon, and I was an awfully gracious hostess, wasn't I, Nora? But now, you people will have to fend for yourselves. There's plenty of food still and you all know where the bar is. Ah, Wes, you're going to be bartender for a while? Wonderful."

She sat down beside Mrs. Taylor and began talking about grandchildren.

"Things going good in the woods this year, Charlie?" Wes Collins asked his first customer.

"Oh, I've seen it better, Wes. Give me a Scotch, will you? just straight. I know this ole gal don't buy nothin' but the best. May as well appreciate it since I'm here."

Charlie's concession to the party had been a bath, clean though worn overalls and shirt, and no boots. He felt strangely lightfooted in his worn black shoes.

"One thing I will say: the weather's holdin' good for us. I've seen snow up that high before this many a year. I believe we can keep workin' right on into October this time."

Viktor had come up with young Tom Edwards, the newspaperman, and old Rex Terry, the sheriff.

"Can I quote you, Charlie," asked Tom, "that it's been a pretty good year in the woods?"

Charlie snorted. "I never said anything like that. We're jist barely keepin' up. I never seen as many breakdowns as we've had this season, always somethin' out a commission, an' these snot-nosed kids nowadays wants to call theirselves loggers, lord have mercy!"

"He wouldn't admit to a good season," drawled the sheriff, "if the logs rolled down off the mountains and loaded themselves."

"Who's in charge of the show now?" Wes asked teasingly.

162

Charlie grunted. "Ain't much of a show left. I've lost some cutters, college kids goin' back to school, fellers got a blister or two or a stiff muscle an' gone home for the weekend. Shane's up there, but he ain't in charge of nothin'. Prob'ly readin' some book right now."

"Well, it is just about dark," Wes observed mildly, and Viktor asked,

"Will he be taking the job up at High Lonesome?"

Charlie frowned. "Says he aims to. Bunch a' damn foolishness. He's got the makin's of a damn good logger an' they ain't many left, but he wants to manage wildlife."

"Something like your job, Rex," said the editor, smiling at the sheriff.

Rex Terry grinned. "Might think so at times."

"Is old Mrs. Parnell still beating up on her husband?" asked Tom.

"Regular as clockwork," said the sheriff, "every Saturday night, or, that is, early Sunday mornings. But that's not for publication either, Tom. The neighbors call us but the old man never will sign a complaint."

Tom laughed. "Well, guess I'll go mingle around a little. I need to get to know the Rosenzweigs. Glad to see them getting out among us more. He seems an interesting man. I understand he spent several years of his childhood in a concentration camp during World War II. It might make a good human-interest story."

Charlie straddled one of the three barstools. "Lemme have another Scotch, Wes. Squirt a little sody in 'er this time. I knew ole Faye wouldn't have none but the best."

Wes Collins was a slender man, tall and

163

slightly stooped, with thinning brown hair and gentle brown eyes. He looked a little older than his fifty years. He handed across beers to Viktor and the sheriff and mixed Charlie's drink. Wes's wife, Doreen, was trying to catch his eye. She and her family were devoutly religious and she felt ashamed that her husband should be tending bar, particularly with her parents present. She was often ashamed of Wes and he would be sure to have a good piece of her mind later.

"You're really not runnin' for re-election, Rex?" asked Charlie.

"No. No, I'm not. I've had twenty years with the state police and twenty years as sheriff of this county. That's enough for anybody. It's a job somebody's got to do, but you *can* get right tired of it. Besides, there's some startin' to suggest pretty often that I take a little here and there, on the side."

"Ah, some people always say that about anyone in public office," said Wes deprecatingly.

The big, grizzled sheriff grinned. "Well, at least if I get or give anything under the table, I got sense enough to make it a cash transaction."

They chuckled and Viktor said, "And what will you do with yourself?"

"I think Amy and me will just take us a little jaunt. We want to see the grandkids, of course. One of our boys is in Alaska, you know. We been looking at campers, campmobiles, things like that. They're nice, some of 'em, but the gas they use! . . . I hear your boy Mitch has decided to be a doctor."

"Yes," said Viktor, almost without expression in face or voice. "He'll begin premed in January."

Doreen Collins sat with Bertha Sheppard,

her mother, on a loveseat. They were quietly and enjoyably picking to pieces the dresses and reputations of the other guests. When there was a brief lull in that topic, Doreen said,

"I think I've about persuaded Bruce to *do* something with himself, Mama. It's such a waste to think of him spending his life in that old store. Viktor will surely retire pretty soon and then I suppose Wes will want a new partner, but Bruce was so pleased about Daddy asking him to help manage Sheppard Foods."

Doreen was a small woman with thin brown hair, fashionably styled, and a sharp face, which seemed to wear a constantly disapproving expression. Her mother looked very much like Doreen would look in another twenty-five years.

"He'll be better off working with your daddy," she said smugly. "Just being around a Sheppard boosts most people's ambitions. And, you know, your Uncle Floyd might use a bright young man like Bruce one day, and then *he* could go into politics maybe. It's such a shame Floyd and Vera could never have any children." But she looked pleased rather than sympathetic. Then she said sternly, "But what's this we hear about Margaret?"

"Margaret Louise" was "Peggy Lou," Doreen's and Wes's daughter. Doreen sighed, tears sparkling in her eyes.

"She's not going back to school," she confirmed dolefully. "She says if Bruce won't stay on at the store, she will. She *says* she likes working there, and I can't do a thing with her."

"How much has it got to do with the Magnessen boy?" demanded Bertha.

"Oh, Mama, I think that's about *all* it has to

do with. He'll be down from working in the woods soon. I've heard he's been accepted to start college in January, but that's months away, and he'll be around the store so much . . ."

Bertha Sheppard was shaking her head, making sounds of irritation. "She can certainly do better than *him*. That's why we thought she ought to enroll in a big out-of-state school where she'd have a chance to meet more of the right kind of people. I don't want to see *her* throw herself away."

Doreen flushed. Both of them knew Bertha might have added "too" to her last statement.

"I try my best to talk to her, tell her what mistakes young people can make, just on whims, but she says things like . . . oh!" Doreen put her hands to her face.

"Like what?" demanded Bertha. She picked up a magazine, opened it, and held it in front of them as if they were studying a tiered cake.

"Well, just the other day," Doreen sniffled and found her handkerchief, "when I was trying my best to calmly talk some sense to her, she said, 'Maybe you wouldn't still feel like your marriage was a whim if you and Daddy slept in the same bed more times than it took to get Bruce and me.'"

Bertha gasped in outrage. "I can't imagine a child her age . . ."

"I had to bite my tongue," Doreen gulped, "to keep from telling her how Wes went to that awful club place in Alder Falls just right after she was born."

"If she's old enough to talk to you like that, you ought to have told her."

"Well, no matter what, Mama, a child ought

to have some respect for her father. You know how she is about Wes. He just simply can't *do* wrong in her eyes, and I sort of was afraid if I was to say a thing like that, it might upset her so much, she'd maybe—go over the deep edge, as they say."

"You could be right at that," said Bertha, frowning intently, "but I'll tell you this, Doreen, you ought to get her away from here till that Magnessen boy goes off to school. I tell you what, honey. I've been wanting to make a visit to my sisters and cousins back around Kansas City. I could go next month. Why don't I just take Margaret with me for a good long visit? You could come too."

"Oh, Mama, if you could! She's as stubborn as Wes, but you just might be able to get her to go. She's years too young to be thinking about marriage and I wouldn't ever want her in *that* family. Viktor and Nora are all right you know, good, kindhearted people and all that, but he *is* a foreigner, and *nobody* knows anything about him. I can't help always feeling suspicious of somebody who won't talk about his past. They came here in—what was it, '53?—and Viktor's been a partner in the store since old man Collins died in 1961, and still, it's like he never had any life before he came to Cana, or at least before he married Nora. Even Nora doesn't seem to know much more than the rest of us. I've heard he was a prisoner of war in Germany for years but, to tell you the honest truth, when they seem to act so cagey about it, I can't help wondering which side he was really on. I've tried to tell Peggy there's that, and then this awful mess Janet is into."

167

"*That*'s all over the county," said Bertha censoriously. "I've heard they're talking about starting one of those communes up there where they're living, drugs and free love and the Lord only knows what else. We just can't have that kind of wickedness in our county. I talked to Amy Terry about it just yesterday at the garden-club meeting. I expect she went right home and talked it over with Sheriff Rex. If it doesn't look like he's going to do something right away, your daddy, or maybe your Uncle Floyd, can have a talk with him. We don't need a nest of wickedness like that right on our doorstep, tempting the few decent young people we have left, bringing in a bunch of scum from all over, and I tell you right now, I don't intend to vote for Paul Magnessen for county commissioner. Carter and Floyd both are going to buy stock in that Cloud Valley Corporation, but a moneymaking venture with someone is a completely different thing from having him have a say in running the county when he doesn't even seem to be trying to clean the skeletons out of his own family closet."

Paul and Morris Epstein were in another corner talking business. Morris was thinking of opening another mercantile store in a little town called Rose Prairie, some twenty miles to the east of Cana, and wondered if Paul might know of a suitable property.

David Rosenzweig had been talking desultorily with plump, gray-haired Ella Epstein. Now he went obligingly into the dining room to bring her just "a taste more of that lobster salad and a *little* slice of Nora Magnessen's home made rye bread, maybe with just a *touch* of that cream-cheese spread."

Gloria was talking animatedly with Ted Carpenter, the handsome, young, blond attorney, while Ted's pregnant wife, Nancy, sat across the room beside Betty Adams, giving her husband uneasy glances.

Gloria was overdressed for a casual party such as this. Ted found her mauve evening gown delightfully low-cut and neither of them made any secret of knowing he did.

"This is a party for old folks," Gloria said petulantly as Dr. Taylor and Homer Grundy, the banker, walked by on their way to the dining room for refills. "Some of us ought to go to the country club. At least there's dancing there on Saturday nights."

"Let's go downstairs and see what Faye's got for her stereo," Ted said, then loudly, "Paul, Sharon, Chris, Carol, Tom, Lou, dancing anyone?"

"Get me a drink first, will you?" said Gloria as David passed on his way back to Ella Epstein. "An Alexander, if he can make one."

"If the makings are not here, we'll just go right out and get them," said Ted happily.

Perhaps half the guests wandered downstairs. Dr. Max Striker took Wes's place behind the bar, but Dr. Striker was on call at the hospital and the call came soon, so that he and his wife, Mary, left. Then others, the Carter Sheppards, Dr. and Mrs. Taylor, a few more made their good-byes and went home.

Lou Edwards, wife of the newspaperman, his chief reporter, cook, and bottle washer, joined Faye as she said good night to the last of the early departers.

"I'd like to take some pictures of the house in daylight, Faye; sometime soon, for the paper.

I should have done it this afternoon with all the people around, but I had to go to a damned football game while Tom was at a men's-club thing. Cana High lost, forty-seven to three. I don't know why we bother. We sure don't have the teams we used to. Anyway, I can see it's a half-timbered English cottage, but I never heard of one with a columned front porch. Just what do you call this style of house?"

Faye grinned. "Southern English?" she hazarded. "I don't know, Lou, I just had them build what I wanted."

"It's a kind of neat idea, the kitchen downstairs, but won't it be a little inconvenient?"

"Oh, not so bad. There's a dumbwaiter to the dining room and unless I have several people for a meal, the eating will be done in the kitchen. I never cared much for dining rooms, really."

"Will you have full-time help?"

"Oh, no, not unless I really go to work at some business, probably not then."

"It was just about dark when we got here, but it looks like lovely landscaping, with the lawn already sodded and all."

"I wish I could have got bigger trees. I like trees, and this ridge is mostly so bare of anything natural."

"This is a beautiful fireplace."

"I wanted to use it, but it's just too warm tonight."

"Yes, it looks like a good, long autumn. Is it true you've rented that space where the fabric shop used to be on Main Street?"

"Yes, I have, but I still don't know what I'm going to do with it. Listen, Louise, you're making me uneasy. I don't like to feel interviewed."

Lou grinned. "Just relax and remember me as your daughter Barbara's friend who once vomited all over the upstairs hall at Holland House."

"You know, I'd forgotten that," Faye laughed. "You couldn't get in the bathroom fast enough because Judy was in there trying on false eyelashes or something."

"Yes, and that brings up one more interview-type question. What about Holland House?"

"That's still in limbo. I never dreamed it would be so hard to give something away."

"Listen, Faye," said Charlie, coming up to them, "I better be leavin' too. I want to drive back up to the show tonight."

"Oh, no, Charlie," she said imperiously. "I've been waiting for this very time, when everyone's scattered out, doing his own thing. I want a poker game with you."

The old man's face added wrinkles with a broad grin. "I don't know *how* many years it's been, girl. Where's the cards and chips at? Who else is in?"

As everyone milled around, resettling themselves, Faye, looking for the cards and chips, found Wes Collins momentarily alone in the dining room.

"I'd like to sit in on your poker game," he said softly, "but Doreen wants to go home. It's a lovely house, Faye, a lovely party, and you—I'm so glad you decided to come back."

For the briefest of moments, their hands touched and they looked deeply into each other's eyes.

"What I think," she said quietly, with a sad half-smile, "is that we're a pair of old fools."

"Probably," Wes said wearily, "but I swear

it won't be too much longer until... good night, then."

In front of the empty fireplace, Faye, Charlie, Viktor, and Rex Terry set up the card table. Most of the younger people were downstairs dancing, someone occasionally coming up for a tray of drinks.

"You ought to have a bar down there," Tom Edwards complained to Faye when this duty fell to him.

"I'm going to. Just give me time. The walls upstairs aren't papered yet either, and a hundred other things."

"That's a lousy hand you've got," Tom said, grinning, dodging her exasperated backhand and returning to the den.

Nora, Betty Adams and Amy Terry sat on a couch at the other end of the room, quietly discussing children. The Adams were the Magnessens' closest neighbors. Betty's youngest, Carolyn and Patty Magnessen, had been best friends since babyhood. In fact, they were spending this night together at the Adams', with Bert's mother, Belle, as baby-sitter. Amy had the latest pictures of her own children and grandchildren to show.

"Is it true," wondered Amy after a time, "that Fred Petrie's wife is leaving him over that check business at Fannie's place?"

Betty grimaced. "That's what Bert's mama, Belle, says. She spreads every rumor she hears and invents some of her own, but she's been a close friend of Mabel Petrie's for years, so this one may be true."

Nora smiled ironically. "I'd leave Viktor if she did a thing like that. Not necessarily for *going* to Fannie's, but for being so dumb about it."

172

They giggled and Amy said contritely, "I guess we ought to be ashamed for going on about it so, but, my land! Right now, I've got to find a bathroom."

"I spied that out first thing," said Betty. "Come on, I'll show you."

After a moment, Nora got up and started toward the dining room.

"Nora," warned Faye, as if she had eyes in the back of her head, "unless you're getting something to eat, just stay out of there. I've told the girls to leave everything alone until the party's over. In fact, I may send them home and ask them to come back in the morning. People need all they want to eat.... I'll see you, Rex, and raise you one."

"Well," Nora said, "I just thought I'd stack a few—"

"Do you want to sit in on this game?" asked Faye.

"Good heavens, no. I don't know anything about poker."

"Tell her not to keep trying to sneak around and work, Viktor."

"Don't do sneaky work, Nora," he said absently, concentrating on his cards.

Smiling resignedly, Nora went back to the couch and took up Patty's partially finished knitted cardigan. She didn't in the least mind being a little to herself in the midst of the party, but it always had made her jumpy just to sit idly.

Bert Adams came upstairs, puffing. "Those dances are too much for me. Sometimes I just get carried away and forget how old and out-of-date I am."

"You can set in on the next hand," Charlie

told him. "An' while I think of it, that scaler you've got at the mill don't know a board foot from a clubfoot. There's goin' to come a day of reckonin' when we're through up at the show."

"We have one of those every fall, Charlie," Bert said dryly.

"Yes, but Shane's keepin' our tally this year. All that education he's had, an' talkin' about more, he ought—"

"Is Shane your scaler?"

"Just part of the time, when he ain't doin' somethin' else."

"Well, you bring your regular scaler to that day of reckoning and we'll reckon. Yes, I will take a hand, Rex, soon's I get a drink. Anybody else?"

Sharon, looking angry, came upstairs then with Nancy Carpenter. Sharon said quietly to Nora, "I'm going to drive Nancy home. She's not feeling well. Tell Paul and Ted, will you? *if* they ask."

A moment later, David Rosenzweig came into the living room.

"Take a hand, David?" asked Viktor, who was about to deal.

"No, no, thank you," he said absently and wandered over to sit down near Nora.

Gloria was enjoying herself, which usually meant that David was not. He was a poor dancer and disliked dancing. He knew that Gloria could happily go on all night, with men practically waiting in line, as they usually were. Already, she had had too much to drink and she was dancing too often with Paul Magnessen. There was a sourness in David's throat as he recalled that night two months ago when she had murmured Paul's name in her sleep. Suppose, while he sat here, they were to go out by the back door and ... He looked up unhappily to find Nora smiling tentatively.

"Would you like a drink?" she asked. "Or there's still plenty of food."

"Perhaps a little later." He looked worried, apologetic. "Do you dance?"

"Oh, I used to be all right with a waltz or a fox-trot, things like that, but I can't do any of this modern stuff."

"Yes, it's too much for me too."

Strange, she thought, his accent was a good deal like Viktor's, though his voice was tight, tense, not nearly so pleasant. She had not noticed the accent until now, but, then, she had scarcely talked with him before.

She said, "Paul tells us you may be buying a place to build up on the lake."

"Yes, it's really much cooler up there. Gloria, my wife, dislikes hot weather."

As a matter of fact, he was strongly thinking now of *not* buying the property Paul seemed so sure of selling him. David could find other places, handled by other realtors, and prevent Paul's having a commission on this one sale at least. Or perhaps he'd just have the big house in the valley air conditioned. It would not be so very expensive with the heating system it already had.

Maybe consenting to live on the lake even briefly had been a mistake. Gloria had wheedled until, last week, he'd taken delivery of a flashy foreign sports car for her. She was playing some golf, taking part in a few things at the country club now, and she argued that she did not like George driving her, that he, David, needed George and the limousine. And it was true that it was sometimes inconvenient having their summer residence twenty-five, rather than five miles from the mill, so perhaps next year...

Nora was saying, "Are you still living up at the Cullen place? Or have you moved back to the valley?"

"We've decided to stay on at the lake until the beginning of October unless the weather turns a good deal cooler. It's unusually warm for September, I'm told."

"Yes, it is. Some years, we've had frost by this time and quite a lot of snow on the mountains."

Silence fell and Nora felt she ought to say something more. It made her uncomfortable trying to talk with people with whom it seemed she *ought* to talk. Maybe he wasn't such an unpleasant person, really. Maybe a little shy? Preoccupied? Or was it superiority? Nevertheless:

"Paul is so pleased you're interested in his project up at the ranch. I suppose he's told you they've begun some of the surveying work."

Her knitting needles clicked in a moment of silence.

"Yes, but I also understand there is some sort of environmental disagreement that may be dragged through the courts. Well, we'll see.... You have other children besides Paul, Mrs. Magnessen?"

"My name is Nora," she said with her warm smile.

"And mine is David," he responded. His tone was friendly enough but, just offhand, she could not remember ever having seen him really smile.

"Oh, yes, David, we have three others. Young

Viktor, who was next younger than Paul, was killed some years ago, he and his wife, in an accident. Their little girl, Patty, lives with us."

Absently, he made sounds of sympathy as there was a burst of laughter from downstairs.

Rex Terry said, "That's it, I fold," and Bert Adams chortled.

Nora went on, "Our older daughter, Alice, lives in San Francisco, and our other daughter, Janet, is living up near Blackbuck."

"Yes," he said slowly, finding it difficult work to go on with this conversation. "I believe we met her once, at the little restaurant—long, light brown hair, a very pretty young lady."

"And Mitch," Nora said proudly, "our youngest, who's working up in the woods now for Charlie Bonner, has just been accepted to begin premed in January."

"Yee-hoo!" yelled Charlie, beating the table with his fist. "Read 'em an' weep. A full house! I'll teach the lot of you to keep raisin' ole Charlie."

"Your son is going to be a doctor," said David in a strange tone Nora couldn't classify. His eyes, drawn to the card players, were suddenly riveted on Viktor's profile.

... The hair had been straw blond, not white, the face thin and hollowed, usually with several days of blond stubble, the blue eyes hard, weary, full of misery, the mouth a straight grim line, not curved in a small smile of resignation. ...

"He decided all at once," Nora was saying. "Mitch is nineteen and hadn't decided on anything to make a career of, and then one day..."

Her words trailed off. Obviously he was not listening. His face was going pasty with bright, flushed blotches, and why was he staring like that at Viktor?

David gave a visible start and turned back to her. "It must be a wonderful feeling, Mrs.—ah—Nora, to have a son who's going to be a doctor."

"Well, he has a long way to go," she said uneasily.

"Tell me," he said carefully, "does your husband come from Germany?"

"No. Viktor's Danish."

"Do you know if he might have relatives in Germany, named—Koerner—I think it was?"

"No, I don't think any of his people ever lived in Germany, though he was interned there for over four years during the war."

"Ah," said David, glancing at Viktor and away. "I was interned also. I was only a child. My parents and two older brothers were—exterminated."

Nora shuddered. "How horrible!"

"Your husband was in a concentration camp in South Germany?" he asked softly after a moment.

"Yes, it was near Munich. We can ask him when—"

"Oh, no, no. Probably it's a time he does not want to talk about, to recall. We won't bother him with it. It's just a resemblance, a very close resemblance I've noticed to someone else.... Excuse me, please. I must go and ask my wife if she's ready to go home. It's getting very late."

Gloria was scarcely able to stand. She was being held up, held very closely in a dance with Ted Carpenter. David could see that Carpenter's hand cupped one of her breasts so that most of it bulged above the neckline of her dress. Angrily, he tapped the younger man's shoulder and put a supporting arm around his wife.

"Come, Gloria, it's time to go home."

"But I'm not ready," she said loudly.

"It's time."

"You're an old meanie, David," and loudly, to the room in general, "he's an old meanie."

David propelled her to the stairs and halfway up them to a landing. "For God's sake, fix your dress!"

"They like me this way, don't you?" she called, giggling, down to the others.

Roughly, he pushed her breast back into the tight bodice.

"You're hurting me!"

Paul had come to the foot of the stairs with the tray of empty glasses. David half-dragged Gloria on. Over her shoulder, and his, she said sulkily to Paul, "He hurt my boob. You wouldn't do that, would you?"

It was awkward for everyone, saying good night to the Rosenzweigs. Gloria wanted just one more drink, which David curtly refused her. She had to go to "the little girls' room," then to tell Faye effusively how much she had enjoyed herself. David, stony-faced, half-carried her to the little sports car and dumped her into the passenger's seat. He tried a half-apology, a word of appreciation, to Faye, but was too angry for more than sullen, mumbled words.

Faye smiled casually, said, "I'm so glad you could come," and went back inside, closing the door quickly so that he need feel no additional embarrassment.

"What a bitch she is," muttered Paul. He

was at the bar, trying to remember the drink orders with which he had been sent upstairs. Nora was there, making drinks for the poker players.

"I believe she's a real alcoholic," she said. "He's as pathetic as she is somehow. It's sad. But she's as simple as can be; I mean shallow, and he's not. I feel sorry for them both, but he still gives me the willies."

David did not like the sports car and he drove it viciously, tossing the half-conscious Gloria about in her seat.

"That Ted Carpenter is a terrific dancer," she said dreamily, seemingly unaware of the car's erratic motion. "But Paul is still the best-looking, don't you think? Both their wives disappeared. I guess they were jealous. And so did you disappear, David dear. Why was that? ... When I'd had enough dancing—if that ever happened—I was going to do my good old club act for them. They all wanted me to."

Magnessen—Koerner; Koerner—Magnessen. Beneath the surface of his anger and torment over Gloria, the two names kept revolving. Why were the names different? If this Viktor Magnessen were not the Koerner he had known, they must have been twin brothers. A son who wanted to be a doctor ... following in the father's footsteps? But no, this Magnessen was in the lumber and hardware business. Still, it *had* to be the same man. David had struggled for two years, trying to place him, and now he was so certain. ... Dr. Koerner in the prison-camp hospital. And there had been another Dr. Koerner, an older man, the father, no doubt. They had done experiments in that hospital, Nazi-directed experiments.

David could not precisely recall much of what he had heard, but there had been ghastly rumors. Psychiatrists, both of them had been psychiatrists. They had been called merely doctors because of the Nazi prejudice against what was considered to be a strictly Jewish profession, psychiatry, but everyone had known what they were, those Koerners. Yes, it was coming a little clearer to him now. The older one had died. Suicide? Yes, he thought that had been the camp talk. And the younger had disappeared. At the time, the boy, David, had numbly supposed that it was the same sort of disappearance that had befallen the rest of his own family and so many others, to the gas chambers, the crematory, but he recalled now that there had been a rumor among the older men, a furor among the guards, that young Koerner had escaped.... Danish, she had said he was, and David had heard that from others, perhaps even from Magnessen himself. Danish he might be, but...

They were on the lake road now. David was driving too fast, and Gloria, oblivious to everything else, was murmuring sensuously to herself, "There's still one more I've *got* to meet, the grandson of that dreadful old Charlie. We met that time at the mill, but we haven't been properly introduced. Why wasn't he there tonight? I wonder. Probably out fucking somebody. He's beautiful, sort of ascetically beautiful, I think that's a good word. Anyway, I think he's the best-looking thing I've ever seen in pants."

"Shut up!" David said fiercely. "You bitch! Goddamn you to hell!"

"Oh, now, Davey, sweetums, that's no way to talk to your little Gloria. I can't help it, can I, if men want me? That ought to make you want me even more, you lucky, fucky boy."

She was running her fingers lightly over him and the heat and hardening he felt in his loins only seemed to add to his anger.

When they reached the Cullen place, Gloria stumbled blithely into the house, humming a little tune, smiling to herself.

"You do want me, don't you, Davey?" She laughed and tried to pull away teasingly, but he grabbed her fiercely, ripping the mauve gown. She went into peals of laughter. "That little dress, that old rag, cost you three hundred dollars."

He took her viciously, as he had never done before, on the bedroom carpet. She moaned, gurgled, clawed at him, as if in ecstasy, but once he was inside her, she lay still, limp, silent. When he had finished, quickly, he found she had passed out. Her limp body seemed very heavy as he dragged her onto the bed and made a disgusted attempt at covering her.

His stomach, knotting suddenly in a frightening viselike cramp, rebelled at the supper and the drinks and his emotions. He ran for the bathroom, staggering, groaning. When he returned a long while later, shaking with weakness, shivering in a cold sweat, he did what he could to put the room in order. Gloria slept deeply. He found the stomach pills, gulped two of them, and went to sit in the dark living room.

As the pain in his stomach began gradually to lessen, David thought miserably: Cana, Alder County, Idaho, Holland Mill. My God, why did I ever come here? No. Why did I ever marry *her*? He put his face in his hands. Because I wanted her; all of it because I wanted Gloria Daly, Gloria

Dalowitz, an ice-cold, utterly self-centered, prick-teasing bitch. God help me! I still want her!

Strangely, he now remembered being a little boy in Germany, a very little boy, perhaps five years old, a child with a stomach ache. His mother, tender and concerned for her youngest, had made an herb tea and had held him on her lap while he drank it. He even remembered the taste of the tea, not good, but not really bad, the comforting warmth and surcease it had brought, the faint, flowery smell of his mother, the feel of her arms around him, the gentle rocking, and a song. It seemed that, since those long-ago moments, he had known no peace, no true happiness and comfort.

He half-dozed, waking with a start as his head fell against the back of the chair. They would *not* make a fool of him, not Alder County, not Gloria. So Paul Magnessen was good-looking; the Bonner boy the best-looking thing she'd seen in pants; Ted Carpenter a fine dancer?

Somehow, Viktor Magnessen was young Dr. Koerner.... Those experiments—Nazi collaboration. Of course the man had changed his name, managed in some way to take on a new identity. Paul was his son. The Bonner boy, David had heard, the same as a son to him; Ted Carpenter, his attorney and friend. Viktor had a plump, comfortable wife who, no doubt, had never given him cause for a moment's worry about anything. He had four living children who seemed to care deeply for their parents, a son wanting to become a doctor, grandchildren. He was a pillar of the town of Cana, his wife and Faye Holland best friends, a man to whom people went for advice, and whose advice they trusted.

While he, David Rosenzweig, was someone to be laughed at, probably a county joke like that stupid ex-magistrate, a man who, though his wife was virtually frigid and cared nothing for the ultimate sex act, gave the impression to anyone with half a brain that she must be cuckolding her husband at least once a day. Perhaps they were still laughing back there at Faye Holland's new house. They would stop laughing.

David had suffered the loss of everything in the war. He had made money since, a respectable amount of money, but he had regained nothing else, while this Magnessen, this Koerner, had everything: love, respect, friendship, evident security within himself.

... Perhaps he, Magnessen-Koerner, had been the very man who had decided, in whatever ghastly way they had of making such choices, when the members of David's own family should disappear, one by one. Why had *he* been left? Because he was so young? Because his strength did not utterly fail through all those grueling, starving, fear-filled years in the factory? Because, through some bureaucratic mismanagement, he was one Jew who was overlooked?

There had been many times, after he was old enough fully to realize what had happened to his family and so many of the other horrors, that he had wished he, too, had died. The nightmares still came to him occasionally, even now. For a moment, he found himself near to wishing again for death, but he clenched his teeth and spat violent, filthy German words, the names they had called the guards, the officers, the trustees, and the collaborators behind their backs. He would show these smug, bigoted, self-satisfied people who thought him something to laugh at! He would show Gloria, who was worst of all.

He got up and rummaged in a small desk for several minutes before recalling that he did not have a Boise phone book here; it was at the mill office. He took up the phone and dialed state information.

"Idaho," answered a girl's bright voice. David smiled a grim little smile. That way of answering made it sound as if there were only one phone in the state, and that was just about the true caliber of the damned place, he thought.

He asked for Boise, his voice croaking and grating hoarsely so that he had to clear his throat and repeat the request. Another operator came on.

"The number of the regional FBI office," David said. His voice was now coldly under control, but his hand shook slightly as he copied the number.

He hung up, direct-dialed. The far-off phone rang, rang. He counted twelve rings and hung up.

State information again; Boise information. "Another number? Yes, sir, I have an 'if no answer' number, but it's in Butte, Montana."

Christ, what did one do here if there were an imminent crisis? He was almost laughing now at the pure provinciality of his surroundings. "Give it to me, please."

Dialing again; a farther-away phone ringing, ringing, thirteen rings. David slammed his phone back into its cradle. Good God! Not even a recording! Suppose he needed to report an imme-

185

diate conspiracy to blow up the United States, beginning in central Idaho?

Still, he felt better for the bitter humor of the attempt, and surely there would be an answer on Monday. He tore the sheet containing the numbers from the small notepad, carried it to his room, and put it into the pocket of the suit jacket he would be wearing on Monday. Thirty hours; perhaps thirty-six; he could wait.

Magnessen had now had thirty-one years and more since the war ended, more than two of those years of grace while living in the same town with David Rosenzweig. David swallowed two sleeping pills. Otherwise, he knew he would be too restless and excited to sleep. No doubt, if consulted, Magnessen would be willing to wait another thirty-six hours.

14 ○

"Viktor," said Nora, finally a little impatient, getting to her feet, "it's two-thirty in the morning. We've got to go home."

"They haven't even noticed the party's over," said Betty Adams, yawning. "Bert, come on. You'll be mortgaging the house in a minute."

"He did that an hour ago," said Rex Terry. "He's working on the kids now."

Amy Terry had fallen asleep on a couch. Faye, to be sociable with the women, had dropped out of the game earlier. She had sent the hired girls home more than an hour ago and had brought up a coffee pot from the kitchen.

"Ah, you girls go on home," said Charlie. "Faye can go to bed if she wants to. We won't *mo*lest her. Got the sheriff here an' all. It's near too late for me to git back to the show tonight."

Viktor stood up, stretching stiffly. "Somebody at our house has to take Patty and Carolyn to Sunday school in less than seven hours. You just want to go on playing, Charlie, because you're winning."

"That's as good a reason as I know of," chortled the old man.

"I guess we better be gettin' on for the Falls," said the sheriff. "Wake up, Mama."

"You an' me could play a few more hands, Faye," suggested the indefatigable Charlie.

"No," she said a little regretfully. "I'm going to have to throw you out, Charlie. It's been a pretty long day. Winter's coming. We can have lots of games then."

"You can sleep at our house, Charlie," said Nora, yawning.

"Let him sleep at his own house," said Viktor ungraciously, but with a smile.

"Why, Viktor!" she said in startled reproof.

"Well, he can. If there's anything I can't stand, it's a gloating winner."

"I ain't sleepin' anyway," said Charlie resiliently. "I'll git back to camp just about in time to git whoever's left up there up with the mornin' star, like they ought to be."

"Even on a Sunday?" yawned Faye. "I wouldn't work for you for anything, you old codger," but she hugged him good night.

The Magnessens and Adams had come together in Bert's car. They were comfortably silent through most of the drive home.

When she and Viktor were in bed, Nora said, "It seems odd to think the house is empty, doesn't it? except for us."

"It doesn't happen often," he agreed and put an arm around her.

"I wish they'd never have to *all* go away," she said wistfully. Then, after a little silence, "That poor David Rosenzweig. What a tart *she* is! No wonder he seems strange and—aloof, poor man. And he did have an awful time in the war. He talked a little about it. He must be a good bit younger than he looks because he said he was a child then. Do you know, he still keeps trying to place you?"

"What did he say?" Viktor's voice seemed strangely without expression, but the room was dark and she could not see his face.

"Oh, just asked if you were German, where the prison camp was that you were in, things like that. He seems to have you mixed up with someone else. He mentioned some name I never heard, starts with a C, or maybe a K.... That wife of his ought to be tarred and feathered. After Sharon came back, she told me some of the things that had been going on downstairs."

"Tarring and feathering is not done anymore," he said coldly.

"Why, Viktor," she said, a little hurt, "you sound the way you used to sometimes when the children were little and called somebody naughty names. They *do* still tar and feather people sometimes, though you know I didn't actually mean it."

"Of course I know," he said, holding her close. "I'm sorry. Go to sleep now, darling. I'll drive the girls to Sunday school. You have a nice late morning."

"I don't want to miss church," she said drowsily. "Be sure you wake me up by nine-thirty."

"Yes, I will."

She fell asleep quickly. He got carefully out of bed, put on a robe and slippers, and went downstairs. He filled his pipe and smoked with no thought of what he did. After a long time, he slept briefly, leaning back in his chair, but, with first light, he woke with a wrenching start, crying out, "No! I can't go back!"

15

Charlie found Shane up in the woods near noon on a Wednesday. Shane sat on a log, smoking, methodically sharpening his chain saw. Other saws snarled in the near distance, but they had to raise their voices only a little to hear each other.

"This what you been doin' all mornin'?" demanded the old man.

"You badger me, Charlie," Shane accused calmly. "I've cut more than any other two sawyers you've got this morning."

"Huh! That ain't nothin' to brag about, considerin' what other sawyers I got left now. You heard the weather forecast?"

"How could I? What's for lunch?"

"They's one of them depression things movin' in on the coast. They're sayin' a lot of snow for the high country by tomorrow night. Bud Stallings come by, gittin' what Forest Service people he's got left out of up here."

Shane looked at the sky—what he could see of it—drawing on his cigarette. It was a soft, hazy autumn blue, the kind that could mean almost anything, with a few clouds seeming to move about uncertainly.

Charlie had sat down briefly on the other end of the log, but now he sprang to his feet irritably.

"Goddamnit, we've got to move timber!"

Shane filed meticulously.

"Lonnie Martin left with a truck around ten, an' the other two's about loaded out. Leonard Hall's takin' one. I want to git 'em up in here after dinner to drag these logs down. It might be this storm won't amount to near as much as they say, but, then agin, it might be we can't git back in up here, after tomorrow night, till next spring."

Shane drew one last long puff from his cigarette and put it out carefully.

"Where's Mitch at?"

"Just over the other side of that shoulder."

"How many others?"

"Two."

"Well, I want them over to finish limbin' an' cuttin' this stuff to length. Go tell 'em, will you? An' then—"

"They're not going to like that, Charlie. The scaler won't know who to credit the board feet to."

"Christsake, I can't help that. We got to git down as much as we can. Then . . ."

"Then you want me to take a truck." Shane stood up, stretching, trying to ease the stiffness out of his arms, shoulders, back, legs.

"I *do* remember what you said, boy," said Charlie shortly, "that mornin' down at the house. I ain't asked you to drive since then, have I?"

"No."

"You can git to the mill, git unloaded, an' be back here in time to git loaded agin before dark. Then you can run that load down to be ready at the mill first thing in the mornin'. I don't know why they won't put a damn unloadin' crew on their second shift this time a' year. How many truckloads you figure we've got?"

"Eight, maybe ten, if all the cut stuff gets loaded out."

"You see? See what a bind we're in?"

"Ah, hell," Shane said resignedly.

Charlie's face cleared. "I'll keep a eye out all winter for good drivers an' sign 'em up," he promised blithely. "An' maybe you'll feel easier about it yourself, next season. I'd drive Big Red myself today, but there wouldn' half git done up here that ought to be."

"Big Red," Shane muttered, gathering tools and fuel cans.

"That ole truck's in the best shape you could think of since we had that brake job done."

"It uses about two gallons of oil a trip and smokes like a sonofabitch. The engine'll just freeze up one day."

"Naw, she'll be all right. You're stretchin' it a good bit about the oil," Charlie said confidently. "We'll git 'er a ring job done this winter. Listen, you just go on down an' see if they're done loadin'. I'll git them other boys over here. An' leave that stuff. I aim to do some cuttin' myself after dinner."

Driving Charlie's beloved old Big Red took strength, concentration, and a kind of clairvoyance about the truck's idiosyncrasies. "Like a woman," Charlie liked to say, "got her little temperaments." Everything about the old truck seemed to be too tight or too loose. Whatever gear Shane tried did not seem to satisfy. It backfired, whined, groaned, sputtered, tried to stall. The road over and down from Jamison's Saddle was a nightmare, a trail gouged out by bulldozers last year, full of rocks, potholes, deep ruts, and washouts, and mostly a sidehill affair where the truck leaned precariously. Every time Shane drove it, the tall weeds in its center hissing and snagging against the underside of the truck, he cursed the fact that the building of such a "road" had ever been allowed. The truck lurched and banged, deepening the ruts, cutting into the washouts. Could this be modern soil conservation? Then, too, this "road," all six miles of it, frightened him. He put an unlit cigarette between his teeth and drove too fast. All his life, when he had been afraid of a thing that seemed to have to be done, he had clenched his jaw and done it as quickly as possible. He shuddered at the thought of having to drive this part of the road again tonight, after dark.

When he was down off the high ridge, with Cloud Creek brawling beside a better road, he got out, lit the mangled cigarette, and checked his truck and load. The air was still, the sun warm, and the smell of the fresh-cut logs sweet. He stood by the back of the trailer, away from the smoking, sputtering exhaust, and rested a moment, drawing deep breaths.

Back in the cab, he found a Thermos lodged under the seat, but it was empty. Charlie had not given him time for lunch. "Damn it, the truck's ready an' dinner ain't. Don't wait around up here. You can stop at McCrarys', maybe make a little time that way."

As he passed through Cloud Valley Ranch, between its cattle guards, he saw a car—Paul's, he thought—and a pickup; two or three men surveying in a big meadow across the creek. Near the foreman's house, one of the towheaded little Quarles boys, too young for school, rushed out toward the road and gave him the signal. Shane obliged him with a couple of honks, Mrs. Quarles, taking clothes off her line, shook her fist at the cloud of dust the truck raised as it fled past.

Normally, Shane took the road around the west side of the lake. It was a little longer that way and the road not quite as good, but there was apt to be less traffic. Most of the summer houses were on the east side, where there was more room between the lake and the ridge of the old canyon, but all the summer people should be gone now. Now it was hunting season, and hunters preferred the west-side road. Just before the Cloud Creek bridge, he swung the truck left.

Now the road was good, two-lane gravel, but on the better roads, Big Red tended to try to wander, like a hungry, cantankerous old horse, trying for a nip of grass, first on one side, then the other. Shane's shoulders ached, whether from the difficulty of handling the truck or the strain of not wanting to do it, he could not have said. The hell of it was, he *was* a good driver. He put a little more pressure on the accelerator and gripped the wheel. At this speed, he couldn't spare a hand to light the cigarette he wanted. Probably just as well. He was smoking too much anyway.

A storm coming. He hoped the report was true. They wanted him up at High Lonesome Lookout by mid-October. He had a lot of papers to fill out and have certified so he could get some postgraduate credit for the work he'd be doing. There was Charlie's book work to finish up so it would be ready for Holland's and the tax people, some resting to do, and ... Janet.

If a storm was coming, she ought to be down, away from Lucky Streak. It was not quite as high as where they were working, but the road up the mountain would be treacherous with snow or mud. Thank God she'd at least given in enough to keep his little station wagon while he took the motorcycle. He didn't want to have to think of her. He'd been working particularly hard at not thinking of her since he had first heard she was living with Gary Hunt. But, to be honest, the avoidance of too much thought of her had been going on longer than that, a lot longer. . . .

She had always wanted to follow Vik and him, try to do almost anything they did. One night when Vik had just turned nineteen, just before his and Anne's second year in college and Shane's first, the three of them had gone to a dance at the Robin's Nest, south of Cana, to celebrate Vik's birthday. Anne would not be nineteen for a couple of months, and Shane had only become eighteen in June, but they could "pass" because nobody really cared much. ID's were never asked for at the Robin's Nest. Still, they had felt important and adult, having beer and pizza, dancing to the loud, very bad music. Suddenly, Vik had yelled "Good grief!" in absolute outrage. Janet, in jeans and a sloppy sweater, strolled through the door, scared, but trying hard to look nonchalant.

"What the hell are you doing here?" demanded her amazed brother. He had to yell to be heard above the music and everyone else's yelling.

"I just—wanted to see what it was like," she said, raising her chin and sticking it out a little in a defensive or belligerent gesture which was particularly her own. "I thought it would be all right since you three are here."

"Well, it's not all right. You're not even fifteen years old. You're a minor and you're going to get us all thrown out. Now go home."

"How did you get here?" asked Anne.

"My bicycle," she said defiantly and the other three burst into laughter. That made her so angry that tears stung her eyes and she looked away from them, blinking rapidly and biting her lower lip for a moment.

Vik said, "Shane, would you mind taking her home? There's some rope in the trunk of the car. You can tie the damned bicycle on somehow."

When he had finished with the bicycle and got into the car, she was crying, trying to hide it from him.

"Don't," he said gently. "You shouldn't have come, but it's not that bad."

"I want to be grown up," she said petulantly

but unevenly. "Alice is out on a date. Everybody else is older. 'Wait till you're older,' that's all I ever hear.... Is it really a lot different?"

"No. Not that I've noticed. Then you just have to wait for something else."

"Like what?"

"I—don't know. To go to college, to finish going to college, to see—what comes next."

"You don't even sound glad you're eighteen."

"I guess not, especially."

"But you wouldn't want to be a little kid again?" She stared at him after rubbing at her eyes with her fists.

"No."

"Then how old *do* you want to be?"

"I don't know."

He had driven to the parking lot exit. "Do you want to take a little ride somewhere before you go home?"

"Where?" She blew her nose and sounded less wilted.

"Oh, just down to the falls and back."

"Yes, but—Vik's awfully fussy about his car."

"He won't mind."

After a long time, she said, "Shane, why don't you have a girl?"

"Sometimes I do."

"I know nearly all the girls in high school were crazy to date you last year. Alice talked about it all the time. I—I wondered . . . sometimes I feel kind of—afraid of boys, the ones I'm sort of—interested in. Do boys ever feel like that—about girls?"

"Yes."

196

"But you—wouldn't ever be afraid of me, would you? Or somebody like me? Because I couldn't be afraid of *you* or feel silly and embarrassed trying to think of things to say to you or wondering if I'm behaving the way I ought to."

"No, I wouldn't be afraid of you."

But it was a half-lie. As Vik's sister, almost like his own sister, she was no threat; however, anything verging on sexual involvement frightened him.... There had been a trip to Fannie's last year at the end of the football season, a trip he would not have been party to except that the others would have laughed and made cracks about him for the rest of the year. And then there had been two girls from his high-school class. Shane had found sex a joy and a terror; a joy because he discovered it was something into which he could go with such wild abandon; a terror because he was so utterly lost to himself, so helpless during those moments of deep arousal and fulfillment that were almost as much pain as pleasure. In those ultimate moments, he had no real control, no self-will except finding satiation for himself and the girl, a complete vulnerability that terrified him in retrospect. And he discovered he could not merely have sex with a girl and then shrug it away. He felt things for her. Immediately afterward, he was so grateful, so content, so awed by what the girl's body had caused to happen to him that he made a complete fool of himself.

At Fannie's, the girl had been a small brunette at least five years older than he. Her name was Margot and she had made a fuss over his still-taped rib, broken in the football game. Lying in her arms later, feeling more relaxed, more free than he had ever felt in his life, he had said with deep concern, "Why are you here? I mean, you shouldn't have to—work in a place like this." And Margot had laughed, tousled his hair, and said, "Pretty boy, you watch too many movies. What would you be doin' if I *wasn't* here?"

One of the high-school girls, Gladys Parker, who was said to have slept with everybody, had seemed to Shane gentle and kind and sad, with a sort of empty loneliness nothing would ever fill. He had wanted to ask her to marry him; he *had* said he loved her in the throes of completion, but Gladys had held him tenderly afterward and said she understood how it was, that she never held anyone, including herself, to anything they said at a time like that.

The other girl was Marilyn Taylor, the doctor's youngest daughter. She was no virgin either, but she had become very possessive, sitting next to him each time there was an opportunity, touching his hand, his thigh, boasting to the other girls about how "the iron man could be turned to so much putty," finally threatening to tell her father that Shane had seduced her if he would not promise to be her steady. In moments when they lay together, he could believe briefly that he could love her for life, but, later, he began to hate her and himself. Marilyn loved exhibiting him like a prize animal, but he was saved by the death of her mother and by Marilyn's going to live with a married sister in Cheyenne.

Sex made him feel obligation, guilt, and that terrible vulnerability. Once he was miraculously freed of Marilyn, he had decided he never wanted that kind of close relationship with a girl again. At times, if he had to, there were places like Fannie's, where he could discharge some of the guilt and obligation by paying, and where the girl would not give him another thought afterward, would not remember his all-consuming needs and vulnerabilities any more than she would remember anyone else's. Shane had decided years ago that he should never marry. At seventeen, he felt that was one of the wisest decisions he had ever made, though it had been made for other reasons, before he really knew about sex.

"Shane?" Janet's voice, small and timid in the car, startled him. "Shane, could you kiss me? Would you? please? I just want to see what it's like. Nobody ever has; no boy, you know—and I'd rather it was you the first time." Her voice hardened and grew more aggressive. "And if you say, 'Wait till you're older,' I'll knock your teeth out."

He smiled, and when there was room, drew the car to the side of the highway and took her gently in his arms. She was slender, only beginning to develop a woman's body, really, but there was a special softness, a kind of instinctive knowing in the way she touched his hair, his cheek. He put his hand under her heavy pony tail and let the tips of his fingers brush the soft, tender nape of her neck.

She shivered deliciously and snuggled close against him. "That's awfully nice."

"We'll go now." He tried to draw away from her, feeling blood pulsing in his face and loins. He was ashamed. This was Janet.

"You haven't kissed me."

He took her small face gently in his hands, touched her lips with his, and pulled the car back onto the highway.

"I do want to grow up," she said quietly and they were silent the rest of the way to Alder Falls.

And that was when it had first begun, his trying not to think too much about Janet.

They had Cokes at a drive-in and turned back north. She began singing songs and he sang with her. They knew a million songs, she averred, the popular ones and many others they had learned from her parents and old Charlie.

Then there was a red light flashing in the rear-view mirror. Shane had not been speeding; he was driving quite slowly, but it was deputy Bill Householder, who was known to have a permanent grudge against all drivers under thirty. Before he could find a place with room to pull over, Bill turned on his siren.

"Let's see your driver's license," he snapped. "You're old Charlie Bonner's grandson, ain't you. Ten miles over the speed limit."

"But I wasn't—"

"Don't talk back to the law, boy. What's that you're smokin'? Some kind a' dope?"

"It's just a cigarette."

"Lemme see it."

He turned it all around in the spotlight from his car and dropped it on the ground. "Got a pack? Let's see it."

Shane gave it to him. "I'll just confiscate this as evidence, in case I need it." It was an almost full pack and Shane began to get angry. "Yes, sir, I'd be a rich man if I had a dollar for ever' time I've hauled your daddy before the magistrate for speedin'." He peered at Shane. "That is, if Steve Bonner *was* your daddy."

"He wasn't speeding!" Janet cried hotly.

"Who you got in there with you?"

"Could I just have the ticket?"

"Don't start gittin' smart with me. You been drinkin'?"

"No."

"Where's that 'sir,' boy?"

"I had one beer about two hours ago, sir."

"Says here on your license you ain't but eighteen. That makes you still a minor, far as beer is concerned."

"He had a Coke, too," Janet said fiercely, "and it was Sheriff Terry that gave him the beer. It's Ellen's birthday. We were at her party."

It *was* the Terrys' youngest daughter's birthday.

While Householder stood a little uncertainly, a small sedan rocketed by on the other side of the highway.

"Jesus Christ! You goddam kids!"

He flung Shane's wallet under the car rather than through the window, raced back to his own car, turned on the siren, and made a U turn, almost colliding with an oncoming station wagon.

Fortunately, Vik had a flashlight in the glove compartment, but Shane had to crawl far under the car to retrieve the wallet.

"I hate him," hissed Janet fiercely. "He's a great big, fat, fuzzy pig."

"Don't say that," he said dully, automatically.

"He *is* a great big, fat, fuzzy pig. They're putting a new bathroom in their house and they're buying pipe and fixtures from Daddy. I'm going to find out which toilet's theirs and fix it so it won't flush."

Out of his misery and humiliation, Shane burst into laughter.

16

Shane was about three miles from Blackbuck dam with the log truck now. The road was good, with easy curves, and there had been no traffic at all, but up ahead was a car, a low, red sports car, pulled to the side of the road, a woman standing beside it, waving. He brought the truck to what, for Big Red, was a smooth stop, pulling in front of the car.

"Well," said Gloria Rosenzweig with a small complacent smile, "a knight in a stinking log truck." She coughed in the sweeping dust cloud.

"Is something wrong with your car?"

"Do you think I'd be standing here in this damn dust if there wasn't? One of those things —those gauges—the needle's all the way over on the wrong side and a light's flashing."

He got in and switched on the ignition. "Your engine's way too hot. How do I open the hood?"

"How the hell should I know?"

He found the hood release. Wisps of steam came out and he looked cautiously in at the motor.

"Your fan belt's broken. I don't suppose you've got a spare?"

"Look, honey, I'm not a mechanic. This is a

brand-new car. It's got no business having anything go wrong with it."

"I'll tell Dewey at the station in Blackbuck. He'll bring you one if he's got it."

"And meantime, what do *I* do? I've already been waiting here twenty minutes. Suppose your hick friend at the service station doesn't have one of the what-you-may-call-its? I'm supposed to be meeting some people for tennis at the club. At least you could offer me a ride."

"It's against the rules."

"Whose?" she said challengingly. "I know you don't belong to any union."

"Mine," he answered coolly, "but come on. You can ride into Blackbuck. Dewey will drive you back, or you can call your friends or whatever."

"Real chivalry," she said caustically. "Give me a chance to get my purse and things."

She also brought a flask from the glove compartment.

The right-hand door on the old cab was hard to open. Shane banged it loose with his fist and helped her up the high step. She sat sidewise on the cracked, dusty old seat for a moment, her hands holding his shoulders.

"That hair!" she said, her smile soft and admiring now. "I liked you better without the sunglasses and you really ought to do something to stop that sunburn. You've got a face like a Greek god or a monk or a movie star and it's a shame to see it—weathering."

Shane couldn't help a small grin at the trinity she had mentioned but he drew away from her, glad of the sunburn because he knew he was blushing, which was another thing he had always

203

disliked about his almost too-fair skin. He said, "Would you like to check my teeth?" and slammed the door; it took several tries to get it properly closed.

Walking around the truck, lighting a cigarette, he checked the load so automatically that he was not even aware of it.

Gloria looked into her compact mirror, trying various kinds of smiles and other expressions.

Big Red's gears ground horribly. The transmission was going to be the next thing to go, Shane thought, after the rings, and Charlie would look all over the state, or farther, trying to find one he could use. It was as though, if he gave in and junked Big Red, it would be a tacit admission that something was ended for him, for Charlie.

"How about a little nip of Scotch?" asked Gloria.

"I'm sorry, I can't hear you."

It was true. The loose old engine clattered loudly and she liked talking in a low, husky voice. She smiled and slid close to him, offering the flask. He shook his head.

"Just like with the gin and tonic that day," she said, pouting a little, "but I bet you drank that, didn't you?"

"Yes, I did. Thank you." He tried to edge away from her but there was no more room. She turned slightly to face him more directly, and so that her breast pressed against his shoulder.

"But you don't like Scotch? Is that it? Well, I've got gin back at the house, and quite a few other things. We could go back there and I could call and say I couldn't make it for tennis. It's only some women, anyway. Why are so goddam many things around here divided? Just women, or just men. I don't like segregation, do you?"

"I have to get these logs to your husband's mill," he said pointedly.

"That day, the first time we met," she said, unabashed, "you said you knew my name is Gloria. Yours is Shawn or something."

"Shane."

"Well, Shane, you ought to know that there hasn't been a day when I haven't thought about you since that time at the mill. We live back at the other end of the lake, you know, for the summer, and often, when I'm sunbathing, I've watched the log trucks, trying to see you again. I've also had some *very* exciting dreams. I was so damn mad at that car, but maybe this is our lucky day."

She touched the deep, smooth waves of his hair. "You know, if David looked *anything* like you, I just might not be quite so opposed to trying to make him the precious son he wants." She sipped the Scotch and laughed. "It would be half worth getting knocked up, just to see his face if I presented him with a kid who looks like you. What do you think?"

"I think I have to decline," he said.

"Don't want to be a stud?" she laughed, resting her hand on his thigh. "Well, let's forget that part of it. I'd die if I got knocked up, to tell you the truth. But what about later? After you've delivered your logs? Good old David is going to a men's-club thing tonight."

He made no reply, turning the truck onto the dam, never gladder in his life to see Blackbuck.

"I'm going to eat at McCrarys'," he said. "If you want to stop there, I'll go and ask Dewey—"

She was staring at him incredulously. "You're not *queer*, are you? Gay? whatever they call it. God, what a crying shame that would be."

"I've never thought so," he said, the anger in his voice and eyes now, "until the past ten minutes."

"Why, you bastard!" She struck at him, but he had stopped the truck in front of Ruby's place and was sliding down out of the cab. Somehow, Gloria managed to get her door open for herself and he did not help her down because she was waiting to slap him.

Shane crossed the highway to the service station. Paul drove in while Dewey was searching for a fan belt.

"I ain't got one'll fit," said Dewey in his thick drawl that could be so comical with his deadpan face. "Have to git it in Cana. I been thinkin' for some months now, there wasn' hardly nothin' wouldn't fit that there womern, but I guess her car's more partic'lar."

"I thought that was Gloria's car back there," said Paul, laughing. "I'll drive her into town if that's where she wants to go."

"Thank God!" said Shane half under his breath.

Paul kept smiling. "If I didn't think I knew you better, I'd say you look a little scared. She's harmless, you know. A little pitiable, really. Just go along with her a little. She lives on flattery, even if it's self-administered, flattery and liquor."

Shane went around to the back of the cafe and came into the kitchen.

"You hidin' from that Rosybush woman?"

206

asked Ruby. "I heard her call you some kind of naughty name when she come in, but she's gone in the bar now."

"I'm starved, Ruby. What's good? and fast."

"Well, that stew's been simmerin' all mornin'. It smells all right, an' the coffee's hot. Leonard Hall's out there, finishin' off his second bowl of stew. He says ole Charlie's got a flea in his ear or words to that effect."

"There's supposed to be a storm."

"So I heard," she said, ladling stew for him.

"How's Janet?" he asked, getting his own coffee.

"Seemed just fine on Monday, but she can't stay off up there with snow comin'. What are you goin' to do about it?"

"I don't know yet."

"Well, I think her folks ought to know. She can't keep it secret forever. I git half a notion sometimes she's thinkin' about *stayin'* up there, winter an' all."

"Don't tell anybody else," he said. "Please. She doesn't want them to know yet."

A few miles below Blackbuck, Shane passed Leonard Hall, driving the green truck. Leonard was a slow, deliberate, fat man in his fifties, who had been with Charlie longer than anyone now, driving for him for thirty years. As the two trucks drew abreast, he gave Shane the finger, grinning, and Shane, pursing his lips primly, answered with a peace sign.

"What are you going to do?" Ruby had demanded. Because Paul couldn't do anything, Janet would never let him; because Mitch was too young; because they were all trying to save Nora and Viktor what they could; because Ruby had always been able to read people too well.... He'd see Janet tomorrow. Somehow he'd have to manage it, in spite of Charlie and everything else.

That night, a month ago, when they had driven to Boise, had been a little like that other time he had been thinking of earlier, that time when they had both been eight years younger. Neither of them had mentioned the baby or Gary or any of it again that night. She had been almost entirely silent until they had passed through Cana, then she had begun humming songs, and all the way down the valley to the interstate they had sung, one song reminding them of the next. Shane found he had almost forgotten many of them. At some point, she had slipped her hand into his.

"I'm so glad you're here," she said softly. "You're so good to me, good *for* me."

"No, it's only—" he had almost said "only that I love you," but quickly substituted "only that almost anything can make you glad."

"I always have loved just being alive," she said. "Even when it's sad, it's worth it."

As he swung his little car smoothly onto the interstate ramp, she said, "I hate superhighways."

"So do I. Why don't you take a nap?"

"You won't, will you?"

"No."

At the motel, he carried the small bag she had brought and his own. Desperately, he wanted to stay with her that night—not for sex, though he knew that wanting would, inevitably, come, too—but to hold her, to stay close to her so she wouldn't have to be alone with it all for a while. Her eyes looked large and sad, a little lost in the bright lights. She was the one who had to live with it all, her family's finding out, the county's knowing, carrying and bearing the child, and he wanted desperately, somehow, to take some of that from her slender shoulders for a time at least, to see her sleeping quietly and at peace. But abruptly, there was something like a stabbing, breath-stopping pain through his body—the recollection that it was Gary Hunt's child.

She had unlocked her door and stood looking at him, meekly, uncertainly.

"You take the car tomorrow," he said, handing her his keys. "The places I have to go aren't six blocks away.... Is there anything else...?"

"No," she said softly. "Good night, Shane. Thank you."

Thank you. My god! when he was standing there with his arms aching to hold her, and a conflicting something that came very near to hate rising up in his throat.

He retrieved Big Red now from a meander into the left lane. The little back-country state highway was almost empty. Not much going on on a Wednesday afternoon. In his rear-view mirror, he could still see Leonard's truck far back, with a car passing it, Paul's car. The road ran along with the river here, in a shallow, narrow canyon, a steep, shaly bank going up on one side, down to the water on the other. The Alder was low now, but there had been a lot of high water last spring, despite what the dam could hold. The river had taken out part of the shoulder on its side of the road, leaving boulders of all sizes strewn along the steep bank.

Far ahead, Shane could see a car pulled into a small turnout cut into the up-bank on the right side of the road, a brown station wagon. A boy of about ten toiled and slithered up the bank from the river and crossed the highway. Shane's truck was a quarter mile away, but he began braking gently. Big Red was moving on the gentle downgrade and there was a curve a short distance ahead of where the car was parked. The boy was taking something from the back of the station wagon, a tackle box. He closed the tailgate and waved Shane an all-clear when the truck was perhaps three hundred yards from him. Paul's car was coming up fast. He'd pass after this next curve.

Then suddenly a little white dog scampered up over the bank from the river. The boy cried out. At the same moment, a car came round the curve, heading toward them, slamming on its brakes to avoid the dog.

I'm going to hit it, Shane thought, nausea rising up in his throat. I can't do anything else. He was braking as hard as he dared, thinking of the tons of logs behind him, feeling the trailer sway threateningly, hearing the screech of Paul's tires behind him. And then the boy, screaming, ran into the road, trying to grab the curly, frisking little dog.

If Shane turned the truck to the right, he'd hit the bank and the station wagon, probably jackknife the trailer, and dump the load on the child —and himself. He could not use the left lane because the driver of the oncoming car was not going to think fast enough to move over and let him have it. The bank down to the river was steep, but maybe, just maybe there were enough big rocks to stop the truck before it rolled, if he could hit them at just the right angle. Shane almost laughed; hell, Red would never hit anything just right. He even had time to know how quickly and clearly he was thinking.

The boy had captured his crazy little dog, but he had fallen on the blacktop and lay petrified, his mouth open in a scream Shane couldn't hear, yet could. He eased what had become a painful grip on the wheel and let the old truck swing left. The boulders were not struck at the right angle. The trailer went over, pulling the tractor with it. They separated and the tractor rolled again, stopping on its wheels in the edge of the river.

17

Old Charlie Bonner looked his age as he came into the hospital that evening. His face—he had forgotten his false teeth—was shrunken and haggard, and he stumbled a little so that Mitch, who had driven him down, took his arm at the door.

Viktor and Nora were sitting on a couch in the small waiting room just off the entry. They got up immediately and came to Charlie.

"How bad?" demanded the old man dully. "They radioed to Bud Stallings up at the ranger station an' he said—where is he?"

There was a kind of frantic terror deep in the old man's eyes. Viktor took his arm.

"Come and sit down, Charlie. He's still unconscious. You can see him in a little while."

"I don't want to set down," said Charlie petulantly. "They said it was bad. Where's he at?"

Gently, Viktor propelled him to the couch,

talking, so that Charlie sat without seeming to realize he had done it.

"He's got a skull fracture, just a hairline one, a bad concussion, a bad cut on one thigh, shock from loss of blood. That's the worst of it. He's pretty well bruised and scraped all over, but I think he's lucky."

"Lucky," muttered Charlie with no conviction. "Good God!"

"We saw the truck in the river as we came down," said Mitch softly. He was pale, his hands shaking a little as he held a hard hat he had forgotten to leave somewhere.

"I'll get some coffee," Nora said.

"What are they doin' for him?" demanded Charlie with a little more strength in his voice. "It's been five, six hours since it happened. Why is he still out?"

"He's getting closer to consciousness now," Viktor said. "It's the blow on the head, the shock. Dr. Striker's with him now."

There was a little silence and Charlie said shakily, "I've been too hard on him. Always have. He never liked haulin'. He told me so, but . . ."

"What happened, Dad?" asked Mitch. "Do you know? Did something go wrong with that old truck?"

"He was avoiding hitting a little boy. Paul happened to be driving right behind him. He saw it. So did Leonard Hall and some people driving up toward Blackbuck. Shane did what he had to. They brought the little boy in, hysterical, but he's all right. Nothing touched him. He was trying to get his little dog off the road and fell in front of the truck. They're a family from California and they were up there fishing. The boy had come up to get something out of their car and the dog followed."

Nora came back with the coffee.

"I don't want that," Charlie said querulously. "I want to see the boy."

"You'll have to wait until Dr. Striker is finished." Viktor said. "He just got here."

"Just got here, for Christsake!" cried Charlie. "Why in hell has he just got here?"

"He was assisting at an emergency surgery in Alder Falls. Dr. Brown had gone fishing and Dr. Taylor is out of town. Young Dr. Dugan's been looking after Shane, and he's done well."

"Dugan!" said Charlie truculently. "He ain't even a doctor, is he?"

"He's a resident, Charlie; he is a doctor. The hospital's lucky to have him. This is the first year our hospital's been able to have a doctor right on hand at all times."

Max Striker came out to them. He was a big man with grizzled black hair, direct blue eyes, and the hands of a farmer.

"He's starting to come round. Yes, you can see him, Charlie, talk to him a little, but don't worry him about anything. I want him awake for a while. It's a good sign. I've got a baby to deliver now." He looked sharply at the old man. "After you've seen him, you better get yourself some rest. I can order a pill, some sedation."

"I don't want no goddamn pill. How *is* he? Will he be all right?"

"Right now, he's a very sick young man: nausea. Shock and concussion do that. We've got bandages on his eyes because he's not seeing prop-

213

erly just yet and that adds to the nausea. He's being transfused and he's pretty well banged up. Things actually look worse than they are, what with the IV's and all. He's going to be fine, I think, barring complications, but it will take a little time." He turned to Viktor. "Young Dugan says you were a help to him. Have you seen a patient like this before?"

"Yes," he said quietly, looking down at the linoleum tiles.

"Well, try to get him to talk a little. He's got a hell of a headache, not to mention other aches, but I'd like him to be fully awake before we give him anything for pain. Maybe you know about shock and concussion cases." And to Charlie he said, "But he's lucky. If whatever he hit his head on had been a couple of inches lower, it could very well have broken his neck. The girls will keep a close eye on him. You go home and rest when you've seen him."

"What do you mean he's not seein' right?" demanded the old man.

"It's a natural thing that will pass," said the doctor brusquely, "but this baby won't wait much longer. I'll be in to check on Shane again when I've finished."

"What's he mean," Charlie asked fearfully, "about his eyes? He won't be . . ."

"A blow on the head can cause vision problems for a while, especially when it's in the immediate area of the optic center, as this one was. Edema—swelling," Viktor cleared his throat and swallowed. "It will clear up in a few days. Let's go in now, you and I, just for a few minutes."

After a moment, Mitch said to his mother, "I

could give some blood." His voice was not quite steady.

"Yes," she said. "Your dad and I did. The lab's just down that hall, I guess there'd still be someone there."

Mitch picked up one of the untouched cups of coffee. "I'll drink this first," he said, a little embarrassed. "I'm not sure I *can* be a doctor, Mom. It's made me feel a little sick, just coming in here tonight."

She nodded a little absently. "Doctors get used to it, I guess, and it's always harder when it's someone you know."

"Dad knows a lot of things, doesn't he?" Mitch said thoughtfully. "He was almost like a doctor himself, talking to Charlie."

Nora did not reply. She was knitting furiously on Patty's sweater and seemed to have to count stitches.

Mitch put down the cup, half-empty. "Well, I guess I'll go and do it."

Faye came in in a few moments. "I was down at Alder," she explained. "Sharon called almost as soon as I got home. She's coming as soon as she gets Jamie to bed. How is he, Nora? Is Charlie here yet?"

Nora told her about what seemed to be the state of things. "Paul was driving right behind him," she said. "He had that Rosenzweig woman with him. Her car had broken down or something. She hit her head on the dash or windshield when Paul had to make a quick stop to keep from hitting the truck. He brought her in before the ambulance got back with Shane, then he called me, and I called Viktor. Gloria was absolutely

215

hysterical. They were still trying to take care of her when we got here and she was crying and screaming that her face was ruined. David had come. No one could do a thing with her, not even get an X ray until they'd given her something to nearly knock her out. It was just a bad nosebleed, nothing broken or anything, but you'd have thought . . . Karen Martin—you know, the one who was in school the same years as Alice and Barbara—was the emergency-room nurse. She said the doctor suggested keeping Gloria overnight, just to get her calmed down, but you could hear the woman yelling all over the place about hospitals in one-horse towns, how they hadn't given her proper attention, and she wouldn't bring them a cat to be castrated, so David finally took her away.

"They brought in the little boy. He was hysterical too, poor thing, but it was just fright. He didn't have a mark on him except a scraped elbow that he must have got when he fell. He'd been trying to get his little dog out of the road and, for a while, they couldn't get him to let go of it, even in the emergency room. The family's from California, staying up in one of McCrarys' cabins for fishing and hunting, the parents and the one child. They seem like such nice people, so concerned about Shane and so grateful. They want to pay all his bills."

Tears sprang to her eyes. She sniffed and wiped at them with the sweater. "Then—they brought Shane in. Oh, Faye, they keep saying he's lucky, but I saw him, right at first, just covered with blood and dirt, then white as paper when they'd got him cleaned up—and so still. I—

I couldn't help thinking of Vik and Anne, of course. I had to run to the rest room and be sick.

"Viktor," she said slowly, "I don't know what to think about Viktor."

"How do you mean?"

"Well, we've been married twenty-eight years and I keep finding out things about him I didn't know before. I never dreamed he knew so much about—doctoring. When he found out none of the doctors was here except young Danny Dugan, he wouldn't let them keep him out of the emergency room. Karen Martin had to be going in and out all the time. She told me Viktor watched every bit of the examination and looked at the X rays. And the way he's been talking... I know it can't be from watching those doctor shows on TV because he hardly ever watches TV. I even heard Dr. Dugan ask him things once or twice, after they'd got Shane into a room—just naturally, you know, as if he were another doctor. Viktor has got some medical books, I know. He's got every kind of book in the world, but... he just—surprises me."

"I've always known he's a brilliant man," Faye said thoughtfully. Absently, she picked up a cup of coffee, stone cold by now, and took a sip.

"I've been worried about him lately," Nora said, feeling a little guilty about bringing it up just now. "He's not been sleeping right. He's so quiet. He goes for long walks by himself almost every evening and he's beginning to look so tired."

"Suppose," Faye said gently, "that when I've given some blood and we've looked in on Shane for a minute, you and I go to one of our houses and fix supper for everyone. It's late. Charlie must be in an awful state and it won't do anyone any good for all of us to stay here."

Nora smiled wanly. "I was right in the middle of making apple butter. Patty had just come home from school when Paul called. I called Betty Adams to see if Patty could go and stay with them, but instead, Betty came up and finished the apple butter. She and Bert were here for a few minutes just a little while ago."

In the two-bed room, old Charlie had sunk down dizzily on the empty bed at the sight of his grandson: white, drawn, moving listlessly, unknowingly now and then, both arms strapped to padded boards to keep them straight and stable for the IV needles. It seemed at least half his body was wrapped in bandages. He had been vomiting and an elderly nurse came in with a clean basin, blood-pressure cuff, thermometer, and chart. When she had finished her checks and written their results on the chart, Viktor took it to read. She relinquished it to him automatically, without question, then looked startled, at him and at herself.

When she had left the room, Viktor put the back of his hand gently against Shane's bruised forehead. A little temperature; better, he thought, than the coldness of the past few hours.

"Shane," he said strongly, "can you hear me?"

"No," he whispered.

"Of course you can. Do you know where you are?"

"I can't see." The voice was a little stronger now with more expression—fear.

"It's all right," Viktor told him quickly. "They've bandaged your eyes because your vision was distorting and making you sicker. It will begin to clear up, probably by tomorrow. Are you listening?"

"Yes, but I can't see."

Gently, Viktor repeated what he had just said. "Now keep listening to me. You must lie very still; try not to move at all. That will help the nausea too. Just try to listen and talk to us for a few minutes. Charlie's here."

"Charlie?"

The old man got up unsteadily and timidly touched one of Shane's scratched, bruised hands.

"I'm here," he said, and his voice shook, as did his hand. "How are you, son?"

"I hurt, Charlie. Everything hurts." He turned his head a little and groaned. "And I can't see."

Patiently, Viktor explained the bandaged eyes again. "Is anything giving you more pain than your head?"

"No. . . . I'm thirsty . . . cold."

"You can probably have some water soon and you're getting warmer now. Do you remember what happened?"

"No."

"Just lie still, Shane. It's all right."

"I remember—is it still Wednesday?"

"Yes," said Charlie. "Seven forty-five Wednesday evenin'."

"I remember eating in the kitchen at Ruby's—talking to her, and then—I don't know. . . . I guess I didn't get the logs to the mill or—"

"No, there was an accident about halfway from Blackbuck," said Viktor. "You've got yourself a hairline skull fracture, concussion, a cut on your leg that bled a lot and took sixteen stitches to close, and you're going to be very sore from bruises and other minor cuts. If you can stay awake until Dr. Striker comes back, I think he'll be prescribing something for the pain."

"I hope he prescribes a lot," Shane said dully, and then, abruptly, he was struggling to sit up.

"Son, don't do that!" Charlie cried pleadingly.

Viktor forced him gently back, checking the IV needles.

"Did I—God, did I hit somebody?"

"No," Viktor said firmly. Shane began to retch, and Viktor held the basin. "You went off the road to avoid a little boy and his dog. No one else was hurt. Now you *must* lie still." He pulled the covers straight as Shane began to shiver again.

"Trailer went over on its side," said Charlie shakily. "Chains broke, a' course, logs all down the bank. Big Red went clear over, standin' on her wheels in the edge a' the water. Leonard had to use a crowbar on the door to git you out."

Shane struggled against the nausea, the pain that was beginning now almost to madden him, and his recalcitrant memory.

"That—that Rosenzweig woman—I gave her a ride. Her fan belt was broken. She wasn't still—"

"Paul was driving her down from McCrarys'," Viktor said. "They were right behind you and saw the accident. I swear to you, no one else was hurt."

Mitch came to the door and grew even paler. A few moments later, Nora and Faye were standing with him.

"He's awake," said Viktor, more to reassure

220

Shane than the others. "Here are Nora, Faye, and Mitch."

Each of them spoke to him briefly. He turned his head, because of the pain and the fact that he could see nothing, and the nausea rose up again.

Viktor said, "There's no need for us all to stay."

"Faye and I will go home and fix some supper," Nora said softly.

"You may as well go, too, Mitch," said the father. "Charlie and I will be along when we've seen the doctor again."

18

Gloria sat shaking in front of her mirror. She had refused to be taken back to the lake house, insisting she hated it, wanted to go to the big house down the valley. David had sent George to bring Bessie down, and they had stopped in Cana to buy a few grocery staples.

Despite the sedation and reassurances, Gloria had never quite stopped crying since the accident. Her eyes were fearfully swollen now, her nose seeming to her to enlarge by the minute as it turned dark with bruising. Gently, Bessie had coaxed the distraught Gloria out of her clothes and into a hot bath. Hot baths were soothing, Bessie said, and a little food would be a calming thing, but Gloria did not want to eat, nor did David, so Bessie had left them alone for the moment.

"Oh, God, David, I'm *ugly!* I'm *hideous!*" Gloria wailed. From somewhere fresh tears welled up as she sat there in a black lace nightgown, mesmerized by the horror of her distorted face.

"Come, my dear girl, get into bed now," he said with the tenderness and patience he had maintained for hours. "Here's Bessie with another of the pills the doctor prescribed. I swear you will be all right in a week or so when the swelling and bruises go away. There are no cuts. There will be no scars."

"How can you swear it? What do *you* know?"

"The doctor said—"

"That bastard quack! He's not old enough to wipe his own nose."

"Take this, Mrs. Rosenzweig," said Bessie kindly. "Then I'll help you to bed. You can sleep an' ever'thing'll seem better in the mornin'."

"And what do *you* know?" snapped Gloria fiercely, but she swallowed the pill with a little water. "Get me a hot toddy; a big one."

"Come on, darling." David half lifted her from the vanity bench. She sat on the edge of the bed while he removed her slippers, then lay back on several pillows as he drew up the covers.

"I know my nose is broken," she said tragically, her voice catching on a sob. "Oh, it hurts so much! You can't imagine . . ."

"If it still worries you so tomorrow, we'll go to Boise, or wherever you like, to see another doctor."

"If *I'm* worried! Aren't *you* worried? Don't you *care?*"

"Of course I care, my darling, but, truly, it's not broken. They X-rayed."

"Bunch of lousy hicks!" she spat. Then, after

a moment, brokenly, "But I can't go anywhere. I can't bear the thought of having anyone see me —like this."

Bessie came back then with two toddies in large, heavy mugs. "I thought you might want one, too, Mr. Rosenzweig."

"That was very thoughtful, Bessie. Thank you."

"Can I get anything else?"

"I think not, just now. I may want some supper later on. Perhaps an omelet."

"Yes, sir, whenever you're ready."

"You can think about *eating!*" Gloria cried accusingly.

"I missed lunch," he explained apologetically. "I may need something later, but I'll sit with you until you're asleep."

"I don't think I ever *can* sleep. Oh, David, it's so *horrible!*"

Her hands were shaking. He held the mug to her lips and she drank.

"Bessie always puts too much sugar," she complained and drank again. More tears came as she touched her grotesque nose tenderly.

"Do you want to tell me all about it?" he asked. "Perhaps talking will help."

"He stopped so fast! Why in hell did he have to stop like that?"

"To keep from hitting the log truck, I understand. Perhaps if you'd been using a seat belt—"

"Oh, for God's sake, don't start nagging at me. I just can't stand it, with everything else. You know I hate those things because they wrinkle my clothes. . . . It's a padded dash, I think, for all the good that was, or maybe I hit the windshield, I don't know, but he was following too close, the fool. I hope you're going to sue him." She gestured for more toddy.

"Drink it slowly, darling. It may not go well with the sedative. Paul said he was getting ready to pass the truck in a moment."

"Well, then why in hell did that stupid truck driver have to screw everything up?"

"There was a child in the road, Gloria. Not many people want to run down a child."

"Oh, shit!" she said miserably and sipped again. She was beginning at last to relax a little.

"That brand-new, fancy, expensive car had something go wrong with it, you know. Something broke. Of course they didn't have the part at that hick station in Blackbuck. That Bonner picked me up in his filthy log truck. I told you I was supposed to play tennis with Carol Drew and some others this afternoon. I'd never have ridden with him, but I'd been waiting forever and there just weren't any cars on that godforsaken road. He's a hateful, nasty person, David."

"How so?"

She thought about it, forgetting her throbbing nose for a moment. After all, the whole thing *was* Shane's fault. "Conceited; typical male chauvinist. Like when he makes a pass, any woman's supposed to be honored beyond words, dirty, sweaty, foul-mouthed..."

David sipped his own drink and the anger in his face made her feel just a little better. Somehow, she'd get back at that bastard for snubbing her, and for the rest of it.

"I was glad to see Paul at that crummy cafe, I can tell you. At least he has a little courtesy —decency—at times. But then, after it happened ...oh, David, there were people all over the place: Paul, another truck driver, two women from another car, and that brat's parents. I was bleeding and bleeding and they all just glanced at me a minute at one time or another and went sliding off down that damned riverbank. I was screaming—I couldn't help it—all that blood, and I felt like I was choking to death and it just seemed as if I was all alone in the world. It must have been hours before Paul came back to drive me to the hospital. He didn't even apologize for leaving me alone, or for what had happened or anything!" She gulped on dry sobs.

"Try to sip the rest of the toddy, love. Try to relax. It's over now and you will be all right in a few days."

"I'll have nightmares forever," she said, "but I suppose if that's the only scars I have, I'll be lucky." She sipped the last of the large drink and said wearily, "Take the extra pillows, will you? Thank God, I think I *am* getting just a little sleepy." She was even able to smile wanly at a new thought. "Paul had been up watching the surveyors at that stupid ranch. He had to meet a client and then he said he was going back up for a while. I mentioned you had that men's-club dinner. He said he was supposed to go too, but he could skip it, and how would I like some company till you were due home? How's that for nerve?" Somehow, she would get even with all of them. Maybe, for once, David would even help her with something.

"Try to rest, darling," he said unevenly and in a few moments she was sleeping.

David went to his study. On the way, he told Bessie to go to bed, never mind the omelet. He paced the room.

225

He had changed the slip of paper, along with the other things he carried in his pockets, from the blue, to the brown, to the gray suit. On the Monday after Faye's party, he had decided not to make the telephone call after all. Things had been very busy at the office that day and he had told himself halfheartedly that he probably was mistaken and, even if he were not, what good would it be after all these years? Nothing could bring back his family; nothing wipe out the horror that was the most of the memory of his childhood; nothing make up for all he had lost then and since.

Still, he had not thrown away the slip of paper and, at the hospital where a nurse was trying to soothe Gloria while people rushed in and out of the emergency room where the Bonner boy was, David had noted—though he was scarcely aware of it at the time—Viktor Magnessen's self-assurance, his calm help in handling the situation. He had even heard Viktor ask a nurse for something and seen her bring it without question. Of course he was right about the man, and the man's son had propositioned his wife, or perhaps ... already ... It was almost ten o'clock. No point in trying those numbers now, but first thing in the morning ...

He looked in on Gloria and went to the kitchen. The house was poorly provisioned, since they had expected to be staying at the lake for perhaps another week, but he found some milk and crackers—food for an old man with an aching ulcer.

Idly, he switched on a television set. The news; the Arabs and Israelis ... Abruptly, David knew he was going to sell the mill and take Gloria to live in Israel. He never should have come to the United States in the first place, and he certainly should never have come to Cana. His talents would be appreciated in the relatively new country and perhaps his wife would be better understood, in a more sophisticated, platonic, sympathetic way. And she would see how important he could be among his—their—own kind.... The way she had turned to him in her fear and misery today, only to him.... Why hadn't he seen that Israel was the answer all along? There were wars and threats of wars, but they surely could not be more miserable, more—estranged and at odds with each other—than they had been in Alder County. She was still young enough to give him a son. Perhaps, if they could find only bits and pieces of happiness together at times, she would come to realize the importance of that.

Selling the mill, wrapping up other business matters would take some time, but he would begin tomorrow. First, though, he would contact the FBI. And second, he would call Paul Magnessen and say that he was withdrawing his promised investment in the Cloud Valley project. He would begin this new kind of life by handing poor Gloria, figuratively, at least one Magnessen head on a silver platter. And he would notify old man Bonner that the mill would not need his logs next year. Perhaps a new owner would reinstate the order, but it would do the old man—and the grandson, if he lived, God blast him—good to worry about it.

19

"I don't want him left by hisself," Charlie said pathetically, moving the food around on his plate.

"I'm going back to stay a while in just a few minutes," Faye said.

"And then Viktor or I will go," said Nora, "but you try to eat, Charlie, and then go to bed. Take the pill Dr. Striker gave you."

"Is Shane going to die?" asked Patty softly. She was not eating. Her eyes were wide with sudden fear and her lips trembled with the question.

"No," said Viktor firmly, putting an arm around her. "He's been hurt badly, but he'll be all right. Now try to eat your supper."

"I already ate a little bit at Carolyn's house. Could I go and see him?"

"They don't let young ladies your age into the hospital as visitors."

"Then I'd like to send him my picture I made at school—you know, the one with the mama cat and three kittens, where the mama looks like my Fluffy."

"He'll like seeing that in a few days, honey," Nora said. "If you don't want to eat any more, maybe you ought to see about doing your homework."

"Mitch," said Charlie, seeming to come out of his haze of worry for a moment, "I wish you'd git back up to the show tonight if you can, try to see the rest a' them logs is loaded out. If he seems to be doin' all right, I'll try to git up there a little while tomorrow, if it ain't started to snow. Christ, I've got to think about gittin' all that equipment out an'...." He remembered then and turned pleading eyes on Viktor. "His mind, Viktor, the way he don't seem to remember the wreck...?"

"It's typical of a head injury, Charlie, fairly typical. He may never remember those hours. What if he doesn't? It's probably better for him that way."

"I'll go back to camp, Charlie," said Mitch, not wanting to, "but if—if anyone needs—anything, call on the Forest Service radio again."

As Mitch was leaving, Viktor followed him outside. "Does Janet have a radio?"

"You mean a regular radio? I don't know, Dad."

"Stop by up there and see if they know about the storm. She'll want to know about Shane."

They got Charlie to go to bed by agreeing carefully on the shifts they would spend at the hospital: Faye would stay until midnight, Nora till four, then Viktor. They would call him immediately if necessary, and as soon as he woke in the morning, he could come back to the hospital himself.

"Take a glass of brandy with your pill," said Viktor. "Come on, I'll get it for you."

Faye and Nora looked at each other. "My lord," said Nora sadly, "Charlie's aged ten years today."

Shane was sleeping restlessly when Faye reached the hospital. "The sedation's not doing as well as it ought to," said the nurse who had just looked in. "I'm about to call the doctor and ask if he wants it increased. Maybe he won't, after shock, I just don't know."

Faye brought magazines from the waiting room and sat leafing through them. Shane started and moaned in his sleep. The IV drips, blood in one arm, glucose in the other, continued. The nurse came in at half-hour intervals to check his pulse and blood pressure. Once, when she was trying to take his temperature, he fought her fiercely for a few moments, and seemed terrified. Faye grabbed his hands, trying to protect the nurse and hold his arms so that the needles would not be pulled out.

"Fever's going up," said the nurse, frowning at the chart. She was new to Cana and one of the few nurses unknown to Faye. The nurse had introduced herself as Irene Blevins. "That's not a surprise in a case like this, but I do hope he won't get delirious. We're always so shorthanded here at night."

"Someone will be here," Faye said, "some of the family—all night."

As the hands of her watch crept close to midnight, Faye looked up at a slight sound and saw Janet standing in the doorway. The girl tiptoed in and stood by the bed. "Oh, Shane!" she whispered. He moved a little, as if he had heard.

"How did you know?" Faye asked softly.

At first, she thought Janet had not heard, but finally the girl moved dazedly away from the bed to the corner where Faye sat. "Mitch came and told me on his way back to camp."

"I hope you're not still riding around on that damned motorcycle."

"No. Shane traded me his car for it several

weeks ago. Aunt Faye, Mitch said—do they really think he'll be all right? He looks so terrible."

"Yes, they think he'll be fine," she said, though there was more certainty in her voice than she actually felt just now. "He looks better now than when I first saw him; a little more color, I think. You sit down, or lie down on that other bed. You look sick yourself."

Janet sat down and another nurse—the late shift had come on—came into the room.

"Hello, Julia," said Faye, feeling a little better about everything.

"Why, Faye! And *Janet!* I haven't seen either of you for ages."

Julia Carter had been present at Janet's birth and she kissed her warmly on the cheek before going to her patient.

"Dr. Striker's ordered more sedation," she told them, fitting the blood-pressure cuff. "Maybe he can rest a little. We're to stop the transfusion after this bottle is empty and see how it goes."

When Julia had finished, chatted with them a few moments, and left the room, Faye said gently, "You know Ruby told me?"

Janet nodded and held up her chin in the little unconscious, defiant gesture.

"What are you going to do, Janet?"

"I'm going to go on working for Ruby until the end of October. They're busier than they expected to be with hunting season this year. After that . . . I'm not sure."

"Well, you can't stay on at Lucky Streak with snow coming."

"Ruby has offered me one of her cabins."

"Would you rather use my house up on

Blackbuck Creek, now that I've moved back to town?"

"Oh, Aunt Faye, could I? I just—like to be by myself sometimes. I can't seem to think very well with all those people around all the time." She smiled a little grimly. "I guess I don't seem to be thinking much anyway, but all I can seem to do is take one day at a time."

"Would you like me to tell Nora and Viktor?"

"No, please don't. It's my mess and I have to do whatever I can to take care of it myself. I'll tell them as soon as I can now."

Nora came then and, finding Janet there, hugged her and cried. They had not seen each other since the beginning of July. Faye, somewhat to Nora's puzzlement, kissed them both before she went home.

Shane seemed to sleep more deeply now. They sat in the corner farthest from his bed, speaking almost in whispers.

"I brought a Thermos of hot tea," Nora said. "Let's have some."

She had also brought her knitting basket and took out some new work, socks for Mitch. Janet turned the pages of the magazines Faye had left, not seeing them. Every few minutes, she went to stand by the bed, and each time Julia came in to check vital signs, Janet, unabashed and unhindered, read the chart.

Finally, Nora said awkwardly, "Gary didn't come down with you?"

"No, he didn't."

"I don't remember seeing your old bus when I came. The parking lot was almost empty and I—"

"I'm driving Shane's car, Mama, his little green station wagon. It's parked right out by the front door. He traded it to me for the motorcycle at the Labor Day weekend."

"Yes, I remember thinking that looked like Shane's car, but I don't . . ."

"Mama, Gary left," she said gently. "He's been gone over two months."

"Oh, Janet!" Nora's expressions changed rapidly. "Honey, I can't help saying it—I'm glad."

"So am I," the girl said levelly and Nora, looking into her eyes, knew she meant it.

"Won't you come home now?"

"Not yet, Mama. I've promised to work for Ruby until the end of October."

"But that cabin—"

"Aunt Faye just gave me the key to her house. I'll move my things down there tomorrow, in case that storm does come. I was listening to the radio, driving down, and they seem to think now it may go north of us. Did you know I have a puppy? Tell me about everything at home. How are Patty and Dad?"

Nora talked about Patty for a few moments, her schoolwork, her sweetness and rapid growth; then she told Janet the things she had told Faye earlier about Viktor's surprising behavior at the hospital that afternoon and that he had recently seemed unwell or very troubled about something.

Julia came in again and Janet, reading the chart, consulted with her in whispers by the bed.

"His temperature keeps going up a little," she told Nora. "That's usually to be expected. The pulse and blood pressure look good."

"Janet, you could have a nursing job here

any time you wanted," said Nora, delighted with the thought. "They're always shorthanded. After October, why don't you do that? Stay home with us a while."

"Let's walk around the halls a little, Mama. These chairs are hard."

When they were at one end of a corridor where a window looked out toward the Forest Service buildings in their surroundings of lawn, Janet said slowly,

"This is not the best time, but I guess there never will be a best time. I'd like to stay and work here, but I can't, for a while. I'm pregnant, Mama. The baby's due toward the end of January."

Nora was silent. In the dim light, Janet could see she had begun to cry.

"It's why Gary went away when he did—though he'd have gone soon anyway, I think. He wanted me to get rid of the baby and I couldn't."

Still no words.

"Mama, I'm hurting you and I hate doing it, but I can't keep hiding. I'm glad about the baby. I've been thinking I'll go away somewhere and have it, give Cana to understand Gary and I got married. . . . Mama?"

Nora put her arms around her and they were both crying now. After a few moments, Janet said,

"I'm going out to Effie's truck stop for a hamburger or something. I didn't have much supper. Besides, it'll give you a chance to think what you want to say—if anything. Can I bring you something?"

When she came back, Janet went straight

to Shane's bed, touched his forehead, took his pulse herself. She was half-afraid to face her mother, sitting, knitting in the corner.

"Janet?" Shane asked weakly.

She started. "How did you know?"

"I don't know. Is anything broken?"

"Just a little crack in your head. You'll be all right."

"Why can't I have these things off my arms and my eyes? You know I'm claustrophobic." He had trouble with the word. "I've got a hell of a headache."

"I know," she said tenderly, brushing his bruised cheek with the backs of her fingers. "It'll all be better tomorrow."

"What time is it?"

"Two thirty-five."

"In the morning?"

"Yes."

"Then it's tomorrow now and nothing's better."

"That was sneaky. Don't quibble."

"I have to have these bandages off my eyes," his weak voice was suddenly desperate. "I don't think anyone is telling me the truth."

"Everyone is telling you the truth. You can see, Shane, but your eyes won't focus right for a while yet and it would make you very, very sick. I don't like that kind of nursing work. Do you want some water? You can have a little now. No, lie absolutely still. We have a nice curved straw here. Just a sip at first."

"It's not enough," he said petulantly. "Not nearly."

"More later. Try to sleep again."

"I don't remember—"

"Don't talk."

"Why are you here?"

"Because I want to be, but if you say one more word, I'll go away."

In a moment, while she still stood touching his cheek, his breathing grew slower and even.

Nora was standing by the foot of the bed when Janet turned. She put an arm about the girl and led her back to the end of the hall.

"I don't have anything to say, Janet, except that we love you very much. I hope you're not disappointed if you expected me to rant and rave. I think I've lived long enough to know that men and women are apt to have sex and what can come of it. I've worried this would happen. I've prayed it wouldn't—for your sake, not because of the town or anything else. You're a grown woman. You've got every right in the world to decide what you're going to do on your own. If you're strong and healthy, I guess working at Ruby's is all right, but what I wish you'd do after that is just—come home. Let us help you *and* the baby till you're on your feet again."

Janet was crying. "I guess," she gulped, "that kids have to grow up a lot before they can really get to know their parents."

Nora smiled through her own tears, hugging the girl. "I think your dad will feel just exactly the way I do when he knows. He's been awfully bitter about Gary, but that won't matter to him now. Only, Janet, if you're going to stay on at Blackbuck most of the time for a while, let's not tell him just yet. I mentioned before that he's had trouble sleeping and all. I'm going to make him see the doctor himself if he's not back to normal soon. He'll be coming here around four. You come home with me then and get some rest till you have to be back at work."

20

Charlie was back at the hospital by six on Thursday morning. Shane drifted in and out of consciousness, his head aching mercilessly, his whole body now feeling stiff and battered. When he was awake, he fretted about the bandages on his eyes, pleading to have them removed. One of his arms had been released from the IV apparatus and, in the late afternoon, in a feverish semiconsciousness, he tried to tear the bandages away himself. Janet was with him and stopped him sternly. He did not understand her words, but heard the angry command in her voice. They stayed with him again that night, in shifts.

By Friday, the headache was relenting a little, though the rest of his bruised and scraped body seemed more sore than ever. He was more awake now, more conscious of what went on around him for longer periods.

When Dr. Striker came in on morning rounds, he said chidingly, "They tell me you won't keep still. I know you're sore and miserable, but what's making you so restless? Everything's going to be better sooner if you do as you're told."

"It's the bandages," Shane said pleadingly. "I want to *know* if I can see."

The doctor sighed. "You're damned hard to convince. We've all told you—"

"Please take them off."

Without another word, the doctor ripped off the tape. "I've got another patient in the next room, a co-operative one. I'll be back."

After five minutes of trying to cope with double vision, lack of focus, and blurring, Shane was dizzy to the point of losing consciousness and violently ill.

"Did that prove anything?" snapped the impatient, unsympathetic doctor, who had been called back hurriedly.

"How long will it be this way?" Shane gasped miserably, his voice sounding strange and distant in his own ears.

"A few days, maybe a little longer. Your brain's got healing to work on. It can't be bothered with translating visual images for a while. Now what I *hope* you'll do today is keep still. Don't be moving around at all if you can help it. You can talk some when you feel like it, but stop this restlessness when you're awake. I'll have Dr. Dugan rebandage your eyes."

"No."

"What?" The taciturn doctor frowned and the nurse making rounds with him looked very surprised.

"I'll keep them closed," Shane promised earnestly. "I can't stand the bandages."

Max Striker looked down at him angrily. "I wonder who's the doctor around here?"

"I won't look at anything. Those bandages..."

The doctor shrugged his big shoulders. "Have 'em left off," he said curtly to the nurse, and to Shane, "But I don't want to hear another complaint out of you, not about anything."

Sharon, who had been sitting with him in company with old Charlie until they were banished for the examination, came in from the hall smiling.

"You're a naughty, naughty patient, Shane Bonner. Nobody gainsays Dr. Striker. He's afraid word of this will get around and undermine his reputation. Ah, ah, don't you dare open those eyes."

His lids were swollen and bruised. She raised a hand to touch them with cool fingertips, but let it drop, not wanting to startle him.

By evening, when he woke from a sounder, natural sleep, the headache had lessened a little. Charlie was there again—still? Shane opened his eyes just long enough to see the old man, who didn't happen to be looking at him, and to note that it was dark outside. Then things blurred and the room seemed to be tilting crazily. Shane took deep, slow breaths, his eyes so tightly closed they ached.

He heard the whistle of the freight that came up every weeknight to take away the mill products from Holland's. When the train was loaded, it stopped beside the town's drive-in restaurant while the crew had their supper. If the train was on schedule, which it rarely was, it would be about eight o'clock.

Irene Blevins was back on duty. She came in to check the things they kept checking and to give him another shot.

"You've got so many bruises," she told him pleasantly, "that the ones from the shots don't even show."

Shane thought that was a great comfort, but said nothing. When she had gone out, humming, Charlie said,

"I couldn't tell if you was awake or not. They don't seem to give a damn about wakin' a feller up in a hospital, do they? Half the county's been through this place today. Doc Striker give orders nobody was to be in your room but me an' Faye and Magnessens. I ought to have wrote down a list of who all has come by."

"Where did you leave your falsies this time?"

"You been openin' your eyes?" demanded Charlie.

"I can tell by the way you thound."

Charlie grinned, but his voice was rough with closeness to tears because, obviously, the boy was feeling better. "I left the damn things up at the show some place. Didn' have time to hunt 'em up when Bud come to tell us about the wreck."

"Have you been here all day?"

"No, I had lunch at Viktor's an' then went to the house an' took a good long nap. Janet was here then. You don't remember?"

"I'm not—sure. . . . Isn't it Friday? I thought she'd be at work."

"She did leave in time to git up there an' help Ruby with supper."

Mrs. Blevins rustled back in again. "More flowers," she said cheerfully. "You're going to have a lovely surprise when you're up to looking at all the nice things people have sent. This is a bouquet of red roses and lilies of the valley, and the card says—why, it says, 'David and Gloria Rosenzweig.' . . . By the way, you're going to have a roommate tomorrow. We have a gall bladder coming in."

Shane looked startled, then smiled grimly as she rustled out. Even the muscles required for smiling were stiff and sore.

They heard the steam whistle from the mill, like that of a big ocean liner, a single blast, signaling the beginning of lunch hour for the second shift.

"People oughtn' send flowers," said Charlie. "It's like a—" he had almost said "funeral," but didn't want to.

"Money would be better," Shane said dryly. He coughed, and it felt as if it would tear the stiff, sore muscles. "I always liked that whistle."

Charlie nodded. "Not many steam-powered mills left. . . . That storm, you know? It missed us. Just a little powder a snow up there, the Forest Service people tell me, but I think we'll start foldin' 'er up. I guess I'll be gittin' back up there tomorrow."

"I'm sorry about Big Red."

"You remember the wreck now, do you?"

"No, but I left camp driving Red, and then I was here."

"Well, sir, I'll tell you, son, I didn' git the best look in the world on Wednesday, but I believe we can git the other trucks an' maybe some other good heavy equipment down there an' salvage tractor an' trailer both. The trailer's on its side, about halfway down the bank, an' the tractor standin' on her wheels, right in the edge of the water. She's bunged up, but I believe they's many a mile in 'er yet."

241

Shane groaned.

"Somethin' hurtin' you worse?" demanded Charlie, immediately solicitous. "You want me to git the nurse?"

"No, just let me have some water."

Charlie held the glass, feeling a vague embarrassment, but smiling a little because there was something he could do.

"Charlie, could you close the door?"

"Why, sure." He did it. "What's the matter?"

"I want to talk to you. No, I mean I want you to talk to me. You'll be going back to camp tomorrow, and there's this—gall bladder coming. This seems like the time."

"For what?" asked the old man guardedly.

"For talking to me—really telling me about my parents."

Charlie went to the window and watched old Mrs. Hobson across the street, locking up the library.

"Shane, it's no use talkin' about it. You've heard—"

"I just want to hear it straight through, from you; who they were, what they were like. It's important that I know—right now."

"Son, you're yourself. It ain't got nothin' to do with—"

"If you won't talk about it, I'm going to get up," he said quietly.

He moved, dragging himself to a sitting position, desperately fighting the dizziness and nausea, trying not to faint. Charlie had whirled from the window.

"Shane, for Christsake!"

"I'm sorry," he said, his voice vague, "but I want you to tell me."

"Lay back, lay back! or I'll have ever'body in this hospital in here."

"Will you do it?"

"Yes, goddam it! Now be still."

There was a long silence. Shane was glad of it. The dizziness passed slowly, the ringing in his ears stopped gradually. He shivered in the cold sweat he had broken into. Charlie saw and pulled up the covers, muttering, "Goddam stubborn kid." He sat down and began slowly, unwillingly.

"Steve was five when your grandma died. Georgia wanted a lot of kids. She died havin' a little girl, an' the baby died too." A long pause.

"Me an' Steve just—never did hit it off some way. I don't know. Maybe I was too hard on him, expected too much. He was always a tough little sonofagun, gittin' in fights an' such, but he—sometimes it seemed like he enjoyed life a lot.... All the time he was growin' up, he said he wouldn' stay here. Said he was goin' off to some big city. Be somethin' big. He never did say what.... He didn' like school. He never finished but the eighth grade up at Blackbuck, an' that was just because I said I'd beat the blood out of him if he didn't. He knew I'd do 'er, too.... He ranted around the country a lot. They was some said he was like me when I was a young buck, before I married your grandma, but...

"Well, the war come an' he wasn' but seventeen in '44, but nothin' would do 'im but to join up. So I signed the papers. I didn' want him in the fightin', God knows, but I thought the Army, that kind a' life, might do his good."

243

A long silence and Charlie said, "I'm fixin' to smoke my pipe. You reckon it'll make you sick?"

"I don't think so. Have I got any cigarettes?"

"I seen what was left of 'em. They had 'em with the rest of your stuff. A body just had to guess they'd been cigarettes. I'll see you git some tomorrow. I expect you oughtn' be smokin' yet anyway."

Shane waited, very still.

"They sent him to the Pacific, to Okinawa an' them places that come toward the end. In '46, after he'd finished out his service in occupation duty, he come home, an' he was—bitter... mean. It seemed like he used to fight an' such just for the hell of it, but after that, seem like he wanted—to hurt people. It seemed like he'd do or say anything to git a fight started. I'd had a while in the First War, an' I could understand, a little, maybe. I thought he'd come out of it.

"He never stayed around here long at a time. Mostly, when he'd come back, it was to see about gittin' money, an' we'd always—have a fuss. ... Said he couldn' stand this whole part of the country, full of hicks an' hayseeds an' dumb loggers.

"In '49—he'd been up here a week or so an' was on his way somewheres else—when he got in that fight at Bill's place down at the Falls. Bill's place ain't there no more. They tore it down an' put up a fillin' station.... The fight got to be pretty much of a free-for-all, I guess, the way bar fights will, but the man Steve had started it with—some salesman from Salt Lake—Steve cut him in the neck with a piece of a bottle an' he

244

bled to death before they could git him to the hospital."

Charlie relit his recalcitrant pipe and sucked at it for a while.

"Shane?" he said softly.

"I'm listening."

"I thought you might of gone to sleep."

He opened his eyes. Just for a moment, Charlie's face was clear to him and he felt like crying. The crumpled old face reflected unadulterated misery.

"Don't do that!" Charlie said querulously. "You'll make yourself sick, an' I ain't goin' to talk with you lookin' at me."

A long silence, and then in a steady voice, "So they had the trial an' they sentenced him for second-degree murder.... After the sentencin', this girl come to me—they'd already took Steve to the state prison, an' she come up to the ranch. I remembered seein' her once at the trial. She wasn' but sixteen or seventeen. Her mother come with her. She said her name was Billie Sue Nolan an' she was carryin' Steve's baby. The old lady was a tough ole piece. She wanted the girl to git rid of the baby, but said the girl wouldn' do it.

"I went to see Steve about it an' he said it might be his, so I went to where they was livin' in Boise. The mother was a—well, a whore, an' she was bringin' the girl up to the same thing, but I tell you, that was the prettiest girl I've ever seen. Her hair was like yours an' she was real fair-complected, a sweet, delicate-lookin' little thing, but the mother was a reg'lar bitch. I said I'd pay the expenses an' send along somethin' now an' then to help her with the baby.

245

"Four or five months after you was born, Steve got killed in a fight. One of the other prisoners had managed to git a knife somehow.

"A few weeks after that, I got this letter from the ole lady, Billie Sue's mother, said they was goin' to put you up for adoption. I figgered she wanted more money, an' that's mostly what it was. She said if you was a girl, they might raise you, but they didn't have no use for a little boy around. Billie Sue cried, but she'd give you up for adoption.... It was the first time I'd seen what you was like."

"Do you think he was my father?" Shane asked tonelessly.

"Yes, son, I do. I did from the beginnin', when I first saw you.... Would you rather he hadn' of been?"

"I don't know."

"Well, you've got her hair an' complexion an' build, someways, but you look like Steve in the face when you smile, an' you've got Georgia's eyes, gray an' sort of changey, that steady look you can give a body an' them long dark lashes. Them eyes was what made me know....

"I said I'd adopt you an' the ole lady said that would be all right, providin' I paid over a good sum of money. I went to this lawyer an' had the papers fixed as legal as I could. But when it come to signin', the ole lady decided I ought to send Billie Sue some money onct a month to help her live, considerin' what they'd been through an' all, so I agreed to that, though I wouldn' go as high as they wanted. I fixed it with this lawyer so I could send him the money an' he'd send it on to her. They was fixin' to move on an' I didn' care about knowin' where they was or hearin' from them.

"I don't know how she come to name you Shane. I think she said it was from some movie she'd seen, or maybe a book she'd read. When I was havin' your last name changed to Bonner, I thought about changin' the first to George, but you'd got used to Shane, so I let that go."

"Are you still sending her money?"

"You been keepin' the books. You ought to know I'm not. When you was about eight or nine, the lawyer sent me a letter from her, from Billie Sue. She said her mother had died an' she was about to marry some feller that was pretty well fixed. She said the money might make him ask questions she didn't want asked, an' she thanked me for what I'd been sendin'."

"Did she—?" He couldn't stop the beginning of the question. He opened his eyes momentarily to see the water glass and took it to drink.

"She asked about you, said she hoped you was well an' a good boy an' all like that, an' that she wished she could see you sometime. But I didn't answer the letter, Shane. There wasn't no use of it. Besides, I—well, I always worried, till you was grown, that she might decide to try to git you back some way. People do that, you know, an' she seemed real broke up about givin' you up."

"Where was she then? when she wrote the letter?"

"Austin, Texas, I think, but you ain't thinkin'—"

"No, I wouldn't want to find her."

Another long silence. Two blasts of the old steam whistle at Holland's, the end of the lunch hour. Mrs. Blevins pushed the door open brusquely.

"Mr. Bonner, you're not going to spend the night, are you? Shane's doing just fine. He won't need anyone but us. He's going to have another shot in a little while and sleep the night through this time. Besides, you look awfully tired yourself."

Charlie heaved himself up out of the chair. "Yes'm, I was just about to go."

He laid his hand on Shane's for a brief, awkward moment. "Night, boy. Don't be lookin' around now. I'll be by in the mornin' before I go up to the show."

Shane sneaked a quick peek to make sure the nurse had left. "Charlie, I—I'm sorry, but thank you. Sometimes, when other kids would say things, and other times, I did wish Steve wasn't my father, but I always did hope you were really —my grandpa."

"Shit, now," muttered the old man and left unsteadily, his own eyes blurred.

21

Gloria spent Thursday and Friday in bed in a darkened room. Her nose and upper lip were turning ghastly colors. She made Bessie cover the mirrors. Each time she woke, she swallowed another sleeping pill, so that by the time David came home in midafternoon on Friday, the pills had stopped working and she had a dull, throbbing headache. Nothing pleased her. She was as fretful and difficult as a small, spoiled child.

"Mrs. Epstein—Ella—called the office," reported David. "She'd like to come try to cheer you up a bit."

"Tell her to go to hell. She just wants to come so she can gabble all over town about how awful I look."

Almost, he told her about his call to the FBI. She sometimes showed indications of a rather bizarre sense of humor, and she might find the anticipation amusing, but the call had not been all that satisfactory. He had spoken with two agents in the Boise office. The first, very young-sounding, had seemed as excited and flustered as if he were getting the first word of World War III. The second, an older, brusque man, had seemed only vaguely interested and not at all sure where the jurisdiction of the matter might fall. He suggested David call Washington, and David said shortly that he was trying to do his duty as a good American citizen, that the agent could, he knew, call Washington himself, toll-free. The agent finally said vaguely that he would try to see that somebody got up to Cana "sometime next week," and would call back when the matter was sorted out. David decided to say nothing about it to Gloria just yet. She made it abundantly clear that she didn't want him around now, so he went to his study to read the paper.

Gloria, lying in a half-stupor, found herself thinking languorously of Shane Bonner. Better, David had reported, probably out of danger, but still quite ill. If she were herself, Gloria thought, she might just make a little visit to the hospital—late evening would be best. There would be no way of his getting away from her there. She could make him want her; she was certain of it. There wasn't a man in the world who could *not* want her.

As she sipped the Tom Collins she had had Bessie bring, Gloria thought of sending him flowers. It made her laugh a little, but that hurt her mouth and nose. She cursed as she reached for the bedside phone, which had been turned off for two days.

22

"It's me," Janet almost whispered. "Don't look unless you can."

Shane opened his eyes. It was past ten on Saturday night. "How did you get in here?"

"I'm a nurse and I know everybody in the world, remember? I just got off work."

"You look tired."

"Well, I'm not, and I wanted to see how you were. Mrs. Blevins didn't think you were asleep yet, and Dr. Dugan said I could come in for a few minutes."

"But you don't know Dr. Dugan."

"I didn't ten minutes ago, but I do now. He thinks I'm nice. I think he's nice."

"I'd think you were nice if you'd brought some cigarettes. Charlie forgot them this morning and nobody else will help me."

"No, no. Not yet. Maybe you can kick the habit while you're in here."

"I don't *want* to break the habit. I like giving in to vice and corruption. Besides, I'm going stir crazy and nobody will tell me when they'll let me out."

"I hear you sat up for a little while today and you're really looking much better. We're getting some color in our face: purple and greenish—"

"All right, that's enough. When do you think I can go home?"

"I'm not your doctor, my dear, but I should say, all in good time."

"You're a help."

"Your eyes are hardly crossing."

"I can tell that for myself."

"You're also in your usual foul mood. I think they'll let you go home earlier than they would a normal patient. I only came to cheer you, and you make a nasty, smart-ass response to every single cheery thing I say. Patty sent you a picture. Can you look at it? She's mad because they won't let her come in."

The picture was of a large yellow cat with three varicolored kittens climbing over her. At the bottom, in neat red crayon block letters was written: FOR SHANE FROM PATTY I LOVE YOU.

He smiled softly. "Put it there where I can look at it, and will you *please* make them take away some—all—those damned flowers? I keep sneezing and they won't believe it's the flowers. They whisper in the hall that I'm coming down with pneumonia."

"I'll take the plants to Mama. She'll love having them."

"But why do they *send* them?"

"Because they *love* you."

"I'd rather have cat pictures."

"You're impossible. Did we eat today? I see our chart said we could."

"We had broth and Jell-O—three times," he said grimly.

She laughed. "Never mind. I know how we feel about those."

"Well, we're getting damned hungry."

There was a little silence. He closed his eyes to rest them as things began to turn fuzzy. "You're staying at your folks'?"

"Just for now, so I can visit you at odd times. Aunt Faye is letting me use her house until I'm finished working for Ruby. On Thursday, I moved Loki and our things down there. It's warmer and much better equipped than the cabin. But then it didn't snow."

The elderly man on the other side of the drawn curtain moaned and snored more loudly.

"He's the gall bladder," Shane explained dryly. "He hasn't really come out of the anesthetic yet. God, people get hardened in hospitals, don't they? He's The Gall Bladder. What am I?"

"The Skull Fracture? The Cracked Nut? I don't know."

"I hope to God I never really have to be a patient of yours."

"So do I," she said, giggling.

"Today," he said, suddenly sober, "the people came—their name is Rollins—whose little boy I didn't hit. I still can't remember anything about it, but they were very—kind. They want to pay the hospital bills and, of all things, buy Charlie a new truck. The hospital people wouldn't let the boy come in—his name is Kevin—so he sent me a letter. It's there in the drawer."

Janet read:

"Dear Mr. Boner,

"Thank you for not killing me and my dog. I love him very much. His name is Zip and he is a good dog but sometimes very dum. Your truck looked very big to me. I would like to ride in a truck like that some day but I would not like to be run over by one and Zip would not either.

"I hope you are getting well soon. Maybe you could come to Oakland and visit us. We like it here but it would not be a good place for us to live. My mother says she can hardly stand to go over that part of the road any more. Your truck is still in the river, so maybe we cant come back here again next year.

"I'm very glad you did not die.

"Your Friend
"Kevin Rollins"

Janet had tears in her eyes and was smiling. "You're right. There are better things than flowers."

She replaced the letter and, after a little silence, said, "Mama knows about Gary and the baby. She asked me to wait a little while to tell Daddy. He hasn't been sleeping much lately and he doesn't look well. Do you know that when they brought you in and only Dr. Dugan was here, Daddy went into the emergency room and helped with everything? Karen Martin was there and she just keeps talking about it. He's a remarkable man, my father."

"Yes," he said, then, intently, "Janet, how long do people go on having identity crises?"

253

She looked at him carefully, glad his eyes were closed. "I don't know, Shane, maybe, off and on, all their lives for some people."

"I thought I'd had mine when I was seventeen, and before that. I'd been fighting a lot in high school, and it finally dawned on me that I was just wasting blood and adrenaline and things, that I couldn't help who or what my parents were, that I should just be myself and I ought to start trying to find out who that was. Pretty soon after that, I decided I wanted to go to college, major in wildlife management, so I did that. But I haven't *done* it. It looks now as if I'll lose out on the job at High Lonesome.... Still, instead of fighting, I did other things, like playing football, and I always felt I ought to work for Charlie during the seasons, as long as he's able to keep it up. In the spring, when you came back here... you asked me not long ago, remember? If I used to love you?"

"I remember."

"It's not that I *used* to, it's that I almost always have, I do, but..."

"But you hate me, too," she said gently, "because of Gary and the baby."

"I don't hate you. It's just that I can't—forget. ... Back when I was seventeen and thought I had my mind settled about a lot of things, no, even before that, I'd decided I'd never marry, because of not knowing anything about my parents. Sometimes, I was sure I was going to turn out just plain mean, the way Steve seems to have been. I had no idea, no way of finding out things about what kids of mine might inherit, so I thought I shouldn't have a wife and children. And now—I don't know how to say it without sounding like a bastard," his eyes tightly closed, he smiled grimly, "but I—want to marry you."

A nurse came in to check the other patient, frowning at Janet.

"I'm going in just a minute," she murmured abstractedly, then, when the nurse was gone, she said unevenly, "How can you sound bastardly saying you want to marry somebody?"

"Because I'm saying it all wrong," he said miserably. "Everything seems so mixed up.... Last night, I made Charlie tell me about Steve and my mother. There wasn't really anything all that new. Her name was Billie Sue Nolan, and she was a whore, just as we've all always known she had to be, but ... it's made me feel more— confused, for some reason. I came from stock like that, and yet, because you lived with Gary and you're having his baby, I feel—superior." He shook his head angrily, miserably. "Goddam it, that's a lousy word! I'm sorry, it just—"

"But I do understand," she said shakily, her eyes filling with tears.

"I *would* forget," he said painfully, groping for her hand, "because you're just Janet, the way you've always been...."

"Not quite, Shane," she said, her mouth trembling. "Maybe we all change, just a tiny bit, with everything that happens to us."

"Please don't be angry."

"I'm not," she said, squeezing his hand, "truly."

"I want to marry you, but I have to try to be as honest as I can. It's only fair. That same day you asked if I used to love you, you said something about our always being honest with each other, brutally honest, you said, something like that."

"Yes."

"Well, I feel I'm being really brutal now and I'm sorry as hell. I love you. I'd like to marry you soon, partly for the baby's sake, and your family's. But . . . I can't be—glad about the baby. I'm sorry. It will be hard to forget it's not mine. Maybe, once it's born and comes to be a person in its own right, things would be fine, but I can't *know* that. I can't make any promises about it and I won't say a lot of things that I don't truly believe yet. Even if you loved me, too, that could stand between us, maybe even forever. I'd promise to try, but—"

Her tears were falling on his hand. "Please, little Janet." He reached for her and, half-kneeling, she lay against him. "I've said it all so *damn* wrong. I don't *want* you hurt, ever again."

"I'm hurting you," she said brokenly, gently moving a little away from him. "I know how sore and stiff you must be. . . . Shane, I don't know what to say, except that I do love you. I never loved Gary that way, honestly. It was a trip, a revolution, some kind of stupid rebellion—I don't even know against what. You were the first boy who ever kissed me. Do you remember?"

"Yes."

"I think I've loved you since then, maybe before, but we've always been so close, almost as if we're brother and sister. Sometimes things that are too close get—blurred."

She stood up, wiping her eyes with a corner of his sheet and managing to make her voice steady and lighter. "I have to go. They'll be throwing me out. Let's think about it. I don't know anything else to say, except—thank you for asking me, *and* for being honest."

She bent quickly, touched his lips with hers, and was gone.

23

The affair between Wes Collins and Faye Holland had been going on for years. It had begun sometime more than a year after Faye's husband, Dan, died, and at about the same time Doreen, Wes's wife, newly pregnant with their daughter, told him she never wanted to share a bed with him again.

They had married, Wes and Doreen, because Doreen had allowed herself to become carried away after a dance one Saturday night in Alder Falls twenty-eight years ago. It was the only time in her life when she had felt strong sexual attraction for a man, and she didn't actually realize that was what she was feeling. She had not come to the dance with Wes, but with Amon Perry, a well-landed farmer from down the valley, a man ten years older than she, a widower with two half-grown children. Doreen and her parents had liked to think for the past several years—though they never quite discussed it—that Doreen was "the most eligible young lady in Alder County." She was not especially pretty, but she was not ugly. She was not particularly intelligent, but she was not stupid, and there was the Sheppard name, the Sheppard money. Doreen had met many young men outside her home county. Her Uncle Floyd was new in the state legislature then and she was often a

257

guest in his home in Boise. She had almost been engaged, once, to a son of one of the wealthiest families in the state, with timber, agricultural, and mining interests far exceeding those of her own family. But they had quarreled and, when the disagreement had been almost made up, their mothers had quarreled over wedding plans. Doreen would have liked bearing that family name, but that had been almost the only thing that had attracted her to the young man, though she had secluded herself for a decorous amount of time after the almost-engagement had been broken off, with her mother berating the other family to anyone who would listen and her father buying Doreen a sealskin coat.

On that night at the dance at Alder Falls, Doreen had realized she was twenty-four, that many of the young men who had used to court her had stopped calling, that she wanted nothing more to do with the widower, Amon Perry.

Wes, who was normally quiet and a little shy, had been drinking a good bit that night. Doreen did not at all approve of drinking, but she liked the way he held her while dancing, closely, but with respect and gentleness. The way he would sometimes smile into her eyes when she looked up at him made her feel strange and shaky inside. There were men handsomer than Wes Collins, men with more money or better prospects, but hardly any in Alder County who were not married now. Doreen's mother was talking more and more about a long visit with her relations in Kansas City, the opportunities there. Doreen didn't much like Kansas City or the relatives there. On the other hand, she had not planned to spend her life in Alder County, nor even in Idaho. She had had bigger dreams, San Francisco, New York, perhaps Washington. But as her twenty-fifth birthday approached, she couldn't stop a growing fear and depression. She was her parents' only child, the only one of her generation in the family, since Uncle Floyd and Aunt Vera had no children. It was time, for everyone's peace of mind, that she married and had children of her own.

Wes was an easygoing young man, eager to take life as it came, interested in what might be, tomorrow. He had a large capacity for enjoyment and contentment, a kind of mild complacency which, for that night at least, gave Doreen a sense of security and safety. He was quiet and gentle, seemed malleable. She was convinced that, should matters develop, she and her parents could eventually convince him to give up his interest in his father's pokey old lumber and hardware business up at Cana to go into the land, cattle, and food-processing business with her father, or perhaps even into politics, as Uncle Floyd had done. Wes was not a dynamic person —he was too quiet to be that—but everyone liked him, knew him as honest and trustworthy and intelligent. Just possibly, Doreen might still, some day, have one of her dreams come true and be the wife of a congressman.

The dance was a benefit to raise funds for an addition to the Alder Falls hospital. Wes had come down from Cana simply for something to do on a Saturday night. In his calm, easygoing way, he was having a good time. He was no more interested in Doreen Sheppard than in two or three other girls there, but they danced together several times, and when they were dancing with other people, he sometimes noticed her eyes following him. He was not particularly flattered, as she thought he must be, only mildly interested and curious. Wes, when he thought of it in passing, believed it was a good idea for a man to wait until he was around thirty before he married. If he had reasons for this idea, they were that it was what his own parents had done and they had had a good marriage, and that he liked his own life as it was just now. He was twenty-two.

Doreen, whose religion forbade drinking, let herself be persuaded to have a glass of punch. After all, buying punch was another way of contributing to the hospital fund, and they told her it was very mild. It made her feel daring and she rather liked it. Later, she had another glass. Some of the boys had spiked this last batch very heavily. So often, she felt awkward and unsure of herself, despite who she was, and tended to be snappish and curt because of the feelings, but the punch relaxed her, and all at once she made up her mind. Wes, having no idea with whom she had come to the dance, had asked casually if he might drive her home. She danced once more with the widower, told him she was developing a headache but he mustn't let that spoil the evening for him, that she had arranged to be taken home by someone else who was leaving anyway.

It was not far to her house, the finest in the county; just down the valley from Alder Falls; not far enough.

"Wouldn't it be fun," she said brightly, daringly, "to drive all the way to Boise and have breakfast?"

Wes had thought it would be fun and that

was all they did, but it was noon on Sunday when he brought her home. Her father was standing on the front steps of the big house and he might as well have been holding a shotgun; her mother was crying.

It was a very large wedding, the most elaborate Alder County had seen. A number of people speculated that it was a bit precipitate, but it was more than a year before Bruce was born. By then, Doreen loathed sex and her husband. He had had a new house built for them, encouraging her to have it as much the way she wanted as possible, but it was not nearly as grand as she wished because Wes refused to accept Sheppard money for the building, though he had had to take a good bit of it for the furnishing of the place because they called that a wedding gift. He went along in many ways, great and small, with what Doreen wanted; the house was decorated and furnished in an ultramodern style he did not like; there was a maid, whom Wes could ill afford, though Doreen did almost nothing at all with her own time; he agreed to separate bedrooms as soon as a short, tense honeymoon was over. Wes did not feel tricked by or resentful toward his wife because she *was* his wife—after all, he was a grown man and should have been able to take care of his life better—he only felt a little puzzled and more than a little sad that the marriage had happened, and he tried to do what he could to make the best of it. For Doreen, it was openly declared warfare, almost from the time of the wedding reception. Wes, who had seemed, and still seemed, with other people, so pleasant and easygoing, showed her a streak of stubbornness like a thick steel rod running through him. He *would* stay on in his father's business; he fought against having any part of the Sheppard money or influence for anything that remotely included him; he was not the least interested in politics and, most irksome to his wife, he coolly and calmly maintained the privacy of himself. She could find nothing in him at which to grasp and claw, to fasten her arguments on, no points of vulnerability.

Doreen felt it an absolute necessity that she produce a child, not so much for herself—certainly not for Wes—but for the potential grandparents and for the inheritances there would be one day. She learned, with embarrassment, about taking her temperature first thing in the morning and, when the signs were right, vouchsafed her husband "sex" two or three times a month. She lay inert, withdrawn, completely unresponsive except for revulsion, under his lovemaking. Wes felt like a stud being used, and not a prize one, but he badly wanted children. Surely, something good could come from the marriage.

Doreen began, as soon as Bruce was born, to try to make his father insignificant in the boy's eyes. She wanted Wes to have no part in his upbringing. When there was a decision to be made about Bruce's life, she consulted her parents or Uncle Floyd. Bruce had a mind of his own and he liked manipulating people. He was a business administration major in college, but for a few years thereafter, he worked in his father's store, so as to enlarge the share of profits and responsibilities given him when he finally "gave in" to the Sheppards' persuasions and went in as manager of the food-processing plant at the age of twenty-five. Bruce began by knowing little about farming and food processing, but he could learn, or seem to learn quickly, and he knew how to delegate authority to those who knew more than he—and drew lower salaries—without the least besmirchment of his position as manager. Bruce felt a degree of contempt for his mother and grandparents because they were so childishly transparent. He rather liked his father, though there was some contempt there too, a wondering why Wes had put up with it all for so long with such seeming detached meekness.

Margaret Louise—Peggy Lou—was born when her brother was almost eight, because Doreen was, one day, suddenly seized with a terror that something might happen to Bruce, who was now the only Sheppard descendant of *his* generation. Doreen was bitterly disappointed when the child was not a second son. She never liked her daughter, though she was hardly consciously aware of it. Peggy Lou was a pretty, clever, vivacious child, popular with her peers and with people of all ages. Doreen saw in the girl, unconsciously, so much that she had never had, had never been. She dutifully saw that the child was well cared-for, had what she needed, and more, but this was Wes's child. It made Doreen furious that Peggy and her father were so close almost from the girl's first cry. Wes began to feel a little less of raw disappointment and hopelessness. Something good had, after all, come to him from the marriage. At first, Doreen believed Peggy might be the key, a way of "getting at" Wes, but she quickly found that the girl had that same thin, inexorable stubborn streak as her father, that same ability to go on being her own person, no matter how much her mother, grandparents, brother, uncle, nagged, nattered, cajoled, or threatened.

Wes and Doreen Collins, Dan and Faye Holland, were near to the same ages; their marriages had taken place within the same year. Doreen had had few friendships in her life; she had never had a "best" friend. Few people in Alder County were "worth putting herself out for." Wes and Dan had grown up together, with a warm liking for each other. Doreen decided that the Hollands were worth a little exertion on her part. The mill was important in the county. When old Jeff died, it was just possible he might leave all of it to Dan, since Dan was the only one of his sons who showed a working interest in the business. Doreen had plans and high hopes of far better things for Bruce, of course, but he and Barbara Holland were almost of an age. She did not approve of Faye, of the way she threw herself into the interests of the mill; it was unladylike, unseemly, but Dan and Faye were the only couple in Cana who seemed worthy of her frequent company.

Viktor and Nora Magnessen had come to town. Viktor had begun as a clerk and sometime manager in Wes's father's store; then the old man had died. Wes and Viktor agreed that the place should be expanded, the stock greatly increased, so they had formed a partnership. Doreen did not care at all for the Magnessens. They were people no one knew. Since Viktor was quiet, a little aloof, and very well-spoken with that foreign accent of his, Doreen thought him a snob. She thought Nora frumpy and weak-willed because she did her own housework almost all the time, always seemed to be deferring to Viktor, and kept having children. A business relationship was one matter. Since Viktor had put his money into the store, profits had certainly risen, but socially, Doreen wanted nothing to do with the new family. She could not understand, and resented, Wes's and the Hollands' fondness for them.

The Collinses and the Hollands played bridge or canasta together once a month or so. The games were Doreen's idea because she considered them fashionable; she played most seriously and least flawlessly of the four. Faye preferred going fishing with the men, which Doreen considered repulsive at the very least. Alone together, Faye and Dan commiserated with Wes.

Faye and Dan had been married only eight years when Dan died and Faye's life, though it was so full with the girls and the mill that no day was ever long enough, became a raw, inner barrenness.

One day, Wes had come to visit Jeff when the old man was recovering from one of his frequent and worsening attacks of asthma. Jeff was napping and Faye gave Wes coffee while he waited. She had some of the mill's office work spread round her in the study at Holland House and she went on with it, though they talked, a little about timber, the expansion of the store, the town, the weather. At one point, she glanced up, smiling a little, and found him watching her; their eyes met and held for a long moment. It came to them both, though they did not speak of it until a good deal later, how comfortable and right they felt there, alone together.

Wes spent a little time with old Jeff, all the

while distracted with trying to fight down the urge of the need that kept rising within him. When Faye came out of the study and walked with him to the door, he said huskily, his eyes on the polished hall floor,

"Would you ever, *ever* consider—meeting me somewhere?"

And Faye said softly, simply, "Yes."

Those first years had been joy and torment so inextricably mixed together that they felt utterly helpless, sometimes angry, ready to give it all up, sometimes desperately, tenderly terrified of losing it. In the beginning, they had liked and respected one another very much and each had been the other's salvation in the aching need for sexual companionship.

Those first years had been such difficult ones. Wes was freer than Faye because Doreen would often take the children to spend a few days with her parents or even on vacation with them. Even if she had been at home to rail at him for being out late, or all night, Doreen would have been secretly almost glad of his supposed infidelity. It would have proved her martyrdom beyond a shadow of a doubt. But Wes would not meet Faye when his wife was in Cana. It was too much in Doreen's nature, he feared, to follow him and, trying not to cast aspersions on herself, ruin Faye's reputation.

For her part, Faye had her daughters, the mill work, and old Jeff with which to contend. Very occasionally, she and Wes went separately to Boise on business for the same day or two, but someone in Cana would have been sure to notice if it had happened often. They were so desperate for each other in those first years and there was never enough time. Even meeting in Boise, they had to be very circumspect because both of them were known to so many people.

The best solution, they had finally found, was that sometimes, when Doreen and the children were away, Faye would say to Jeff and the girls and the housekeeper at Holland House that she was tired—which was true—that she must get away by herself for a while. She and Wes would meet at the summer place up on Blackbuck Creek. Occasionally, they managed almost an entire weekend alone together.

Wes had first spoken to Doreen of divorce when Bruce was two years old, long before he had begun the affair with Faye. Doreen was scandalized. Her family, her religion, did not condone divorce. He spoke of it again when Peggy was a baby. They were miserable together, had nothing in common. Why go on with the marriage? She refused to discuss it.

As the years passed, Wes's and Faye's relationship deepened. It became not so frenetic with passion. Other things grew to have as much importance and they, of necessity, learned patience, so that when they could find a few hours to spend together, they relished them, moment by moment, rather than chafing bitterly that they were so few.

Wes asked again for a divorce when Peggy was four. Doreen threw a cup of soup at him, screaming hysterically that she knew he had a mistress somewhere, that if he didn't stop pestering her, trying to scandalize her family's name, she would get a divorce, all right, and she would have it arranged so that he would never see his children again.

"Oh, let it go, Wes," Faye pled when he told her. "I don't care if Doreen and the whole county know it's me, but let's not make things worse for the kids."

So now, on a late Thursday evening in October, a week after Shane Bonner's accident, they sat together on a couch in front of the small fireplace in Faye's cozy little "room," shut securely away from the large living room of her new house, which she used only for entertaining. They had just come up from having dinner in the basement kitchen and were having coffee. The air outside was clear and frosty after a few showers of rain; the fire felt good. They sat and sipped their coffee in a companionable silence, like, as they in fact were, a couple who had been together for many years.

A part of the miracle of their togetherness was that, so far as they could ascertain, no one knew of their affair, or ever had known, though Doreen was certain there was *someone*. She had been certain of that since the first month of marriage. In a town like Cana, such a long-kept secret was very near to achieving the impossible. Wes had not come up to the East Ridge house until after dark. He had put his car straight into the garage and closed the door. He would leave before dawn.

"Is it really true?" Faye said finally, smiling dreamily.

"Is what true?"

"That you can come here now, maybe for weeks."

Wes put his arm around her. "Bruce is living with his grandpa, being a big manager tycoon. Doreen and Peggy Lou have gone visiting in Kansas City with Granny. I think I can't come every night; that would be asking for trouble, but as often as I can..."

"Wes, I missed you so while I was away. We don't see each other often, not really *see* each other, but when we're both in Cana, I know you're there. I can feel it. I know when you're probably shaving, leaving for the store, having lunch..."

"You needed to go away," he said, "to get some rest and change after Jeff died and the mill was sold. You'd been under too much strain and pressure for too long, but—well, I guess I never thought you'd stay almost two years. It was pretty bad sometimes."

"I did it because, for all these years, from time to time, I've tried to convince myself what a couple of fools we are. I thought if I stayed away, we could get it out of our systems."

"I don't want it out of my system."

She sighed and leaned against him. "I know. Neither do I."

"Faye, in another year or two, when Peggy's just that much older and can understand just that much better, I'm going to be divorced. It would look better for Doreen if she did the suing. For the sake of all the nothingness that's so important to her, I hope she will, but, if she won't, well, men can go to Reno, too, can't they? What would your girls think if we married and were the scandal of Alder County?"

"They'd be surprised, I guess, maybe a little upset at first. They'd be more understanding, more empathetic, I think, if we were a couple closer to their own ages, but they'll get used to it."

"The Sheppards won't get used to it," he said grimly, "and they'll do their damnedest not to let my kids accept it, but I don't think it will matter to Bruce, one way or the other. I just feel I have to wait a little longer for Peggy's sake. She's having a bad time as it is, just now."

"I thought she wasn't going to go to Kansas City."

"The original idea was that she was supposed to go there with her grandmother for a long visit, maybe as much as two months. She wasn't having any of that, but then this family wedding came up and she was asked to be maid of honor. It was a put-up job, of course, and she knows it. She'll probably only be gone a couple of weeks."

"Are they doing all this because of Mitch Magnessen?"

"Of course they are," he said, smiling, "and Mitch and Peggy Lou have been having a picnic out of it."

"Then it's nothing serious between them?"

"It could be, someday maybe. I don't think I could wish Peggy a better husband, when they've both done some more growing up, but they're sensible about it. I think they're making kids more sensible these days than they used to. Peggy has told me they want to wait a good while and see if it's for real. Right now, according to her, they're very good friends."

"Very good friends can be very nice people," she said; then, drawing herself a little out of the languor and comfort of his nearness, she said, "Why isn't Viktor enthusiastic about Mitch's wanting to be a doctor? Nora's so thrilled, and she's hurt—Mitch is, too—by his seeming—indifference."

Wes shrugged. "I think Viktor Magnessen is my best friend, but if ever there's something you don't understand, or Nora doesn't understand about him, for God's sake, don't ask me to explain it. He can be a damned strange person sometimes. Just when I think I've finally got him all figured out, he does something that knocks all my figuring into a cocked hat. Just as an example, we've got a screwed-up order at the store. It's got to be straightened out in a hurry so we can have the things we need in stock. One of us will have to go to Boise tomorrow. Viktor never seems to give a hang about going anywhere, so I just took it for granted I'd be the one to go. As we were closing up tonight, he mentioned something else he'd take care of while he's in Boise tomorrow."

She said thoughtfully, "He's not enthusiastic either, it seems, about Paul's running for county commissioner, but there always has seemed to be a little—constraint between them, and I guess Paul's turned absolutely chilly since Viktor won't invest in Cloud Valley."

"I don't know," Wes said worriedly. "I do think I know him well enough to know something's been bothering him lately, a lot."

A half hour or so later, Faye stacked the coffee things on a tray and took it down to the kitchen while Wes locked up.

As they lay drifting toward sleep, he said, "Did you talk to Nora this afternoon? after she brought Shane home?"

"Yes, he's all right. I mean, he'd rather be on his own, but with Charlie away, Nora wasn't about to let him go home alone. You know Nora. When she makes up her mind to take care of someone, they may as well resign themselves. He's still having trouble with his eyes, and headaches, but the doctors said that would happen."

They lay silent for a time until she gave a little start.

"I meant to tell you, Wes. Just as I was cooking supper, Blanche Moore called and told me an odd thing."

"What was that?" he said drowsily. "It has to have been something about the mill, I suppose. Blanche can't know much of anything else. She's had to do with the office there even longer than you did."

"Well, it was about David Rosenzweig. An FBI agent came to see him late this afternoon."

"FBI?"

"Yes. Isn't that curious?"

24

"Did you make a list of the things you'd like from Boise?" Viktor asked Nora as she got into bed.

"Yes. It's down in the kitchen."

He had been reading while she had her bath and now put the newsmagazine aside.

"You could come with me."

She sighed, stretching out wearily. "Oh, I suppose I could, but I really don't want to. I hope you don't mind. There's Patty, before and after school, and then we brought Shane here to be properly looked after. It would be a little silly for me to go running off the very next day, especially since he didn't want to come. Did you look in on him, Viktor? I hate to just open his door, and I don't like to knock, in case he might be asleep."

"He is asleep," said Viktor, smoothing her brow with one finger. "Try not to fuss over him too much, Nora. A hospital is a tiring place. Mostly, he needs rest and quiet now."

"Well," she said, "I did feel as if we were forcing him, a little, against his will, but he couldn't have just gone home and been all alone. He's still so weak, and that trouble with his eyes...

"You know, I'd forgotten Charlie even had a brother. It almost seemed like he had, too, until he got that wire about his having died, down there in New Mexico. He had a big family, Charlie said, five or six children, and they hadn't seen each other for more than twenty years. He had something to do with the oil business—the brother. It's sad the way some families separate and practically forget about each other until someone dies....

"Anyway, about Shane: I'd never feel easy about depending on Maxine Shelton to look after him right. She's all right as a cleaning woman, I guess—that is, if you don't much care whether the work gets done on the day it's supposed to—but she's no cook, and I just don't believe she'd show up every day....

"I thought Janet might be down today. I called her at Faye's place this morning to tell her Shane was getting out of the hospital this afternoon and would be staying with us for a while....

"Mitch and the boys may be home from hunting by tomorrow night. I've got to clean out the freezer and do some rearranging, in case he brings any meat....

"Sharon may be over in the afternoon. We've been trying to get together to do some sewing. She's the *best* seamstress and I've got material for three dresses for Patty. I hope we'll feel about all the people our children marry the way we feel about Sharon. And, oh, I almost forgot, there's a chili supper at Johnston on Saturday night, a political thing for Paul's campaign. They want us to come."

Suddenly, she felt awkward and self-conscious, running on like that. She always talked too much and he could be so quiet. She was worried about him and that seemed to make talking necessary.

He said, not seeming to have noticed anything different, "Yes, Paul was at the store today. I told him we probably would come. We haven't taken enough interest in the campaign, Nora."

"I know, but it seems like there's always something.... Well, I suppose if Mitch isn't back by then, Patty could stay over with Carolyn. I don't want Shane to feel he has to baby-sit.... Viktor?"

"Yes?"

"I was a little surprised when you said you were going to Boise. You usually want Wes to take care of things like that, and I just wondered..."

"I only felt like getting away for a day."

"It wouldn't *have* to be on business, you know. You could just take a day off now and then, or even two or three."

"Not now. We're shorthanded since Bruce has left, and Peggy."

"Is Mitch going to work at the store?"

"He said he would, as soon as he's through hunting. He'll be there until the middle of January. If Doreen can keep Peggy Lou away, she will. Maybe we can persuade Shane to come do some of our book work when he's a little stronger."

"Not the way his eyes are. I heard Dr. Striker tell him he's not to read or watch television or drive..."

"That's only for now. It will clear up."

She looked at him thoughtfully in the soft lamplight. He turned his eyes away to the half-drawn drapes.

"You've been wanting new drapes in here," he said. "I wouldn't know what to look for in the way of materials. Maybe, in a few weeks, you and I could go to Boise to look for that—and there's Christmas shopping."

"Yes," she said a little sadly. "Time passes faster every year."

"If we should do that, maybe we could make a two-day trip of it, stay overnight. I'd like to hear a symphony concert."

"Why, yes," she said, pleased, then sobering, "but there'll be Patty and Mitch, and I should be..."

"Arrangements could be made, my girl," he said, meeting her eyes with a half-smile. "You were only just saying how *I* should take some time off now and then."

Nora laughed a little. "Well, when you seem willing to do it after all this time, I have to admit it leaves me not quite knowing what to think. I know you haven't been sleeping well and you look tired. Viktor, please tell me truly, are you feeling all right? You're not—?"

"I'm all right, Nora. It has come to me, though, that you and I have never really had enough time together, with raising the children, the store, and all the other things. Time does seem to pass faster each year. I think we ought to begin having some little trips of our own now and then. Perhaps, rather than doing the shopping I was talking about in Boise, you'd like to go to Portland, or Salt Lake?"

"Why, Viktor!"

He switched off the lamp and lay down, putting an arm around her. "To tell you truly, I'm tempted to tell you just to pack a couple of bags and leave with me tomorrow. Not to Boise. That order could be unsnarled later."

"To where then?" she said, taken completely aback.

"I don't know," he said. "Anywhere."

He had never been a particularly impulsive person and now, rather than sounding gay and carefree, there was something like an edge of desperation in his voice. Nora felt frightened. There *was* something he was not telling her. Did he have an illness? She said a little tremulously,

"That would be just wonderful, Viktor, but I don't...."

"I know," he said gently. "We shouldn't get hasty about such things. It was just a—passing thought.... I hear Faye's decided it's a bookstore she wants."

"Yes," said Nora, still deeply troubled, with only half her mind on what she was saying. "I thought I'd told you that. She's going to start having the shop redecorated next week, and she's already begun ordering. She's counting on having it open by Thanksgiving, for the Christmas trade, you know."

After a little silence, he said, "There are so many books I haven't read."

Nora shivered; she couldn't help it. There was a note of something too close to finality in his tone, as if he never expected the chance to begin reading those books. He noticed and held her closer, drawing the covers around her shoulders. She said, trying for lightness,

"I'd better get out the electric blanket the next time I change the bed. I don't believe my blood circulates as well as it used to.... Why don't you start making a list of books you want and have Faye order them for you?"

She was going to call Dr. Striker tomorrow, ask if Viktor had been in to see him. Was it possible he was being sent to some kind of specialist? Was that the reason for the trip to Boise?

He said, "How was Janet when you talked with her?"

"She was all right. She likes staying at Faye's place and I'm so glad she's down out of that old cabin."

Janet, when she had spent several nights at home after Shane's accident, had told her father Gary was gone, had been gone since July, but she had not told him the rest of it. "Let me be the one to tell him, though," she had said determinedly to her mother. "I want to, and it's not right that you should be the one who has to do it. I will, the next time I'm home, if he seems to be feeling better." Perhaps, Nora thought now, that was why Janet had not come down today, but she said,

"You know, Viktor, I've been wondering if Janet and Shane have quarreled over something. She was at the hospital every minute she could be until after Saturday night. I know she was in for just a few minutes on Tuesday, but that's all since Saturday. She hasn't been back."

"When is the baby due?" he asked softly.

Nora started and did not speak for a moment. "I didn't know she'd told you."

"No one told me. It's getting fairly obvious. I've been wondering why no one *has* mentioned it to me. Does Janet—do you—think I'm going to rave? Foam at the mouth? Cut her out of my will . . . ?"

I've only known for a week," Nora said defensively. "She asked me not to mention it because she wants to tell you herself. I don't think it entered her mind that you'd rave or any such thing. You know Janet. She hates hurting people, disappointing them, worrying them, and she takes her own responsibilities very seriously. She's very much like you, really. . . . The baby's due toward the end of January, and she's talking about going away somewhere to have it. We can't let her do that, Viktor, not all alone—can we?"

"Certainly not," he said vehemently.

"What I really think," Nora said wistfully, "is that Shane wants to marry her. I've been thinking a lot about it and I wonder if he hasn't wanted that for years, maybe without quite knowing it. Janet says now that she knows she never really loved that Gary, but you know how proud she is. If Shane has mentioned marriage to her now, she'll be thinking it's just because of the baby—to try to make an honest woman of her, or whatever it is they say. If that's the way it is, maybe you can get her to listen to reason. You always have been able to do more with her than—"

"She's hurt him very badly," Viktor said with compassion. "He's been in torment ever since she and that boy came to live at Lucky Streak."

"I didn't know," Nora said, tears springing to her eyes. "I mean, I didn't see it. How could I be so stupid? Here I'm the one saying he may have been in love with her for years. Of course he's been hurt and, if anything, he's more proud than she is. Do you remember how they used to have such arguments about everything or anything, then be laughing over it later? ... Maybe you could talk to both of them ... ?"

He smiled sadly. "I'm not a magician, darling. They're both adults. I think about all you or I or anyone else can do now, in fairness, is listen if *they* want to talk."

After a silence, Nora said dubiously, "If nothing comes of that, then do you suppose she'd want to go and stay with Alice—"

"Good *lord,* no!"

"Well, she says she's going away and I just thought ... I know how Alice is, but I also know she'll always come through for her family. I can't bear to think of Janet having the baby without some of her family. ..."

"When she gets around to talking to me about it, I'll try to persuade her to stay here—where she belongs."

"There'll be an awful lot of talk. She's trying to spare us that."

"Yes, I understand that, but she's going to have to let someone think of her, too. Will you mind the talk terribly, Nora?"

"Not if I can have Janet here to take care of her," she said passionately. "I feel like I won't mind anything about any of it, now that that—boy is gone."

"Yes," he said. "That's the good in all of it, that he left. He caused Janet a good deal of turmoil and doubting, I think, with his bitterness and destructive talk and thoughts. Until she got involved with him, she was always such a *sure*, optimistic person. Gary was one of those pitiable young people who are just—lost. He has all the answers and no questions."

After a moment, she said slowly, "That seems an odd thing to say, but I guess I see what you mean."

He kissed her. "I've got the clock set for five. I want to be in Boise when the suppliers open up and I should be back for supper."

Was this it, then? she wondered, beginning to feel relieved. Was it worry over Janet that had made him so troubled lately? She said, "I'm glad you told me you know about the baby. Some of my worry has been not being able to talk to you about it."

He held her close for a moment and she could feel his understanding. He moved away a little and each of them turned, settled covers, prepared for sleep, but sleep did not come. After a long while, Nora said softly,

"I'm so proud of all of them, Viktor. Even

this that's happening to Janet; she'll work it through and be all right."

"Yes."

"I wouldn't be a bit surprised if Paul is elected a county commissioner," she went on. "I'll be glad of it, awfully proud of him, though I sometimes worry that he and Sharon aren't as happy as they might be. I'd like to see him spend more time at home, though of course I know it's none of my business.... And Alice: her letters are always so full of how happy she is with her job. It looks as if it's always going to be the biggest thing in her life. I wouldn't have chosen exactly that kind of life for her, but then I'm just old-fashioned, and she does seem happy, doesn't she?"

It's the middle of the night, she thought tensely, and here I am, running on and on again, but she couldn't stop. There was still something...

"And Mitch: He's so pleased about beginning premed."

"All in all," Viktor said quietly, "we've had a very beautiful life."

Nora did not notice just then—though she recalled it later—that he used the past tense.

Now that she had broached the subject, her mind was on it only for the moment, and she had to say, "You haven't seemed pleased about Mitch, Viktor. He's noticed it, too. I remember how proud and happy you were when Vik decided to study engineering."

She waited what seemed a very long time. Finally he said, "It's a great responsibility to be a doctor."

"I've always thought Mitch is a pretty con-

281

scientious person," she said, a little defensively, "especially for a young boy. He has years for more growing up and settling down. Surely you're not worried that he won't do well with his studies? He always has."

"No, I was thinking of—later."

Another silence. Nora turned on her back and said tentatively, "That day at the hospital when they brought Shane in . . . you seemed to know . . . ?"

"Dr. Dugan was alone," Viktor said, almost too quickly. "He was a little flustered with the Rosenzweig woman in hysterics and a nurse new to him working in emergency. He needed some help—reassurance—even if it was nothing more than someone who could keep reasonably calm."

"But you . . ."

There was a longer silence before he began slowly, "Nora, there are things we haven't talked about—*I* haven't talked about. . . . When I met you in Fox Falls, *that*'s the time, I've always felt, when my real life began."

He stopped. They both lay very still, waiting. She said tentatively, "Viktor?"

"I've told you that when I left Denmark as a very young man, I went to England, France, Austria, Germany, studying things, working at various jobs. When you, or the children, have asked what studies, what jobs, I've been—evasive."

A long pause.

"I was a doctor—a psychiatrist."

Another silence. Nora reached dazedly for the switch of the lamp on her side of the bed.

"Why, Viktor, I never dreamed. . . ." Tears sprang to her eyes. "Why didn't you ever men-

282

tion it? Surely that's not a thing to hide? How could we have been married all these years and I never had an idea—and you never said a word? ... The *years* of your life that education must have taken! How could you just want to forget it, or ... ? Why didn't you get licensed again in this country? I don't know what it would have taken, some more schooling, maybe, but we could have ... Why, that's a *wonderful* thing! I've always known you had an incredible mind, but ... the lumber and hardware business for someone with that kind of training! ... My lord, Viktor, you didn't give up all that because I'm such a frumpy old small-town thing?"

She was crying. He turned quickly and put his arms around her. His voice was not steady.

"My dear love, no. I gave it up years before I knew you ... in the war. I never had the least desire to practice any kind of medicine again.... Having Mitch decide to become a doctor was a shock to me. I've worried him unnecessarily about my feelings. Of course I'm glad, proud of him. It's only that it was a—a surprise to have him decide so suddenly like that, you see. It—brought back so much. He's still so young. It's possible he may ultimately decide on something else after all."

"You don't *want* him to be a doctor?" she said incredulously.

"Yes," he said firmly, trying to pull himself away from the memories. "Of course I do. It's only—I've kept thinking that my own father didn't want me to go into medicine and there were many times—later—when I wished I'd listened to him. But it's not going to be like that for Mitch. This is a completely different situation —almost a different world. I'll tell him how glad I am when he's back from hunting."

She said slowly, gently, "You were a doctor in that prison camp."

"Yes." The word sounded choked.

"Oh, Viktor, my poor, poor darling!" She stroked his face with one hand and held him tightly with her other arm.

"People died," he said quietly. "It was a small camp in relation to many of the others, but people died there every day, from malnutrition, ill treatment, overwork—and I could do nothing. Even if treatment had been allowed, and sanctioned, I had—my own work assignments."

"What were they?" she asked softly.

His voice was harsh. "I was assistant to— another psychiatrist. We had—experiments to conduct. For the most part, I took care of the records, paperwork, and reports." He was silent, smiling bitterly, a smile that was closer to a sneer. "They insisted on very complete, very detailed records, to be used for the benefit of the master race in the future. But their records were ultimately destroyed. At the time of the liberation, the entire camp was burned.

"That's one of the reasons I've never mentioned it, Nora. I thought there was no evidence left. After I met you and Paul and your mother, when we were married and the children began coming, all I wanted from those other years was to be able, for portions of the rest of my life, to forget them."

"Is it Mitch making up his mind like that," she asked, her fingers wandering gently in his thick, springy white hair, "bringing back all those memories? Is that what's had you so upset lately?"

"It's being reminded, yes." He was speaking with difficulty. "I've said that people died every day, people who should not have had to die. It's bad for any human being with feelings to see such things. Perhaps it's a little worse for a doctor because of his specific knowledges, because he can see more clearly the complete waste.... Even worse was that, after a time—I was there more than four years—and what is worse is the time when a man, particularly a doctor—stops caring."

He drew her hand away from his face, kissed it hurriedly, and got out of bed to prowl about the room. He was scarcely aware of what he was doing, his face distorted with torment.

"Viktor, love," she said tenderly, "anyone with sense could see how that could happen, how it would *have* to happen. I mean, it's a little like reading the papers every day. There are always so many reports of disasters, wars, horrible accidents, tragedies, cruelties that people do to one another. If we let ourselves dwell on all those things, get all wrapped up in every one of them ... even worse, if we had to *see* them happen, and feel, and care, how could any of us go on living with any sanity? It's a thing of—of defense, isn't it? Of self-protection?"

"A man who swears the Hippocratic oath gives up rights like that."

"No," she said with gentle reproof. "A doctor isn't above being human."

After a time, she said, "Won't you come back to bed now?"

"I'm sorry. No."

"I could make some coffee—or tea?"

"I don't want anything, darling."

"Do you want to talk some more? Sometimes, talking *can* help.... Oh, Viktor, when I think of all those years ... !"

"I don't want to talk," he said stiffly. "I've never wanted to. I thought—except for the refuse of it in my mind—I was through with it until ... Nora, I didn't want you to have to know any of it, ever, but ... somehow, David Rosenzweig has recognized me. You've been right all along about his trying to place me. The other night, at Faye's party, when you were talking to him about Mitch's going to be a doctor and he asked you about that other name. Remember? You told me.... It was Koerner, wasn't it?"

"Yes," she said slowly, "yes, I think it was, but..."

"I was using that name then because Magnessen was obviously foreign in Germany, and we —I—thought another name might keep me from being interned, so that I could just go on with the work I was doing, the life I was living."

"I always have wondered why you didn't just leave."

"I had—ties. Someday, when I can, if I can ever again feel a little less of a coward and destroyer, I'll tell you, and the children, all of it I can. Since Rosenzweig has turned up and seems to be going to do—something, it seems the only remotely fair thing I can do for you all."

Nora had sat up in bed, shivering, the covers hugged around her. "You think David Rosenzweig was in that same—camp?"

"It's all I *can* think." He was fumbling his pipe from the pocket of a shirt that hung over a chair. "So far as I can recall, I've never seen him before in my life, but he was only a child then."

His hands shook so that he made a bad job of filling and lighting the pipe.

"But Viktor," she said pleadingly, "what if he was? What difference can it possibly make? Everyone in the county knows you were a prisoner of war. No one knows you were a doctor, of course, but . . . ?"

There was a sudden sinking feeling in her stomach, then a rising of nausea. "Oh, Viktor, they didn't . . . ?"

He sat down abruptly, laid the pipe in an ashtray. His contorted face was suffused in tears before he covered it with his hands.

"I had no direct part in killing people," he said brokenly. "I made no decisions about the gas chambers and crematories at other camps. I did no killing, but I aided in experiments that were damaging to human minds. No, I did no actual killing, but, on the other hand, I did no saving."

"Viktor, Viktor, darling!" She was beside him, her arms around his shoulders, which shook with sobs, her own tears falling on his hair.

After a long while, he grew quieter and finally he said in a muffled voice, "I think I'll go now."

"To Boise?"

"Yes." He raised his head to look at the clock. It seemed to Nora, her own chest rending with his pain, that he had aged in those moments his face had been hidden from her.

"Yes," he said more steadily, "it's past three. There's no point in trying to sleep now."

"I wish you wouldn't go at all when you're so—"

"You should want me out of your sight," he said dully. "I'm going to have a shower and—"

She began to cry almost hysterically then. "How can you say or even think a thing like that about *me?* That I'd want you out of my sight . . . ?"

"I'm sorry, Nora. God knows I don't want to hurt you. The truth is, *I* feel I should be out of your sight, that I should find a rock somewhere to crawl under and never be seen again. . . . When I knew I was falling in love with you, even up until the time of our wedding, I was always so near to running away, because of—this."

"But Viktor, *why?*"

"I didn't want you ever to have to know, and . . . I didn't want myself to remember."

"You've said you had no part in killing. I know you. You could never, never have done things to be so—ashamed about as you seem to be. In horrible situations like that, people do what they have to. My darling, I can't bear seeing you torture yourself like this."

"It's Rosenzweig," he said, shuddering. "He seems to remember. Perhaps he even remembers things I've managed to forget. The conscious mind is a fantastic defense mechanism, and I've had so many *good* years since, for trying to forget."

He left her and was gone for what seemed a very long time. Nora put on robe and slippers, turned up the thermostat, and went down to the kitchen to put on coffee. Viktor was dressed when he came down, his jacket over his arm, a briefcase in his hand. Nora put her arms around him.

"The coffee's almost done."

"There are the other things I must tell you," he said doggedly, "sometime later, when I can. They aren't things that should worry you, nothing to do with anything—criminal, nothing I would expect Rosenzweig to know or care about. They are just—parts of my life I've never told to anyone, and since this has begun, I think you have a right to know it all. I shouldn't mention the existence of anything more now because you'll only worry more. It's just that I feel you should be—warned that there is more. First, you must think of what I've told you now and give yourself time to know how you truly feel about it."

"I *know* how I truly feel. I truly love you. You're the man I've lived with for more than twenty-eight years. There's nothing you or anyone else can say that will change any of that. Won't you wait for the coffee? I made rolls yesterday."

"I'm sorry; I don't want anything. I have to be alone for a little now, to move around, to *do* something—"

"It's all right," she broke in as his tone grew more desperate. Her voice was gentle, but she was frightened for him. "Just two things: I don't ever want to hear you refer again to anything that has to do with you as 'criminal,' and please, please promise me you'll be very careful of yourself today."

25

David Rosenzweig was not at all pleased with his interview with the FBI agent on that Thursday afternoon. Though he was probably nearing thirty, the agent seemed excessively youthful to David. What could he know of the war? He had not even been born then. Also, though he asked many questions and seemed to be taking copious notes, David did not like his attitude. For one thing, he seemed to take his work, and this job in particular, very casually. For another, he seemed uncertain of what he ought to do with the information David had given him. Worst of all, his name was Ken Borman. Borman, for God's sake! David could see no humor, nor even irony in this; it only added to his weariness and feeling of futility.

After about an hour, young Borman got up to leave the mill office, saying he would report to his superiors, "get back to Mr. Rosenzweig." In answer to David's irritated question of when, Borman had shrugged and said, "Sometime next week, I would think."

"Aren't you going to talk with Magnessen?" David asked. "His store's just—"

"We'll have to check out some things first, Mr. Rosenzweig," the young man had said reasonably. "These are pretty serious charges we've been talking about."

David sat on in his office, doing nothing. He

found he had had visions of a stern, elderly agent who would remember things about the war firsthand, perhaps even another Jew, someone he might have felt inclined to invite home to dinner where the two of them could have disclosed, for Gloria's interest, what David was in the process of doing. He still had told her nothing.

Gloria was getting very restless now. The swelling of her injury was gone, and, though discolorations lingered from the bruising, she could cover them reasonably well with makeup. She was depressed, listless, dissatisfied, and, what worried him most, not nearly as voluble as usual about the feelings.

David buzzed for Mrs. Moore, then noticed it was past five-thirty. She and the rest of the office people would have left a half hour ago. Well, he hardly required a secretary for phone calls and personal reservations. He took up his phone and dialed for an outside line. He would, after all, have a nice little surprise to bring home to his wife.

26

Faye spent Friday morning with the contractor and decorator who were redoing the interior of her bookshop. She went for lunch to a small restaurant out toward the mill, and there she met Blanche Moore, David Rosenzweig's private secretary.

Blanche Moore had worked in the office at Holland's for thirty-five years. The lives of the mill people were her life.

"I'm so glad we ran into each other," she said, leaning eagerly toward Faye when they were seated at a table together. "I almost called you at home again this morning. I just had to tell you last night about that FBI agent coming in to see Mr. Rosenzweig yesterday. But now, something even stranger has happened. He was still there, the FBI man, when I left, and then, at about a quarter to six, Mr. Rosenzweig called Bert Adams to tell him he and his wife were taking a night flight to some place in Mexico, that he wouldn't be back in the office until Tuesday. He left a note on my desk, saying they had suddenly decided to take a little trip, that I should cancel his appointments for today and Monday. Now, isn't that *odd*, though? Do you think he's been mixed up in something? Or what in the world do you suppose?"

Over the weekend, speculation spread like a brush fire all through the county.

27

On the following Tuesday morning, Shane woke with less of a headache than usual. The accident had happened almost two weeks ago and it seemed to him damn well time he began to feel better. Except for a bout of pneumonia that had come when he was almost too young to remember it, he had never been really ill before and he tended to take the weakness, constant exhaustion, dizziness, headache, and continuing trouble with his eyes as personal affronts. The forced inactivity was driving him crazy. Charlie, before rushing off to New Mexico, had scooped all the books and papers pertaining to his business into a cardboard box, which he left at the Magnessen house. "In case," he told Shane solicitously, "you're up to doin' anything, there'll be somethin' for you to do."

Still lying in bed, hearing Patty clatter down the stairs, chattering something, Shane thought, I never knew how busy I've always been, and I wish to God this was done with. If I could get back to things—anything. He mightn't have minded the inactivity, might even have welcomed a part of it, if he had been able to read. His voracious reading had always been one of Charlie's chief complaints: "Always hidin' out some place with a book!"

But Charlie, who had quit school in the middle of the sixth grade, had a love for reading, too, if it were done by someone else. Many winter evenings when they were shut in alone together, at the ranch or the house in town, Charlie would stretch himself out on an old divan and say, "Whatever it is you're readin', I better hear some of it, see if it's fit for you." This had begun when Shane was about twelve. Charlie's personal tastes ran to Westerns, mysteries, and adventure novels, but he would listen, for a while, to anything. They discussed Shane's school books and argued over his own choice of reading matter.

"You'd read the dictionary," Charlie had grumbled once when Shane was reading him a dust-dry book of philosophy, "didn' have nothin' else handy. That there book's a pure waste of time—Stoics, Platonists, all them words! What kind of a philosopher you reckon you are?"

After a moment's thought, Shane had said he might be a hedonist.

"What's them?"

"People who take their pleasure when and where they can and don't worry much about paying the piper."

Charlie snorted. "That may be what *I* am, but you ain't. If you was, you wouldn' be readin' books like that."

Viktor had such a lot of books Shane longed to get at, but he could read only a few pages before the words began to blur and his head to ache worse. He had worked a little on straightening out the mess Charlie had made of his carefully kept business records, but that was even worse. He could keep his eyes in focus long enough to eat a meal with acceptable manners, to shave, to read his own mail, of which there had been two pieces—a postcard from Charlie, saying he wouldn't be back from New Mexico until the following weekend, and a brief note from the Bureau of Wildlife Management, with their regrets that they could not hold the High Lonesome job for him until the beginning of November. They had another applicant who could be there at the time they had specified.

Shane was sorry about the job, but he knew he probably would not have taken it anyway. There were so many things on his mind. He wished Nora would let him go home where, perhaps, some of the things he was trying to think out might come clear. She was a dear, good woman, but she would fuss over him, try to think of things to keep him entertained. The distractions here were sometimes almost as bad as those at the hospital.

He was worried about his eyes—frightened, no matter what the doctor kept telling him. His visual acuity was returning so slowly that he might not have been able to take the High Lonesome job, even if they had been willing to wait. . . . But mostly, there was Janet. . . .

Charlie had put Leonard Hall in charge of folding up the show, of knocking apart the flimsy buildings that were bunkhouse, cook shack, office, getting the boards under cover; bringing all the machinery down before it was snowed in up there. Shane had heard nothing from Leonard, had got no answer at his house the few times he had tried to call. He felt he ought to go up there, make sure of what was happening. Mitch, back from his hunting trip, was not yet working full-time at the store. He would be coming home early this afternoon to drive Shane to the doctor's. Maybe they could go up to camp tomorrow. Shane chafed miserably at having to make such requests of anybody, though Mitch would probably like the trip.

There had been several phone conversations with Vince Kucharski, the mechanic. Charlie had managed to have Big Red dragged out of the river and hauled to town just before he left.

"The only place," Vince had reported wearily, "where there's a guy *might* have what we need for that front end, is Brigham City, Utah."

"Then I guess someone will have to go and see about it eventually."

"Shane," Vince sounded close to tears, "I been

mechanicin' around here for twenty years, an' it seems like I must a' spent five a' them years workin', or tryin' to work, on that one goddam ole truck. He's goin' to end up this time spendin' more than enough to buy a new one. Good Christ, as far as I'm concerned—the insurance people, too—you totaled it. God knows I don't wish *you* any worse luck, but I do wish that ole truck would of caught fire."

He couldn't really care much, though, about Big Red or the folding up of the show, or the records. Those things were just diversions from Janet, that conversation on the Saturday night in the hospital. Some of it he was not quite sure he remembered clearly, but he knew he had said everything all wrong. He had waited tensely for her to come back so he could try again. When she did not return until Tuesday afternoon, he supposed things must be even worse than he had feared. Old Mr. Muller, the gallbladder patient, had had his daughter visiting him, and everyone knew that Lottie Franklin was one of the best, or worst, gossips in the county. She had eyed Janet avidly, not listening at all to her father's tenth recounting of his operation until Shane, who was sitting up in bed, had got up and pulled the curtain that closed the beds off from each other.

Janet had seemed oblivious to Lottie, to his action, to the pleading in his eyes. She was bright and brisk, almost brittle, in that way of hers that let those well acquainted with her know a storm was brewing. Worse of all, she kept giving her head that sharp little lift that rippled the hair down her back and stuck out her chin. "Hit me! You wouldn't *dare* hit me!"

They had had little to say to each other, though she chattered almost feverishly for fifteen minutes, about the weather, her pup Loki, the hunting and fishing business passing through Blackbuck. Things had been too hushed and listening on the other side of the curtain for him to say anything of any significance. Besides, he was afraid, from the way she was looking and acting, that anything he said might be used against him.

So now it was Tuesday again. She should be through with working for Ruby until Friday. And if she didn't come down today or at any time? That was one place he simply couldn't ask Mitch or anyone else to drive him.

He heard Patty going off to school and got out of bed, wishing he had got up earlier. Nora would insist on cooking him a breakfast he didn't particularly want, and it would have been easier for her if he had been down to eat with Patty. This afternoon, when he had seen Dr. Striker, he was going to tell Nora and the others that it was all right for him to be on his own now, and go home. Besides his own desire to be alone, there was a tension in this house he had never known before. Viktor looked older and tired, Nora's temper was short. Almost every day, she dropped at least one dish and broke it. She was cross with Patty. Mitch seemed oblivious to it, whatever it was, but for Shane it was almost a palpable thing and he felt in the way. Was it worry over Janet? *What* it was was none of his business. The fact that the household might be more comfortable without the extraness that was himself, was.

He dressed slowly—he had learned to do

everything slowly and with caution—and went downstairs.

It was a dismal morning, dark, with thickening, lowering clouds. "You can surely feel fall this morning," Nora said, trying to be cheerful.

She was moving about the house with her own particular, slow deliberation, getting things done, beds stripped, loads of laundry in washer and dryer, the dishes done, almost without seeming busy. Shane asked for something to do. Nora could see his desperation with being idle and she said,

"Well, Viktor picked his late peas yesterday evening. If you'd want to shell some of them . . ."

He did want to. He wanted to do anything.

"This will be about the end of the garden," she said. "I expect when this weather clears out, we'll have a real frost."

She wished, a little absently, that the rest of the pears and apples were in, but would not mention them for fear he would want to go and get them.

At lunchtime, she made soup and sandwiches, which Shane ate out of courtesy.

"Now you've got those peas ready," she remembered, preoccupied with other thoughts, "I don't believe I've got any freezer bags. I'll just run down and see if I can borrow a few from Betty. No use going to the store for just that."

Shane wandered aimlessly through the house and out on the front porch. Thank goodness, Nora had forgot, so far, to insist that he go up and take a nap. She was right about fall, the feel of it in the damp, chill, heavy air. A reluctant, misting rain was beginning. The mountains were obscured, but he knew there would be snow up there today, that when the clouds moved on or broke up, the mountains would emerge covered in fresh, bright whiteness.... Maybe he ought to try calling Leonard Hall again. Oh, the hell with it. It was Charlie who couldn't, or wouldn't, delegate authority. If Leonard hadn't seen things folded up and put away by now, it was too late to worry.

He picked up an armload of wood—bending made him dizzy and the dizziness made him angry, he had had enough of this weakness—and went to make a small fire in the living-room fireplace. When it was blazing and snapping, he sat down to read bits of the Boise paper, resting his eyes by looking, now and then, through the big window at the solid, restful gloom outside.

The back door slammed. "Mama? Where is everybody?"

It was Janet. The dampness muffled things and he had not heard the car go around the drive to the back of the house. He went into the kitchen.

"Well," she said, smiling brightly, "you still look pretty awful."

Her chest ached at his thinness, the bruises that discolored his pallor, the frown that puckered his straight, dark brows because he had concentrated too long on the newspaper and was now having trouble controlling his eyes.

She had Loki with her, on a leash, behaving reasonably well. "Did I see smoke from the chimney?"

He nodded.

She went past him, the dog trying to lick his hand, and stood in front of the fire, enjoying it. Then she told Loki to sit while she took off her coat, rearranged the fire, and put on more wood.

"It's starting to rain."

"I know."

"Where's Mama?"

"At Adams'. She'll be back soon, I guess."

She told the dog to stay several times and flitted out onto the porch to get more wood.

"Don't do that," he said, following her. "I can . . ." He brought his own armload.

"It's nice," she said, letting her wood drop with a crash and adding still more to the fire. "I'm almost out of wood up at Aunt Faye's."

"Is that why you came home?" He couldn't keep the bitterness out of his voice as he put his wood down more carefully and went to sit on the couch, drawing deep, slow breaths because he was dizzy and his vision blurring.

"Oh, Loki, you *are* such a *good* boy! Is there any coffee? No, don't move, silly. I'll get it. Do you want some?"

"No."

He closed his eyes while she was in the kitchen and regained most of his physical equilibrium. It would be better if he said nothing at all now, or as little as possible. There were sparks in her eyes and he knew too well the quick, nervous movements, the veneer of busyness. They would quarrel if he said much. He wished Nora would come home.

Janet came back with her coffee and the dog. "Loki, sit. Good boy! Now stay." Her eyes flicked up at Shane with unnecessary challenge. "Isn't he good? And smart?"

"He's almost miraculous," Shane said dryly, lighting a cigarette. Now he had done it, already.

"Well, you needn't get nasty," she said, giving her head that little defiant lift, then sipping her coffee. "I thought you liked dogs. The reason I came home was to bring you your car."

"Keep it for a while. I can't drive yet."

"Where's my motorcycle?"

"Janet, for God's sake, you're not—"

"No, probably not. I might borrow Mama's car, or Mitch's. There are plenty of vehicles around here, but you can at least tell me where my very own property is when I ask you as civilly as possible."

"I can't exactly. It was up at camp and—"

"What was that?"

"What?"

"Something just shut off."

"The washing machine, I suppose. I—"

"I'll go down and see, put the things in the dryer. Loki, stay."

She hurried away. Loki stayed for only a moment, then came to put his paws in Shane's lap, licked his face. He scratched the dog's ears absently.

"You aren't much help with him," Janet said irritably when she came back. She made the dog return to his place. "What do you mean, you can't drive? Are your eyes still that bad?"

She came to him, took his face in her hands, and tipped it up to scrutinize his eyes. He closed them.

"Shane Bonner, you always could be more aggravating than anybody in the world. Let me look."

"Why? You don't know anything about—"

"Just let me *see*, that's all! You're behaving like a two-year-old."

"*I am!* You've kept to yourself all this time when I—"

"My lord! They look like you've been on a two-week drunk! What's Dr. Striker doing about them?"

"He says—"

"Listen, I'm going to take you to Boise to an ophthalmologist. It's been long enough—"

"Will you sit down? Just sit down and be still a minute?"

She went back to her chair and coffee and said sulkily, "You're talking to me as if I were Loki."

"I want to talk to you as if—what I said the other night in the hospital ... I'm not sure I remember it all, but I know almost none of it came out right—"

"*Now* I think you're using your bad memory as an excuse. You do remember saying you felt superior," she said bitingly.

"I didn't mean it like that and you know it. It was the wrong damned word. I feel—"

"Hurt?" she said with sudden gentleness. "Mad? Frustrated to hell?" Then hotly, "Well, so do I."

"Janet, I do want to marry you."

"But you're not sure you can love me now, the way you think you ought to, and you're even less sure about the baby. At first, the other night, I thought I *did* understand what you were saying, but the more I've thought about it, the madder I've got. You just want to smooth things out a little for your dead best friend's sister."

"Goddam it! I can't help what's happened lately any more than you can."

"But isn't that how it is? how you feel?"

"Yes," he said fiercely, "that's some of it, but not nearly all. If you'll just shut up—"

"I told you the other night I'd think about it," she said tautly. "Well, the thought that's been uppermost in my mind almost ever since is: Don't do me any favors. On the other hand, maybe I don't have as much guts as I thought, but it would be for the folks' sake. Everyone will know, of course, when I got pregnant, but maybe it will be a little easier on Mama and Daddy if the baby is even a little bit legitimate. . . . We can go down to Nevada someday when you're feeling better, and then, when I'm over having the baby, I'll get a divorce."

"Janet—"

"You needn't worry that there'll be child support or anything like that. I can perfectly well—"

He was standing over her, shaking her shoulders.

"Damn! Now look! You've made me spill coffee on Loki. I wish he'd bite you. Loki—" and she was crying.

He drew her to her feet and put his arms around her.

"It's a strange way to accept a proposal," he said, still half-angry, his body aching with love.

"I took it as a proposition, not a proposal," she sobbed, furious with them both because she had started to cry. "I've only laid it on the line, exactly the way you did the other night. The baby's between us now and it'll be between us when it's born. You'll never forget. Worse than that, you can't forgive. I know you."

"You evidently don't know how much I love you."

"Oh, don't be magnanimous!" She pushed at him, trying to get free. "The fire needs—"

"The fire doesn't need anything. If you don't stop and listen—"

"What? Then what? You wouldn't dare hit a pregnant lady."

"A spanking is what you need."

She flashed a look up at him through her hot tears. "Well, don't try it. Your condition is as delicate as mine. I'll bet you two to one I could—"

The slow smile spread over his bruised face, into his reddened eyes, and she began to laugh with her crying, half-hysterically.

"Please give me a chance," he said tenderly, his cheek against her hair. "I haven't had much to do these past days but think. It was pride that made me say things the way I did the other night, all wrong. Who am I to—?"

"Don't be humble," she sobbed. "I can't stand it. It's *not* you. I'm the one who ought to be saying 'please.'"

"Then don't you be humble, because if you are, it's not you at all."

She laughed again, shakily. He led her to the couch and they sat down with their arms around each other. She had no handkerchief and he gave her one, saying, "I love you."

"I love you, but all this past week, I've been afraid you'd change your mind," she said, blowing her nose. "You can be so stubborn."

His lips opened, but he closed them in a firm, straight line.

She said, "The baby's a fact, Shane, and my wanting it is another. You still feel the same about the baby."

After a moment, he said slowly, "Yes, for

now, but can't we take things one day at a time? Feelings change."

"If we're married, we'll fight," she said desolately.

"Well, you see, there's one thing we can count on. We always have fought, sometimes. What would you say we've been doing just now?"

"I just wanted you to know how I feel," she said. "*I* wasn't fighting . . . but feelings *do* change."

He kissed her. Her mouth was warm and trembling, her breath still catching on sobs.

"I hate it when I cry," she sniffled. "And what I hate most is when you're hurt. I've been so stupid. For ten days now, I've been thinking back over the summer and spring and how I've hurt you. It was there, in your eyes, I can remember, but I just wouldn't see then. And I mean it about a divorce. Maybe things won't go right. Maybe you can't ever . . . if it's a mess, then we can just—"

"I don't think that's the way any marriage ought to start."

"But I can't go on hurting you. If you can't come to feel—at least to accept—"

They heard the back door. Nora was home.

"We'll work it out," he said softly.

"Yes," she said slowly, "maybe we can because we love each other. I'm going up to wash my face before Mama sees me. We can't say anything to any of them yet. I haven't even talked to Daddy about the baby." She ran upstairs.

28

A little later, Janet called Mitch at the store to say she'd be driving Shane to the doctor. She came back from the phone looking puzzled.

"Mitch left a half hour or so ago. He was going to deliver something before he came home. Daddy's up at the lake, helping someone figure out what he'll need for a house he's building.'"

Nora nodded. "A Mr. McCormack is having a summer place built, doing most of the inside work himself."

"Well," Janet said perplexedly, "Wes says there's been a man at the store, looking for Daddy, and he's on his way up here now. He was asking all sorts of questions and he's from the FBI."

Nora had had to spend an extra, nerve-wracking twenty minutes at the Adams' house, listening to old Belle speculate about what the FBI might "be after" David Rosenzweig for. She twisted her hands together now. "No, oh, no!" her lips said, though no sound came.

"Mama, what is it? Do you know what it's about?"

The pickup Mitch was driving and Ken Borman's car came to the house one behind the other, and the two of them came up to the front porch together.

"Mom?" Mitch said quizzically, "this is a Mr. Borman. He says he's from the FBI."

Ken Borman showed her his identification. "I was looking for your husband, Mrs. Magnessen, but I'd like to talk with you, too, if I may."

Shane had gone upstairs for his jacket. He stopped on the way down and would have withdrawn, but Nora said, "You've met our son Mitch. This is our daughter Janet, and Shane," she gestured him to come down, "Shane Bonner, our very good friend. Would you like some coffee, Mr.—uh—Borman?"

Nora's hands were shaking but she kept them gripped firmly together. The three young people kept looking askance from her to the strange young man.

"No, thank you, ma'am.... Maybe you'd rather we talked alone for just a few minutes?"

"No," she said decisively, "we'll all go into the living room."

He asked her when she had first met Viktor, when they had married, what she knew of his life prior to their meeting. Nora answered readily, quietly, but with very little detail.

"You know that Mr. Magnessen was in a prison camp during World War II?"

"Of course I knew."

"Mom," said Mitch, giving Borman a belligerent look, "I don't think you *have* to answer any of these questions, whatever they're about."

"That's right," Ken Borman agreed. "No one has to answer anything, right now, but there are a few things we're going to have to find out and it's so much simpler for everyone if we can just talk this way."

"It's all right," Nora said to Mitch. "I know Viktor would talk with him if he were here."

"Has your husband told you much about his war experiences?"

"No. He's never wanted to talk about it."

"But you know he was in the prison camp for more than four years? That he was a psychiatrist there, using the name Viktor Koerner?"

"Yes," she said almost inaudibly.

The others were staring at her, at Borman, at each other. She wished pityingly they might have known before, been warned, but Viktor had not mentioned the matters again since last Thursday night and she had not found the strength to bring it up again herself. She would never have told anyone without his consent, but what choice was there with this man here?

"Can you tell me why he changed his name and profession some time after leaving the camp?"

They heard the closing of a car door and Janet, at the window, said, "Here's Daddy now."

Viktor came in and shook Borman's hand with grave, seemingly calm politeness.

Wes had told him about the man who had come in, asking all manner of questions, until he, Wes, had asked a few of his own and been shown the official identification. "I thought," Wes had said, "he must be trying to find out something about Rosenzweig, though I couldn't think what I could tell him, but you know the talk that's been going around. But then—" his voice and manner became apologetic, embarrassed—"it seemed like everything he asked had to do with you. I didn't have any idea when you'd be back, so when he asked how to get up to the house, I thought I might as well tell him, because, if I didn't, someone else would. I was going to call Nora and tell her, but just then Janet called...."

"It doesn't matter," Viktor said quietly. He had taken hold of the edge of a counter and his knuckles were whitening.

"Viktor... if there's anything I can do..."

"McCormack wants the copper pipe ordered, beige fixtures, beige and white ceramic tile. These are the figures."

He supposed he must have driven home without speeding or breaking any traffic laws. Later, he could not remember the drive. All the while, he was thinking my poor Nora, and of each of the children; Paul, bitter and, perhaps, ready to believe; Alice angry, sure there was a mistake in the snarls of bureaucracy; Janet, furious, heartbreak in her big blue eyes; Mitch stripped of illusion, longing to strike back. And Nora, trying to balance them all, among each other, with him, trying to juggle the pieces of her family, her life and his, back to some semblance of what he had, all this time, let her believe it was.

He said now, to the young people in his living room, still speaking with calm equanimity, "Shane has the appointment with Dr. Striker. It's already late. Why don't you all go along?"

29 ℭ

Doreen Collins was giving a birthday party, just a little supper for her friend Clara Elkins. Clara had married Elvin Loomis thirty years ago and Elvin was now a regional representative of Pacific Slope Lumber. They had a son, Ronnie, who was following his father into the business.

There were only the three Loomises at the supper party, Doreen's parents, Bertha and Carter Sheppard, Peggy Lou, and Doreen herself. It was a Thursday night and Wes was keeping the store open late. Doreen was furious with him. *Anyone* could have kept the store open.

When Peggy Lou had flatly refused to stay on with the relatives in Kansas City—unknown to Doreen, Wes had given the girl money to pay her fare home when she was ready—Doreen had, sighing, decided she'd better come home to Cana, too. Wes wouldn't half-look after the girl. Bertha, after all those odd rumors they had been hearing by letter, had chosen to return as well. The rumors, hints, and speculations had come from Clara Loomis, who lived in Alder Falls, and who freely admitted she couldn't find out the straight of things for sure herself.

Since their school days, Clara had been Doreen's only good, long-lasting friend—though there were even now weeks at a time when they were not on speaking terms over some little tiff. The travelers to Kansas City had been back almost a week, and the occasion of Clara's birthday made an excellent excuse for getting together. Doreen and her mother agreed that the little party would be better held at the Sheppard home, but they wanted Peggy Lou present, and the girl refused to go to Alder Falls.

"Mama, you just want to get me together with Ronnie Loomis and you know I hate his guts," she had said calmly. "I always have, since he shut my cat up inside that old icebox and tried to kill him."

"You're just being silly to hold a grudge like

that," her mother had said petulantly. "He was just a baby then, and he didn't mean—"

"If he was a baby, then I was unborn. He was all of ten years old because I was in kindergarten that year."

Doreen had a cleaning woman once a week. She felt she should still have a live-in maid as she had when the children were small, but Peggy was what her mother ruefully called "the domestic type," and when Doreen had fired the last girl for "insubordination," Peggy had insisted she could do most of the kitchen work, and Wes, naturally, had agreed with her, paying her most of the maid's salary. She had stayed home from the store today to prepare the birthday meal, except that Doreen had decorated the cake and arranged flowers in living room and dining room; she could do those things beautifully.

And now, with the meal ready, Peggy Lou kept hinting that she could take some of the food to her father at the store, help him out until closing time. The girl was so fidgety, Doreen could have screamed.

As they sat down around the dining table, Carter Sheppard said grace. Everyone commented on how good everything looked and smelled and Doreen said,

"I only wish Bruce could be here. It seems like just forever since we've seen him."

"He ought to be back by Monday," said her father, who was meticulously carving the roast. "Floyd and I are thinking it might be a good idea to buy that sugar-factory interest that's available down in Utah. I wanted Bruce to go down and make a judgment all on his own so we can see what sort of businessman he may be turning into."

"I'm so *proud* of him!" said the mother happily. Dutifully, she asked Ronnie Loomis a few questions about how he was getting on in his own job. He answered in his laconic, bored way, taking large helpings of everything.

"Now," said Doreen eagerly, the amenities over, "Clara, I want you, or any of you, to tell us what's going on."

"Why you mean about Magnessens?" asked Clara mildly, but her eyes sparkled at being the center of attention. After all, there ought to be something to take a little of the sting out of being fifty-two years and three hours old. "But you're right here in Cana, Doreen, honey, and I'd think Wes—"

"Wes!" Doreen spat his name. "You might *think* anything about Wes, but all of you know good and well how close-mouthed he can be. And that one there"—indicating her daughter, who was looking innocently down at her plate—"is just as bad or worse. She's been at that store every day, and not a word."

"Mama, I don't know anything," said Peggy Lou reasonably. "I've told you and told you: Nothing's different at the store."

But she did know a few things. She knew she was worried half to death about Mitch. Something terrible had happened in his family while she was away, something that had caused him to move out of the house and go to work at Vince Kucharski's service station, rather than the store, something that made him unwilling to discuss their attendance at the same college in Janu-

312

ary, when they had both been looking forward to it so much.

"We-ee-ell," said Clara Loomis, enjoying herself, "I don't *know* much, but we have *heard* a lot of things."

She paused and Doreen demanded almost frantically, "What? What things?" More than Wes's silences and Peggy's lack of co-operation, Doreen was irritated and deeply hurt by the fact that, after all these years in Cana, she had no confidante here.

"Just after you went off to Kansas City," said Clara, "there were strange people all over the place—*federal* people. The first one went to the mill, Holland's, to talk to that Rosenzweig man. And all of a sudden, practically within the hour, those Rosenzweigs took off for a four-day trip, they said, to Mexico. Old Belle Adams found out about that and was telling it all over, and some heard it from Blanche Moore."

"Bert Adams is Belle's boy," pointed out her husband, Elvin, mildly, "and Blanche Moore's been working at Holland's since the beginning of time."

"They ought to look into that Rosenzweig man," said Bertha Sheppard righteously. "He's a strange one. I always have said so."

"There's talk he's putting Holland's up for sale," said Ronnie Loomis smugly and got a frown from his father.

Carter Sheppard gave a little start and looked sharply at Elvin Loomis. "Is *that* right? Now, *I* hadn't heard anything like that. I suppose PSL wouldn't mind . . . ?"

"We're looking into it," said Elvin smoothly but with just an edge of impatience.

313

"I'd say good riddance to bad rubbish if that pair did get out of this county," said Bertha, "him with his nose always stuck in the air and her flirting like a—well—with everything in pants."

"But it *wasn't* Rosenzweigs?" cut in Doreen with nervous impatience. "*Was* it?"

"Nooo," said Clara, having a thoroughly good time, "or at least not *just* them. It's something about Viktor Magnessen too. There was an FBI man in to see Sheriff Rex Terry—that is, while Rex *was* sheriff, before the elections—and one came up to the Adamses, I suppose because they're the Magnessens' closest neighbors. He went to the chief of police here and, I suppose, to Faye Holland, since everybody goes to her about everything. And I just *know* he must have gone to the store, Doreen."

Doreen was flushed with embarrassment, near tears. Wes would never talk to her about anything important.

Bertha Sheppard said, irked, "Well, if any federal people talked to Rex, Amy Terry's not saying anything about it. I was with her the other day at garden club and couldn't get a word out of her about any of it."

"Belle Adams is the best source of information," said Clara knowledgeably. "She knows pretty nearly everything that happens at this end of the county."

"Or thinks she does," muttered Elvin.

"Oh, hush up now, Elvin," she said impatiently. "You'll make me forget where I was with my story. It was Ona Farrell that told me about them coming to see Rex Terry. Ona works right

314

across the street at the bank, and she saw the FBI car—"

"I don't think they mark their cars," broke in Peggy Lou, tensely, too loudly.

"Oh, just be still!" snapped her mother.

"Ona Farrell," said Clara complacently, "is Belle Adams' niece. They compared notes. It's the same car that's been at Magnessens' and the same one that came to Adamses."

"What did they say to Bert and Betty Adams?" asked Bertha avidly.

"That's one of the aggravating things," said Clara, a little deflated. "It seems like they must have called and made an appointment without Belle knowing about it, because it was on her missionary society meeting night. Their oldest girl—I can't remember her name—took Belle off to the church. They met that same strange car not a block down Tamarack Road and Belle saw it turn in the Adamses' driveway. She began to tell her granddaughter she'd forgot something, but I guess the girl had had her orders because she started driving faster. She'd just got her license a few days before and Belle was afraid to do much. When she got home, they wouldn't tell her anything about any company."

"Then," said Ronnie, with his mouth half-full, "some different federal guys started coming around besides the FBI."

"How do you know it was the FBI in the first place?" demanded Peggy Lou.

"Who else *would* it be?" he asked, smirking at her. "Some people say this new man is from the CIA."

"My land!" breathed Bertha, awed. "Car-

315

ter, why can't you keep up with a thing like this? I turn my back and go to Kansas City for just two weeks—"

"Now, hon, I've been in Boise and Idaho Falls and clear down in Utah—"

"Have they been into something *together?*" mused Doreen, "Viktor and that Rosenzweig?"

"It could be something from as far back as the Second World War," said Elvin Loomis. "Everybody here knows they were both in Germany then. At least, some people think it could have to do with that."

"PSL might just get a pretty fair bargain on the Holland Mill," said Carter softly, and the two men smiled knowingly at each other.

"I think you're all just making mountains out of molehills," said Peggy Lou lightly. "Do you want me to bring in the cake now?"

"I certainly do not," snapped her mother, "but I do want you to stop your rudeness. You can see nobody's through eating yet. Eat your own dinner."

"Molehills some of it may be," said Clara Loomis comfortably, "but it's no molehill that Paul Magnessen withdrew from the county commissioners' race just a few days before election time, and almost everyone thinks he could have won, too, if those stories hadn't started getting around."

Peggy Lou said staunchly, "Daddy said he withdrew because there was going to be a conflict of interest about the Cloud Valley project. They're going to bring it up for county approval soon, and if Paul had been a commissioner, somebody might have—"

"All that may be so, miss," said Clara snappishly, "but he *did* withdraw just at the time these other things started coming out in the open, and I hear he and Sharon are about to separate, but I expect that's over Cloud Valley, or it may be all of it together."

"And it's not so much of a molehill," added Ronnie with malice, "that your very good friend Mitch has moved out of his folks' house and won't work at the store."

They were all looking at her now, and Peggy felt her face going hot.

"Get some hot rolls," Doreen said curtly. "Can't you see there's just one left on the plate? And it's bound to be stone cold."

When Peggy was in the kitchen, her mother said, "That's one thing I've got to be thankful for, that she's not seeing so much of that boy. The way she acts, I think he may have changed his mind again about going to school. I'd thank God every minute of my life if I could get her off to college and clear away from him. I get the notion—not that any of them *tell* me anything straight out, mind you—that he may be giving up his la-de-da notions about being a doctor."

"Has this—whatever it is—hurt business at the store?" asked Carter as his granddaughter returned with the bread.

"Wes says," reported Doreen dubiously, "that it's better than ever."

"It is," affirmed Peggy Lou angrily. "People came in to snoop around, trying to find out things, and we make them feel like, since they're there, they must have come in to buy something. Shane's awfully good at that."

"Shane Bonner?" asked Clara. "I didn't know—"

"Oh, yes," said Doreen petulantly. "They got him to start work down there as soon as he could see straight after that accident. I don't like for Peggy Lou to associate with people like that. Everyone knows what Steve was, and . . . well, thank the lord that Bruce is doing something worthwhile now."

Bertha was shaking her head, clicking her tongue. "Surely, with all this other that's going on, they could try to find a worker with a better reputation."

"What's wrong with *Shane's* reputation?" cried Peggy Lou. "What's he ever done? He can't help who his parents were, or are, any more than the rest of us can. I never heard such a bunch of picky old—"

"Now, that will be enough, young lady," said her grandfather sternly. "That's no way to talk to your elders."

After a little silence, her enjoyment only slightly and briefly subdued, Clara said, "We did hear once—oh, a week or so ago, wasn't it, Elvin? —that he was going to marry Janet."

"Well, he hasn't," said Doreen righteously, glad there was *something* she could tell. "He's been living at their house since he got out of the hospital, and *she's* been living there since the end of October. I always did say Nora and Viktor spoiled those children, but that's just a little too much."

"You mean," said Clara, opening her myopic eyes wide, "you think they're—"

"Clara, I wouldn't be surprised at anything anymore. That's why this investigation business —whatever it is—doesn't surprise me one bit, and whatever comes of it won't be any surprise.

I just wish my family wasn't so mixed up with them in business. I've been thinking for several years now that Viktor would be retiring and maybe we could—borrow the money to buy out his interest...."

She had glanced significantly at her father and Elvin Loomis said, smiling, "That might turn out to be another good, reasonable business proposition, Carter."

"I've heard he's sick," said Clara, "Viktor, I mean."

"I saw him once at the store since we got back," said Doreen. "He looks like a ghost. I've called Nora twice, just trying to be friendly. The first time, I could hardly get two words together out of her. The second time, that snip Janet answered and said her mother couldn't come to the phone."

"Well, I think that's as much as anyone could be expected to do," said Bertha. "After all, the way some of that family has been carrying on, and still seems to be, and now this other business, two phone calls is as much concern as they deserve."

Peggy Lou, without asking, went to get the cake now, before she started crying and screaming at them in anger and frustration. It was the talk about phone calls that had been the last straw. Why *wouldn't* Mitch call her? Mitch, please, please! I just want to help. Somehow, I know I can. Please let me!

She had called him several times when she had the store office to herself, both at old Charlie's where he was now living, and at Kucharski's station, where he worked. She had seen him only once, very briefly, since her return from Kansas

City. Both at that meeting and on the phone, he had been gentle and considerate, but somehow preoccupied, as if only half his mind were aware of her. He had said they shouldn't see each other for a while, that he didn't know anything now about any plans for the future. The hurt in his eyes, even the memory of it, seemed as if it would break her heart. She had talked, a little, about him to both her father and Shane. They hadn't said so, but both of them, particularly Shane, seemed angry with Mitch, and they gave her essentially the same advice, that the best thing would be to leave him alone for a time. Peggy Lou was trying, but it wasn't easy. Surely he needed to talk to someone. Her love could help him, help rid his eyes of that hurt bewilderment. She would like to have talked the thing over with Mr. and Mrs. Magnessen; they had always been her friends; but it was true when her mother said Viktor looked like a ghost. He had become, almost overnight it seemed, a sick old man, and Nora had that same absent, bewildered look as Mitch. Whatever was happening was falling chiefly on them, on Nora and Viktor; it was something they, or one of them, had done. It wasn't right, then, that Mitch should be suffering so.

Peggy Lou had tried talking with Janet once, but Janet had been very abrupt, evidently impatient and angry with Mitch, preoccupied in that same way they all were.... If Wes knew precisely what was happening, Peggy Lou believed he would tell her. It couldn't be *that* bad. He knew she wouldn't spread any talk, but was only interested in Mitch.

Well, she *would* find out somehow, and she *would* do something. If he didn't call her soon, then one night when old Charlie was out drinking...

"Margaret Louise!"

"Yes, Mama," she answered meekly and went into the dining room to gather up the dishes.

"So they've just sort of changed places," Ronnie Loomis was musing.

"Who?" asked his mother.

"Mitch and Shane."

"If the Magnessen girl doesn't marry somebody soon," said Elvin, leering, "there won't be a bit of need in it."

Peggy Lou wheeled out a cart of dishes and Doreen said angrily, "They've got *her* working at the store, too."

"*Janet!*" cried Bertha, "in that shameful condition? Doreen, honey, I'd give anything if you could get Peggy Lou to stay away from that store."

Doreen was close to tears. "Mama, you know I can hardly do a thing with her. Wes has never let me give the child a proper upbringing. You know how contrary he can be, and he has always encouraged her to be just like him."

Ronnie said, smiling speculatively, "I'll bet it's not even that black-bearded hippie kid's baby. Maybe it's Bonner's after all, or—"

"Ronnie!" cut in his mother.

"You may well be right, son," said the father, "but I don't like the frank way you young people talk about such things these days, and I'll thank you to remember there are ladies present."

"Well," said Bertha, clicking her tongue, "*this* lady says that if she can get anyone to marry her *now*, she'd better grab the chance, no matter who or what he is."

Peggy Lou carried in the cake with its lighted candles and moved her lips as they sang "Happy Birthday," though in truth, and probably unfairly, she hoped Clara Loomis was having a lousy birthday. Peggy Lou tried to leave unobtrusively without having any cake, but then almost lost her temper when they tried to stop her.

"You've hardly touched a bite of anything," fretted her grandmother.

Peggy Lou went back to the kitchen, put on a pot of coffee, and began loading the dishwasher. Her mother's and grandparents' and all their "good" friends' religion forbade the drinking of coffee or almost anything else, but she always tried to have a pot ready when her father came home, if she were there before him.

Ronnie followed her to the kitchen before she was finished with the cleaning up and asked her to come for a ride in his new sports car. Her refusals, less and less polite, were getting her nowhere, and she was menacing him fiercely with the meat platter when her father came in by the back door. Ronnie faded away to the living room, where the others had gone.

Peggy gave Wes a cup of coffee and he rested a hand briefly on her head.

"Thanks for doing all this for your mother," he said. "I guess she's had a nice time."

"They've all had just a lovely time, gossiping and gossiping," said the girl, tears springing to her eyes. "Daddy, did you see Mitch today?"

"No, Peg, I didn't."

"Do you know anything more about—?"

He was shaking his head. "Just that we've had a shipment canceled. Is Elvin Loomis still here?"

"Yes."

Wes went to the living room to greet the guests, coffee cup in hand. Peggy Lou followed and stood just inside the door.

"I'd like to bring up a little business talk, Elvin," Wes said when he had briefly greeted the others. He did not sit down and he looked tired. "We got word, last thing this afternoon, that Holland's—Rosenzweig's—won't sell us any more new lumber. We'll have to see about buying from PSL."

There was a little silence and Elvin Loomis, not quite able to conceal a triumphant little smile, said, "Time was, Wes, way back, when you and Viktor Magnessen told me you wouldn't buy from us if—"

"*I* don't think you ought to sell to them, Elvin," snapped Clara. "You don't know what you might be getting into, with the CIA and—"

"What do you know about whatever this is that's going on, Wes?" demanded Carter Sheppard.

"Nothing," Wes said, "except all it has to do with Alder County is in the pretty nearly empty heads of a bunch of tongue-waggers. Whatever those people are snooping around about happened a long time ago, and far away."

"Well, is it mostly Magnessen, or mostly Rosenzweig, or—?" began Elvin Loomis.

"What I know for sure about it right now," Wes said calmly, "is that we need a lumber supplier, Elvin. Do you want the business, or not?"

"Where else would you go?" Doreen tried to ask the question sweetly and with concern, but couldn't hide a little note of triumph.

They waited. Wes said coolly, "We could

323

look for another supplier, or we could cut down most of the lumber part of the business until—"

"You'd let that man, somebody under investigation by *federal* people, ruin your business!" cried Bertha.

"I never knew you thought it was that much of a business, Mama Sheppard," said Wes, smiling faintly.

"Make him sell out to you, Wes!" cried Doreen, "before we're all ruined. Think of Uncle Floyd's political career. Think about your own children, for the lord's sake!"

Wes was seeing Viktor Magnessen's stricken face ("I'll have to get out, Wes, before the whole business is ruined.") He watched Elvin Loomis's face, waiting.

"I've heard some people are canceling orders *from* your store," said Ronnie.

"That's hardly going to put PSL into bankruptcy," said Wes coldly, not bothering to look at the younger man.

"Well, I tell you, Wes," said Elvin, leaning back expansively in his chair, "I expect you'd have to pay a little steeper price than you've had from Holland's, what with longer delivery distance and all."

"Yes. We thought we might."

Elvin nodded soberly. "You can tell Viktor I'll be in my office all afternoon tomorrow."

"Viktor?"

"Why, yes, he's the senior partner, I believe. I just supposed—"

"I'll come and see you, Elvin, around two. Happy birthday, Clara. You'll all excuse me now, I think?"

324

"Where are you going at this time of night?" Doreen was fighting to control her voice.

"Peggy Lou and I are just going to run up and let Viktor know that—providing the terms aren't too outrageous—we're going to be dealing with PSL for a while. Yes, sir, by God, just like the big boys."

30

At three o'clock on the Saturday afternoon following Thanksgiving, Nora was putting a casserole into the oven. This was the last of the turkey and she supposed the family would be glad, though this year there had been almost none of the usual comments about how long the bird's remains lasted. Faye and old Charlie and Shane had been with them for Thanksgiving dinner, but fewer of the real, blood family than ever before. Sharon and Jamie had come, but not Paul, not Mitch, and of course it had been a long time since Alice had been able to spend a Thanksgiving at home. Nora, sensibly, had not bought quite such a large turkey as in former years. By next year ... Oh, God! What? By next year? How many of them would be together? *Where* would they be?

A heaviness had been growing in Nora these past weeks; not of physical weight—her plump face was looking thinner. They said you didn't really feel pain or joy, love or hate in your heart, that it was some glandular reaction and the feelings you got more probably came from your stomach, but this heaviness in Nora *felt* like her heart. It dragged at her, hurting, sometimes making breathing seem difficult, wearing her down, awake or asleep. She straightened up slowly, then turned quickly at the sound of feet on the back steps.

"Viktor?"

He came in quickly and closed the door against the cold. His face was gray and drawn. Even some of the crispness seemed to have wilted out of his white hair. His eyes sometimes had a blank look, as if he were trying to shut in the hurt and confusion and questioning, to bear it all within himself. His voice was the same, deep and quiet, but he often spoke with a slight intonation of apology.

"Charlie came into the store a while ago," he said. "You know Charlie. If he's going to be around, he's going to be helping out with the work. Wes and Shane and Peggy are there. Business was slow, so I thought..."

Nora couldn't recall when he had come home in the middle of a business day, except for an emergency, the illness of a child, or something very special to be celebrated. He was shivering. She went and put her arms around him, saying nothing because she wanted more than anything to make a fuss over him and he never liked that.

"It's damp out," he said, leaning his cheek against her hair, speaking with that edge of apology, almost as if he were asking her to forgive him for being. "I don't think the heater in the pickup is working right. I can't seem to get warm."

"Why don't you have a nice hot bath?" she suggested.

"Yes, I was thinking of that and—maybe a nap before supper."

She looked at him fleetingly, trying not to show the fear and concern. Viktor almost never took naps. God knew he needed the rest, but...

"I suppose it will be turkey?" he said, smiling wanly.

"Yes, but this will be the last of it. I hadn't planned that we'd eat until around seven. You could get a good long nap."

When he came from the steaming bathroom, warmed, though still shivering sporadically, she was just finishing making up their bed with fresh linens. The book he had been reading, or pretending to read last night, was on the night table, and beside it a glass of brandy.

"Nora," he said tenderly, gratefully.

"Here, just get in bed," she said matter-of-factly, holding back the covers, "before you get cold again. You don't suppose you're catching a cold...?"

"No, I'm only—a little tired."

He caught her hand and she sat beside him on the bed.

"There was a letter from Alice today," she said.

"And what does she have to say?"

Nora held the brandy for him.

"I'm hardly an invalid," he said, but, smiling a little, he drew himself up on the pillows and sipped, not taking the glass into his own hands.

"Her letter is mostly about her job," said Nora. "You can read it when you come downstairs—and that she expects to have about a week at home at Christmas. She's already seeing about reservations and things."

"Poor Alice," he said softly.

"She's got to know things some time. She's part of the family." Nora tried to smile. "Maybe you ought to say 'poor us' for when she comes home and gets hold of things and starts straightening them out."

"I think," he said, "she might at least have been told about Janet's baby."

"Yes, but Janet doesn't want it. She says Alice would be calling once or twice a week, trying to see that something proper is being done, and she's right, of course. Alice loves us, but she's such a mother hen.... I've supposed for the past month or more that Janet and Shane would be married well before Christmas and that Alice would just have to draw her own conclusions, or maybe even keep her mouth shut. Why *don't* they get it done, Viktor?"

"You know neither of them will have the wedding in this county. They want to go to Nevada and they—well, I think they're a little afraid of leaving—us, among other things."

"We could go with them, for the lord's sake, if that's all it is! Every other minute, they're quarreling. Sometimes I think it won't ever work out at all. If he were acting nasty about it, like he were doing her a favor or something, I might understand Janet. But Shane's not like that. He loves her. You can *see* it, and there's no question anymore of keeping the baby secret any longer. She's seven months along, maybe a little more. She's really got no business making a trip like that now. I just don't know ..."

"Would it bother you terribly, having an illegitimate grandchild?"

"Of course it would bother me," she said

curtly, "when there's not a reason in the world why it has to be that way. If it was that Gary Hunt, I'd do anything in the world I could to get her *not* to marry him, but Shane—well, we've talked before about how long he may have loved her, and she loves him, I *know* she does, but she's so stubborn. She needs a good spanking is what she needs. I've heard her accuse him of only wanting to marry her because he's fond of the family."

"Pregnant women can sometimes be very perverse," he said, moving her hand a little so he could sip the brandy. "Do you remember before we were married—?"

"*I* wasn't pregnant," she said vehemently.

He smiled. "No, but what we talked about more than anything else was Paul. You were afraid I was just feeling sorry for a poor, lonely, pretty young widow."

She laughed a little. "I never thought anything about *pretty*." Then, sobering, "Well, there's still Paul. I just know he's not living at home now, Viktor. I couldn't bring myself to ask Sharon on Thanksgiving. She looked so miserable and was trying so hard not to let it show. Have you seen him?"

"Not to talk to, really. He was in the store a few days ago, but..."

"Is he just trying to stay away from us now because...?"

"I think he thinks it would be good business practice just now," he said wearily.

"I've brought the bottle," Nora said. "It's on the dresser. Do you want some more?"

"No, thank you, my darling girl."

"Then I'll go so you can sleep."

"You needn't hurry," he said. "Thank you for . . . it's good to be here with you."

Tears stung Nora's eyes. She got up and poured just a bit of brandy for herself.

He said quietly, "Charlie says Mitch is fine, doing well with the new job."

"I wasn't going to ask about Mitch," she said shortly. "He knows where home is."

Viktor was thinking back to that day when Ken Borman of the FBI had first come to the house, when he, Viktor, had sent the three young people away to keep Shane's appointment with Dr. Striker. But they had already heard his questions to Nora. It was the fact that Viktor had once been a doctor that was so difficult and bewildering, particularly for Mitch. The boy had gone straight up to his room when they came home that afternoon. Janet had busied herself in the kitchen with Nora. It was Shane who had come out in that cold, misting drizzle and helped Viktor get in the rest of the pears and apples, lest there be a freeze that night. Shane's hands shook and he was white with exhaustion.

"You shouldn't be doing this," Viktor had said after a time. His own hands were trembling.

"Nor you," Shane had answered softly and gone on gently putting the fruits in his basket.

If they had been complete strangers at the beginning of it, Viktor would have loved Shane Bonner after that hour together in the cold rain. He wondered if his own son Viktor would have been capable of such understanding, such sensitivity, of showing such empathy with two words and the gathering of pears and apples.

Mitch had scarcely spoken at home until the next evening, after Patty was in bed.

"Well, aren't you going to tell us anything?" The question seemed ripped from him.

After a little silence, Viktor said, "You heard Mr. Borman's questions and your mother's answers. They were a part of the truth."

"But what's the rest of it? What are *you* going to say?"

"Mitch, I would like to say nothing more for a while. I must think. These things—I've tried for so many years to push them down in my mind, to forget what I could. Now I must begin sorting through them again, and I must know what these people are going to do—about me. Mr. Borman thinks probably this is not a matter for the FBI to handle. He must talk with other people. I tried, last night, to tell your mother all of it. She has the first right to know. Before I talk with the rest of you, I need—a little time."

"For what? Are you a war criminal? Is that why you've been hiding? Were you one of those doctors who—"

"Stop it!" Nora cried.

She, too, had said almost nothing through that day. She had said almost nothing during Viktor's recounting of that other life. She had dropped and broken three dishes today, and scorched a hole in Patty's best dress. It would be days before she could get back to any semblance of her old self.

When he had finally finished with it, Viktor had offered to sleep in one of the other bedrooms and she had said stonily, "Only if it's what you want."

331

But when he would have gathered his things and gone, she had cried out miserably, "Oh, Viktor, don't! I can't talk about it now. There's so much I never dreamed...I'm just numb.... You seem—a little bit of a stranger to me now, after all these years, but it's not because of anything you've done. It's only that I didn't know.... I—I just need some time, but—in that time, we still need to be close to each other. I couldn't bear it if you went away."

And on this next night, she went on fiercely to Mitch, "Don't you talk to your dad like that."

Mitch said desperately, "I thought my life was all set. Now I don't know. I just don't know about anything. Maybe there's something to be ashamed of in a Magnessen's being a doctor."

"Oh, stop feeling sorry for yourself," Janet snapped. "Can't you think about—"

"Leave him alone, Janet," Viktor said gently, and to his son, "When I've had some time to bring it into the light again, when I know what's to be done about it by the authorities, then I will tell you."

"You've just said you told Mom. I don't know what you mean about bringing it into the light and—"

"I will tell all of you all of it I can, you, Paul, Alice, Janet, Shane, maybe a few others who have been very close to us and have a right to know because of friendship. Maybe you will think it weakness, Mitch, cowardice, but I can't tell these things over and over and over, and I won't have the burden of discussing it fall on your mother, not even once."

"All at once, you're saying we have a right

to know. If that's true, then why didn't you . . . ?"

Viktor said, "I didn't think it was possible that it would all come up again after so much time. I had thought I was protecting you—and myself."

Nora said, "It was all really so long ago, Mitch. It really has nothing to do with your life."

"The hell it hasn't!"

"Don't you—" began Janet, but Viktor held up his hand.

"Please let's not quarrel now."

After a little silence Mitch said, "How much time? How long do you have to think and wait?"

"I can't say, son. A few weeks at least, I'm afraid, until we know what the authorities decide."

The boy stood up. "Well, I can't stay here. I won't, and I can't go on working at the store until I know—something. The thoughts that keep going through my mind... I've heard about those concentration camps and the things—"

"Just shut up and get out then!" cried Janet, tears spilling down her face.

Shane spoke for the first time then. He said roughly, "Here's a key to Charlie's house. When he comes back tomorrow, tell him we've decided to switch living places for a while."

Nora said now, tentatively, as she swallowed the last of the few sips of brandy, "Viktor, did you hear from anyone today? The immigration people or . . . ?"

"No," he answered gently, "I don't think we can expect that for another week or two. I did hear from Harvey Grant, though. It seems he's found he can get a better price on the plumbing and other fixtures for his house at Corley's in Alder Falls. It's the third fair-sized order we've had canceled this week, and with having to get our lumber from PSL—"

"*Damn* them!" cried Nora, and for a moment he thought she would fling her glass against the wall. "They haven't got the least idea of what's going on. They're making up bogeymen to scare themselves with, like little children. Oh, Viktor, if you'd only get *mad* . . ."

"How can I, Nora? I'm the one who—"

"You haven't done anything! *I* could kill David Rosenzweig for dragging up all these things that he doesn't know much more about than the people in Cana."

"Some of the things he has said are true," he said wearily.

"They are *not!* Not the way he's twisting them."

After a time of silence when he would not meet her fierce eyes, he said stiffly, "You know I can't let Wes's business be ruined."

"It's *your* business, *our* business, not just Wes's."

"But Wes isn't old enough, or ready, to retire."

"And neither were you, a month or two ago."

"When we know, Nora, the town will know. If they don't know the truth, then they'll make up something. If I'm not deported—"

"You will *not* be deported, Viktor Magnessen. The man told us there's a statute of limitations and it's run out. Even if you *had*—"

"On everything except murder," he said almost inaudibly.

Nora burst into tears. "Viktor, I can't bear this load of guilt you *will* carry. I just can't. You couldn't kill anyone or decide anyone should be killed. I've lived with you too long. I know things were different in that camp—horrible—and that you can't remember a lot of it clearly, but I know David Rosenzweig is lying. Maybe, if we *have* to be charitable, we can try to believe he doesn't know he's lying. He was only a little boy at the time... but you! For God's sake—and mine—you've got to get hold of yourself, to know yourself again and have a little faith. You can*not* just give up like this! I won't let you.

"I suppose the next thing, you'll be talking about one of those awful retirement communities or something. Well, *I* don't want to be run out of our home—away from friends that count and everything we've worked for—by a David Rosenzweig and a few old granny gossips who'll have something else to occupy their tongues in another few weeks.

"Now, I want you to drink another glass of this brandy and have a good nap. The lord knows when you've had a decent night's sleep, with those dreams and...."

"Nora, Nora," he said tenderly, his face still averted.

"We've provided enough talk for this county," she said angrily, spilling some of the brandy on the dresser as she poured it and mopping at it fiercely. "Besides being a Bicentennial year and Cana Year, it's been a Magnessen year, with Janet's carryings-on, Paul and Sharon maybe breaking up, Mitch running away from home, and this other thing that they just clack and yak about without knowing a thing for sure. I've had enough. You retire if you want to, but it'll be a cold day in summer before I tuck my tail between my legs and start hiding from the likes of Cana, Idaho."

Viktor's face was buried in the pillow. The strain was telling on him so heavily that he felt near hysteria, not knowing if he would laugh or cry in the next instant.

"I don't remember," he said, his voice muffled and breaking. "I've tried for so long to forget so many things about the camp that I'm not sure anymore about some of it, what's true and what isn't, but you—you are so marvelous. I have to try to fight because—because I can't expect you to do it all alone."

"The first thing you have to do," she said, and her tone was angry, though tears had begun to run down her cheeks, "is believe in yourself again. Then you can worry about me and the children and Wes and the business and Cana and the rest of the world. Now drink this. Don't just sip it; drink it down so it'll make you sleepy. It's easier to feel confident about anything when you've had a good rest. Nobody's going to bother you. It would be the best thing in the world for you right now to sleep straight through until tomorrow morning."

"I may never know," he said bleakly, his face still turned away from her. "I may never remember it all."

She was kneeling by the bed, forcing him to a half-sitting position and putting the glass in his hand. "But you know who you are. Nobody changes from a good person to a—a ghoul and back again. People just aren't made that way. You

Indulge your fantasies with The Doubleday Book Club.

Here's how our Club Plan works:

You'll get your six books for only 99¢ plus shipping and handling—and a FREE Tote Bag—when accepted as a member. If not satisfied, return the books within 10 days to cancel your membership and owe nothing.

About every four weeks (14 times a year) you'll receive our magazine describing our two Club Selections and at least 100 Alternates. The Extra-Value Selection is always just $2.98 (up to 60% off publishers' edition prices). The Featured Selection and Alternates save you up to 50% off publishers' edition prices. In addition, up to four times a year you may receive offers of special selections, always at big discounts. A charge is added for shipping and handling. If you want both Club Selections, do nothing—they will be shipped automatically. If you'd prefer only one Selection, an Alternate or no book at all, indicate this on the order form and return it before the date specified. You'll have at least 10 days. If you do not have 10 days and receive books you don't want, you may return them at our expense.

Once you've purchased just six books during your first year of membership, you may resign or continue with no further purchase obligation.

The Doubleday Book Club offers its own complete hardbound editions, sometimes altered in size to fit special presses and save members even more.

The Doubleday Book Club
Makes your fantasies affordable.

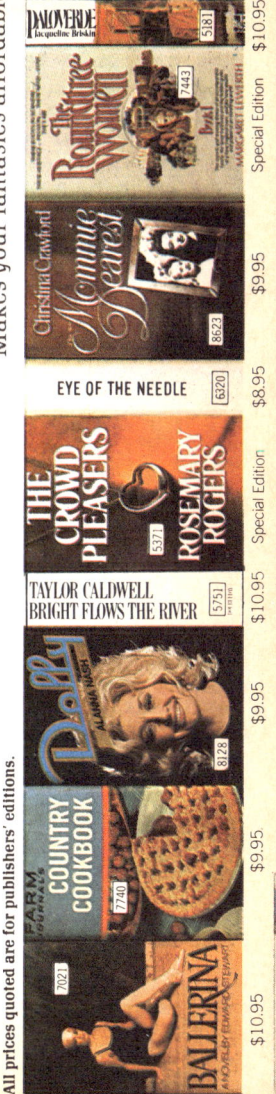

All prices quoted are for publishers' editions.

7021	7740	8128	5751	5371	6220	8623	7443	5181	0869
$10.95	$9.95	$9.95	$10.95 Special Edition	$10.95	$8.95 EYE OF THE NEEDLE	$9.95	$10.95 Special Edition	$10.95	$10.00 Warning Sexually Explicit

At 6 for 99¢, you can afford 6 new fantasies this month.

Title	Price	Code
LOOKING TERRIFIC	$10.95	6445
John Travolta Scrapbook	$4.95	4752
O/786 4 Volume set	$3.95	—
THE ESSENTIAL GUIDE TO PRESCRIPTION DRUGS	$25.00	3277
YARGO — Jacqueline Susann	Special Edition	8904
War and Remembrance — HERMAN WOUK (2 Volume Set)	$15.00	7278
Same Time, Next Year	Special Edition	7922
THE INSIDERS — ROSEMARY ROGERS (Warning: Sexually Explicit)	Special Edition	8425
A Necessary Woman — Helen Van Slyke	$10.95	8516
Betty Crocker's COOKBOOK	$9.95	5322
By Myself — LAUREN BACALL	$10.95	3011
THE FAR PAVILIONS — M.M. KAYE (2 Volume Set)	$12.95	6536
Wifey — Judy Blume (Warning: Sexually Explicit)	$8.95	6957
NORMAN ROCKWELL'S Counting Book	$6.95	6502

know what a good life we've had, and that there's some of it left."

"There may be a hearing..."

"Then there will be."

"How long can you stand things to go on like this? or maybe worse?"

"As long as I have to, Viktor. As long as we have each other."

Nora went downstairs, the brandy bottle in her hand. She took the kitchen phone off the hook and, taking up the afghan she was crocheting for Janet's baby, sat where she could see if anyone came up on the front porch, to forestall their ringing the doorbell. Then she realized she still had the brandy bottle. Smiling a little sheepishly, she went into the dining room for a glass.

Nora had had perhaps two dozen intoxicating drinks in her life. She came near to hysteria, thinking how funny it would be if the children came home and found her falling-down drunk, baby afghan, burned supper, and all. She dropped the glass, one from a set that had been her grandmother's. She began to cry then, and to mutter words that had never before passed her lips.

When the broken glass was cleaned up, she determinedly took several swallows of brandy straight from the bottle and put it away. She began to feel calmer then, though strangely not quite herself.

Back in the living room, she turned on the television set, very low, to have something to occupy her mind a little while she worked on the afghan. It was Paul whom she stopped from ringing the doorbell.

He kissed her cheek perfunctorily and looked around as she switched off the TV set.

"It sure is quiet. Isn't that Dad's pickup outside? They said at the store he'd come home."

"Yes, but he's upstairs—sleeping, I hope. He needs rest."

"Where's everybody else? I don't think I've ever heard this house so still."

"You know, of course, that Mitch is living at Charlie's for a while. Shane is at the store. Janet and Patty are at your house. I'd think you'd know that."

"I—uh—haven't been home all day."

"Sharon's helping Janet with some maternity clothes and some things for the baby. Sit down Paul. There's coffee, or maybe you'd like something else to drink. You're a little late for Thanksgiving dinner, but we are having the last of the turkey for supper tonight if you—"

"No, I can't stay, Mom. Maybe time for a cup of coffee. I really wanted to see Dad for a few minutes."

"Well, Paul, you've hardly seen him for a few minutes the past six months. There's been time, and there'll be more of it later."

He followed her uneasily into the kitchen while she got the coffee.

"It's about time Janet did something to get ready for that damned baby," he said edgily as they sat down again. "I thought Shane was going to marry her."

"It's not his fault that he hasn't, but I expect they still may get to it."

"My God, when? She's a scandal to the whole county, going around acting like the Virgin Mary or something. You'd think she'd jump at the chance to marry anybody who'd have her."

"Sometimes I'm surprised at how old-fashioned you are, son," she said calmly.

He stared. "You can't mean you don't *care*?"

"Yes, I certainly do care, but I'm not going to be ashamed of Janet."

"Well, I think I'd better have a little talk with her, maybe with Shane, too, if—"

Nora smiled gently. "I think you'd better just leave them both alone. They're both a little bit what old Charlie calls 'ringy' right now, and you might get more than you bargained for."

"Mother," Paul said slowly, incredulously, "when I came in, I could see you'd been crying. Your eyes are red and puffy, but you're—you're not yourself. If I didn't know better, I'd almost think you've been drinking."

"Only a little," she said placidly. "Where were you for Thanksgiving dinner?"

"Why, didn't Sharon or Charlie mention that Mitch and I watched some football games over at Ted Carpenter's house that day? Nancy was visiting her folks in Salt Lake. We just went out for fried chicken and things."

"You could have watched the games here."

"Well, Mitch . . ." he stopped.

"Mitch isn't acting his age and I'm not sure you are either. I'll be glad if the two of you can get to be better friends. Mitch has always thought of you as a much older and awfully bossy brother—which you are, of course—but he needs friends right now and maybe you do too. But you should have been with Sharon and Jamie, Paul. Thanksgiving is a family day."

"Sharon—gets tired of football."

"And of a lot of other things, too, I think," said Nora, "though she hasn't said a word about any of it."

"She'll be all right, once she lets herself get used to the idea that the Cloud Valley development is really going to happen. We'll be bringing it up for an initial vote by the county commissioners in a couple of weeks."

"Is that really why you resigned—withdrew —before the election?"

He nodded. "It was just plain dumb that it hadn't occurred to us, but conflict of interest is what that Blackbuck bunch would have started yelling right off the bat. I can run for the commission another time—maybe."

He took a cigar from his pocket and toyed with it. "Mom, I'm going to a meeting tonight, a supper and kind of smoker for businessmen at the country club. I wanted to talk to Dad before I have to face all those people, but you two have always shared things—talked things over, I mean—so maybe you can—"

"I doubt that I can tell you any more than Mitch has, or Sharon, if you've talked to her about it. David Rosenzweig was a little boy in the same prison camp where your father was in Germany. He's brought outlandish, horrible charges, and they're being investigated. Viktor has told me what it was really like—what he did and why. He never did more than touch on the surface before because he wanted to forget. I think when you know the whole, real story, you'll understand that. He's told me, and he's talked with people from the FBI and the Bureau of Immigration and Naturalization. He thinks— and so do I— that rather than telling the things to each of you separately, or one or two at a time, over and over, one time is enough, after we know what's going to be done. I can't believe anything will be done because your father did nothing to be punished for, but he wants to wait until it's been thoroughly looked into and cleared up. After that, I hope this county will be ashamed of its suspicious nasty-mindedness, and will maybe want to run David Rosenzweig out on a rail." She snapped a thread with vicious scissors. "So, maybe when we're all together for Alice's Christmas vacation—"

"But he really was a psychiatrist once? And he used another name for some reason?"

"Yes."

Paul waited, but she was going to say no more. "Mother, it wasn't just the conflict of interest that made me withdraw from the election. Word about this mess had started to get around. ... Listen, I've lost three sales in the past month and I know it's because of this. I ought to be able to know where I stand."

"Paul, *you* stand just where you did last year or last month."

"No, I *don't!* This is affecting my business— my life.... You know Rosenzweig is going to put the mill up for sale."

"Yes, we'd heard that."

"That's mostly what this meeting tonight is about: what may happen to business interests in this county. Everything I've got is tied up in the business interests of this county; everything you and Dad and your friends have. If people are suspecting..."

"Suspecting what?"

"Well, that he's a—war criminal or something—I could lose everything. So could you two, and the Collinses and..."

"It'll be enough to satisfy me if we can lose David Rosenzweig," said Nora coldly. "Your father is *not* a war criminal and I don't want those words used in this house. Have I ever lied to you? To any of you children? Has he?"

"He—he never told us any of these things. Neither of you is telling us all the truth now."

"But we've told you we will, when we can. Have I asked you directly if you and Sharon are talking about divorce? No, I haven't, and I won't, because, though I'd like to know, you're adults and it's really not my business. Your father and I are adults, too, and I'd appreciate it very much if you'd let us handle this thing—which is basically our problem—as we see fit."

"Mom, I know the store is already losing business. Isn't that important? I know Mitch is like a hurt little kid who's found out his idol is clay. I know... if there's really nothing bad to hide, then why not let everyone know?... Mom, I don't have anything to *say* to those people tonight."

Nora stood up and put her hand on his shoulder. "Paul, I'm sorry, but I can't be bothered too much with your problems right now. Your father comes first, he always has. I'm very worried about him.... If you have to *say* something tonight—make explanations or excuses—say you're not responsible for your parents, particularly for things that happened before you were born. If you have to *do* something, drop in the store on Monday, not to badger your dad, but because he'd like to see you and it would be good for Cana to see you going there. If—"

But the door burst open before Patty then and Nora had to go quickly to shush her.

31

Perhaps three-dozen businessmen gathered for dinner in the country club's private banquet room. Afterward, while the tables were being cleared away, they went into the bar. When they came back, chairs and small tables had been arranged about the room for an informal county and Chamber of Commerce sort of meeting. They would discuss how business had been that year; David Rosenzweig would make his formal announcement that the mill was for sale; then they would discuss how business might be next year. The Sheppard brothers were there, the editors from newspapers at Cana and Alder Falls, real-estate men, local Chamber of Commerce officers, Elvin Loomis and another, much higher executive of Pacific Slope Lumber, owners of some of the larger stores, controllers of large blocks of land, representatives from banks and savings and loan associations. When the men drifted back to their private room, they found two people who had not been present at the dinner, Faye Holland and Charlie Bonner. They sat in a corner, a small table between them, Charlie smoking his rank old pipe. They tried to look decorous and properly impressed, but, now and then, catching the look of surprise on someone's face, they would exchange grins like a couple of kids who had managed to sneak into a dirty movie. Paul tried to ignore them, but one or another kept catching his eye until he finally had to grin. Floyd Sheppard, the unctuous politician, went and spoke to them just before the meeting began. Most of the other men had spoken to them matter-of-factly, but Floyd said,

"Well, this *is* an unexpected pleasure: Miss Faye, Charlie."

"It was in the paper an' all," said Charlie a little belligerently, "businessmen's meetin'. She ain't a man, but we got businesses. By right, anybody in the county could be here. We're most all in some business, tryin' to stay alive."

"You're absolutely right, Charlie," said the senator soothingly; he patted his shoulder and went away.

"Straddle-ass sonofabitch!" muttered Charlie, and Faye tried to turn a giggle into a cough.

Not much of any moment happened at the meeting. After the Rosenzweig announcement, the executive of PSL assured them that, should his company buy the mill, everything and everybody in the county would be improved.

Faye and Charlie left early. They had come in separate cars, and as they stood in the parking lot, Charlie said menacingly.

"All right, *now* what are you goin' to do?"

"*Me?*"

"Yes, ma'am. It's your mill. Jeff must be spinnin' in his grave. If PSL gits ahold of it—"

"But Charlie, I haven't got the money. It's *not* my mill. It never was *my* mill. If I had the money, I wouldn't—"

"What'd you make me come with you to this damn dudey meetin' for then?" he demanded, scrambling up into his old pickup and screeching away, just touching Floyd Sheppard's Cadillac enough to leave the tiniest spot of yellow paint in a little dent on its gleaming blue surface.

Getting into her own car more slowly, Faye remembered Jeff talking about the way old Charlie Bonner used to handle mules: "Take a ten-mule hitch an' knock a nit off the leader's off ear with a piece of limp rope."

He could still do it, she thought, sitting there, sighing. I wonder if he'd give up Big Red for stock in the mill? She shook her head. I can't do it; nobody can do it. If everyone in the county gave up something as precious to them as Big Red is to Charlie, we still couldn't overbid PSL. Holland's is the only independent mill of any size left in this part of the state. They mean to have it.

She would have given almost anything at that moment to be with Wes. He would understand that she understood that poor old Jeff probably was spinning in his grave, and how much it hurt. She had half-expected Wes, or perhaps even Viktor to be at the meeting, for defiance's sake if nothing else. Seeing Wes tonight was impossible, of course, but she didn't want to go home yet. She'd just have a look-in on Nora.

After the general meeting broke up, six or eight men lingered on in the banquet room, sending a waiter for more drinks. Each had been asked, separately, by David Rosenzweig to stay. They talked desultorily for a little, each wondering what this might be about.

Abruptly, David said, "Gentlemen, I will tell you why I am selling the mill just at this particular time. You have all been friends to me, good business associates, and I feel you have a right to know.... My wife and I have not been particularly happy with this part of the country, I'm sorry to say, but I had planned to stay another five, perhaps ten years here. But—there is a man—Viktor Magnessen, you know—whom I had been trying to recall since we first came to Cana. Once I did remember who he was, I knew I could not stay in the same town, perhaps not in the same country with him. You all know, I think, that the FBI and other agencies have been looking into some matter here. I will tell you now what I have told those people. I feel it is your right to know."

The waiter had brought a fresh round of drinks and David drained his glass before he went on speaking.

When he reached home, Gloria, sulking at being left alone on a Saturday night, and at being still in Alder County, was in bed, a pitcher of martinis on the night stand, a movie magazine, and the TV on. David flipped off the television set.

"What did you do that for?" she demanded petulantly. "It was Paul Newman. A person can't even finish watching a movie—"

"I want to tell you some things," he said with a quiet exaltation she didn't notice.

"Well, then, for God's sake, pour me a drink. I can't reach with you sitting there in the way."

She sipped steadily, but a light grew in her eyes as he talked.

"I'd heard the FBI was around," she said slowly. "Somebody even said they were after you and I said, 'It'd serve the sonofabitch right,'" but she was laughing and she kissed him heartily on the cheek. "It'll ruin them, won't it, Davy? Serve that Paul right for almost ruining my face—and those others, the way they've snubbed us. Will they make him go back to Germany? Put him on trial and everything?"

"I don't know, Gloria. I want you to understand, though, as I told those men tonight, it's truly not spite on my part. I'm so sure it was those two psychiatrists in the camp hospital, perhaps along with a few others, who decided which prisoners were to be sent away to..."

"I know, I know, honey bunny," she said, the words slurring as she stroked his balding head and tormented face. "Get another drink, my poor Davy. *We'll* show 'em, this whole goddam place!"

He told her then that he was selling the mill and she was literally wild with happiness, shrieking with laughter, throwing pillows and things about the room, until Bessie, wakened by the noise, knocked timidly at the door to ask if everything was all right.

"In a week or so," said David, laughing, holding the still-chortling Gloria in his arms, "we'll go to New York and stay until after the holidays."

"You mean we have to come back here?" she fretted groggily.

"Only for a little while, until all the business matters are settled. While we're in New York, we can start making arrangements for our move."

"We going to live in New York again, Davy?" she asked drowsily, beginning to tug at her negligee and his clothes.

"No, darling, not New York."

"Oh, my God! are you finally going to move to Monaco? I can't believe—"

"Gloria," he said a little breathlessly, "we're going to Israel."

"What?"

"We're going to have a beautiful, brand-new life in a place where we can truly belong."

"Israel?" She was vaguely troubled, but the martini pitcher was too low for her to give it much thought now. "Let's just go to bed now. I guess we know how to fix hicks."

"Yes, dearest, I'll be right back."

Through the open bathroom door, he could see her lying naked on the bed, her beautiful skin glowing a little in the dim light. He looked at the bottle of pills. The level was dropping at its regular rate.

Bless Harry Goldman. Harry was a doctor whom David had known for many years. Harry and his wife had spent a few days as the Rosenzweigs' guests several weeks ago. In return for a good tip on some stocks, Harry had obtained for David some sugar pills—placebos, he had called them—that looked exactly like Gloria's birth-control pills. David smiled tenderly. The poor darling would be so furious, so absolutely raving, but she would come to accept it and, ultimately, to be glad.

"Know what, David?" she murmured as he came back to the bed. "There's just one thing wrong with what you were saying."

"And what's that?" he asked, beginning to caress the luscious curves of her body.

"Even in Monaco, we couldn't have a really brand-new life, or start over. It could be different, maybe, and, God, it's got to be better, but nobody, once they're born, or even conceived can really start over. That feels good.... My psychiatrist told me that; about how you can't really start over. You know, the one I told you about that got such cases of the hots I had to stop seeing him."

32

The Cana *Clarion* was published twice weekly and, in the issue of Friday, December 3, there was an editorial that was a gentle, almost apologetic piece of writing: "As an organ of news and commentary for Cana and Alder County, we believe it to be our duty to report all matters of interest and concern to our fellow citizens. It is not our intent in this reporting to be rumormongers, or to stir up dissension, unrest, fear, or animosity. That is not the business, not the wish of a good and worthwhile newspaper.

"There is increasing talk in our town and in

our county concerning some events which may or may not have taken place more than thirty years ago, in a faraway country, one might almost say in another time. Some of the talk is bitter and calls for retribution of some sort as we approach the season of 'peace on earth, good will to men.' Some of the talk, we feel certain, is completely without foundation. Newspaper people are no more omniscient than anyone else, but we feel the time has come when we must make a report to our readers upon the facts we do know."

Tom Edwards, then, without naming names, recounted the story that there had been a small concentration camp in the South of Germany during the Second World War. That, after all these years, two former inmates of that camp were living in Cana, Idaho, that one was making harsh claims concerning the part of the other in the operations of that camp.

Tom Edwards had been one of those singled out by David Rosenzweig to stay at the country club to hear his story the week before. Tom had been a schoolmate of Paul Magnessen's; his wife, Lou, of young Viktor's. Both of them, over the years, had been in and out of the Magnessen house a good deal. Their eldest son was now a classmate of Patty's.

"When contacted," Tom wrote, "a regional agent of the FBI told us that the matter does not fall under FBI jurisdiction. We have learned an investigation is being conducted by the Office of Immigration and Naturalization and, possibly, by another agency of the federal government. The man making the accusations, who was a small boy at the time of his horrible imprisonment, has told us his story. The man being accused has no comment at this time, preferring to wait until the investigations have been completed."

The truth was, Tom had not pushed Viktor for comment. On the day preceding the night when Tom stayed up, writing his report, he had gone to the store and talked, briefly, alone in the office with Viktor, and Viktor had told him gently that he simply had nothing to say now, for publication or otherwise.

"Some reporter I am," Tom raged at Lou as he had paced the kitchen floor, trying to put off beginning the editorial. "I should have been right in there, hard-nosing out the facts."

"Shit," she said laconically. "Those things Rosenzweig told you men just can't be true, Tom, and you know it. I suppose the paper has to say something, but David Rosenzweig must be sick in the head. Do you remember that time when the little Drew boy's dog ran in front of Viktor's pickup? He rushed it to the vet and visited or called every day for a week. Do you remember when we were kids and their house was like a year-round summer camp for everybody? Remember—"

"Will you just shut up?" he said angrily. "You're not making any of it one damn bit easier."

"Some of the finest people in the world live here in this valley," wrote Tom (though if he could have typed with crossed fingers, he might have done so for just that one sentence, the mood he was in). "We are not people who jump to conclusions, who make judgments before we have all the facts. Let us go on with our preparations for the extra love and generosity that the holiday season always engenders. The Bible"—Tom was not a churchgoing man, but it never hurt to bring in the Bible—"tells us the three greatest things are faith, hope, and charity, and the greatest of these is charity. The Alder Valley has always been a stronghold of these three fine qualities. Let us trust it will continue to be so."

Now that he had started thinking of the Bible, Tom was tempted to add another quotation, but he had to stop writing some time. Surely his message was clear enough, but what he was strongly tempted to finish up with was, "He that hath an ear to hear, let him hear."

On that Friday, late in the afternoon, when most people had gotten their *Clarions,* Tom went to Alder Valley Lumber and Hardware. From Wes Collins, he bought two small bicycles with training wheels for his two small sons. Tom had to go to Boise the next day and had planned to buy them there, where there would be more selection and prices perhaps a little lower.

"Has he seen the paper?" he couldn't help asking Wes. Viktor was in the office.

Wes nodded. "He understands you had to do something, Tom. It's your job, and I know he appreciates the way you handled it."

"Did he—say anything?"

"Not much, but I've known him a long time. Sometimes I think I can pretty well tell what he's thinking. He read your editorial and then, a little later, he said, 'I remember when a lot of the good people of Cana got all up in arms because Paul and Tom Edwards and several other boys were swimming naked in the river, just below the only bridge the town had then.' Then he just—went on with what he was doing."

Viktor came out of the office then, with a sheet of paper in his hand.

"Hello, Tom. These are our Christmas specials. You or Lou can do the ad layout. None of us here knows much about that sort of thing. Let's run it two weeks, four issues, wouldn't you think, Wes?"

Tom took the sheet and tried to study it. He could think of nothing to say, as a newspaperman or otherwise.

"You'd better start putting those bicycles together early," said Viktor, smiling a little. "As I recall, you're not much good with a wrench and screwdriver."

At about that same time, Lou Edwards had dropped in at the house, where Nora was cooking supper. Lou had her two boys with her.

"We brought you a couple of pomander balls," she said, hugging Nora. "The boys and I have been making a lot of them, at odd moments, for our friends."

"Have some coffee, Lou. I don't see how you find time for all the things you do. Oh, what a lovely smell!"

"Yeah," agreed Lou, grinning, "they make your drawers smell good."

They giggled, but Nora's eyes made Lou want to cry. They sat at the kitchen table, sipping coffee, while Patty and the boys went into the living room. They talked of inconsequential things, Lou wanting painfully to apologize that there had been anything in the paper, Nora wanting to tell her she understood.

33

Nora did not want to tell Lou about the unsigned letters that had begun to come, or the phone calls. She did not want to tell her that, last Wednesday, old Joe Withers, who had delivered milk and butter and eggs ever since they had lived on Tamarack Road, had told her he was retiring.

For a change, Nora had been up as early as Viktor that morning and, while he showered, she got the coffee on.

"Why, come in, Joe," she had said warmly, hearing his truck, then his step on the back porch. "My goodness, it's cold this morning. The coffee's ready."

"Yes'm," he said, shambling in and putting her order on the table. "My thermometer said six above when I left the house. The—uh—mister not around?"

"He'll be down in a few minutes."

Somehow, Joe seemed relieved that Viktor was not there, and he looked, still standing, at the coffee cup she set before him as if he didn't quite recognize what it was, or as if it might be something faintly repulsive.

"I can't take the weather like I used to," he said, with something of anger or challenge. "I've decided to retire, Miz Magnessen. Today's my last delivery."

"Why, Joe—"

"If it wouldn't be too much trouble, I've got your bill here, what you owe for this month..."

Puzzled, even worried about Joe, Nora got her checkbook and paid the bill.

"Aren't you well, Joe?" she asked with concern. "I didn't dream you were thinking of—"

"Not what you'd call well atall," he said shortly. "You folks has been right good customers, ma'am, but a time comes when a man's got to call a halt."

He pocketed the check and left, the coffee untouched.

"Isn't it too bad about Joe Withers?" Nora had said later in the day when Betty Adams had come to borrow some flour.

"What about him?"

"He's retiring. Right now. You mean he didn't tell you?"

Betty looked at her closely and began to frown. "No, he didn't, but he'd better."

Nora knew then. She felt her face go hot, then cold. What a fool she was! Tears burned her eyelids. Betty took her flour and left quickly.

On Friday morning, Joe's next delivery day, Nora heard his old truck at the Adams'. She had not told the family about the letters or the phone calls, but she had told them about Joe at breakfast on Wednesday, before she realized the truth.

Later on Friday, when their households had settled down after breakfast, Betty came to return the borrowed flour. They had been talking about Christmas trees when Betty said casually,

"By the way, Joe Withers retired from our house this morning."

"Betty, you didn't have to—"

"Bert told him if he saw his truck up here again, he'd put sugar in the gas tank. The stuff's cheaper at the store anyway."

34

On the Saturday after Tom's editorial was published, Patty called to see if Carolyn Adams might come to spend the afternoon. After a long pause, waiting for Carolyn to ask, Patty said a few half-audible words into the kitchen phone and hung up. Nora was making fruitcakes.

"What's the matter?" she asked, half-frightened by a glimpse of the child's stricken face.

"Carolyn can't come. Her grandma says we can't ever play together anymore. She wouldn't even let Carolyn say much on the phone, but she says we're not the kind of people she wants her family to have anything to do with. Oh, Grandma, what's the *matter?* Some people have been acting funny at school . . ."

"It's just—something that won't last long, Patty. Really, it doesn't have a thing to do with you. Wasn't Carolyn's mama home?"

"No, she's downtown, and her daddy's not there either."

"Well, when they come home, I think things will be all right. Anyway, for now, I wish you'd help me with these fruitcakes. Just look at all these things that have to be mixed up."

"I'd rather not, right now," said Patty bleakly. She drifted out of the kitchen and upstairs, but in fifteen minutes was back to help, looking sad, saying little.

Before the fruitcakes were done, Carolyn had arrived, saying breezily that her mother had returned and, after some loud-voiced private conversation with the grandmother, her mother had told Carolyn that sometimes, when people got as old as Granny, they got things a little mixed up in their minds; it had just been a little mistake. Carolyn announced that she could even spend the night if it was all right.

35

On the following Wednesday afternoon, Charlie came into the store and stood around with his hands in his pockets for a time. Business had not slowed down much; some people came in out of curiosity, others from friendship, but most bought something. In a free moment for Viktor, Charlie said,

"I'm goin' up to the Blackbuck ranch tomorrow. Thought you might come along."

Viktor looked at him with appreciation. "I'd like to, Charlie, but I can't. Thank you. It would be good to get away. Nora..."

"Oh, I'd planned we'd take her, too. Might as well have ourselves a decent cook if we can. Looks to me like you've got enough people here an' at home to take care of things. I planned to stay a week, maybe more. Long enough to git the ole house warmed up an' see to things up there."

"We couldn't go now," Viktor said quietly. "I have an appointment with some people in Boise on Friday afternoon."

Charlie nodded, not understanding, but wanting to.

"Well, I'll prob'ly stay till about the seventeenth or eighteenth. I can bring Christmas trees for ever'body if that's not too late. You want a big one, I guess, like always?"

Viktor looked down at the floor. "Yes, and that won't be too late. We'll appreciate it."

Charlie shrugged. "I'll be gittin' one for Faye an' some others. Have you heard what's goin' on about the mill? Workers is comin' to Faye in droves, wantin' to put their life into stock, to form a corporation."

"Yes, Bert Adams has told us. He says you've offered quite a contribution."

Charlie grinned deprecatingly. "Rosenzweig wouldn't make me no contract for logs for next year. That happened some while back, an' if the thing goes to PSL, they don't care much for independents, especially me, so . . ." he spread his hands. "But, hell, we can't outbid PSL. What else the workers is talkin' about doin' is gittin' in the union an' throwin' a big strike if PSL buys."

"I don't really see how that would help anything."

"I don't neither, but it would be somethin' to do. Sometimes a man just needs to *do* somethin', you know? . . . I've got my snow cat parked up at McCrarys'. If you an' Nora change your minds after you've had that meetin' on Friday, Shane can find some kind a' vehicle to git you up to the ranch. Where's he at anyway?"

"I think he's out on the dock, loading some lumber and insulation for someone. Charlie, Shane has been like—a son to us. You know he always has been, but these past weeks, we've . . ."

"I guess he's not turned out so bad," said

Charlie, trying to mask his pride. "Hard to see how, the raisin' he ain't had."

"Mitch," Viktor began painfully.

"Well now, Mitch says he'll stay on at my place, look after things there for me while I'm up at the ranch."

"I ought to see him," Viktor said.

"Yes, you surely ought, but if I was you, I'd let the stubborn little whelp come to me. He thinks he ought to see you, but he's too stubborn to just come home. He says you won't talk to him. Don't say anything now. He's done told me how you want to wait till things are settled before you talk the thing out, but kid's got no patience. Mitch'll be all right.... You an' Wes still figgerin' to make another addition to the store next year?"

"I don't know, Charlie. I—we may be leaving Cana."

"Good God, Viktor, you've got more grit in your craw than that!"

"It's something that may be necessary, one way or another."

"Well, I just ain't about to believe a thing like that.... Looky yonder's ole lady Parnell, wantin' somebody to wait on her. I expect she got a screw that wouldn' fit or somethin'. Now you an' Nora come on up there if you've got a mind to. I'm goin' to see Shane a minute."

Shane threw the last roll of insulation on Herb Warner's truck. "I been talkin' about puttin' walls an' insulation in that garage for years," Herb had explained, seeming almost defiant about it, "an' May an' the kids been after me to do it. Things are a little slower at the farm right now, an' I got my boy home from college to help, so I says to myself, 'Might as well just git 'er done.'"

"Well, boy," was Charlie's greeting as Shane turned from the departing truck.

Charlie was missing Shane, more than he would have cared to admit. There had been his time at college, and other times the boy had been away, but he had always come back home. It had come to Charlie in the past few weeks that Shane might never really come home again, to stay. The old man had not known until the accident how much he counted on Shane—for work, yes, but also for just being around, for things like those crazy books he'd read aloud on winter nights.

Charlie still had nightmares about that accident, but Shane was looking good now, his face worried and tired, too thin, but flushed a good color from working in the cold, his eyes steady and direct, all the redness finally gone, a sifting of snow on his bronze hair.

"Looks like they keepin' you busy."

Shane lit a cigarette and leaned against the wall. "How are things, Charlie?"

"Fair to middlin'. I wisht you'd come down in Utah with me to have a look at that front end for Big Red."

"I wouldn't know anything about it. You're the mechanic."

"Hell, I know that, but you could drive, couldn' you? It's gittin' so these long hauls gives me a pain in my shoulder, right in here."

"I'm sorry, Charlie, I just can't. You know—"

"Yes, yes, I know," Charlie said roughly, but he understood. It was in his eyes.

"Maybe Mitch—?"

"Lord, no! Vince seems to need him at the

station an' he's out tomcattin' so much at night, he'd likely go to sleep as soon as he set down to drive. It was after three when he got in this mornin'. You ought to talk to him."

"He doesn't want to talk to me. *You* talk to him."

"Well, I'm afraid he's fixin' to git hisself in some kind a' trouble an' they don't need no more a' that. I'm goin' up to the ranch for a week or two. I jist got done tellin' Viktor you'd find a way to git him an' Nora up there if they want to come. What's this thing in Boise he mentioned?"

"It's a meeting with the immigration people. That's all I know."

"Looks like they could have the decency to come here instead of makin' him do the comin'."

"I think he wanted it somewhere else, maybe to keep the gossip from gettin' any worse."

"After that, is he aimin' to tell his side a' things?"

"I don't know, Charlie."

"You know he's talkin' 'bout leavin' here?"

"Yes."

"Well?"

"Well, it's been their home a long time and there are quite a lot of people ready to stay their friends through anything, but—there are some real bastards."

"Like who?"

"Oh, people who come in and say or ask things you wouldn't believe; anonymous letters, phone calls. One of the suppliers in Boise that they've been doing business with for years, refused to send a shipment and bill in the usual way. He wanted payment in cash or a cashier's check and we had to go and pick the stuff up."

"Goddamn sonsabitches!"

There was a little silence and Charlie said, still vehemently, "But he's got to stick it out. Oh, I nearly forgot. I want you to be sure an' be at that county commissioners' meetin' when they bring up the Cloud Valley business. You know how people in the upper valleys are, most of 'em, won't hardly stir their stumps in the wintertime. I want to know what's said an' all."

"All right; unless something really drastic comes up."

Charlie looked carefully out through the stacked lumber, as if he were trying to spot something specific, cleared his throat, and said sternly, "Where's Janet at?"

"She's shopping with her mother today."

"Are you aimin' to marry her, or not?"

"Let's go inside, Charlie. It's cold out here."

"Wouldn' be cold if you wasn' in your shirt-sleeves an' had a hat on."

"I came out here to work. I wasn't cold while—"

"Le's just stay out here a minute. Are you aimin' to?"

"I'm aimin', but—"

"For Christsake, git it done then. That might help things a little, for all of 'em."

"It's not all that easy."

"Don't she want to?"

"Yes, but . . . no."

"Now, that don't make a lick a' sense."

"Still, it's about all I can tell you because it's all I know."

"If I thought you was just stayin' up there, waitin' for her to change her mind back an' forth, I'd beat your butt, old as you are. That ain't no kind of a position for a man to let hisself git put into, but I reckon it's, partly anyway, that they need another man on the place right now.... Ain't it?" he demanded sharply.

Shane nodded, not looking at him.

"Well, I hope to God you've got it done by the time I git back from the ranch. If you don't, maybe I'll have a talk with her. I never had no daughter, but I think I might know how it'd feel to—"

"I really hope you won't," Shane said fervently.

"Well, is she aimin' to have that young-un—"

"Shane?" Peggy Lou was standing in the doorway. "There's somebody here wanting cement. Daddy and Mr. Magnessen are both busy and I don't know a thing about it."

36

Wes had hired an extra boy to work at the store, at least for that Friday and Saturday. Viktor and Nora had to leave before noon on Friday to keep the appointment in Boise. Peggy Lou was also in Boise, Christmas shopping with a girl friend. Janet left the store early to be with Patty after school. They were keeping open until eight-thirty now for Christmas shoppers, but when there was little business by seven, Wes said,

"Maybe you ought to go on home, Shane. Janet looked like she was feeling pretty bad...."

Janet heard the car and met him in the kitchen, her eyes red and swollen.

363

"It's Patty," she said hoarsely. "She was supposed to stay after school today to practice the Christmas play, but when I went to pick her up, the other kids said she'd come home on the bus. When I got home, she was in her room, crying, but she wouldn't tell me anything. She said she didn't want to upset me." Janet's laugh was more than a little hysterical and there were tears in her eyes. "She couldn't eat any supper. We were going to watch one of those Christmas specials on TV, but she started crying again right in the middle of it, and went to bed. She promised she'd talk to you when you came home, if she was still awake. Shane, her heart's just broken. She's too little to have to suffer all this crap. And then ..."

"Then what?"

"Oh, just another of those shitty phone calls."

He took the kitchen phone off its hook and laid it on the counter.

"Don't!" she cried with a frantic note. "Mama never will do that because somebody might need us or—"

"Just until we talk to Patty, all right? You *can* hang up on those people, you know, and throw away the damned letters as soon as you see—"

"I know, but there's something—some horrible fascination—about how loathsome people can be. I had no idea how many letters and calls were coming here, to the house, until the other day when Mama—well, never mind that now. I'll tell you about it later."

Patty lay huddled small in her bed, the covers pulled close. Her hair was wet with tears but she was not crying now. There seemed nothing left except a dry sob to shake her now and then. The big yellow cat lay on the foot of her bed, raising its head with what seemed a look of disdain as the others came in. Shane stood by the bed, looking silently down at Patty.

She said bleakly, "I wanted Fluffy to cuddle in bed with me. Sometimes she does, but she won't now."

"Cats can be very independent people," Shane said softly.

He picked up the pajamaed little girl, pulled a blanket from the bed, disgruntling the cat, wrapped Patty in the blanket, and sat on the bed with her in his arms. Janet came and sat beside them. Patty looked at her uneasily.

"Grandma says when people are having babies, they shouldn't get upset."

"Pattycake," said Janet, trying to keep her voice steady, "I won't be upset, I promise. It's *not* knowing what happened to you..."

"What did happen?" Shane asked. "Something about the play at school?"

"We wrote it ourselves," the little girl said dully. "I mean, we made it up and Miss Perry wrote it down because some of us can't write very much yet. Instead of a Pilgrims' Thanksgiving, it's a Pilgrims' Christmas—all about how they didn't have much and it was so cold and everything, but they still wanted to have a good Christmas, so they made little presents and put their food all together and then, at midnight, when they were all in one of the houses, they all sort of had a dream about when Jesus was born, how he was so poor and maybe cold and everything too.... I was going to be Nancy Hawkins. She's one of the main people, with a husband and some children; the Christmas thing is partly her idea and it's her house where everybody gets together. Aunt Sharon is making me a long, old-fashioned dress and a bonnet, and Grandma's been teaching me to crochet, just a little, so I could do that when I'm sitting down, to look real, you know."

There was a little silence. Janet pulled a wet lock of hair from the child's cheek and stroked it between her fingers. Shane was utterly still in that attitude of complete attention and listening that was one of the things Janet loved about him.

"We had practice today," said Patty, speaking faster, her voice uneven now. "The play is on Tuesday night before Christmas, the night before the last day of school before vacation.... Miss Birchard came in our room. She called Miss Perry out in the hall and then they called me. Miss Birchard said—I couldn't be in the play. She said there was too much talk and people wouldn't like it. She said she'd had phone calls and—and—Miss Perry was going to give the part to Debby Householder."

"What did Miss Perry say?" asked Janet after a silence.

"She said she was sorry. I know it's not *her* fault. Miss Birchard's the principal, her boss. I didn't look at Miss Perry much then, but when I looked back at her, I thought she looked like she was going to cry. I asked if I could have another *little* part, because of my costume and everything, but Miss Birchard said no. When I went back to get my coat and things, it seemed like some of the kids already knew. Billy Malone said it was because my grandpa was a Nazi, and Teri Freeman said Nazis are awful people; they kill people and torture them and do terrible things. I—I didn't cry because they made me so mad, even if I didn't really know what they were talking about. Besides, I felt kind of—funny, kind of dizzy and numb at the same time. Miss Perry yelled at them that she wouldn't have that kind of talk and —and then I left and the bus was still there. . . . Oh, Shane, what *are* they talking about? *Why*. . .?"

Shane sighed and held her closer, looking steadily down into her face.

"A long time ago, Patty, before you were born, before Janet or I were born, there was a big war, called the Second World War. Have you heard of it?"

"Yes, but I—"

"We fought in that war—our country did. Some people who fought on the other side, who were our enemies then, lived in Germany and were called Nazis. Some of those Nazis were cruel in the ways the kids said, and—"

"Not *Grandpa!* Not my grandpa!" She was fierce.

"No," he said firmly. "Your grandpa was a prisoner of the Germans' during the war. He was not fighting on their side; he did none of those bad things, but he has never wanted to talk much about it. It isn't a good thing to remember and talk about, having been a prisoner anywhere for four years."

"But he's from Denmark. He tells me about his grandpa's farm."

"He was working in Germany when the war began so he was put into prison. Many foreigners were. Some people here are just finding out some of these things. They're behaving like little kids, making up ghost stories to scare themselves with."

"But *why?* It was ages and ages ago and Grandpa—"

Janet was about to speak angrily, but he cut

in, "None of us really understands why, Patty. It's just how some people are about some things. You remember when you've been up at the ranch, watching the calves, how one would start to run, then they all would? Probably, sometimes it was just because they were happy and felt like running. Other times, maybe something frightened one of them. People will do that kind of thing too. But probably this won't be a thing that will last very long. People always find something new to talk about pretty soon. Now suppose—"

"I—I wasn't going to say anything," she said, looking away from their faces, "but Timmy Jackson, he's a minister's son, and he said . . ."

"What?"

"That you and Aunt Janet are—are living in sin, that you're wicked. Do they think you're Nazis, too?"

"No. Some people are just not very happy with any of us right now."

"Carolyn called me before Aunt Janet came home. Grandma told me not to answer the phone when there's nobody here, but I was afraid it was someone looking for me. Carolyn said Chad, her big brother, you know, would beat up Billy and Timmy and that Tommy Edwards—he's in our class—would help him."

Shane smiled a little. "Why don't you call Carolyn and thank her, but tell her it won't be necessary. Probably, all it would do would be to get Chad and Tommy in trouble."

"But the play," she said, and suddenly began to shake with fresh tears.

"Please don't cry, Patty," he said, hugging her. "We'll see about the play, and if you cry any more, you're going to make yourself sick."

She sniffled, trying to control the tears. "Will the baby know I'm crying?"

"He might," said Janet, stroking her cheek.

"Is it a he?"

"We don't know for sure yet."

Patty sat up, brushing at her eyes. "I just can't *wait* until it's born. I wish it would be in time for Christmas. That would be so neat! Can I help, Aunt Janet? I mean, when it's time to feed it and things?"

"You certainly can. I'll need lots of help."

Patty's brief animation faded. She looked back at Shane, her face setting grimly. "I'm not going back to school. That will be the best thing."

"No, it won't," he said gently after a moment. "I want you to do me a big favor, Patty. Try to go on with things just as they have been. Don't mention, for a few days anyway, about the play to your grandparents. Things are a little bad for them. People are saying mean things to them, too, and—"

"That's why Grandpa looks so sick and Grandma cries sometimes," she said, startled.

"Yes. It would help them not to worry about the play or your going to school. We'll see what can be done—"

"You mean you can fix it? I can still be in it and—"

"I don't know if I can do anything at all. I just said we'll see. Now I don't think anybody in this house has had any supper. Suppose I go and get some pizza?"

"Will Grandma and Grandpa be back tonight?"

"They said they might," answered Janet. "I

369

hope they'll stay in Boise and get a good night's rest."

"Yes," Patty said bleakly, "that would be a good thing for them to do, but I sort of wish they'd come back. Sometimes it seems like our house gets emptier and emptier all the time. I wish Uncle Mitch would come home."

"Why don't both of you get up," asked Janet, trying for gaiety, "so I can remake the bed? Then, when Shane brings the pizza, we'll all eat here in your room, where it's nice and cozy and full of people. Maybe even Fluffy can have a bite."

"I'm not even sure Fluffy's my friend anymore," said Patty tremulously.

Shane had stood up and given Janet the blanket. Now he put Patty down on a chair and left the room briefly.

"Shane!" the little girl squeaked as he came back, offering a huge floppy teddy bear.

"He was for Christmas," Shane said, "but you see I didn't even get him wrapped. I think you can always be sure he'll cuddle, where Fluffy's not always so dependable."

"Oh, I *love* him, and I love you!" She tried to jump up and put her arms around him, still holding the bear. "I love Aunt Janet and the baby and—just about everybody. And our house doesn't seem nearly so empty anymore."

When they had eaten, Patty, tucked in with the teddy bear, and with a repentant Fluffy curled against her shoulder, wanted to sing Christmas songs. Shane, saying he didn't know many songs, couldn't sing very well, and had some things to take care of, excused himself, and went downstairs.

Patty called after him, "I'm going to name this bear Shaney, okay?"

"I'm honored," he said and closed the door.

37

A half-hour later, Janet found him sitting on the living-room couch, absently turning the stiff, crinkled pages of the Boise paper.

"You were wonderful with her," she said, tears starting again in her eyes. "You've got some kind of—innate thing with kids—rapport, I guess."

He got up and drew her down to sit beside him. "You weren't half bad yourself. I couldn't have stayed up there to sing Christmas songs. Not now."

She tried to smile. "She finally fell asleep right in the middle of the third round of 'Rudolph.' Oh, Shane, imagine her not wanting to upset *me*."

"How did the newspaper get wet?"

Janet clenched her teeth. "Because that damned Hendrix kid won't try to hit the porch anymore." She gave herself an impatient little shake. "God, look how paranoid I'm getting. He never could hit the porch. I heard the phone . . . ?"

"It was just Rex Terry, making a friendly call. He wanted to talk to your dad, but he said he and Amy would come for a visit one evening next week. They've bought their campmobile and are going to visit their daughter in Texas for Christmas."

"I thought it might be the folks calling," she said, "to say they were going to stay over."

"Yes, I hoped it was."

"Will this be the end of it, Shane? Can they tell us . . . ?"

"Didn't your mother say they were trying to get in touch with people in Europe? Viktor hasn't mentioned it, but it seems to me that could take a long time."

"Well, whatever they find out, I think it would be good for them to stay away from Cana for a little while."

"Maybe they'll still call. It's just past nine."

"But their meeting was at four. You didn't leave the phone off?"

"No. I was going to after I called Miss Birchard, but then I remembered—"

She was staring at him, beginning to smile. "*You* called Miss Birchard?"

"She wasn't home," he said.

"But you *hate* Miss Birchard."

"If I didn't before, I do now. She was my third-grade teacher up at Blackbuck and she used to keep me after school and ask me questions about my parents. Also, she said things in front of the other kids. If I'd had any sense and been a little older, I'd have spit in her eye, or, better yet, told Charlie, but she was the terror of my life. She's got no business having anything to do with kids. She's a shriveled, disturbed, voyeuristic old maid. I never have been able to understand why they made her principal of the grade school here."

"Well, she taught twenty years first. I don't guess the school board gets much feedback from scared little kids. Wow! Were you going to tell her those things if she'd been home?"

"Damn right and some others too. I'm still going to talk to her."

"That might do Patty more harm than good," she said gently.

"I've got other plans about Patty. It'll do *me* good after all these years."

"It *is* Miss Birchard, of course," Janet said. "Ellen Perry wouldn't do a thing like that to Patty, or any child."

"Well, the school board is going to hear about it," he said grimly. "I happened to remember, when Rex called, that Amy Terry's been on the county board for years, so I told him. It seems the board is having a little Christmas gathering next week, but he thought Amy would want to talk to several members before Monday. Then, too, this Householder kid who's to take her place is the granddaughter of our new sheriff. I suspect it's this Debby's parents who have been bringing most of the pressure. The whole family's not worth tying up in a sack and drowning."

She laughed. "The more you're away from Charlie, the more you talk like him. I didn't know you had so many grudges."

"Do you remember, years ago, when you were fourteen and you followed us to the Robin's Nest one night? Viktor asked me to take you home."

She frowned, then smiled, putting her hand in his. "That was when I asked you to kiss me and you did."

"Yes, and then, later, Bill Householder stopped me for speeding when I hadn't been."

"And *he* said nasty things to you," she said gently, "and threw your wallet under the car. Yes, I do remember."

"I also talked to Faye," he said.

"About—about Patty?"

He nodded. "She'll be back in the play on Monday."

"Why, Shane I—you're awfully special. And she does so love the teddy bear. Where did you get it?"

"In Boise the other day when I had to go and pick up that shipment of small appliances.... Janet, I bought a ring, too—well, two rings. I wanted you there, but you haven't wanted to talk about it and ... They're upstairs. I could—"

"No. We can't get married."

He sighed and lit another cigarette. The ashtray was overflowing. He emptied it into the fireplace and stood looking out into the gloom of the cold, cloudy night.

They had both almost believed the matter was settled that day in October when she had come down while he was still at the house because of his illness. Soon, in a few days, a week or two at most, they would go to Nevada where there was no waiting period, and be married. They talked about it in their brief moments alone. She said she would not expect anything from him about the baby, that she understood what his feelings must be. He told her he felt almost certain all his reservations would be dispelled once the baby was born. Janet finished her promised working period at McCrarys' and came home to live. Things concerning Viktor's difficulties had begun to crop up.

Janet was going through a period of feeling nervous and ill. One evening, after she had locked herself in her room to cry in solitude, she encountered Shane in the upstairs hall. He had taken her in his arms and held her gently close. She had leaned against him, almost physically drawing upon his nearness, his strength and love.

"It's going to be all right," he had said softly. "It's—"

Then the baby had given a great lurch and, reflectively, he had started, drawn away from her.

Janet had run back to her room, crying more heartbrokenly than Patty, and she had been very ill all night. Nora had made her see the doctor the next day and Janet had felt too unwell to return to the store until two days later. She would not speak to Shane or meet his eyes for almost a week, until one day when they were momentarily alone in the store's office, she had said abruptly, in a tight, hard voice,

"It's inside me, Shane, but it's a human being. It didn't ask to be there or to be born. It will always come between us. I realize you can't help that. I can't blame you, but—"

"Janet, I'm so sorry," he had said abjectly. "I—I never felt a baby like that before. If it were mine, I might have been as—"

"If it were yours," she said tightly, "you'd want to feel it move. At least I'm told most fathers do. But it's not yours and you'll never forget."

Gradually, their relationship had grown again; sometimes it was very close to love. Sometimes she seemed on the verge of agreeing to the marriage.

He said now, turning from the window, "Can't you please try to forgive me for that—"

"It's not that I don't forgive you. I've told you I understand. But what the hell good would I be as a wife for—for months? And then—"

"I don't like it," he said between his teeth,

"when you act as if all I'm after is your body. Of course I want to make love to you. Sometimes I ... but I can wait. That's a hell of a long way from being all I care about you or all there is to you. In your room, the one you and Alice used to share, there are twin beds. We could have that room and I wouldn't ... Janet, I want to be with you. You've said sometimes you're afraid of things in the night. I want, legally and with your family's blessing, to be with you at those times, to hold you. I want to be with you, legitimately, at the hospital.... God knows there's not much I can do, but you don't have to be alone."

"I have the family," she said dully, then smiled grimly. "Well, not Paul and Mitch, maybe not Alice when she knows, but ..."

"Has Mitch done something? said something?"

"He told Paul that I'm one of the reasons he won't come back home—not the major one, you understand—but he thinks maybe Peggy Lou's mother won't think quite so harshly of him if he keeps completely away from the likes of me."

Shane spat a shred of tobacco. "That sounds like something Paul made up. It would be a hot day in January before Mitch considered what Doreen Collins might think."

"Have you seen him?"

"Mitch? No."

"I wish you'd talk to him. He's always been close to you—closer, I think, than he ever was to Vik."

"He won't talk," Shane said. "You run out of steam pretty fast with a monologue, at least I do."

"But you haven't seen him at all lately? Shane, he's breaking Daddy's heart."

"I saw him picking up Peggy Lou at the store the other night—I think it was Tuesday. When I left the store tonight, I drove by the house. There weren't any lights and I didn't see his car at Vince's. When I went back to Effie's to get the pizza, I asked one of the boys at the station. Mitch hasn't been in today."

"Oh, my God!" she said, covering her face. "What now? He's too old, technically, to run away from home, but do you think—"

"I think he just took a day off. It seems he's been working pretty hard and Charlie says..."

"What?"

"That he's keeping pretty late hours some nights."

She got up heavily and went upstairs. The phone rang. A woman's voice. Perhaps she had been drinking; perhaps she was just high on what seemed to her the daring or righteousness of what she was doing.

"I want to talk to Mr. Magnessen."

"I'm sorry, he's not here."

"Well, his wife then."

"They're both away."

"Who's this?"

"Would you care to leave a message, or—"

Then he could hear her words clearly, holding the instrument at arm's length. "*I know who you are!* You're that Bonner bastard that's shacked up with their whore of a daughter. This is a clean town... moral people... the likes of you ought to be... Nazi fascist and the rest—"

He replaced the phone, shaking, and got himself another cup of coffee.

"What was it?" asked Janet wearily.

"Nothing."

377

"It was another of those... I can tell by your face. Oh, people aren't even animals, they're—"

"Remember that Rex Terry called tonight, too. People are all different."

"Come back and sit down," she said petulantly, "and for God's sake, stop trying to be so blasé about all of it. Blasé people's hands don't shake and their faces don't turn red and then white."

There was a little silence and she said in a more controlled, gentler voice, "It's the phone calls, the letters, and other similar things that are the reasons why I won't marry you."

"What the hell kind of sense does that make?"

"Maybe none, to you or anybody else, but it does to me. I had no idea, until a couple of days ago, about how much crap Mama's been getting. She didn't want to tell anybody because she was afraid Daddy would find out and be more hurt and worried. Poor darling, it had hardly occurred to her that the same things might be going on at the store.

"I went shopping with her, you remember? On Wednesday. Well, first we went to the bank, dear old Mr. Grundy's bank. She had a deposit to make. They were a little bit busy and we stood in a line by Alma Jeffreys' window. Just when we came up to it, Alma closed for lunch. Then we went to another window, Sally Tilly's, and she would hardly say a word, though poor Mama was trying to be friendly, just the way she always is.

"Then we went to the drugstore and that was all right. Carol Drew waited on us herself.

She even followed us around while we were getting things, talking about the weather, church, things like that.

"But after that we went to Epsteins. You know how Mama is about Christmas. She enjoys it every bit as much as Patty. This year, she says, even with all the trouble, everything has to be perfect for Patty and Jamie, and as good as can be for the rest of us. She always orders from the catalogs and spends a day shopping in Boise, but then, when it gets to be December, she always thinks of a dozen more things she just *has* to get. So we looked around Epsteins a long time and she found all sorts of goodies. 'Don't you think this scarf would look nice with Alice's hair? What a sweet little picture for Patty's room! Do you think Jamie has a car like this for his train? Oh, look, their yarn's on sale. We'd better lay in a supply for the baby.' On and on till we had almost two carts full.

"When we got to the checkout counter, Shirley Epstein was running the register, Morris and Ella's daughter. Business must be either awfully good or awfully bad because I've never seen any of their kids working in the store before. When we got up to the register, Mama started asking Shirley about college and things. Mama took her checkbook out of her purse. Shirley took one thing out of a cart; it was a new sewing basket Mama thought Sharon needed. She set it down on the counter and left. Mama said she must have to check a price or something, so we took the other things out of the carts and put them on the counter. People were starting to line up behind us.

"Mr. Epstein came back instead of Shirley,

and stared at us. Mama said, 'How's Ella, Morris?' She had her checkbook in her hand and he said, 'I'm sorry, we can't accept your check, Mrs. Magnessen.' She looked like she was going to cry, but she got out her wallet. She only had a few dollars and so did I. I said, 'Do you mean you're afraid of a hot check from us after all this time?' He said, 'It's a new policy with all our stores. No more checks.' I said, 'I don't see any sign that says that.' His face had got very red. He leaned over the counter and said, 'When we came here, so many years ago, we used to thank God every day that we'd got away from anti-Semitism. Now we find that, right in our midst, all this while, in this beautiful little town, there is a Nazi. We don't want your business. You can see the people waiting. We're very busy today. I'd appreciate it if you'd just return the merchandise and leave my store.'

"I returned his goddam merchandise to the floor and brought Mama home. She was nearly hysterical and she told me about the calls and letters and things. After a while, she remembered we hadn't bought groceries and she couldn't face that, so I went down. I got all kinds of breakable things, like baby bottles, things we didn't even need, in case our money wasn't good enough for Scarsdale's, but that turned out all right. When I came back, Mama made me promise three times not to let Daddy find out about Epsteins' or any of the rest of it."

There was a silence. The mill whistle blew two blasts, end of second-shift lunch period.

"I'm sorry," Shane said gently, "that you have to be subjected to things like that. Maybe Viktor's right and they really ought to leave here when things are cleared up. There's Patty to think of and it takes some people a hell of a long time to forget. There are a few, I suppose, who never will stop being suspicious."

"Now, that's a hell of a note!" she cried angrily. "What ought to happen is that you and Wes and Charlie and every friend we've got ought to wreck Epstein's mercantile and Grundy's bank and half the town. We haven't *done* anything! Can you imagine anybody less anti-Semitic than my parents? I'm not even sure Mama knows the real meaning of it. If people wanted to go back far enough, Daddy's great-grand-something was an Orthodox Jew. Can you imagine anyone who's ever known him even slightly, having the least conception he could be a Nazi, or—oh, hell."

"I know," he said quietly. There was no more he knew to say.

"Anyway, maybe they will decide to leave sweet, clean, kindly Cana and maybe it would be best for them, but *I'm* not going, and I'm not going to marry. People have called me a whore so often and with such conviction lately that I'm beginning to believe them and I don't care. If I had the money and the real professional know-how, maybe I could start a Fannie's place for Cana. It would be damned interesting to see who all came in. But since I'm not quite ready for that, I'll have my bastard child, then I'll get a nursing job at pure Cana's hospital. They're always desperate for nurses and they'll take just about anybody who's qualified. I'll stay here the rest of my life and spit in the eye of half the people that look at me *or* my baby."

Shane exhaled smoke from a fresh cigarette

slowly and she said shortly, "You're going to kill yourself, smoking so much."

"I don't see," he said carefully, "how a decision like this is going to help the family."

"Oh, they'd like me to marry you. They love you very much and it might help a little for the baby to be suddenly legitimate, but everybody would know it was just a minor formality. Everyone in this half of the state knows I'm an unwed mother. The folks have already taken the shock of that, so what difference can the rest of it make?"

"It makes a difference to me."

"Don't, Shane. I can't stand any mushiness. I love you, but—won't you try to understand?"

"I don't know if I can, Janet. It looks like I'll have to try, but—it seems to me that if we get married, if the baby's born with my name, people would soon forget—"

"Some don't ever forget anything," she spat. "You were saying so yourself, just a few minutes ago. For God's sake, at least be consistent."

"But this is another situation—"

"These fine, upstanding, good Christian citizens! If they can't think up anything cruel and dirty to remember, they make up something. And besides, that's half the point. It's not only that I want something to throw into the kindly moral face of Alder County, it's that I want my baby to be born named Magnessen. I'm *proud* of the name. I'd bet you anything Paul will be leaving here sooner or later. I *know* Mitch will. This damned place *needs* Magnessens."

Another silence. He put more wood on the fire. With her face averted, she said, "I'm sorry, Shane. You've been more loving and patient and—all the good things than I deserve. I love you. I guess I always will...."

"Is it worth that much in principles?"

"What?"

"I love you. If you love me, mightn't we, someday, be married if we still feel the same? Do you think it's going to hurt a few small, stupid people more than it hurts us if we ruin our lives?"

"Don't be melodramatic."

"I don't think I am being. And then—there's the baby."

"Oh, God! We've been over this so many times."

"Not quite all of it," he said quietly, turning to the window. "By refusing to let him have legitimacy, you're putting a kind of heavy load on him, you know. I was adopted, eventually, but I'm a bastard, Janet. I know what it feels like. Most of the time, it doesn't feel good. To me, it doesn't seem fair—"

The phone rang. She started violently. "I can't stand this!" She almost shrieked.

"Go up to bed," he said. "You're worn out and there's no point—"

"Oh, *please!* Just answer the goddam thing!"

"Shane?"

"Mitch?"

"Yeah. Hi. It's me."

Silence except for a crackling in the lines that told Shane it was a long-distance call.

"Well, where are you? What do you want? Is something wrong?"

"You sure as hell aren't very friendly, polite, even. Who's home?"

"Just Janet and me, and Patty."

Mitch sounded drunk, but complacently happy. "What did they find out today at that meeting Dad was having?"

"We don't know yet."

"Nothing for publication, I guess. Not even to his own family."

"Mitch, I said we don't know. What—"

"Well," he hiccoughed happily, "I just called up to tell you me and Peggy Lou got married. We're in Elko. I lied about my age. You're supposed to be twenty-one in Nevada, too. Guys are. Did you know that?"

"No."

"Do you think they'll find out? The authorities, I mean."

"I don't think they'll care, Mitch."

"We'll be home in a couple of days. Will you tell 'em at Kucharski's?"

"All right."

"And—uh—do you think it'll be all right to bring Peggy Lou to Charlie's, just for a few days? I mean, he's not there and we'll be looking for an apartment or something."

"Yes, I suppose it'll be all right. You might bring her home, you know."

"No, can't do that. I thought that was understood. Aren't you even going to say 'congratulations' or 'many happy returns' or anything?"

"Sure. Sorry. Congratulations, Mitch, to both of you."

"Oh God!" said Janet, who had come to stand beside him. "Did he and Peggy Lou—?"

Shane nodded.

Mitch was saying, "I'm glad you're the one answered the phone because I wanted to ask you to do me a little favor. See, Peggy Lou told her

384

folks she was going to Boise today to Christmas shop with Iva Lee Pearson. They're probably worried, thinking she ought to be back and—uh— I don't seem to have change enough for another phone call, so I thought maybe you'd..."

"No way."

"What?"

"I said no. There'll be plenty of places where you can get change."

"Shane, her mother's going to be a wild woman."

"I know that, but she can hardly get at you in Elko. Talk to Wes."

"Suppose he doesn't answer the phone?"

Shane grinned resignedly. "*Ask* for him."

"Maybe he won't be home."

"Mitch, there's no point in talking about it all night. You knew this would be part of getting married. Why don't you just make the call and have done with it?"

Mitch sighed. "You're probably right.... How's the weather up there? Is it snowing or anything?"

"No."

"Tell Vince I'll be at work Monday morning."

"I will. I'm going to hang up now."

"No, wait, Shane. I have to ask you something. It's a word we can't think of. We're afraid Peggy Lou's mother will start in trying for an annulment or something, but they can't do that, can they? If you've already—well, fucked?"

Shane's shoulders sagged, his smile widening. "I don't think they can, Mitch."

"Well, we have, but I don't think I can say it just like that to the Collinses, and Peggy doesn't either. There's another word—"

385

"Consummated."

"What?"

"The marriage has been consummated."

"That's it!" he said, sounding vastly relieved. "I better write it down. Peggy, babe, you got a pencil? Could you spell it, Shane? I never was any good at..."

A moment later, Shane and Janet had dropped to the couch together, their arms around each other, consumed with cleansing, near-hysterical laughter.

38

Around noon of the following Wednesday, Nora called Viktor at the store to tell him Alice had come home. They had not expected her for another week, but she had flown into Boise early that morning and rented a car.

"We thought maybe you could come home and have lunch with us," Nora said tentatively.

"I'd like to, but Wes and I have to see Walt Philips in a few minutes. I'll try to get home early this evening."

"Walt Philips," she said tensely, but asked no questions. "All right, Viktor. I'm going to invite Paul and Sharon for supper."

"Yes, that will be a good thing. Is Alice all right?"

"Oh, fine," Nora said so brightly that he knew Alice was nearby.

"Tell her I'm glad she's come. She had a letter from someone, I suppose?"

"Yes, I think so."

"I'll try to be home by five."

Wes came into the office, wearing the quiet little smile that had been on his face for the better part of the past several days.

"Doreen wanted the police called," he had reported to Viktor, concerning the wedding that had linked their families. "The kids didn't tell us where they were in Nevada, but they did say they'd already been to bed together. She called your house, trying to find out where they were and I kind of suspect Shane told her to go to hell or something of that nature. I tried to tell her calling the police wouldn't be any good, but of course she wanted her parents' opinion, and Bruce's. She even called Floyd around midnight. He told her an annulment might be possible, with Mitch being under age, even for Nevada. But not likely, without everyone's co-operation.

"There was no sleep at our house that night, none at Sheppards', either, with phone calls back and forth and Doreen raving and packing in between. Bruce came and picked her up at seven on Saturday morning. She was too nervous and upset to drive and didn't want me to take her down. Sunday, Carter called me to say she was going to sue for divorce, that the kids' marriage was my fault because I've always spoiled Peggy and refused to let Doreen have a hand in bringing her up. I understand the grounds are going to be incompatibility. It's a good, all-encompassing word. I know they'd like to make it something more—salacious, but there's never been a divorce in that family, or a marriage like Mitch's and Peggy's, to hear them tell it.

"I think you may already know I was going to divorce Doreen in a year or two anyway. I was only waiting till I thought Peggy would be old enough to understand, a little. The kids are too young to marry. I'm worried about that, but, strictly for me, it may be the best thing that ever happened. I don't know of any other family I'd rather have for my girl's in-laws."

Peggy Lou had come back to work on Monday morning, exuberantly, and she had kissed her father and father-in-law with equal vigor. "Now I've got two daddies," she had laughed.

A little later, she said privately to Viktor, "Don't you worry about Mitch. He just needs a little more time to get himself together about some things. I think I've already persuaded him to go ahead and start school in January. We both will, and we'll both work part-time so there won't be too many money problems. And don't worry, either, that we're going to start presenting you with a bunch of grandchildren. We both like kids, but we want to wait a long time before we begin a family. Mr. Magnessen—that meeting you had with those people in Boise—?"

"Not much came of it, Peggy. They're still trying to contact people. Perhaps in another week or so, we'll hear something more."

In the office now, Wes temporarily lost his smile. "Viktor, Walt is coming about his note."

"I know he is and I have no idea what to do about it. Wes, if I left the business right now... you could pay for my share as the money is available. I don't care about terms. Nora and I have some savings—"

"I wish you wouldn't talk silly," Wes said shortly. "There's enough nonsense going on around here without you starting to act like you're going soft in the head."

Several years ago, when they had decided on further enlarging the store, they had borrowed money from Walt Philips. He had been a long-time friend of Wes's father and had offered them the loan at a slightly lower rate of interest than the banks were charging. The yearly payment was due in April, and in another three years the loan would be paid off, but it was a demand note, the only way Walt ever lent money. At any time, he could ask for payment in full with thirty days' notice, and this was what he was doing. Alder Valley Lumber and Hardware, it seemed to Walt, might be falling on hard times. He was a good, solid, cautious businessman.

"Going to the banks is no good," Viktor said wearily when the other man had left, "not while I'm associated with the business."

"We've got till the middle of January," Wes said blithely. There was nothing, it seemed now, that could really, deeply disturb or upset him. "Something will turn up."

To Nora's surprise and pleasure, Paul and Sharon and Jamie all came to supper together. Shane was not there. He was working at the store, glad to avoid the meal because of Alice's management, which he had been dreading for weeks. He had tried in odd moments since Friday night to talk further with Janet about marriage, but she was brusque and adamant, and, at his last attempt, she had cried and said that if he was going to be such a pest, she wished he'd go away and live somewhere else, which was precisely what he had decided to do if Mitch ever got out of Charlie's house.

Mitch and Peggy Lou were absent from the supper, too, though Peggy had taken a few minutes from the store in midafternoon to come up and say hello to Alice. As she was leaving, while they stood briefly alone on the front porch, she had kissed Nora and said, "I promise, we'll be here for Christmas."

Before she and Jamie went off to watch a television Christmas special, Patty told her Aunt Alice in some detail about the play at school, and asked Sharon for reassurance that her costume was almost finished. It was Sharon who refilled the coffee cups as the grown-ups sat on around the table.

Alice kept looking covertly from one to the other. They all looked so tired and strained and she was beginning to feel she, too, must look the same. She had had a letter, all right—in fact, she had had three of them, all in Monday's mail. The first had been a brief note to the effect that, if she didn't, she really ought to know what was going on with her family, and had enclosed the editorial from the *Clarion*. The second, too, was brief, saying that her family was in trouble and might find her presence helpful. But the third, poorly spelled and written, was a filthy tirade about how her father was an active member of the Fascist and Nazi parties, and had been the murderer of hundreds during the war; how her mother was, to all intents and purposes, running a whorehouse by allowing Janet to live under her roof with Shane Bonner, while Janet was pregnant—"big as a barrel," the letter had said—by the lord only knew who; that Mitch was drunk every night, seen often at Fannie's place in Alder Falls, and living with old

390

Charlie Bonner, who could pollute the morals of any young person; how Paul and Sharon were on the verge of divorce because things were catching up with Paul and his shady business dealings, and because both of them had been sleeping around for years. The letters were, of course, anonymous, except that the third was signed "A FRIEND."

Alice, whom the family had been trying to spare everything until they should see her face to face, was dazed and horrified. She did not sleep that night, and, the next day, after saying she must have immediate emergency leave, she made a terrible job of putting her work in order for someone else to take over.

She had been home several hours now, had had time to think and to see things for herself. Of course, she had not for a moment believed much of that third letter, but, to a slight degree, some of it was true. Her mother had told her, almost immediately, all that the other children knew about their father's troubles, and Janet had answered calmly that her baby, Gary Hunt's child, was due toward the end of January. No, she had no notion as to where Gary might be, and her fondest hope was that she might never hear his name again. Yes, Shane was living at the house, but not *with* her—how could Alice ask a thing like that in front of their mother? Yes, they had talked of getting married, but they weren't going to. At first appearances, it seemed to Alice that Paul and Sharon were getting on no worse and no better than they ever had. The news about Mitch's and Peggy Lou's marriage, which the letters had not been able to include, seemed unimportant, anticlimactic.

"Well," Alice said briskly into the silence that had fallen around the table, "isn't it time we made some decisions? Got some things *done* around here?"

"What did you have in mind?" asked Viktor after a moment, with all their eyes on him, waiting.

"I was thinking about it on the plane and Mama says you've been thinking about it too: about your leaving Cana."

"We may do that," he said. "In time, it may develop that we have to, one way or another. It hasn't been easy for the family, these past weeks, but we do still have friends."

Nora nodded. "Ruby McCrary drove all the way down from Blackbuck this morning, just to visit for a while. She brought Janet the most beautiful homemade quilt for the baby. I don't see how she finds time to do things like that, with Bill and most of the children never turning a hand."

"Where were you thinking of living?" asked Alice, getting back to the point with her father.

"We hadn't thought that far yet, Alice."

"There's Patty's school," said Nora almost pleadingly, "and the store..."

"The store's going to lose just about all its business," said Paul curtly. "I've heard talk that Morris Epstein may go into competition. They say he's thinking of beginning a new building up in the next block in a month or so. As for *my* business, it's practically nothing. Some of the people who were going to invest in Cloud Valley have withdrawn. If there's trouble when we present it to the county commission tomorrow night, it may as well just go down the drain. If that happens, I'd do better to leave the damned state."

"As for Patty's school, Mama," said Alice, "you *know* she isn't having an easy time either. Children can be the meanest things with what they pick up from their parents. I always have thought Patty is precocious and I believe she's keeping things to herself, almost like a grown-up would, trying to spare other people worry. You know the way she talked about that play? Pleased as she was, I'd swear there was something she wasn't telling. It showed in her face. I think they tried to take her part away or something."

Alice sipped her coffee, then looked around at them brightly. "Everyone could resettle in California, a regular old family migration."

There was no response except a slight, dubious, thoughtful nod from Paul.

Alice went on matter-of-factly. "I know selling the house and making business arrangements will take time. I don't have to be back at work until the third of January. I'll do all I can to help between now and then, and when I do go back to San Francisco, Janet can come with me."

Janet, who had been toying with a knife, only half-listening, looked up at her sister sharply.

"That will be a beginning," Alice told her brusquely, "getting you out of here before the baby's born, a little less on everybody else's mind. I've got a nice guest room and there's a good hospital just—"

"No!" Janet cried harshly.

"What?"

"Just—no, Alice. Mama and Daddy said, when they first knew, that I could stay here and I believe them when they say it's all right. I mean, I know it's *not* all right, but... Everybody else may leave Cana. I'm staying here."

"Because of Shane?" asked her sister quickly. "Are you—?"

"No, not because of Shane."

"I never have approved of him much," said Alice judiciously. "Lord knows what kind of scum he came from, and raised by that crazy old Charlie—"

"I don't want you talking like that about Shane," Viktor said gently. "He was your brother's best friend and he's another son to your mother and me now."

"He's been so good," said Nora, tears springing to her eyes, "staying here and helping with everything, working at the store when Mitch—"

"She only talks that way," said Janet scathingly, "because she's jealous."

"Jealous!" cried Alice, flushing.

"When you were in high school, you were crazy about him. I seemed so much younger to you then that you didn't care if I overheard things. You'd have given anything for dates with him, you and half the other girls at Cana High. Well, all of you were right to feel that way. He's just about the most wonderful person that ever lived."

"Then *why* don't you marry him? Good lord, if *any*body's willing to have you after—"

Viktor was shaking his head somberly. "Please, Alice, it's not necessary to talk like that to your sister. We've never been a cruel or vindictive family."

"Vindictive!" began Alice, "*Me*—"

But Paul said, "She won't marry *or* go away because she's got some damned-fool notion of bringing retribution on Cana and Alder County simply by her unwed presence—hers and the baby's. She tried to explain it to me on Sunday when she was at the house, while she and Sharon were supposed to be working on clothes. It makes just about as much sense as running under the tallest tree around when there's a lightning storm."

"Oh, you couldn't have understood ABC," Janet said wearily. "You were all wrapped up in a football game and half-drunk besides."

"Janet," Viktor cautioned gently.

It was a little like old times, Nora thought sadly—the arguments, the bickerings, with their father as arbiter—only a little.

"Well," Paul said, "no offense, Alice, but we didn't come over tonight *just* to welcome you home. We've had an idea." He turned to Janet and said calmly, with a touch of magnanimity, "Sharon and I are willing to adopt the baby."

She stared at him, her mouth all but dropping open. Viktor watched her worriedly. He had been thinking for some time that she was too thin, too pale and drawn. On Monday, she had had a dizzy spell, almost fainting at the store. She had wanted it kept from him, but Peggy Lou had found her in the rest room. Viktor had driven her home himself and had forbidden her to come back to work until after the baby was born. Now her face had turned a blotchy red and she clutched the knife until her knuckles began to whiten.

"Of course you'll give it up for adoption," Paul said coolly, and Alice said, "Oh, honey, there's nothing else *to* do; absolutely no question. You're so young, and if you won't marry, you don't want to be saddled—"

"I *won't* give it up for adoption!" Janet cried. "I never ever *thought* of it. All the time, *some*body's been trying to make me get rid of this baby. It's *mine!* Do you think I've gone through all this, put everybody else through it, just to—"

"Janet," said Sharon softly, shyly, "it would have the best care ... all the love ... I want other children so badly."

"You and Paul may not even stay married," cried Janet. "You've said so yourselves, or as good as—"

"Will you show some *sense?*" snapped Paul. "Suppose—just suppose we didn't. There'd be money to take care of the kid; there'd be love, she's just said that. There's legitimacy—more or less. I do know that on Sunday you were talking about how all-fired important it was that the baby be named Magnessen; well, it would be—"

"Shut up!" She was almost screaming. "It's *my* baby. Half the people in the world want to take it away from me. Don't any of you mention—"

Viktor had risen and taken her arm firmly. "Come upstairs, little girl. You should rest." He spoke very gently, but he glared at Paul and Alice.

Alice stood up and he said sternly, "No. Your mother needs help with the dishes."

Lying on her bed, Janet moved fitfully. No position was comfortable anymore, and she was so violently nervous.

"They can't make me do anything?" she demanded challengingly.

"No," said her father firmly.

"Daddy, I'm sorry. I'm just always making extra trouble—"

"There's nothing for you to be sorry for, my darling girl. I'm going to go now. I want you to promise you'll get into bed and try to sleep. Where are the pills from Dr. Striker?"

She indicated two bottles on the dresser. Viktor brought water and she took what was given her docilely.

"You do make me feel like a little girl," she said shyly, her mouth trembling.

"And so you are. My baby daughter."

"What time is it, Daddy?"

"About eight."

"When—when you've had another meeting with those people, will you tell us?"

"Before Christmas, Janet, I promise you'll know all I can tell you. Now, will you try to sleep?"

"Yes, but I—I want Shane. Please tell him when he comes home. I can't help it if it scandalizes Alice or anyone else to have him in my room. I just—"

"Alice is not so easily scandalized, I believe, as she would have us think. She really is a fine girl, you know, perhaps a bit too helpful sometimes, but—"

They smiled at each other wanly.

She said, "I don't know if I can ever stand to see Paul again."

Viktor stroked her hair. "I'll tell Shane. He'll come."

"I'm still not going to marry him," she said warningly, "just because I want to see him . . ."

"Yes, I understand that."

"Daddy, can you make them leave me alone . . . please . . . ?"

"We're going to talk about that right now; when I go back downstairs. Good night now. Rest. You'll feel better in the morning."

Almost before he was out of the room, she was crying. The drawn, aged face, bending over her with such love and concern, made her ache with pity and guilt for the additional worry she was to him. Getting up, walking unsteadily, she went to the bathroom. When she came out, Alice was standing there.

"Don't you talk to me, Alice Magnessen!" Janet said fiercely through her tears.

"Well, good grief, Janet, I just came up to use the bathroom," said her sister, hurt, slamming the door.

Janet's room was dark. Shane's tap on the door was almost inaudible, but even in restless sleep, she had been waiting for it.

"Shane?"

He went in and closed the door. "Can I turn on the light?"

"I'd rather you didn't. Will you just sit here for a little while?"

He groped his way to the bed, sat down, and took her hand.

"They—they want to adopt my baby."

"Viktor told me."

"Did you see Alice? Has she started in on you yet?"

"She's in bed. It's past eleven."

"It is? I must have been asleep. Where were you?"

"At Mack's."

"Are you drunk?"

"No, not quite."

"Shane, I'm sorry. I know I'm using you shamelessly, but when they started talking the way they did downstairs, I just—wanted you with me. I know you're going to go away, with Alice home and—and the rest of it...."

"Try to go back to sleep."

"You didn't answer my question."

"You haven't asked me anything."

"You're going away."

"When Mitch and Peggy find a place to live, I think I'll have to move back to Charlie's."

"Oh... but will you stay here now, just for a little while? I—I guess I need a teddy bear."

39

Faye came to the house on Thursday afternoon, bringing armfuls of wrapped gifts.

"I mustn't stay long," she said to Nora's offer of coffee. "I've got that Lennox girl at the shop. She's just fine when I'm there to be asked about everything, but she's so unsure on her own. Where is everybody? I expected to see Alice."

They sat at the kitchen table, having coffee.

"Some of the girls Alice knows—Lou Edwards, Carol Drew, and some others—were having a little get-together this afternoon. Lou called to invite her this morning. Poor Alice! I think she was half-afraid to go. She doesn't think we have any real friends left. Janet's upstairs, lying down. She was invited, too, but didn't feel up to it. I'm worried about her."

"Do you think she might have the baby early?"

"I wouldn't be a bit surprised, with all the tension there's been."

"I'll be going down to the county commissioners' meeting tonight," Faye said. "Would anyone want a ride?"

"No, I guess not. I think Charlie asked Shane to be sure and go, but I know he'd want to take his own car. None of the rest of us ... probably, someone ought to go for Paul's sake, but—well, I'm afraid we really can't care much just now what happens about Cloud Valley. I think Sharon is bringing Jamie over to spend the night so she can go. But the rest of us, it seems we're always so—tired lately, and there's always so much to be done. Now, with Christmas—I haven't wrapped a thing. We haven't done any decorating. I still have an order of things coming from the catalog. I hope they get here in time."

"Oh, it's ten days yet—well, nine."

"Alice really will be a lot of help with getting things done," Nora said, smiling wearily. "She really can accomplish a lot, though the way she goes about it, all fuss and feathers, always has made me nervous as a cat. What she'd like to do, of course, is put the house up for sale, things like that."

"Nora, you won't leave ... ?"

"Viktor talks about it more and more often. I think it's his way of trying to protect me and Patty and whoever else of the family might want to come away to some new place, to try to start over. Faye, we're too old for starting over. It will kill Viktor if he tries to retire now, if he just tries to quit everything all of a sudden, after all this strain. *I* don't want to go. I agree with Janet that the nasty people around here ought to be stuck with Magnessens; they deserve it. But Viktor can't get mad. I think if he would just get absolutely furious with everybody, it would be—cleansing for him, for all of us. Then maybe he wouldn't feel so much that we have to run away. Does that make any sense?"

"Of course it does. I don't see how you're standing it all. Do you get absolutely furious?"

Nora looked away through the window, birds at the feeder, Janet's dog romping happily with an old shoe in the backyard.

"Every day, I get—hurt—right to the quick, every time I see what's happening to Viktor and—well, so many things, but, yes, sometimes I get so mad I could smash everything in the house. I have to go and lock myself in the bedroom then, for a while, so I won't just start screaming and biting and..."

After a moment Faye said gently, "Wes said Viktor mentioned something once about—deportation...?"

Nora shook her head. "They've been checking into his citizenship, why he used another name when he was in Germany, things like that. They've contacted his sister, who's lived in Norway since the war. His older brother, who had the family farm in Denmark, died five years ago. Viktor's sister, Christiana, has written to us. She has three grown children and a grandchild.

"When Viktor left Denmark after the war, he went to England first for several months before he came to the States. His mother's people were in England. But after he left England, he *tried* to lose contact with everyone he knew. I know now that's mostly why he didn't want to stay on in Iowa, because the English relatives knew he had come there.

"Anyway, those federal people are also trying to contact other people who were in the prison camp. Until they can do that, all of this is just Viktor's word against David Rosenzweig's. But the talk about deportation is just from all the guilt he's been carrying all these years, and misery. He did nothing that could be called a crime, not under the circumstances."

"When do you think you'll hear from them again?"

Nora shrugged tiredly. "Viktor thinks maybe a few more days. I don't know. It just seems as if it's going to drag on forever. When I think back, I just can't believe what a short time it's really been. They're not really *bad* people, I suppose, and they seem to be trying to get things done as fast as they can, but there's this one man in particular who seems to—relish it so much. They just have a job to do and I don't think it's very pleasant sometimes, for most of them, but this one is like a little kid playing spyhunter or something. He talks to Viktor as if he —the investigator—is a movie Nazi questioning a prisoner. I could smash his face in every time I look at him."

After a little silence, she went on more calmly, "Janet told me this morning that Viktor promised her last night to tell them all of it before Christmas. I think he'll want you here, Faye. I know I do. A few of our special, close friends, it seems to me, have a kind of—right to know, and it's such a bitter, miserable thing for Viktor. Telling it to me was ... well, I don't want him ever to have to talk about it more than once more. I'd tell the children and the others we want told, but he won't let me. He says he has to do it now, himself, after all he's put people through. I'm worried so over him, I just can't seem to think straight half the time."

She got up to refill their cups, staring absently at the coffee pot for a moment before remembering to pick it up.

"Tell me how it's going at the bookshop."

"Well, really not bad. It's the Christmas trade, of course. By next month, business will be down to a trickle, if that. This town is not what you could call filled with avidly addicted readers, and most of the ones there are patronize the library entirely too much. It'll be a long time, if ever, before the place shows a profit, but it's kind of fun."

"And what are all these things we've been hearing about the mill?"

Faye sighed. "They want to form a corporation. It's just beautiful, really, the way almost all the workers are willing to give nearly everything they have for stock. Bert's been to see me a lot, and Tim Mallory. You know Tim's been a foreman for twenty-five years. He's talking strike and all manner of wild things, says he and a lot of the others won't work for PSL. They want me to come back into it. I've frittered away a good bit of my share of the money from the sale on those trips and the house and shop. I'd buy what stock I could, of course, but I just couldn't go *back* to the mill, not personally. That place was something around my neck for so many years. I loved it—and hated it at the same time, if you know what I mean. I still hear all the whistles and notice when the train comes and goes. It's almost as much a part of my life as breathing, but I couldn't go back there. I'm just really finding out what freedom is. There are plenty of people who could run the place. Bert Adams could. Tim himself could, with a lot of good office help.

"But it's just a pipe dream, you know. No matter how much money we got together, PSL would overbid us. They can afford to take a loss and they mean to have Holland's. They've been trying for so long. I think, when we put it up for sale before, they were just in shock when David Rosenzweig showed up, interested. That's the only reason I can think of that he ever got hold of it in the first place. I hear he's got a meeting in Boise with them right away. They say he was going to be in New York by now, for the holidays, but he's after a fast sale and PSL wants records in order and all the figures and statistics they can get. They can't close a deal like that so fast, but they're certainly not going to waste any time. Some lawyer has told some of the people they might try filing an antitrust suit, but I doubt they could win. PSL is just into too many things in this state, has fingers, and money, in too many political pies. Anyway, the workers are trying, and I'm doing what I can to help. If

David knew what Bert and some of the others are doing, I know they'd be fired on the spot; they've been going into his files and doing what they can to sabotage his dealings. Certainly the new owners will fire them. I'm afraid we're going to see quite a turnover in residents in this town before the thing's done with. PSL can send in their own people with no problem at all."

"I'm sorry," Nora said slowly. "I can't really get much worked up about what happens to the mill. As long as David Rosenzweig gets out of here, I..."

"I know. Of course I understand that."

"That's another thing about Viktor," she said fiercely. "He keeps saying we shouldn't blame him too much. Faye, I never would have believed, three months ago, that I could ever in my life even think of feeling like I wanted to kill somebody."

Faye nodded her understanding and there was a long, empathetic silence. She took a sip of her coffee and almost seemed to be squaring her shoulders.

"I came to tell you something today, Nora. Everybody will know soon enough, or I suppose they'll certainly have their suspicions. I wanted to tell you first because—well, you're special, and I thought it might help, just a little, to know the county will soon have a new topic for gossip."

Nora waited, beginning to smile faintly.

"Since Doreen Collins has decided to divorce Wes, she's decided to do it right, Reno and the whole bit. She and her mother left yesterday. Doreen's taking everything, of course, except his interest in the store, which he arranged she couldn't get at a long time ago, though she will get some more in alimony if the profits go above a certain amount. That doesn't matter, though. As soon as it's legally possible, Wes and I are going to be married. I guess we'll just run away to Nevada the way so many of the kids do."

Nora laughed softly. "You *look* like a kid right now, Faye. Why, you're even blushing. I'm glad for both of you. I'm *so* glad. You both deserve wonderful things."

"Well," Faye said firmly, "that's not all I wanted to tell you." She laughed a little, shyly. "I didn't know it would be so hard.... Wes and I have been—living together when we could, for a long, long time."

Smiling softly, Nora got up, went around the table, and put her arms around the shoulders that had become stiff and defiant. She said, almost whispering, "I've known that forever."

Faye stared up at her and, after a moment, they both began to laugh.

"*How* did you know? We thought—"

"Viktor told me. My Lord! It must have been fifteen or sixteen years ago. No," she said, holding up a cautioning hand, "Wes didn't tell him. There are a lot of things Viktor just—doesn't have to have anybody tell him. You've been very discreet, my dear. I truly believe that not another soul suspects, though of course they'll *say* they knew all the time."

"I sort of wish you'd told me," Faye said ruefully, but still smiling broadly. "There were times I could have used somebody to talk to about it."

"Yes, I would think so," Nora said with sympathy. Then her smile came back. "But, you see, you didn't tell me. There *are* times when I can mind my business and keep my mouth shut."

Faye got up, laughing. "Sometimes you very nearly make me mad, and I do have to go now. Wes is taking Peggy Lou out to supper tonight to tell her we're going to be married, that we've wanted to for a long time."

"Peggy came by here on Monday," Nora said. "She promised she'd have Mitch home for Christmas, but I just don't know if . . ."

"I think she just may do it, Nora. She really is a wonderful little girl, all Wes's child, not a bit like her mother."

"Of course," Nora said wearily, "we wish they hadn't married so young. We're afraid it's partly a kind of—reaction as far as Mitch is concerned. Vik and Anne married almost that young and it seemed to be working out all right for them. I do know Peggy's a lovely girl. I couldn't wish for a better daughter-in-law. You and Wes come to Christmas dinner. We *will* have a good Christmas, in spite of everything."

They were at the front door, Faye going out, when Nora grabbed her arm and swung her around sharply to look into her face and begin laughing again. "Faye, have you thought you're going to be Mitch's mother-in-law? My lord! talk about all in the family!"

40

Shane left the store at four-thirty that Thursday, showered, put on a fresh sports suit, and went to Kucharski's. Mitch wasn't there. He had gone home, they said. He was in Shane's old room, lying fully dressed on the bed, looking at a mechanic's manual.

"That you, Peg?" he called. "I didn't expect you'd be home this early."

"Take your shoes off my bedspread," Shane said curtly, jamming a cigarette into his mouth.

"Well, Christ, Shane—"

"That's genuine Navajo wool, not treated or anything. It won't even stand much dry cleaning. Look at the mud!" He was brushing at it.

"I was just in here because it makes a good place to study. We've been using Charlie's room. Didn't you even notice the rest of the house? Peggy's been scrubbing and working on it like crazy."

"Yes, I can see she has. It looks great, but haven't you found an apartment or something, or couldn't you go live at Peggy's dad's?"

"Well, yeah, I guess we could, but it's kind of nice, being by ourselves, you know, what time we're not working. Before Charlie comes back—"

"Listen, Mitch, I don't see why *I* should have to go out and find a room to rent when you can—"

"You mean you're not... Did Alice chase you out or what?"

"Don't ask me anything. I don't like you. Just change your clothes."

"Well, who the hell do you think—"

"I know Peggy's having supper with her dad tonight. I'm going to that commissioners' meeting at Alder Falls. I want you to come with me. Well, no, I don't *want* you to; I think you'd better. We can eat somewhere."

408

"Why in hell should I?"

"I thought you might be interested in seeing what happens to your brother's project and I want to talk to you. No, I *don't* want to talk to you, but I'm going to. Hurry up, goddam it!"

"What's the matter with you? You're acting like—"

"Will you just come on?"

They had driven, in Shane's car, halfway to Alder Falls before Mitch spoke sullenly, "You're ten miles over the speed limit."

"Just shut up." But he slowed down a little.

"Shane, what the hell . . . ? I can't imagine why I'm doing this, putting up with—"

"Last night, your dad told Janet he's going to talk to all of you about whatever the things were that happened to him. He said he'd do it before Christmas. Go and see him, and your mother, before he does it."

"I don't want to. I can't. And I don't see how it's your business."

"What do you mean, you can't?"

"I—I thought I had everything figured out about my life. I really wanted to be a doctor, once I realized it. God, it was *so* important! . . . Now it seems there's something criminal about being a doctor named Magnessen, and I don't—"

Shane had raised his right hand, but he put it back on the wheel, gripping it hard.

"I'm not at all sure you're even half-bright. You've known your dad a long time. Don't you know he could never—"

"If there's nothing to hide, then why has he been hiding?"

"Why shouldn't he keep some of his life private if he likes? When you have kids, are you go-

409

ing to tell them about every breath you drew before they were born? Before you married their mother? Would you tell then, particularly if remembering those things was like turning a knife in a wound?"

"How do you know it's like that?"

"My God, Mitch, go and look at his face!"

"Then it must have been something—criminal."

"If you use that word once more... Don't you know there are things that hurt, very nearly kill people that have nothing to do with criminality? Are you *that* young? He wasn't even using the name Magnessen in the prison camp. You know that, but if you're so damned concerned that the name is somehow—besmirched, why in hell don't you do something about it? Peggy Lou says you're going ahead with school."

"Well, maybe, but—"

"Mitch," he was pleading now, the anger momentarily gone, "go home and see them, *before* he talks to you about it. Let them know you care about them, no matter what even *you*'ve been thinking. Show some loyalty. Do you think they'd treat you like this? Under any circumstances? You *do* care?"

"I—yes, but—"

"You're their son. Don't you know they need you? You don't have any idea what they've been going through. Family deserters are just about more than they can take. Is your head so thick that—"

"I don't have to listen to any more of this. I want to go back."

"Well, I'm not taking you back. We can eat right down there at Joe's Place. I could stand

410

four or five drinks, and, no, you don't have to listen to any more because I'm finished. You're just like some other people we've run into lately, who wouldn't recognize common sense and reason if you fell over it in broad daylight."

"I always thought you were my friend," Mitch said, his voice going suddenly ragged. "When I was a kid, you were a better brother sometimes than Vik or Paul, because you didn't *treat* me so much like a kid. You could understand things—at least you'd try.... Can't you—"

"No. Now *I* don't want to talk."

He parked crookedly and slammed the car door. After a time of silence, except for orders, at their table in the restaurant and bar, Mitch tried.

"Peggy Lou and I will be out of Charlie's house by tomorrow night."

Silence.

"Are they—pretty much all right at home? I mean..."

Shane sipped his drink methodically, looking away from him through a foggy window.

"Do you think it'll snow for Christmas?... Shane, you're making me feel like an absolute—"

A flash of fierce gray eyes stopped him, made him helplessly furious. He began to eat, cutting viciously at his steak.

"*Don't* do that!" Shane said between his teeth. "You haven't got to cut half through your plate, have you? I can't stand what you're doing with that knife."

Mitch went on, bringing the knife down gratingly for every bite.

"Mitch!"

"*You're* gritting your teeth. *I* can't stand

411

that. Aren't you going to eat anything?" he asked in sugary, fake solicitude.

"I am eating. If you don't stop it—"

"You're not. You're just drinking. You won't get a thing out of the meeting and I'll have to drive."

"Not my car, you won't. I'm going to take that goddam knife and—"

"Well!" A hand fell heavily on Shane's shoulder and they both stared up at Gary Hunt. "A couple of old buddies! It didn't occur to me I might run into you two here, but I was thinking of coming up to Cana to check on old friends. Just passing through, you know, but I've certainly heard a lot of stories. That's my sports job out there. Well, you can't really see it through the fucking dirty window. My mommy gave it to me so I wouldn't come home, so I've just been cruising around the country and I ran into a girl from here, in Boise, an old college friend of Janet's. She told me some *shocking* things. Mind if I join you?"

He reached for the other chair at their table and Shane kicked it over.

The record playing on the jukebox had ended. Other customers turned at the sound of the falling chair, to look and listen.

Gary kept smiling, swaying on his feet. "That's okay. I'll stand. I think Janet's still got some papers of mine. Would you fellows know about that? I need them."

"You'd better get out of here while you can still stand up," Mitch said fiercely. The room had grown very still.

"I hear *nasty* things about your old man being a fascist or much worse." Gary still smiled through his beard. "Of course, I always knew this whole valley was nothing but a bunch of shit. ... Janet's not still living up at that old shack, is she? I'd hate to have to take my car over that road. Has she had the kid yet? I forget when it was due. If she's all through with the breeding bit, I wouldn't mind seeing her at all—just for a one-nighter, you know. This girl I met in Boise said you were going to marry her, Bonner. Have you saved her good name? It seems like there's not really too much point in that, not with the stuff that's going around about the old man."

Shane and Mitch had both stood up. People nearest them moved away a little. Shane's hands, doubled into hard fists, were shoved deep into his pockets, but he jerked them out to grab Mitch.

"Don't!" he said sharply.

"I'll kill the sonofabitch!" Mitch cried, "and you ought to—"

Through the haze of blind, mindless fury in Shane's brain, Charlie's words from the hospital room came whispering insanely:

"When Steve come home, he was bitter, mean. It seemed like he used to fight and such just for the hell of it, but, after that, seemed like he wanted to hurt people. Seemed like he'd do or say anything to git a fight started. ... That last fight got to be pretty much of a free-for-all, I guess, the way bar fights will, but the man Steve had started it with ... Steve cut him in the neck with a piece of a bottle an' he bled to death before they could git him to the hospital. ..."

Gary was going on softly, "She's a hot little number in bed and she doesn't have to be married. She's especially good if you let her talk about love and crap like that, strictly establishment—well, pretty strictly." He smirked at Shane. "Would you believe I used to be a little bit jealous of you, logger boy? I still doubt that kid's mine. You know a girl, once she's started sleeping around, it gets to be a habit, pretty much like for a guy. You can't ever tell—"

Mitch was fighting Shane's grip on his arms. "Goddamn you! If you won't stand up for her, you bastard—"

"Do you want to go to jail?" hissed Shane between his teeth. "Joe's already called somebody." He was white and his hands, holding the boy, were not steady enough.

"Won't fight, huh?" said Gary pleasantly, leering. "All you asshole hicks are cowards, some more than others."

He picked up Mitch's plate and flung it at Shane. It would have struck him because he couldn't seem to move, but Gary was drunk, his aim uncertain. The heavy crockery plate struck the window and smashed through. Abruptly, Gary had stopped smiling. He swept everything from their table and the one next to it. Turning to the bar, he began throwing bottles and glasses. Everyone was moving now, trying to find any sort of cover. Shane dragged Mitch behind the bar.

"Crazy sonofabitch!" yelled the bartender, crouching beside them. "Joe's called the cops. I never had no idea he was that loaded or I wouldn't have served him anything. My God!"

Two Alder Falls policemen came in. One held a pistol menacingly in Gary's face, but he seemed oblivious of it, still grabbing things from other tables and flinging them about the room.

It required both policemen and some help from customers, to hold him, get him handcuffed and out of the place.

"Let me have our bill, Roy," Shane said hoarsely under the noise of talk and speculation that was rising louder and louder.

"Joe said you don't owe nothin', Shane," said the bartender, awed. "I purely believe he'd of killed one or both of you if he'd been half-sober. Look, somethin's cut your hand. You better—wait! Those cops'll want to ask you . . ."

But they had reached the door, both of them gulping painfully at the cold air. They drove away while the policemen were still struggling to get Gary into their car, customers streaming out to watch.

"You're not still going to that meeting?" Mitch cried angrily as Shane turned the car into town. "Your hand's bleeding all over the place. Look at it!"

Shane looked, briefly, as if it were not a part of him.

"Shane, let's go home!"

"No, not yet. I told Charlie—"

"Goddamit, why didn't you fight him? Why wouldn't you let me?"

"My dad," Shane said tonelessly, "went to prison for killing somebody in a bar."

"Those things he was saying—good Christ! I thought you *cared* about Janet."

"Leave me alone, Mitch. I can't—"

"No wonder she won't marry you!"

"If you don't shut up, I'll—"

"You'll what?" he cried, thrusting out his face belligerently.

"I'll knock hell out of you."

Mitch laughed harshly. "If you think you can take it out on me, you're crazier than even *I* thought. I've got size on you, and weight, a lot more than that sonofabitch had."

Shane said, still quietly, dully, "You can ask anyone who's old enough to remember, Mitch, and they'll tell you I could take on anybody when I was in high school, for a while—until I quit fighting. I'm still in good enough shape to mop up this street with . . . I—I'm sorry."

They were silent for the rest of the short way to the courthouse. It was early. The parking lot was empty.

"Honest, Shane," Mitch said, mollified, half-pleading now, "let's not stay for any meeting. I feel sick and you sure as hell look it."

Shane fumbled at his cigarettes. Mitch took the pack and lit one for him. He drew deeply, twice, then reached for the keys in the car's ignition. As he held them, he seemed to notice his hand for the first time, dripping blood onto his trousers and the floor of the car. He got out swiftly, dropping the cigarette and, leaning weakly against the car, was sick for what seemed to Mitch forever. Finally, Mitch got out and walked around the car, gulping down his own nausea.

"Let me drive you over to the hospital emergency room. That cut needs some stitches and there might be glass slivers . . ."

Shane had wrapped a handkerchief around his hand but it was already blood-soaked. He still held the car keys, but he let Mitch take them, though he shook his head dazedly at the offer of help getting back into the car.

"But we have to come back to the meeting," he said thickly.

"Yes, all right," Mitch agreed shakily. "We won't miss the goddam meeting. Don't pass out on me now. It scares hell out of me when people do that."

41

The meeting went badly from the first, as Paul had been almost certain it would. He had come down with Ted Carpenter, who was helping to make the presentation. They had fortified themselves with several drinks against the disintegration of their hopes and plans. The five commissioners, seated around their table, kept glancing at each other, shaking their heads slightly from time to time as Paul talked. When he finished, a little lamely, and went to sit down for Ted's part of the talk, Paul looked at the crowd. There was quite a turnout. Paul knew practically all of them more or less well and felt that most were against his plan.

Sharon was there, having come down with Nancy Carpenter. Sharon looked sullen and miserable. He was so sick of seeing her look like that. Faye Holland seemed to look smug, except that she began casting glances of concern when Mitch and Shane came in by a side door and sat down, both of them looking glassy-eyed and vague, as if they were on drugs or something. There was a contingent of students from Alder Valley Junior

College who wanted to talk about the environment, and even two or three old people from the northern end of the county, ranchers from the Blackbuck area.

Paul slipped out by a side door and took a good slug from a pocket flask. It wasn't going to go. Sharon could have her damned ranch kept the way she wanted it. There was that land-development company in Boise that had offered to take over a part of the project if he couldn't swing it, but their price offer was laughable—or cryable, however you felt like looking at it.

A few farsighted businessmen did speak in favor of the project, but not nearly as many as had been for it back in the summer. Then the environmentalists and nonprogressives got started.

"Shit, we may as well go home," muttered Ted in the hall as they passed the flask between them. "Those old buzzards had their minds made up a long time before they came to this meeting. All this talk is just for the sake of formality. Old man Baldwin is practically snoring with his head on the table."

"No," Paul said tiredly, "I guess I'll stay till it's really finished. What do you think I could get for my business, Ted? and the house?" He laughed bitterly, swaying a little.

"This county's sure given you the dirty end of the stick."

"It's not the county," Paul said petulantly. "Not really."

When everyone had said what they had to say, old Sam Baldwin, commission chairman, began droning. It was the consensus of the commission that, for the time being, it would be best not to go ahead with the Cloud Valley project.

What with the various objections voiced right here in the county, the threat of a court fight over possible environmental disagreements, the adverse feeling of the residents of the area most concerned, the uncertainties where the Forest Service and conservation people were concerned, constantly rising costs, the state of the economy generally, and its particular uncertainty right here in the county with the difficulties that could arise over the Holland Mill ...

Paul took the flask from his pocket and swallowed the last of its contents, not bothering to go into the hall.

"All right," he said angrily, standing up to face the commissioners. "You don't need to go on about it all night. I think everybody's got the message. Some have already left.

"You must know in your stingy little hearts what this backward hick county is going to be missing out on. All the reasons you've been expounding, Mr. Chairman, at such length and with such yawning clarity, no doubt have their grain of truth, validity, common sense, and feasibility. But a lot of people—most of you sitting at that table—were ready to go on this thing as short a time as two months ago, when all those same reasons existed and were just as valid. I've had the word of some of the finest, most upstanding citizens of this fine county, which I was stupid enough to believe could be trusted. 'Go ahead, Paul boy. We're behind you 100 per cent. *Fine* thing for the Alder Valley.' I sunk all the spare money I could scrape together on surveys and the like. Worse than that, I also sunk some other people's money—*and* my business and personal reputation.

"And it was all just fine until, say, the beginning of November, when talk really got going about the Magnessen family. Now you're going to let this kind of economic promise for the future slip through your beloved county's fingers out of fear, or prejudice, or perversity, or just plain ignorance. Hold on, Mr. Chairman, I've got just one more point. I think you can afford to spare me that much time.

"The talk, the gossip, the suspicions—hell, the truth, for all I know—some of you may know more about it than I do—is that my father, Viktor Magnessen, is or was or has been a Nazi, that Alder County's been harboring a viper in its pure bosom. Well, you're fools to drop the project without even giving it a chance, whether there's truth or not to this talk, these rumors. This is *my* project, basically, and I'm not Viktor Magnessen, but you're going to see that all of us pay. Yes, my name is Magnessen, but it wasn't, always. He's not my father. He adopted me when I was four years old and he married my mother. And, no, I wasn't even a bastard. My father was named Paul Kirkwood. He came from Cincinnati, Ohio, and he died in France, fighting for America in 1944. His war record is as good as any of you American Legion or VFW people can boast of. I've got his medals at home. You're throwing away an economic opportunity of a lifetime for this stagnant, backwater county, chiefly because of what you think *may* be the Magnessen history, and he's not even my father. Really, when you think about it long enough, and you're in just the right frame of mind, it gets to be goddam funny."

Paul turned and walked unsteadily from the room, not looking back.

"How could he *do* it?" Mitch cried when they had driven several miles in silence. He choked. "You have to stop the car a minute, Shane. I—"

This time it was Mitch who was sick, in the dry winter weeds at the side of the highway. It had begun to snow lightly. Waiting, Shane got out of the car and held his face up for the gentle, cold touch.

Later, Mitch said, looking at the dash clock, "It's past eleven. Do you think they'll be in bed?"

"I don't know."

"Even if they're asleep—Mom and Dad—I think I'll have to wake them up just for a few minutes. I just want to see them, ask how they are and things. I know they need their rest but ... if it's all right with them, Peggy Lou and I will move up there, just till time for school to start. That's only a month...."

"What about going back to work at the store?"

"Yes, I'll tell Vince they need me. By Monday—"

"How about by tomorrow morning?"

"Well, it doesn't seem fair not to give any notice at all."

"You didn't give any notice when you left the store, and they're going to be shorthanded for the weekend."

"Why? I don't understand—"

"I'm going away for a couple of days. Janet and I are. Tonight."

"Does she—?"
"No."

42

Janet was in bed, reading. She had slept a good deal that day. Earlier, Patty had come in to say goodnight; then Alice to talk some more about the coffee gathering she had attended that afternoon and to fret that Janet had stayed downstairs such a short time and eaten so little supper; then her parents, Nora bringing a glass of hot milk.

She heard them come in, Shane go to his room, and Mitch at their parents' door, knocking softly, then saying, "I just—uh—came by for a minute to say hello. Tomorrow, if it's all right—" then he went in and closed the door behind him.

Tears of relief sprang to Janet's eyes; then there was a knock at her own door.

"Shane, Mitch came back with you! Oh, what in the world did you say to him, do to him . . . ?"

She stared briefly at the small suitcase in his hand, then turned her face away, trying not to let the tears spill over.

"I—found the poem this morning. It's beautiful."

Last night, after she slept, he had written the two lines on the flyleaf of the book she was reading: 'What I do what I dream includes thee As the wine must taste of its grapes.'—E. B. Browning."

"It's beautiful," she said again shakily, "but at the same time, after all that's happened, it was like a kind of—good-bye, and now you have that suitcase..."

"How do you feel?"

"I'm all right; much better." She had turned back to try to face him. "What have you done to your hand? Oh, there's blood—"

"Yes, I have to change my clothes."

"You and Mitch didn't—?"

"I cut it on some broken glass. While I'm changing, get dressed, please, and put some things in here, whatever you need for a couple of days—"

"What on earth are you talking about?" Alice was standing in the open door behind him. "What are you doing with that suitcase?" she demanded.

"It's our week for going to Nevada. Get up, Janet."

"But she can't make a trip like that when she's—this far along," Alice said sternly.

Janet, in surprise, had sat up fully; Alice hurriedly and decorously put a robe around her shoulders.

Shane put the bag on the foot of her bed. "You've got about five minutes."

"Let me see your hand," she said curtly. "There must be stitches under that big a bandage."

"Seven," he said. "It's a lucky number, and I've got pills in case it starts to hurt."

"*You* can't make a trip like that," fretted Alice. "You look sicker than she does right now."

"Well, I'm not. Janet, if you're not ready,

I promise I'll dress you and carry you downstairs."

"Shane, please," but he was gone.

She sat there, beginning to be filled with a bewildering mixture of fear and joy, not hearing Alice's assurances that of course they couldn't go. She was still sitting like that when Shane came back in clean shirt and trousers and thrust a few of his own things into the suitcase.

"I told you," he said warningly. He began to open and close drawers at random, flinging things at the bed. "Damn it, Janet, I don't know what you need or want. Will you please get up and be just a little help?"

"You can't drive all that way with the back of your hand cut open," cried Alice, "and she—"

"You're right," he said a little wildly. "I'll get blood poisoning and be dead inside of three days. *Then* she'll be sorry."

"He really is a wonderful driver," Janet murmured dreamily. Then, suddenly, she began to laugh, a cleansing, good-feeling laugh that she couldn't seem to stop. "Not *that*, Shane," she gulped as he flung a gauzy nightgown at the bed. "I haven't worn that since I was about fifteen," she choked. "I couldn't possibly—"

"I *told* you, I don't know," he said doggedly, still throwing garments.

"Will you just get *out* of that dresser," she said, weak with laughter. "Here, I'll *do* it."

"Janet," said Alice worriedly.

"You want her married, don't you?" demanded Shane, but he had begun to smile as he picked up the things he had flung at the bag.

"Yes, of course, but it may be too late, for going all that way, I mean. Or—maybe I could go along to help drive and things. Shane, she's liable to have the baby right—"

"Alice," Janet said, still spluttering, "you are my dearest sister, but even the *very* dearest doesn't go along on one's wedding trip."

"But the baby . . ."

"I'm a nurse, remember, and Mr. Bonner is so goddam masterful, he can just deliver it in the car if it has to be that way."

"You don't think," he began worriedly. "I've already got blood all over the front."

"You are the tenderest, most concerned person I ever saw," she said, pushing him out of her way. "No, I'm not going to mess up your car any more than you already have. Now, are you going to get out of here so I can dress?"

It was a tumultuous leave-taking, with Alice, Mitch, and their parents calling after them long after they could hear. They drove in silence for a long while, until he said tentatively,

"It could have been better. I just didn't know any other way."

"It's probably a mistake," she said softly, "but . . ."

"Well, there's not a chance of your going back now."

"No," she said in a small voice, "and I'm glad—I think. But you look awful."

"I *am* awful," he said, suddenly frightened. "I think I forgot the damned rings."

He stopped the car and searched his pockets frantically, then finally found them in the bag. He took them out and buttoned them into a shirt pocket. She began to giggle again and he laughed, sighing, "My God!"

Later he said soberly, "If you get too tired or

want to stop for any reason, we can manage that."

They passed through Alder Falls and over the fifteen more miles of state highway to the interstate.

She said gently, "Shane, tell me."

"I'd rather not, now."

"But you'll have to, some time."

He drew on the cigarette she had lighted for him and exhaled slowly. "At the place where Mitch and I went for supper, Joe's Place, there was—a fight. I wasn't in it, neither was Mitch, but bottles and things were flying all over the place, and that's where my hand was cut. I started thinking after that, about Steve, my dad. I used to wish when I was a kid that he wasn't my father —a man in prison for murder who was killed there, fighting. I used to hope it hadn't been Steve, but just somebody unknown, and I used to make up—well, never mind that. Then we went to the commissioners' meeting."

He told her some of the things Paul had said.

"He *couldn't!*" she cried, tears starting to her eyes. "Not even Paul. Oh, poor Daddy!"

"I'm not so sure it was all that bad, Janet. Maybe it got through to somebody there that some of these people are a bunch of ... anyway, I'll have to think about that when my mind's clearer.

"The point I'm trying to make right now is that I want you. And there's the baby. I do understand how you feel about its being a Magnessen, but I want to marry you and I want it to be named Bonner from the beginning, if it's to have the name. I—I don't want it ever to have to feel ashamed of being named Bonner, or—to wish it's not mine."

"Shane," she said tenderly.

He cleared his throat and put out the cigarette. "Put the seat back and try to sleep now, all right? It's a long way and I'd hate like hell to *need* Alice."

It was a grubby little town, the first they came to after crossing the state line. Next to a casino, the wedding chapel and the office for purchasing marriage licenses were the easiest things to find.

Shane had to wake Janet; it had taken her a very long time to get to sleep. She stumbled to a service-station rest room to wash her face and comb her hair. She was so groggy and tired that he led her by the hand into the licensing office.

The wizened old clerk peered at them disapprovingly through his dirty glasses and Shane, who was feeling a half-wild elation that sometimes came to him with total exhaustion, had to struggle to put down an urge to wink at the old man. He let it go at an inane smile and turning his eyes away for a minute.

"We have a scheduled wedding at ten," said the minister in the chapel, "but I think we might fit you in before that."

He glanced meaningfully at Janet, who said groggily, "You'd probably better."

Shane began to laugh and the man said sternly, "Do you want a civil or a religious ceremony?"

"Well, we hadn't thought about that," Shane said, trying to pretend he was coughing. "Why don't you choose, just so long as it doesn't interfere with the next one."

"What about music? And I think we have some flowers you could—"

427

"No, that's all right. I don't think we'll need anything else."

Shane had got himself reasonably well under control, but a stifled giggle from Janet threw him into another coughing fit.

"Do you have rings?" asked the minister, most soberly and severely.

"Yes," Janet had to answer this time.

"And have you brought witnesses?"

"No."

He summoned two elderly ladies from somewhere who were, evidently, perennial witnesses.

As Shane paid the minister, Janet stood a little aside, stifling a yawn. The two ladies were signing as witnesses and one whispered righteously, "It looks like it's high time." The other said, "If he'd made them wait till after the next wedding, it might have been too late." The first said, "A couple of those hopheads, if you ask me."

"Where did you nice ladies ever learn about hopheads?" Shane asked mildly and they left.

He came back from the first motel office, swaying with exhaustion. It had begun to rain.

"There is no room in the inn," he said, getting stiffly back into the car. "Not with twin beds, that is. It seems people don't use them much around here, but he thinks there may be some at the next place down the road."

"You have to stop being so silly," she said, giggling helplessly, "especially sacrilegious. You should have seen yourself through the wedding. You just stood there, grinning like an absolute idiot."

He began to laugh again. "Should I have cried? Besides, I thought you were asleep. You didn't hear a thing he said."

"I did, too. He said, 'Please don't hold hands until the part of the service where you are asked to join hands.' And you wouldn't let go."

It was twilight in the room when Shane woke. He lay, as he often did, without opening his eyes, trying to place himself in time and space. Then he remembered. Only maybe it was a dream. His eyes snapped open. He was lying on his back, half facing a dingy yellowish wall. He turned his head. Janet lay on her side in the other bed, watching him, smiling softly.

"Hi," she said. "You're beautiful when you sleep, or any other time. It's just that I've never watched you sleep before. Why, Shane, you're blushing! All right, you're not beautiful, but you're terrifically handsome. Everybody who ever saw you must have told you that. It's a wonder you're not spoiled worse than you are. You may as well be warned that I'm always going to be a little jealous and—worried."

"You're nuts."

"No, it's true."

"*You*'re beautiful," he said softly, "and sweet and pretty and stubborner than hell and—nuts. Have you been awake long?"

"Just a little while. Does your hand hurt?"

"Only a little. Are you all right?"

"Yes. This is a very odd honeymoon, isn't it?"

"We'll try for another sometime."

"Do you think we'll ever really remember our wedding?"

"Maybe not. Maybe we ought to have another of those, too. Sometimes you can't remember the most important things, like I never have been able to remember running that log truck off the road."

She laughed. "You draw some very odd comparisons. But we did get married, didn't we?"

"I think there's a paper that says so, if I can remember what I did with it, maybe two papers, and we're wearing the rings."

Their eyes met and held for a long moment in the dimness. She said, almost inaudibly, "I really am your wife."

"Janet, I want you so. I—"

"Oh, Shane, there *are* other ways. We wouldn't have to . . ."

"No," he said roughly. "Let's wait until everything is right." He lit a cigarette. "What time is it?"

"Not quite six. It's raining. . . . Shane, I want to tell you something. I don't know, maybe you won't want to hear it, but—for months now, when I think of the baby—almost with*out* thinking, you know, it just seems, automatically for an instant, that it's—ours."

"It's a good thing to hear," he said softly.

He came and sat beside her, bending to kiss her, gently at first, then drawing away when they both began to tremble and cling to each other.

"We—we really better go," she said in a small, wistful voice.

"Where?" he asked shakily.

"Back home. With all that's going on, you can't tell what may have come up. They may—need us."

"When you were asleep this morning, I called your mother to tell them you seemed to be all right, and where we were, in case they did need us. They don't expect us back until tomorrow night. I don't know if I could drive back tonight. I'm still really tired. You must be too."

"I do think you're feverish," she said, putting her hand against his cheek in sudden concern. "You'd better take that bandage off and let me see your hand. We can get things at a drugstore to make another bandage, if they have a drugstore."

"If I'm feverish, it's you, it's not my hand. Suppose I go out and bring back something to eat. Unless you especially want to get dressed and see the town."

"I think I saw it this morning."

He began dressing. "Here they are."

"What?"

"The papers."

"Let me see them."

"Just a minute."

"What are you looking for?" she asked after a moment.

"The date and the name of the town."

She laughed. "You said you told Mama where we were."

"I'd forgotten it, though."

He handed her the papers and she clicked her tongue in disapproval because he'd practically crumpled, rather than folded them. She smoothed them lovingly.

Shane stood looking from the dusty window. All that was visible among cinder-block buildings was a small space where a few cars were parked on wet asphalt. It was raining, the heavy drizzle that was almost like tears, or blood. Music from a bar or casino came faintly.

"It's a nice wedding day," he said with quiet

sincerity, turning back to her. "But turn on the light. You can't read that stuff in the dark."

"You were," she said, but she reached obediently for a reading lamp. "Are you always going to be as bossy as you have been for the past night and day?"

"Yes."

"And how far do you think it will get you?"

"Just as far as I can make it go." He combed his hair and put on his coat. "What would you like to eat?"

"I don't know. It doesn't matter. . . . You're right that we should stay here tonight and—and rest, only I do so want to make love. What will we *do?*"

"Janet, please be some help. I can't . . . We'll eat and watch TV and—and sleep. Just—don't let's torture each other."

"I'm sorry," she said miserably. "I mean I'm sorry we can't because . . ."

"And don't say that anymore either," he said gently. "Please don't. It won't be forever."

She smiled dreamily. "Last night at this time, I wouldn't have dreamed . . ."

"You see, things do change," he said, trying for a smug grin as he closed the door.

43

Paul did not come home after the commissioners' meeting on Thursday night. On Friday, Sharon called Nancy Carpenter, who said he had driven Ted home very late. It was 2 A.M.

on Saturday before he returned to the East Ridge house. Sharon, sleeping uneasily, woke at the sound of his car. He came upstairs after a little time, walking unsteadily, and went into the guest room, where he had been sleeping for months.

"Paul?" she said through the door, shivering though the house was warm.

"Go away, Sharon."

"Is—is there anything I can get you? . . . Have you had anything to eat?"

"I don't want anything, except I'd like to know what the hell happened to all the Scotch."

"You drank it," she said quietly.

"Never mind, there's bourbon."

"Paul—"

"Leave me alone."

He looked ghastly when he finally came downstairs toward noon.

"Daddy, look at the Christmas tree," urged Jamie eagerly. "We're just getting it all fixed up."

Paul did not answer, did not glance into the living room. The little boy looked at his mother and, suddenly, his eyes brimmed with tears.

"Go and put on some more tinsel," Sharon said, hugging him. "I'll be in again in a minute."

She followed Paul, who was going a little unsteadily to his office.

"Let me fix you some bacon and—"

"God!" he groaned, putting his hand to his mouth. "Just go away."

"You've got to eat some time," she said desperately. "And Paul, it's the Saturday before Christmas. Jamie—we—"

"I'm going out. There are some things I have to take care of."

"But—"

"Goddam it, I don't want to talk. I can't care about Christmas right now, and I am not ready to have you start in about—"

"I'm not going to start in about anything," she said curtly. "Can't you give anyone half a chance to—"

He was sorting through papers, not seeming to know she was in the room.

"Your mother called yesterday and this morning."

"Yes, I'll just bet she did."

He had the bourbon and he drank from the bottle a little desperately, gulping when he had finished as if he were going to be sick.

"Yesterday, it was to tell us that Janet and Shane have gone to get married."

He smiled, but it was more of a grimace. "Phyllis is at the office downtown," he said absently. "She agreed to work today and I've got to get this stuff to her so it can be taken care of, wound up."

"I could take it down. You need—"

"No. I don't know when I'll be back."

"Nora called this morning to ask if we'd come to church with them tomorrow. She'd like all the family to be there. It seems Mitch and Peggy Lou are moving back to use Mitch's old room, just until the second semester begins. He's all enthusiastic again, about school and—"

"Nice," he said bitterly, trying to even up a stack of papers for his briefcase. His hands were shaky. "Everything's coming up roses; red and green ribbons for Christmas."

"Paul, Viktor called, too, just before you came

434

downstairs. He'd had a call at the store from those immigration people. Someone's coming up to see him again on Monday and he'd like us all to come to the house that evening. He called here even before he'd called to tell Nora. He wanted to see if you were home and—"

"When I do come back," he said, seeming not to have heard her, "I'll take some of my things and go away, far away, get the hell out of here."

"I don't want you to," she said quietly.

"You can have whatever's left," he said. "Ted will draw up the papers. Talk to him. I'll write him in a week or two. I can do something to send enough money to keep up the house payments if you don't want to sell it, and there's the ranch. There won't be much coming in in the way of commissions. What little there is left of the real-estate business, I'm turning over to Joe Starbuck. I think everything can be wound up at the office by the first of the year, but if questions come up, problems, Ted will know how to reach me, when there *is* a place to reach me."

"Paul, he called because they've been worried about you. We all have. It was—"

"I don't want to be forgiven, Sharon, taken back into the fold." His voice was loud and unsteady. "Nobody wanted to stand by me before. What is this all of a sudden? When I've done the ultimate, it gets to be a big deal, all at once— let's be nice to Pauly week, let's take him to church and—"

"What do you mean, done the ultimate?"

"I mean, as you damn well know, that I stood in front of all those people and said he's not my

435

father. You were there. I saw the way you looked."

"That was no big thing," she said shortly. "Everybody knew, or they used to. Probably a lot of people had forgotten that Viktor adopted you. You were old enough to remember, and they've never tried to hush it up or anything. My God, why should they? Lots of people are adopted. It doesn't mean—"

He closed the briefcase with a snap, then opened it and tried to fit in the bourbon bottle. It was too big. He cursed viciously, then looked up at her belligerently.

"That wasn't all of it," he said fiercely. "You know it wasn't. Why do you have to make me— I as good as said those things were true, the gossip and—"

"Paul, you didn't; you really didn't. Just at first, when you began talking, it seemed that's what you might mean. I suppose some people will always think you *did* mean that, but they don't matter. When I got home and had time to think about it, I was *proud* of the way you socked it to those people. They needed it and..."

He was staring at her. "You? Proud? You've been crying for years over Cloud Valley. You had to be the happiest person at that meeting to see the thing really and finally go down the drain. Get out of the way, Sharon.... When I come back, I'll try and talk to Jamie, be a little merry for the season, maybe try to explain to him, a little, about why I'm leaving. He won't care. You can have Christmas with the folks. God knows there are plenty of them; getting to be more every day, it seems."

He slammed out of the house, banged his car

door, and scattered gravel in the driveway as he left.

It was almost dawn on Sunday. Sharon, who had not been asleep at all this time, lay tensely listening. He went into his room and in a few moments there was silence. He wasn't packing or going out again just now. He must be completely exhausted, needing sleep desperately.

She got up at nine and went down to the kitchen to drink coffee alone and make some absent-minded preparations for dinner. After a while, she went and woke Jamie.

"Have a bath before your breakfast," she told him brightly. "We're going to church with Grandma and Grandpa and the others."

"How long till Christmas?"

When the little boy was in the tub, she opened Paul's door softly. He was sleeping heavily, the room smelling thickly of whiskey and cigarette smoke. Quietly, she opened the window. The gray, leaden sky looked like snow. She sat on the side of the bed. One of Paul's hands lay on top of the covers, the fingers curled a little the way Jamie's would be. It looked so vulnerable and helpless that there was a lurching in her chest and her eyes stung. She took it in both of hers.

"Paul?"

He stirred, murmured belligerently, pleadingly.

"Paul, Jamie and I are going to church in a little while."

"Great," he said thickly and pulled his hand away to rub at his gummy eyes. "God, there's never been such a hangover. Will you tell me why you had to wake me up? Bring another bottle of something up here. I don't care what.

And close the damned drapes, will you? I suppose if the sun were shining, you'd have opened them just the same."

She closed the curtains and came back to the bed.

"I can't bring a bottle because I don't think there's anything left in the house. Besides, you've got to start drying out some time. I woke you to let you know we'd be going out, but not for long—because I want you to promise you'll still be here when we come back. We have to talk, you and I."

"There's nothing to talk about, Sharon."

"There are a thousand things. I've put a roast in to cook while we're gone. I know you can't stand the thought of food, but you've got to start eating again—and thinking, too. We'll have a proper Sunday dinner, the three of us, like an honest-to-God family. Maybe you'll help Jamie finish off the tree-trimming. He's saved a few special things that he wants his daddy to do. Then, when he's having his nap . . ."

"Will you just get out?"

"Will you promise? Because if you don't, I can't go, and having us all at church today is very important to your mother."

"I can't even *see*," he groaned.

"Then you can get some more sleep," she said gently. "We'll be back soon after noon."

She was at the door when he said angrily, "Well, we're not having any big soul-searching talks. It's way too late for that kind of thing. I told you, I'm leaving."

"Mommy!" yelled Jamie. "Will you come help me dry off now?"

"Just a minute, Jamie," she called and Paul

clutched his head, groaning at her raised voice. She turned back to him. "Anyway, how do you *know* it's too late? We've never tried it, not really. And stop feeling sorry for yourself. I don't mean about the hangover. God knows you must have reason for that. You've always been a little inclined toward paranoia—"

"For God's sake, get *out!*"

"You have, Paul. . . . Go away later if you have to, but don't be cowardly about it. At least give me a chance. It's not *just* your life."

"Mommy!"

"If he yells again," Paul said between his teeth.

When Jamie was having his breakfast, Sharon put a cup, a small pot of coffee wrapped in a towel, and some aspirin on a tray. She tiptoed back into Paul's room. This time it smelled heavily of his sickness, but there was no mess. He had made it to the bathroom all right and was sleeping again, white, his closed eyes looking sunken. Soundlessly, she put the tray on the table by the bed and went downstairs.

It was important to Nora that they all be in church that Sunday. She always saw that Patty attended Sunday school and she rarely missed a Sunday service herself, but it didn't bother her much that the others rarely or never attended; only *this* morning, the Sunday before Christmas, and with all that had been happening to them, it seemed somehow vital to her that they all be there, together. She hadn't pressured anyone, just asked, and they had understood.

There was more than a pewful of Magnessen relations now, and Faye and Wes were there to sit with them. Shane, raised in the heat of Charlie's fine contempt for formal religion, had not been in church since there had been a funeral up at Blackbuck, long, long ago, the funeral of an old timber buddy of Charlie's, killed in a logging accident. Charlie, grumbling all the while, had felt compelled to go and had made the little boy go with him. Even when there was Vik and Anne's funeral, they had been hard at work in the woods; Charlie hadn't wanted to have Shane take the day off and he had been secretly glad, though he had never got over feeling guilty about it, though the family seemed to understand. Now he felt stiff and uneasy, sitting there, completely at a loss as to what, if anything, would be expected of him.

"How long since you've been to church?" whispered Janet, under the opening music.

"I don't know," he said unhappily, "unless you count that wedding chapel..."

She shook her head, half-hiding a mischievous grin with her hand. "Well, you know you're all flushed and guilty-looking. People are going to think you've been terrifically wicked," which heightened the color in his fair skin even more, brought an angry, pleading look from his lowered gray eyes, and broadened her smile.

Some members of the congregation had smiled at them as they trooped in. Some of the smiles were warm, others a bit cynical. Some people had stared; others had deliberately and obviously turned their faces away. The minister, Philip Bennington, noticing them from the front of the church, had seemed a little taken aback and had become very busy with some papers as the choir began its first hymn.

Rev. Bennington and his wife had been at the Magnessen house for a half hour or so one evening last week. He had explained that he liked to make brief calls on all his parishioners during the holidays if there was time. He had been at the church less than two years. Both he and his wife had seemed stiff and uneasy with small talk, but unable to bring up the subjects that loomed so large for the family. Nora had seen them out with one of her fruitcakes, thinking that they were nice, kind, thoughtful young people, but that she still missed the old minister, Rev. Slater. He and his family had been there when the Magnessens moved to Cana, and the families had become good friends. But Rev. Slater had died; his children were all grown up, and his widow had moved away. Nora sighed sadly. Still, the young minister tried hard.

Philip Bennington and his wife, Sara, were both basically shy people, and he was uneasy with his sermon this morning. Yet, he was more uneasy with what he had been seeing and hearing in his community of late.

He began with the Christmas story from Luke, his light voice not quite steady. The congregation looked pleased, comfortable. This was the talk and reading they wanted, expected, at this season. Then Philip's message worked smoothly into some of Jesus' doings and teachings. Briefly, he touched on the miracle of the wine at Cana and everyone was pleased, as always, to have that brought up. Then he got around to "A greater commandment I give unto you, that thou shalt love thy neighbor as thyself." And somehow—it seemed to happen quite smoothly, for Philip Bennington was good at composition—but some of the parishioners who tried to recall later, just couldn't quite recall how he had worked it into a Christmas sermon—he was giving them quotes such as the sins of the fathers shall be visited upon the children, even unto the third and fourth generations; "The fathers have eaten sour grapes and the children's teeth are set on edge"; "An eye for an eye . . ." And, for counterbalance, "Judge not, that ye be not judged"; "Let him who is without sin cast the first stone"; and again, "A greater commandment I give unto you, that thou shalt love thy neighbor as thyself." And finally, shatteringly, "Father, forgive them, for they know not what they do."

Philip's own commentary was very brief, just enough to give the quotations a semblance of being linked and blended.

The final hymn was "Joy to the World." The organist played it and the choir sang it joyously, but many of the congregation, all standing now, murmured the words thoughtfully, or not at all.

They went out of the church quietly. Some greeted the Magnessens in subdued voices, more than had looked on them with warmth when they had come in.

"That was—" Nora began, holding the minister's hand gratefully, but then she could say no more.

Viktor gave him a brief, deep look whose gratitude caused Philip Bennington to flush and feel a warm, engulfing conviction that the ministry could have its beautiful, gratifying moments.

Driving home, Shane said softly, "I never knew all those things are in the Bible. Are they? Or was he just—"

"Of course they are," Alice said placidly. "There's just everything in the Bible. You're always reading, Shane. I can't see how, even with

Charlie the way he is, you've passed up such a beautiful, interesting book all these years."

44

Charlie came in the late afternoon with a pickup full of Christmas trees. They put the Magnessens' on the back porch and Patty, getting into coat, cap, and gloves, insisted on keeping it company. "It's so cold," she explained vehemently. "If we leave it out here long all by itself, it's just liable to isolate." She stroked the tree's branches as she stroked Loki, who was with her, until the slow-moving grown-ups should be ready to bring the tree into the house.

They had had a late dinner, but quickly got together a plate of leftovers for Charlie. There were a few moments when he was alone with Shane and Janet in the kitchen. He had been eying them covertly since hearing about the wedding, grinning one moment, the next looking sober, a little sad. He kept feeling that he really ought to say something so, before sitting down at the table, he took Janet's hand and said brusquely,

"Now, you see he gits treatment like he's used to. He's been raised to a real easy life, you know."

"I have?" Shane said, widening his eyes. They were all smiling now.

"Tell me about it, Charlie," Janet said, "so I'll know just what to do."

"Well, you know, like sleepin' till noon most days, breakfast in bed too, three times a week, not much to do at the timber camps but set around an' wait for them good meals we always have, not havin' to spend his money much on groceries and wasteful stuff like that."

Shane said dryly, "I guess I just got used to it; I've been taking it all for granted all these years."

"Well, you want to let her know about them kind of things right from the start," advised the old man. "A woman, she can git plumb out of hand, you don't see she starts off right."

Sobering, he took Shane roughly by the shoulder. "An' you treat *her* right. If he don't," he said sternly to Janet, "you see I git word of it."

She kissed the grizzled old cheek. Charlie cleared his throat loudly and sat down to eat. Janet left them. Shane got a cup of coffee for himself and sat down at the table with his grandfather.

"What are you aimin' to do now?" asked the old man after a silence.

"Well, stay here until spring, I guess, Mitch is back working at the store, so if you need me for something in the next few weeks . . . but I can't go looking for front ends," he added hastily, forestalling Charlie. "I'll work at the store if they need me, after Mitch and Peggy Lou leave; then, in the spring, we'll go back to the woods."

"You don't want to work in the woods, Shane," the old man said quietly, "not in the timber. You tried to tell me that last fall before you run my best truck in the river."

"Yes, I do. As long as you're running a show, I guess I'll be around for most of it."

"What about Janet? Where'd she be at?"

"She says a tent or a camp shack will be all

right. She thought she could help with the cooking, maybe do all of it, depending on how big a crew you've got."

"With the young-un hung on her back like a papoose, I reckon," said Charlie, grinning in approval.

"So she says."

"Well, see you don't never let things git too hard on her," Charlie said soberly. "I always have felt like maybe I let that happen to your grandma."

"Charlie—"

"I was a young buck when we married, younger'n you are now, an' cocky as hell. I didn't know, back then, that women can't always stand up to just any kind of life. We had that ole ranch to run, an' I was my dad's timber boss in the woods, summers. Steve, your daddy, was born in a camp up on Roan Stallion Ridge. We had a Mexican couple workin' for us. You might maybe remember her, Juanita Garcia. She was one of Effie's cooks till—oh, I guess fourteen, fifteen years ago. He got killed the next year, José did. I nearly never lost anybody out of a crew of mine, but the tree we was usin' for a spar—well, never mind that now.

"Juanita an' your grandma was doin' the cookin' and such things up there on the ridge that summer. We had breakfast before daylight an' Juanita brought us our lunch and water up on a mule. We was still mostly usin' mules an' draft horses then. I remember it was hotter'n a bitch that day. Still, in amongst the trees, not a breath a' wind. I asked Juanita if Georgia was all right an' she says, 'Oh, yes, she's workin' on some of the

445

baby clothes.' When we come back to camp—it was just about dark—there she was with the boy....

"That didn' go too bad, I guess, but Georgia never was what you could call a real stout woman. She never complained about it, but she was kind of—delicate, you know. I don't think I took enough account of that when she was alive."

Shane got them more coffee and there was a long silence. Finally, he said,

"In the fall, I want to go back to school for a while. Some of my master's work can be field work, but I'll need some more classes, too."

"Field work like that High Lonesome business you was plannin' on this winter?"

"Yes."

"An' you aim to drag Janet an' the kid—or kids, I expect there'll be more soon enough—off to places like that?"

"She says it'll be all right."

Charlie grunted, but his eyes looked wistful and blurry. "Right now, it looks to me like she'd say it would be all right to go to hell with you, but you see you do right by her.... Wildlife management! Now, that's a hell of a note. What people like you is goin' to do is manage people like me right out of livin'. 'You can't saw down that tree, ole Charlie. They's a little birdie got a nest up in there.' Christ!... Well, I guess I'll be too old to care much one of these days. You can make a little somethin', maybe, off the sale of the equipment an' such."

"Oh, come on, Charlie."

"It's so. A man might as well be honest with hisself. Besides, I don't even know about no show

446

for next year. PSL ain't goin' to buy from us. I've put burrs under the tails a' too many a' them smart-asses works for 'em. It'd be hell, wouldn't it, if we had to haul all the way to Twin Falls, cut the gizzard out a' profits, if we was to happen to make any.... Git me another piece a' this pie if they is one.... God, ain't they through cleanin' up an' movin' stuff around in there yet? Look at that little ole girl out there, pettin' that tree. She's gonna freeze her rear off."

45

All those living at the Magnessen house left the store early on Monday evening, to get supper over and done with. No one was much interested in eating and, except for Patty's happy chatter and their replies to it, the meal was mostly silent.

Wes and Faye came later, then Charlie and Paul and his family. Paul was gray-faced and ill-looking. His eyes shifted uneasily away from any direct contacts, but he sat on a loveseat with Sharon and agreed with Jamie that it was a beautiful Christmas tree when Patty put on the lights, that, yes, there were certainly getting to be lots of gifts and some of them probably were for Jamie; they could check into that later.

"Now, Patty," said Nora after a time, "you and Jamie must run upstairs to bed. You have a big day at school tomorrow, with the play and everything, and Aunt Sharon says Jamie didn't have his nap today."

"I thought it was going to be like a party," Patty said, looking around at them quizzically, "and we could all stay up late..."

"It's not really a party, honey," said Alice. "It's a—a talk for grown-ups."

"In serious?" she asked solemnly, looking to her grandfather.

Viktor nodded, not looking quite directly at her. "It's something we must take care of, Patty. Then it will be all Christmas and..."

"Come on, both of you," said Peggy Lou enthusiastically. "I'll go up with you for a few minutes."

Nora turned off the Christmas tree lights when the children had gone. She had wished they might wait for putting up the tree until this evening was over, but there would have been no explaining that to Patty. Besides, it had been a good diversion for all of them yesterday evening, everyone talking at once, advising, speculating, not listening to each other, remembering only now and then to defer to Patty. In the morning, when she had the living room to herself, Alice, who really did have a flair for rightness and proportion, had rearranged most of the decorations, but no one had noticed. But somehow, to Nora, for just now it didn't seem right to have the tree here, sparkling and shimmering even with its lights off. She went back and sat beside Viktor on the couch.

He said quietly, "We won't begin for just a little yet. There is someone else coming. I've told Nora and she doesn't think it's right. I called David Rosenzweig just before we left the store and he said he'd be here."

"Oh, Daddy, *why?*" cried Alice. They had all stiffened, grown even more tense.

"He's the one that caused all this," Mitch said angrily. "How can you think about having him in this house?"

"No, Mitch, he didn't *cause* it."

"He made up those lies and—"

"I don't believe he did. Some of the things he said were true; others, I can't remember about. As for the rest, I think he believed it was true. I think he should be here."

David rang the doorbell just as Peggy Lou reached the foot of the stairs. She opened the door and stared at him, but Viktor was standing behind her.

"Come in, David. Peggy will take your coat. We have some brandy here, whiskey, coffee."

Wes gave David a slight nod. The others glanced at him in varying degrees of hostility, not really acknowledging his presence. Shane got up from where he sat on the carpet, leaning against the arm of Janet's chair, and brought another chair from the dining room, placing it, for David, near the door into the hall.

Viktor began slowly, looking diffidently down at his hands, "Now that this time has come, I feel foolish—melodramatic—as if I've been making too much of my life, the things that have happened to me. Everyone has trials, sorrows, uncertainties. I"—he looked briefly around the room—"I will tell you my story now, and I think perhaps it will seem anticlimactic after all that has happened, but I will ask you just to—let me tell it."

There was a moment of silence and he began, self-consciously, looking at no one, his deep voice low, so that they leaned forward a little.

"When I was a young boy, maybe twelve years old, I decided I wanted to become a doctor.

Peter, my older brother, was to have our grandfather's farm. He was the eldest and he wanted it. Our own father was a carpenter, an excellent one, and I think he wanted me to become a carpenter too, though he said little about it. He was a hard man, my father, in some ways. He had been badly wounded, a head wound, fighting in the First World War; then my mother, whom he loved, died young.... He was often away for a long while at a time, working on his buildings. Our grandparents raised us, my brother and sister and me, and they thought it would be a fine thing if I were to be a doctor. They helped me, with money and with their love, when it was time for me to go away to school.

"I worked, and I studied at several schools. I became interested in psychiatry. Psychiatry was relatively new then, not even accepted by a great many people as any sort of science or profession. But there were beginning to be courses available in the field at some of the universities.

"I wrote to my grandparents sometimes—not often enough—but when they heard I wanted to be a psychiatrist, my grandmother remembered a very distant relative of hers, living near Munich, whom she believed had married a man who already was a psychiatrist. She looked into old letters and found that the man's name was Hans Koerner. I was *so* excited. His name was very familiar to me. He had studied with Freud and Jung and some of the other finest men in the field. Finally, I got enough courage to go and see him, using my grandmother's letter as a kind of introduction, an excuse.

"My grandmother's people were originally from Russia. They were Jewish, you see, and the entire, large family had scattered away from the Kiev area because of various troubles there long ago, when my grandmother's mother was a young girl. My grandmother's name was Rachel. Ilse Grossman's branch of the family had gone to the area of Munich at about the same time my grandmother's people came to Copenhagen, and it was Ilse who was married to Hans Koerner.

"In those days, psychiatry was practiced chiefly in a madhouse or in a private sanitorium. If one were lucky, he got to do a sort of internship in a sanitorium, with a fine, learned man such as Dr. Koerner. Eventually, it developed that I was so fortunate, or what seemed to me fortunate at the time.

"Dr. Koerner's sanitorium was in a beautiful place in the mountains of Bavaria. His family's house was on the grounds and I was invited to live with them. It was—it is a beautiful thing to see someone else, or to be, oneself, completely engrossed, happy, excited with one's work, always eager, always learning, sad with the disappointments, delighted over the little progresses, or even the imagined ones. It was like that for me.

"The Koerners had one child, a daughter named Frieda. She was a pretty and a kind girl, and we agreed to marry. When we talked with her parents about it, they were pleased, and Dr. Koerner said that I should become a partner with him. That was in 1937. Things were already very bad in Germany, but I scarcely paid any heed to anything that was happening outside the sanitorium grounds. He suggested, Dr. Koerner, that since I was a foreigner, not German, it might be better if, rather than Frieda's taking my name, I should take the name of Koerner. He had friends who could arrange this easily, and I agreed—after he reminded me of some of the things that were happening. I had new identification papers, but I kept my old ones. I hid them in a hollow tree in the woods, near a place where we sometimes had picnics. I don't know why I did that. Possibly it had to do with pride. I have always been proud of my family, my name."

He had taken up his pipe and was filling it carefully, but without realizing he was doing so. When it was ready to his satisfaction, he looked at it as if a little surprised. Nora reached for a match from the table and lit it for him. He looked at her absently, then with a slight nod of gratitude. It was as if he had not been in this room for the past few moments. The nine-thirty, end-of-lunch whistle at the mill blew, and there was the whistle of the log train, off schedule as usual. A dog somewhere very far away, barked, barked. Mitch put wood on the fire quietly and Sharon, moving softly, offered the tray of drinks.

"They did not leave us alone," Viktor said when the room was settled again. The words were causing him pain now and he looked at nothing. "They used Ilse's Jewishness—though she had never been any sort of Orthodox Jew, nor her family, for generations—as an excuse, and they put us all into a small camp near Munich. What they wanted was Hans Koerner, his knowledge. There was a factory at the camp, for making uniforms, and another for making parts for small arms. The women made the clothes, the men machined the weapons' parts. . . . And there was a hospital. Later in the war, some wounded soldiers were brought there, but it was set up as an—experimental hospital. I know very little about what went on in the surgical wards and other places. I—tried not to know. Perhaps that seems wrong, hard, but there was so much, and after a time... The other doctors there were Nazi sympathizers. Dr. Koerner conducted experiments and I was his assistant. They told us that if we simply carried on with the work they wanted, things would not go badly with Ilse and Frieda. ...

"The camp was divided into two compounds, one for women and young children, the other for men. There was a high fence between that no one was to go near except the guards. Sometimes one of us would catch a glimpse of one or both of the women as they filed in line to their work or meals. We heard things sometimes, rumors or the truth. We were not allowed to talk with them.

"Frieda had a child three months or so after we were taken to the camp, a daughter who lived only a few days. I did not know about it, for certain, for weeks."

He drew on the pipe, which had almost gone out, and cleared his throat huskily.

"Our work, Dr. Koerner's and mine, was in the nature of what has come to be called brainwashing. We two were the only psychiatrists at that particular hospital. We were not called psychiatrists, but only doctors. The Nazis considered psychiatry to be too much a Jewish profession to dignify it with a separate name. It was mental torture; there really is no other name. Sometimes, too, there were lobotomies and other things, but they were handled by other doctors, chiefly. For us, it was... Once when he refused to continue an experiment, they brought his wife into the yard of the women's compound and beat her, while we stood handcuffed at the fence, with the guards' guns. ... She had never been a strong woman, Ilse. Even before the beating, we could see that she was frail and ill...."

"My work, for the most part, was to keep the records. The psychiatric experiments were a new kind of thing and they wanted very thorough, detailed records. I can't begin to tell you the times I was sickened by the profession I had chosen with such hope and happiness, how I came to hate and be ashamed of it, and of myself. Sometimes, days would pass when Dr. Koerner and I could not look at each other...."

"Sometime early in 1943, Ilse died. We did not know, of course, for a while, for certain. When she had been dead several weeks, they let us talk, very briefly, with Frieda, at the fence. She seemed to have aged ten years and she was ... She told us her treatment had been a little better than most of the women were receiving, that her job was not a hard one, and she was being given enough food. The commandant of the camp came to our office that same day. He came often to watch the experiments and look at the papers, but this time he very nearly apologized for Ilse's death. He said if we went on properly with our work, Frieda would be given a job in the office of her factory, that her food ration would be increased secretly, so that the other women would not find out and be jealous. He reminded us that Ilse had been in ill health when we were brought to the camp. I was not sure that Dr. Koerner even heard him, but he went on with the experiments."

Suddenly, Viktor's abstracted eye fell on David Rosenzweig, sitting by the door.

"I don't remember things, names, there were

so many. Sometimes, still, a name or a face comes back to me in sleep or when something reminds me, but I don't remember your family, any of them, or you. I know most of the people on whom we experimented were Jewish, or said to be Jewish, especially in the beginning. It was there, in their records. They always wanted as much background material on the—patients as they could get, but I tried not to know. I could not have stood any more involvement, any more empathy. ... I never signed papers transferring anyone to any other camp or anywhere else, for any reason. I hadn't that kind of authority. I had no authority; I was a—a nothing."

The pipe had gone out and he had let it turn in his hand, spilling ashes on his clothes. Gently, Nora took it and held his restless hand for a moment, but he could not keep still now. He got up and paced the room, not seeing any of them again.

"But Frieda died, late in that same year. I never knew how. There were stories that one of the guards had taken her as ... I didn't want to find out. ... About a month after we knew that for certain, Dr. Koerner killed himself. It was not easy. Those of us they knew not to be sympathizers were always watched very carefully. The drugs, the instruments, almost everything we used were locked away and had to be issued, given, taken, used in the presence of someone they could trust. I don't want to tell you how he died. ... There is so much I have tried to forget, but after that last death, his suicide, I remember almost nothing for months.

"They brought in another psychiatrist, a good party man this time, and I was still to be his assistant. I did my work badly. Vaguely, I remember that there were punishments....

"There was an underground movement in the camp and it kept growing stronger somehow. The war was going badly for Germany by then. Thinking back, I believe some of the guards and trustees were involved in the movement because they could not bear what was going on at our own camp and the stories that came from other places. Sometime in the late summer or fall of 1944, someone told me that if I could destroy the psychiatric records, they would help me to escape. It didn't matter to me. I had been certain for a long time that I would die there and I only wished I had the nerve to do what Dr. Koerner had done, or some similar thing. I thought—such as my thoughts were then—that if I were caught destroying the records or escaping, I would be killed and it would finally end.

"They got some gasoline somehow and I managed to get into the office while the other doctor was having his lunch. I threw all the papers into the middle of the room, poured on the gasoline, lit a match, and jumped from a window. They had arranged that a garbage truck should be leaving the hospital just at that time, and I got into it, among the things that such trucks carry."

He had paused briefly in his aimless pacing by the Christmas tree, and he fingered a tiny bell. Its brief, fairy ringing seemed loud in the silent room. Alice was crying, almost without sound. Janet touched Shane's shoulder with a trembling hand and he reached up and took it between his own. Sharon made a tiny gesture; Paul looked at his mother's ravaged face and got up to go and sit beside her. Peggy Lou had hidden her face against Mitch's shoulder. Faye and Wes had their fingers interlocked, and old Charlie's hands were clenched into fists between his knees.

"There is some saying," Viktor went on quietly, beginning to walk again, "that God looks after small children and drunks. I don't remember what happened after the garbage truck. Something made me go and find my old, my real identification papers and destroy the others. We had not been marked with tattoos or the other things I know were done to many others. Something protected me while I got those papers. People, I don't know who, or how they did it, helped me to cross into France and get through the lines safely. There was little I could do as a soldier. I remember I was weak and ill for a long time, but I had my medical training, which I had come to loathe. I was, perhaps, some help with the wounded in field hospitals.

"The rest you know. I went home to Denmark when the war was over. Most of my family was gone. I said only that I had been interned by the Germans. I heard that our entire camp had burned just after the liberation. I thought there would be no way of anyone's ever knowing that I had been a Dr. Koerner, but still I was afraid. My mother's people were in England. I had never really known them, but they asked me to visit, perhaps to work and live there. Several of their children, my cousins, had died in the war. The part of the country where they lived had hardly been touched by bombing or such things and they were kind to me, but I couldn't stay. I had nightmares, always. They wanted me to talk about it, saying that might ease things a little, but I couldn't. It was too horrible and I was always afraid someone would find out what I had done—"

"But you didn't *do* anything, Daddy," Mitch cried, his voice breaking. "Under circumstances like that, most people would have done a hundred times worse—"

"Hush up, son," said Charlie softly, dropping a hand on the boy's shoulder. "Let him be done with it."

Viktor looked at Mitch briefly, as if he were a stranger. "There *were* people, the brave ones, who did nothing that was remotely co-operative. They killed themselves, or managed to be killed."

"But, Daddy—" began Alice, and Faye whispered compassionately, "Don't, honey, let him say what he has to."

Viktor had turned again to David Rosenzweig. "The immigration people were here again today."

"Yes, I saw them, too," his voice was barely audible.

Viktor looked around briefly at his family and friends, then began pacing again.

"It has become quite the thing, keeping records on people who were in Germany or connected with Germany during the war. There are large record centers in Vienna, Berlin, Ludwigsburg, where files are kept. The records of our camp are patchy because of the fire. However, they have found, in France, a woman who was a girl at the camp. She worked in the hospital's main office. She remembers Frieda and David's mother. In Switzerland, there is a man who was an orderly in the hospital. In Chicago, another man who remembers David, his father and brothers. He was even sent away to another camp at the same time as one of the brothers. Those people seem able to remember more clearly than we do."

David stood up unsteadily. "I must go."

No one moved and Viktor, looking around at them, gray-faced and drained, said, "What has been done with his coat and hat?"

"Sit down now, Viktor," Nora was pleading. She had come to him and she led him to a chair like a dazed child. Paul offered a glass, but he said, "No, I'll go upstairs in a moment."

It was Wes who got David's things for him and opened the front door.

"Will you tell him," David said unevenly, "tell him—I'm sorry."

"Yes," Wes answered and closed the door.

There was silence in the room again until Charlie put more wood on the fire. He walked stiffly all the way out to the kitchen but, even from there, the blowing of his nose sounded loud.

Viktor said stonily, "They have told me that, even if I were considered a criminal, my naturalization could not be taken away because I have a wife and children who are citizens of this country. I won't be deported."

Alice was kneeling beside his chair. "Daddy, darling Daddy, please just try to let it all go away now, as much as you can. You're not guilty of anything, not such a fine, kind, loving man as you are."

He put his hand absently on her head, but his eyes were still dull, vacant, seeing more than the room.

"I *will* be a doctor," Mitch said passionately, his voice breaking. "I'll be the best doctor you ever saw. Maybe you can be—a little glad again."

459

"Come up to bed," Nora said pleadingly. She was more than worried now, she was deeply frightened. "I've got that strong sleeping medicine from Dr. Striker. You've got to have some rest."

He tried to rise, and more hands than could touch him reached out to help. As he stood unsteadily with Nora's arm around him, the girls and Faye kissed him, the men gripped his hands, all of them speaking softly, saying little of any consequence, only being there, together.

Paul went upstairs with them. Gradually, the living room filled with murmurs of the horror of it. Shane said softly to Janet, "You come and rest, too, please."

"Oh, I couldn't! Not now. I couldn't lie still ..." and she began to cry, clinging to him fiercely.

When Paul came back, the room had fallen silent again. Charlie returned and sat down, feeling very tired and old.

Paul said, "He took two of the pills and she's helping him get to bed."

"I guess the best thing all of us can do right now," Faye said shakily, "is just disappear as quietly as possible."

"Wait," Paul said, "please, for just a couple of minutes. I was going to make a—revelation, a kind of apology myself tonight, only now it seems like just about nothing." He looked at his brother and sisters. "When he wakes up, I wish you'd tell him that the saddest thing in my life right now is that I'm *not* a born Magnessen. And then," he said into the deeper silence that had fallen, "we had an idea. It's really Sharon's idea, so she can tell you about it."

"Well," she said shyly, "there's a big land-development company in Boise that wants very

460

badly to get in on the Cloud Valley project. They've got all kinds of power and pull and they can probably just walk right over the county commissioners and such people. We've decided to offer them half the land up there. It won't bring the price it would have a little while back, but it should still be a good bit of money. There'll still be enough of the old ranch left to run cattle enough to pay for a caretaker. If we'd thought of it in time, we could have had the road plowed out and the house fixed up enough so that we could all spend Christmas up there."

"We don't know yet if we'll be staying here," Paul said. "I once had a damn good job offer in Denver. I doubt we *can* stay here if I want to keep on in real estate, but, right now, I'm not even sure if I want to do that. About the only thing I do know is that I'm not cut out to be a rancher, but we will keep some of the old place. That's not all the idea, though, Sharon. Hurry up and tell them. We have to get Jamie and go home."

"It's the mill," she said. "Some of the money we get from the land company will have to go to pay back investors in Cloud Valley, but there'll be some left and we'd put it into stock in the mill corporation. It *could* just possibly make a difference in outbidding PSL."

They were silent a moment and some of them could even smile faintly. Then Faye, who didn't for a moment believe the money would have any effect, but was very proud of all of them tonight, said, "By Gadfrey, you know, it just might."

46

David Rosenzweig prowled distractedly through his house, feeling ill, stopping when he passed the dining-room sideboard for another drink.

Gloria had flown to Denver on Friday to stay with a couple of friends. He hadn't wanted to let her go, but the trip to New York had had to be postponed because of business and she was growing even more restless and irritable than ever. She had called the night she arrived, but, though he had tried to reach her two or three times, he had not heard from her since then. No doubt, she was out every possible moment, doing the things a reasonable-sized city offered for fun and entertainment. Tomorrow he would join her, and Wednesday they would fly on to New York.

David caught a passing glimpse of himself in a hall mirror and thought, you're a bitter, twisted, vindictive old man. After what he had heard tonight, he was even more glad to be leaving Alder County. God grant that most of the people here would soon forget what he had started, and that that good family could go on with reasonably happy lives.

He wondered again, as he had been wondering for the past week about Gloria's seeming acquiescence toward the Israeli move. She had not seemed nearly as angry and opposed as he had expected, once he began to talk openly about it and to make concrete plans. Rather, she had seemed only vague and distracted. Now he could add another reason, to himself, at least, for going. It should be a place where even a warped, frightened, sour man like himself need not be constantly searching for covert anti-Semitism.

He kept seeing Viktor Magnessen's face as it had been for most of the evening, drained, blank, except for the eyes, dazed and filled with the pain of memories. He lost as much as I did, David thought miserably. He went into the dining room and refilled his glass, swallowing two stomach pills with the first sip of the new drink.

He had had the meeting with the PSL people on Friday in Boise, then had badgered and cajoled his office staff into working through most of the weekend to have the necessary papers and records ready. Two PSL executives had been up to look over the mill today. They had made him, in writing, what they called a "tentative but fairly firm offer." It was not what he ought to be getting for the business, but he couldn't seem to care much.

As for the workers' corporation, of which he had been hearing rumors, if they cared to try to outbid PSL, it would be all the better for him. They could take it up with his attorney. He and Gloria would probably have to come back here for a few days before leaving the country, when most of the arrangements for the sale of the mill and the house were completed, but then—

The phone rang and he started so sharply that some of his drink sloshed onto the carpet.

"Hello, darling David!" cried Gloria's voice exuberantly. She sounded as if she had had a good deal to drink.

"Why, Gloria! How are you, darling? I've tried to call you, but—"

"Yes, we've been—out a good deal. *I* tried to call you, earlier this evening."

"I had to go out, too, for an hour or so."

"You're still coming tomorrow, aren't you?"

"Yes, and all the arrangements for New York are made."

"Oh, good! ... Well, David, there's something I have to tell you and I thought it might be better, easier for both of us if we talked about it first on the phone."

His heart lurched as he thought of the bottle of fake pills. "What is it, darling?"

She was silent for a moment; it seemed he could hear her drinking something, the clink of ice in a glass, then she blurted belligerently, "I had an abortion on Saturday. I was about six weeks pregnant and going absolutely mad. I called Lisa several days before I left there and she got her doctor to make all the arrangements. I practically went straight from the airport to the hospital and I just got out today because I also had my tubes tied. I forget what they call the operation, but it's only going to leave a little tiny scar and I'm feeling all right. Oh, it was just awful! But I was so glad to get that—that thing out of my insides that I didn't much care what they did. And now I think I can be safe. Obviously those pills weren't doing their job, were they? ... David, I'm only trying to avoid a lot of argument and worry, telling you this way. It's all done now, all taken care of. I'll bet you wouldn't have thought I could manage such a thing practically all by myself. ... David?"

He put the phone back into its cradle almost gently and gulped at the nausea rising in him. "You can't *really* start over again." Gloria's own words that she had heard from her psychiatrist. My God, my God!

Yes, Viktor Magnessen had suffered as much from the war as he, David, had done, but Viktor had a family now, a close, warm, loving family, and friends. And what did *he* have? It was not jealousy that brought the question, not any longer, only the most excruciating loss and misery and loneliness he had ever known. What had *he* had? Business success to a degree; the respect, perhaps even liking of some of his associates. He had two almost-grown daughters whom he would never know now. He had a wife who had just finished telling him blithely and with vast relief that she had killed their child, a wife whose only smattering of self-assurance and ego-bolstering seemed to have to come from inane flirtations with other men, from lying to him, to David, from torturing him in her petty adolescent ways, a shallow, not-very-bright, pathetic woman whom, God help him, he still wanted to love. Everyone, didn't they? needed to love someone. His face was wet. He could not think what to do about it.

After a very long time, he went into his office and began writing. By the time he had finished, the brassy winter sun was just topping the eastern mountains. He went to the servants' quarters and asked them to sign some papers as witnesses.

"You needn't read them," he said gently. "It's only some legal papers that concern me. I need your signatures to verify mine. . . . No breakfast for me this morning, Bessie, thank you. I'll be leaving in a few minutes."

At their door, he turned back. "I've left a check for you on the kitchen table, and a reference. I'd appreciate it if you'd take a day or two to close up the house properly, and then we won't be needing you anymore. It's been a pleasure knowing and working with you both. The real-estate people can show the house. There's no point in your having to stay on. Maybe you have —family you'd like to spend Christmas with."

"My land!" Bessie murmured to George and shivered. "He looks like a walkin' ghost."

Back in his office, David shuffled the papers together into a briefcase and called his attorney in Boise.

"Sam? David Rosenzweig. I'm sorry to bother you so early and at home, but I wanted to make sure you're going to be in your office today and see if I could have a few minutes of your time. . . . Yes, some papers I want you to make sure are properly executed. . . . Thank you. I should be there around eleven."

He went out to his car, still in the rumpled suit he had worn yesterday and through the night, carrying no luggage other than the briefcase.

47

In their room, Janet and Shane talked, but only briefly, about Viktor's story. Its horror was so crushing, there was little to say. Then, abruptly in the darkness, she began to cry, trying to stifle the wracking sobs in her pillow. He got up and sat beside her, stroking the hair away from her cheek.

"I just can't stand thinking about it," she said chokingly after a time.

"Try not to."

"Will he be any better now?" she asked, almost pleadingly. "I know he can't possibly ever forget—and having it all brought back like this, but maybe talking about it—not having to remember *not* to talk about some things . . . ?"

"Maybe," he said gently.

She scrubbed at her face with a corner of the sheet and blew her nose on a handkerchief he brought.

"Turn off the lamp," she said miserably. "Darling, could you—lie here with me? Please, if you can. I so want your arms around me."

She moved, turning toward the wall, trying to make her swollen body smaller. He lay down, resting his cheek against the heavy coil of her hair, one arm beneath her head, the fingers of the other hand gently massaging the back of her neck.

"If it's too much . . ." she said wistfully, adjusting her body so that they touched from shoulders to hips. "Oh, Shane!"

"It's too much," he answered huskily against her hair. "But it's wonderful. Try to sleep. You haven't got much room. Can you—"

"Neither have you," she said, settling more against him, feeling his desire in the slight trembling of his body. "You're so warm and—gentle. Will you always be?"

"Maybe not, always."

"I like not having much room, when it's—like this. Shane, I'm so tired of being pregnant—for a lot of reasons."

"I know. You're also just plain tired. Please try to sleep."

After a long silence, during which they both tried hard to control themselves, remember rea-

467

son, she said, "Why didn't you tell me about Gary?"

He started slightly. "What about him?"

"About *everything* that happened at Joe's Place last Thursday night, how your hand got cut and—God, it seems like weeks, or even months, doesn't it? Since you came storming home and got out that suitcase."

"I didn't fight with him," he said a little defensively. "He was throwing things around and—"

"Yes, so I was told."

"Mitch," he began angrily.

"Mitch didn't say a word. I brought in this morning's mail and there was a letter for me."

"Goddam it, I've told you not to read—"

"It really wasn't a mean, nasty letter. Just a kind of friendly warning."

"Warning about what?"

"Well, that he was back in the county; making threats; that they'd probably have to let him out of jail soon. Shane, I'm—afraid of him. Even after the first few weeks, I knew that he could get a little—insane at times. I don't know why I had to be so stupid and stay with him, but even then—almost from the beginning, I was a little scared sometimes. I suppose it was some goody-good idea that I could *help* him, something like that. Now, I—the letter said he was very drunk that night and that the police also thought he was *on* something, some kind of drugs."

"Does he use drugs?"

"Yes, he smokes pot every day. I used to try it, but it was just a big nothing as far as I was concerned. He used to want me to try other things, but I wouldn't. Then, while we were still in Spokane, he gave me something, LSD, I think, without my knowing. It was—what they call a bad trip. I can't tell you how horrible.... That scared him and he didn't try it again. He's awfully cowardly, really, in spite of all his talk, but if he's using something for artificial courage, I'm scared to death he might—"

"Do you remember Kitty Kucharski?"

"No. Yes, I do. She's Vince's oldest daughter, isn't she?"

"She and I were in the same class in school. She's married now to a guy named Smedley at Alder Falls. He's the one who had the most to do with breaking my rib in that football game. Kitty's a dispatcher for the Alder Falls police department. I talked to her today on the phone."

"You did? About Gary?"

"Yes."

"Do you always know somebody to call?"

"Janet, everybody always knows somebody. You know that. It's the beauty—and the aggravation—of a place like this."

"What did she say? Is he still in jail? Are they going to—"

"They hit him with a really heavy fine in magistrate's court on Friday morning, drunk and disorderly, disturbing the peace, resisting arrest, assaulting an officer, destroying private property —everything they could think of, it seems. He called his mother, wherever she is back East. She sent some things airmail. They came today, a cashier's check to cover the fine and the cost of things at Joe's, and a ticket, a one-way ticket, from Boise to Honolulu. He'd been giving them such a hassle in jail that they got someone from the sheriff's de-

469

partment to go with him to the airport, make sure he got on the plane."

She sighed. "Thank God!" then stiffened, "but he could come back..."

"Can we deal with that *if* we have to?"

"Yes, I just—"

"You just go to sleep."

She lay silent for a time, then said timidly, "Is she pretty?"

"Who?"

"Kitty Kucharski."

"Hell, I can't remember. I haven't seen her for years. I just happened to hear once that she worked—"

"Did you date her?"

"I don't think so."

"I'll bet you did, I'll bet she—"

"I used to dip her pigtails in inkwells."

"Oh, you did not. They stopped having inkwells years ago, and girls were certainly not wearing pigtails then."

"Kitty was. She had long, shiny, beautiful black braids, and the face and figure of a sexy movie star."

"That's not the way *I* remember her," she said sulkily.

"Then why ask me? I told you I don't—"

"Because I told you, I'm going to be jealous. I can't help it. *I* remember her as having short, frizzy blond hair, kind of fat and dumpy, with a bad case of acne."

"You may be right," he said resignedly, then very quietly, "Do you want to know a secret? I don't like the way I look. People notice me, and that starts them speculating about Steve and all the rest of it. Homosexuals like me. Women I can't

470

stand... well, never mind. It sounds more like bragging than what I really mean. What I'm trying to say is you don't need to be jealous because, for me, the way I look is not an asset."

"All right, you can't help being handsome, whether you want to or not. I'm sorry it bothers you. You ought to be proud and cocky as hell, because you just are, and I can't help being jealous.... Oh, Shane, I'm sorry about the jealousy. It's so unfair of me, after I've—"

"And I thought we agreed you were going to stop pouring ashes. Will you shut up now and go to sleep?"

"I don't think I can," she said apologetically, with a restless movement. "I guess I ought to try reading for a while or something."

"You need more room."

"Please," she said, catching at his hand, "don't go, if it's not too—difficult. It's *so* good having you here, even if you are driving me a little bit mad. It's mostly the baby. He's so restless. He won't keep still a minute."

Tenderly, he slid his hand down her body to rest on her abdomen. Shivering, she moved the hand slightly, so that he got the full impact of the baby's lurchings and pushings.

"God!" he murmured, a little awed. "I didn't know it would be like that. Is it always?"

"He's awfully active," she said tiredly, but with some pride. "Right now, it seems he has been ever since I can remember."

"I've begun," he said shyly, "to think, sometimes, it's *our* baby."

"Oh, Shane, *have* you?"

"Once it's born, I know I'll always feel that way."

"But you'll feel—irritated sometimes," she said sadly. "Little babies need so many things. They take a lot of time and maybe you'll—"

"Maybe we'll both resent—interruptions at times, but I guess we can live with it."

"Yes," she said, smiling softly. She took his hand, held it between both of hers and, in a few moments, was asleep.

Shane slept, too, after a time, but then he woke again to find his arm under her head was numb. He tried not to move, not wanting to wake her, but finally he had to.

"What's wrong?" she murmured.

"It's only that my arm's asleep," he said.

She yawned. "In those romantic books," she said drowsily, "people sleep in each others' arms constantly and their limbs never go to sleep."

"They never have to go to the bathroom or things like that either," he said grimly, turning over to rub his arm.

She giggled. "Let's all turn over. I want to see what it's like to snuggle against your back. The baby seems quiet now. Maybe he won't bother you. All right?"

Before he slept again, Shane heard Loki barking from his doghouse in the backyard. The pup rarely barked when he was shut up, and he thought of going to see if anything real was bothering him, but feared his getting up would wake Janet again. The clock on their nightstand said almost four.

It seemed only a few minutes before he woke again, but it was almost seven. He felt tired and stiff and knew he was not likely to sleep again. Very cautiously, he got out of bed and pulled the covers around Janet's shoulders. She sighed, murmured something unintelligible, and stretched herself unconsciously into a new position with more space.

Shane dressed in virtual darkness. The house was very still. While he was shaving, the mill whistle blew for the beginning of the day shift. He could tell by the whistle—its sounding muffled or clear—if the day were fair or cloudy. This one sounded fair.

Quietly, he went downstairs and put the coffee on, then into the backyard to let Loki out. The young dog was most physically glad to see him. He went back through the house to the front porch. It was too early for the paper, but he looked anyway, on the porch and among the shrubbery, which still sheltered a few little patches of snow.

The light was coming rapidly now. He stood on the walk for a moment, appreciating the eastern sky, then realized it was very cold. It was as he crossed the porch that he saw it, and stopped in horror and fury. Almost the whole of the big front door had been covered with a black swastika.

"Goddam somebody to hell!" he muttered through his teeth. When he could move again, he touched the thing with loathing. It had been done in tar.

"How could anybody *do* it?" wailed Alice, who was the next to come downstairs. "Oh, my God! People are so ghastly! *Do* something, Shane You've got to, before Daddy knows."

"What will take it off?" demanded Mitch vehemently. "Some bastard is going to pay for this."

"Oh, *why?*" said Nora, beginning to cry. "Won't they *ever* leave us alone? He's had more

473

than he can bear. Boys, *do* something, please! Before he wakes up."

The Hendrix boy pedaled up then with his newspapers and, seeing several people standing on the porch, came up the walk.

"Gee, how come somebody messed up your door like that? What is that thing supposed to be, anyhow?"

"Just a mess," snapped Alice, staring at him coldly.

"Well, here's your paper," he said, handing it to Mitch. "Uh—Merry Christmas, everybody."

"Merry Christmas, Danny," murmured Peggy Lou abstractedly, and Mitch began cursing again as the phone rang.

"Oh, *don't* let him know," pled Janet urgently.

"I don't see how we can help—" Shane began.

"Take the door off," ordered Alice.

"Well, that would be a little obvious," said Mitch derisively. "*Why* would we say we'd done that?"

"Call Wes," Nora said. "He may be at the store by now and would have some idea of something to do. Oh, God, let Viktor go on sleeping!"

They thought of an excuse to get Patty to leave for school through the back-yard. It was a shorter way to the house of her friend Carolyn, with whom she always caught the bus, and Nora gave her scraps to take to Loki on her way.

No one wanted breakfast. They were standing around in various parts of the house, trying to think what might be done, when Viktor came downstairs in robe and slippers. His face seemed grayer, more ravaged than ever, his eyes tired and sunken. In

474

reply to Nora's concern, he said he had slept soundly all night, but that the pills had left him with a feeling like a hangover. His voice seemed even deeper, still drowsy and a little gravelly.

"Since there should be enough people," he said, "I thought I might not go in to the store this morning, maybe not until around noon." Then he looked around at them quizzically. "Why are you all here? Didn't I just hear the clock strike nine?"

"I'll get you some coffee," Nora said hastily. "Why don't you just come into the kitchen and—"

He was looking sharply at Janet. "Are you in labor?"

"No, Daddy," she said almost inaudibly.

"Then I don't understand any of you," he said wearily. "You know Wes can't manage alone. I'll go up and get dressed."

They looked futilely at each other and Nora told him then. There was no choice. He went slowly to open the front door and stand staring at it. His face seemed to grow even paler. He bit his lip and a flush, creeping up out of the neck of his robe, began to suffuse his neck and face with a frightening blotchy red.

"Viktor," Nora said, timidly touching his arm, "don't look anymore. Come and sit down. The boys can do—something...."

"What?" he demanded harshly, his blue eyes flashing in turn at Mitch and Shane. "What, precisely, do you propose to do?"

Mitch gulped. "There must be something that will take it off. Wes thought—"

"There is *nothing*," Viktor roared, "that will take that off without leaving the wood stained—ruined! Do you—any of you," and he glared around at them, "have any concept of what a

475

beautiful piece of wood this is? It's solid oak. Do you remember how it sagged, Nora, when we bought the house? And how long it took me to find hinges properly suited for it? It was one of the things I liked about this house, that beautiful piece of wood. Now look at it . . . *look at it!*"

None of them could remember ever having seen him so angry. Alice breathed fearfully to Janet, "He'll have a stroke."

Peggy Lou said timidly, "I'll go on down to the store," and left hurriedly.

"They put one on one of the show windows at the store, too," Shane said with more coolness than he felt. "Joe Wilkerson, the night constable, caught them just as they were finishing up that one. He called to say you could prefer charges, you or Wes. It's a couple of seventeen-year-old boys. They were—"

"I'll prefer charges," Viktor growled through his teeth.

"Wes already has," Mitch said hurriedly, "and there's a cop down there now, making them take it off the window. Also, their parents are supposed to be there."

"It will come off the glass with gasoline," Viktor said curtly. "I don't care about that."

"Well, won't their folks have to pay for a replacement for the door?" asked Alice, trying to sound as if things were being solved.

"There *is* no replacement for this door!" he shouted. "Can't any of you understand that? Have you no feeling for the fine piece of wood this is?"

"Well, Viktor," said Nora mildly and found to her relieved amazement that she was having to work at not smiling, "we can't just stand here all

476

day with the door *open*. It must not be more than ten degrees. Think of the heat bill."

Reluctantly, he went into the dining room and let her give him coffee, which he hardly touched. Mitch and Shane stayed with him, exchanging uneasy glances. Nora and the girls were busy in the kitchen. Viktor sat scowling blackly down at his cup, now and then muttering curses in various languages he thought he had forgotten.

"Dad," Mitch ventured finally, "there's a big door at the store. Wes thinks it might fit, just until we—"

"It can't be sanded off," Viktor cut in, thinking aloud. "There is *nothing* . . . goddamn!"

Shane snapped his fingers and his face became suddenly animated. "We can take it to Luther Andrews at the planer."

"What?"

"You said it's solid. He can shave off a layer, as thin as possible. If it looks as if he's going to have to take off more than you want, we could stain the door a little darker color. Anyway, he could plane it off and then we could sand it down and—"

"That's dumb, Shane," Mitch said irritably. "The door's too wide."

"No, they've got a new machine. I was looking at it one day last summer while I was waiting for a truck to be unloaded. The blade is suspended and supported from above. There are guides, but they're movable; one can be taken off completely."

Viktor had begun to nod, though slowly, dubiously. "Bert has told me about that planer." He was still scowling.

"Well, Jesus!" cried Mitch in eager relief.

"Let's get a screwdriver and stuff, get it off and into the pickup. We'll have to take off the knob and—"

"Get the tools," Viktor said shortly, "but you're not to touch that door, either of you. You can measure, then go to the store and see if there's anything to be had temporarily. I can't recall what may be in stock. But *I* will take the door down. I want newspapers spread in the pickup for it, and *I* will go to the planer to see that they do as little damage as possible. Neither of you knows or appreciates a fine piece of wood like that. Those men at the planer will be the same. Also, from the store, you can bring sandpaper, sealer, and the other things I will tell you."

"It's awfully heavy," Shane said, straight-faced. "Won't you even need us to help carry it?"

Viktor turned sparking blue eyes on him. "I would appreciate it if you were not to be facetious this morning," he said coldly.

Shane flushed and stepped into the hall to hide a smile.

Viktor said busily, "The tape measure is in the pickup, I remember now. I'll get that if neither of you can get moving." He had reached the door when Mitch, grinning, said hesitantly,

"Uh, Dad, wouldn't you like to get dressed first?"

48

They would close the store in midafternoon on Christmas Eve, but all of them—Mitch, Peggy Lou, Shane, and Viktor—were already there when Wes came in that morning. Viktor was giving the boys instructions about rearranging a shipment of lumber that had come in the day before.

"And be sure it's well covered," he finished. "I'm as determined as Patty that there's going to be snow."

The high mountains were deep in white, though, as yet, there had been little snow in the valley. This day was damp and gloomy enough for it.

Wes had the Friday copy of the *Clarion*. Coming in, he had met Lou Edwards, taking the papers to the post office. The front page was all Christmas jollity, but on the second page was the caption "Yuletide Mischief Misfires." Tom had done a fine job with the pictures, or perhaps Lou had taken them. They did not disclose the faces of the two juveniles, the entire configuration of the design they had made, or the name of the store, but only hands, scraping tar from plate glass. Another picture showed a policeman standing behind the boys and a few irate-looking passersby who had stopped to watch. "Police Chief Terry says vandalism will not be tolerated in Cana," began the brief commentary.

They looked at the paper and at each other. Viktor laid it down on the counter by the cash register, opened to the pictures. Some customers came in and, when Peggy Lou would have removed the *Clarion,* he shook his head.

"Leave it," he said softly. "Let it be there all day."

One of the customers was Claude Enright the barber, who had decided all at once to enclose a side porch his wife had been wanting glassed-in for years. He had to know what he needed today, and get it, because he hadn't bought Mary anything for Christmas and this was going to be it. Claude always did things this way, abrupt decisions and rush jobs. He hadn't thought to do any measuring.

"You remember that porch," he said to Viktor with helpful reasonableness. "It's about as long as the house is deep, and maybe ten feet wide."

Viktor went out to the Enright place to get the statistics himself.

After a while, Peggy Lou came to the back where Mitch and Shane were working.

"Paul's in the store. He says he has something to tell you."

Paul was already shut in the office with Wes. He said, "I've just seen Ted Carpenter, Tom Edwards, too. David Rosenzweig shot himself. They think it must have been some time Tuesday afternoon. They found him late yesterday, in his car, on a back road near Boise. Ted has had a call from Sam Greenstein in Boise. He was David's attorney, though Ted took care of a little business for him here now and then. Sam was an instructor when Ted was in law school and they've always been friends. He called because of David's will. He, Sam, saw him late on Tuesday morning and David had made a new will. He named the figure

PSL had offered him for the mill, included a paper they'd given him, and said that if the projected workers' corporation would raise that figure by a dollar or more, they were to have Holland's. He left that money and practically everything else in trust for the two daughters he'd had by a previous marriage. Gloria's only to have whatever there is from the sale of the house. No one seems to know where she is. Not even the housekeeping couple they had is around."

"They're sure it was suicide?" asked Wes.

"Tom's got friends and connections with the state police and at the Boise paper," Paul said. "No one is saying anything for publication yet, but the word is there was a note in the car, saying he was going to shoot himself—no reasons or anything—and the car was locked from the inside."

After a little silence, Mitch said, "Well, I don't think we ought to tell Dad or the women."

Paul nodded, but Wes was shaking his head slightly.

Shane, looking up at them sharply, said, "Why not?"

"Dad asked him to the house that night," Mitch said slowly. "I think he felt—sorry for him or something. It might upset him. Maybe I shouldn't say it but, for my part, I'm a little glad to hear it. Still, you know how women can get about a thing like this, and ... besides, it's Christmas."

"They're going to hear soon enough," Shane said. "It'll be on television and in the papers, if it's not all over the county first. Maybe there's already been a little too much of somebody trying to protect somebody else from things that have to come out anyway."

Wes agreed and when Viktor came in in a

481

moment, Shane going out to keep the hurrying Claude Enright company, Paul told Viktor. All the while, Viktor looked down at a pad where he had the figures and estimates for Claude's porch.

"That's very sad," Viktor said heavily, still not looking up. "He was a tormented man."

Peggy, who had come in ostensibly to look for something in a file cabinet, said vehemently, "It seems to me he might have left *you* something, after all he's done. I'll bet he knew Walt Philips had called that note on the store, maybe even suggested it to him...."

"I wouldn't want any of his money," Viktor said quietly, looking up for a moment. "It would only be another shadow."

He went back to the pad and, after a few moments, said into the heavy silence, "Paul, you and Sharon and Jamie will be at the house tonight, won't you? She has this notion, your mother, and I agree with her, that we all ought to sleep under the same roof this Christmas Eve. The house will be there, *we*'ll be there other years, but we're beginning to be afraid our young ones may scatter."

He tore a sheet from the pad. "Mitch, get Shane to cut this glass. You get the rest of these things together for Claude before he has a hernia or something. I'm going out now. I haven't finished with my Christmas shopping."

49

"Get Charlie, too," Nora had instructed Shane. "No, don't call and *ask* him, just go *bring* him.

No one should be alone on Christmas Eve, or at Mack's Bar. We'll make that couch for him in the little room down here and then everything will be just right. Every bed in the house will be full, with an extra cot set up for Jamie."

So it was a busy, warm, crowded evening, full of talk and laughter and carol singing, with twelve people in the house. It was very cold and looked as if the sky might be clearing. No one had mentioned that fact in Patty's hearing.

She said, "I guess it doesn't matter if it snows anyway. Reindeer are supposed to be able to fly. Some of the kids say Santa and all the other things are just made up, that it's your parents or other people who bring the presents."

"And what do you think?" Sharon asked carefully.

"Really," Patty said, grinning, "I don't care. Look! here comes Aunt Alice with some more of Grandpa's packages. I'd better go check them." She glanced back over her shoulder at those still in the dining room. "Anyway, you have to learn early not to believe *nearly* all you hear."

In the morning, Patty woke very early, as children seem to have a sixth sense for doing on Christmas. She crept from the bed she was sharing with her Aunt Alice and into the next room to wake Jamie without rousing his parents, so that the two of them could go, alone and wide-eyed, down to the living room to check their stockings and the tree. Jamie immediately became engrossed in the things Santa had brought him, but Patty took only a cursory, complacent look and rushed upstairs to knock on every door, shouting, "Merry Christmas, everyone! Oh, wake up! It's *so* beautiful!"

And it was beautiful, inside and out. They

saw, as daylight began to dim the Christmas tree and other lights, that it had, in fact, cleared in the night. There was no snow, but the still, icy air had left a great frost on everything, so that it was like a sparkling fairyland when the sun looked over the eastern mountains.

There had always been a rule in the household that only things from Santa Claus could be looked at and played with before breakfast; no gifts must be opened until everyone had eaten.

"Oh, *do* hurry," Patty begged urgently, dancing around the kitchen. "I just can't stand it if it takes much longer."

"Alice, honey, let me do that bacon," Nora said harriedly. Alice was burning it. "You start getting things on the table."

"Where are Janet and Shane?" asked Sharon.

"Why, I don't know," said Nora, glancing around.

"I knocked on their door," said Patty.

"I'll bet you did, you little monkey," Peggy Lou said grimly. "I'll bet you even went out and knocked on the doghouse door." But she softened her words by tickling the little girl in passing.

"Well, my lord," said Nora, smiling, "if they can sleep through all this, let's let them. Everybody around this place seems to be in need of catching up on rest."

"I hope there's going to be enough butter," Alice worried.

The phone rang then. They looked at each other uneasily. All of them had come to dread and fear the telephone in these past weeks. Peggy Lou, who was nearest, moved reluctantly toward it, but Viktor, coming in from the backyard, picked it up quickly.

"Merry Christmas!... Shane? Why, where ...? She what?... But why didn't you tell anyone?... Just a moment, please; such a crowd has gathered suddenly that I can't hear. No, never mind. We'll be there in ten minutes."

"What in the world?" gasped Nora.

"Janet's in the delivery room," he told them, replacing the phone. "They seem to have argued all night about going to the hospital. He said she insisted the baby would wait until the gifts were opened and only let him take her less than two hours ago."

He smiled gently and kissed Nora's cheek. "Come on, Granny, and where's Charlie? The boy sounds as if he needs support."

Shane shivered, though the room felt hot to him. He went to the window and looked out at the sparkling world, which hurt his tired eyes.

Last night, as soon as he had come upstairs, he had known something was happening. Janet had come up about an hour before him and was propped in her bed, reading, but there was an added drawnness about her face, and her eyes, when she glanced up at him, held an expression that was a mixture of awe, shyness, and pride.

"Janet?"

"I *may* be in labor," she said calmly, looking back at the book. "I'm having contractions regularly about every ten minutes, but—"

"Ten minutes!"

"Shhh! It's probably a false alarm. It's supposed to be nearly a month early. Shane Bonner, if you let anyone find out and they all come in here and start fussing around, I just can't stand it and I'll never forgive you."

Her body convulsed under the covers, but after a few moments she went on. "Christmas day is not the time to have a baby. I don't want to miss out on things and, besides, think of the poor little kid having Christmas for its birthday. People would just forget all about it."

"No, they wouldn't," he said uneasily. "I think everyone's in bed now. I'll use the kitchen phone to call the doctor or—"

"*No!*" she ordered in a sharp, peremptory whisper. "Even if it is for real, I won't need to go for hours yet. It's such a shame the people at the hospital, or anywhere else, have to work tonight. Shane, please don't keep frowning and looking like that. I'm a nurse. Don't you think I know what I'm doing?"

"No."

He was desperate and exasperated, angry and frightened by turns as the night dragged by and her pains grew closer together. She tried to make him lie down and rest for a while, read a book, anything but letting him do something relevant. She showed by turns, but different turns, the same feelings he was experiencing.

At some point, she said, "If it's a boy, I'd like to name him Charles Viktor. Daddy's first name is Karl, but they're the same—you know, Karl and Charles—and this way he'd be named for his Grandfather and . . ."

"Great-grandfather," Shane finished distractedly.

She smiled softly, then her face twisted with pain.

"Janet, now, goddam it, let's—"

"Don't curse at me," she ordered shortly when she could breathe normally again. "Just stop it."

She turned slightly to take a little writing pad

from the drawer of the nightstand. "If it's a girl, we could call her Charla Viktoria. Maybe it's a little fancy, but would you mind?"

She handed him the pad on which she had written the two names: "Charles Viktor Bonner," "Charla Viktoria Bonner." Shane looked at the names absently. At this moment, he could not have cared less what the child might be called. He was so utterly helpless and he had to make her go where she could be properly looked after. The pains were less than five minutes apart now and she could no longer silence the straining moans when they came, possessing her whole body, but she looked up at him between times, waiting, with a wistful eagerness.

He remembered the pad in his hand and said huskily, "They're—uh—beautiful names."

"You don't like them," she accused petulantly.

"I do! But can't we please go now? Tell me where your things are. I'll go warm up the car and help you—"

"Damn it!" she cried in the vehement half-whisper both of them were using most of the time. "It's a little unreasonable of you to expect me to go on talking and talking, reassuring you, when I have everything else to do."

"I'm sorry," he said pleadingly, kneeling by the bed. "It's just that I want somebody else to do something. *I* can't."

"Well, don't go warming up the car. You're just looking for an excuse to wake somebody else up."

They waited out another contraction, he flinching with her, grinding his teeth.

"Don't grit your teeth," she gasped, "and

don't keep looking so scared and everything. People have babies every second."

"That's what I'm afraid of," he said grimly, but was immediately contrite because she began to cry.

"Can't you let me do anything the way I want to?" she sobbed. "It seems to me you're always in here, saying I have to get up and get dressed and do something."

"You do, Janet," he pleaded. "You're not going to have the baby here."

"And just suppose I did?" she demanded, wiping angrily at her eyes. "Oh, Shane, I'm sorry," she said with abrupt tenderness. "I won't have it here. I promise. As soon as the pains are two minutes apart, we'll—"

"*Two minutes!*"

"Shhh! I swear to God, if you wake people up, I won't go. It takes less than five minutes to get to the hospital from here."

"Four," he said, setting his jaw.

"What?"

"When they're four minutes apart, we'll go."

Finally, when the pains were coming regularly every three minutes, she let him go and use the kitchen phone to alert the hospital, which would, in turn, call Dr. Striker. Even when she was briefly ensconced in the labor room and they let him in for a few minutes, they continued to argue.

"You are *not* to call home until you're sure they're up," she told him sternly, coming almost breathless out of a wracking contraction.

Julia Clarke, the nurse who had been present at Janet's own birth, said, smiling, "It looks to me like we're liable to have another patient, you've got him so upset. We had him in here last fall and I don't think we need him for Christmas."

"He can be difficult," Janet panted, holding his hand briefly.

Julia nodded. "Never would eat his Jell-O. I remember that."

Shane turned away from them, scowling out of the window miserably. It was not a time for being humorous, so far as he could see. In fact, he had never felt more serious and rarely more ill in his life.

Cana Hospital was not yet allowing fathers in the delivery room. Shane was ashamed at the relief he felt about that, but he was not at all sure if he could trust his nerves any longer. He walked beside Janet as she was wheeled to the door. At the same instant, they reached for each other's hands and whispered, "I love you," and they both smiled shakily because the spontaneity of it was like a tiny miracle.

Shane began to shiver as the door closed upon her. He went outside and stood for a few moments in the silent parking lot, drawing deeply on a cigarette and of the icy air. Then he went in and called the house.

Viktor, Nora, and Charlie found him alone in the small waiting room, standing dazedly at the window, his eyes momentarily closed against the brightness outside and the unreasoning animal fear that was gripping him. He had two cigarettes burning, one scorching the fingers of his right hand, the other, newly lit, on the windowsill.

"We brought a Thermos of coffee," Nora said gently. "What they have here is always so weak."

Viktor said, "How long has it been?"

Shane looked at his watch, his lips moving like a second-grader trying to calculate time. "Twenty minutes, I think."

"Here, set down," Charlie said curtly. "I

brought along a little of Viktor's brandy to liven up the coffee."

A nurse stood in the doorway. Shane moved the cup at sight of her, making Charlie spill brandy on the floor.

"You have a little girl," she said, smiling brightly. "Six pounds, two ounces. You can have a look at her soon. Julia said to tell you she can already tell she's going to look like Janet and be a Jell-O lover."

"Janet—" Shane said hoarsely.

"Oh, she's fine. She'll be out soon too. I don't think she ever stopped giving Dr. Striker advice and counsel. Merry Christmas, all of you."

"How can they *be* like that?" Shane asked Viktor vehemently. "So calm and—and thinking they're funny?"

Viktor shook his head, looking at him with compassion. "I never have understood that about women at a time of birth, Shane. Sit down now. Try to drink the coffee. It's just about over." He began filling his pipe. "No, there are a great many things I don't understand—about women, or many other things either. I think, the older I get, the less I really understand."

"Little girl," mused Charlie huskily. "How soon you reckon she'll be ready for the woods?"

"Understand or not," said Nora, with just a touch of complacency, "it *is* a merry Christmas."

"*That* I understand," Viktor said quietly, touching her hand. "Perhaps the happiest, most peaceful merry Christmas we've known. You've been flung into all this very suddenly, Shane, but a family is a wonderful thing, and friends. A man doesn't really need to understand, at times, in order to know how fortunate he is."

IF YOU ENJOYED CANA AND WINE, YOU'LL WANT TO READ THESE OTHER BESTSELLING BOOKS BY FRANCES CASEY KERNS...

THE WINTER HEART
by Frances Casey Kerns   (81-431, $2.50)

Two young Scotsmen stood at the ship's rail on the eve of their landing in America. Maxwell has power and wealth waiting for him — MacWinter, a large and loving family. In this saga from the author of THIS LAND IS MINE, destiny will mesh their lives and focus their differences in one boy — Thorne MacWinter Maxwell. A powerful celebration of forbidden love!

THIS LAND IS MINE
by Frances Casey Kerns   (81-704, $2.50)

The author of A COLD, WILD WIND brings you love in a wild country! Against the grandeur of the Western landscape, Frances Casey Kerns tells the story of a special kind of pioneer fighting for an individual way of life and for the beauty of the Indian heritage.

ROMANCE... ADVENTURE... DANGER...
by Best-selling author, Aola Vandergriff

DAUGHTERS OF THE SOUTHWIND
by Aola Vandergriff (92-042, $2.25)
The three McCleod sisters were beautiful, virtuous and bound to a dream — the dream of finding a new life in the untamed promise of the West. Their adventures in search of that dream provide the dimensions for this action-packed romantic bestseller.

DAUGHTERS OF THE WILD COUNTRY
by Aola Vandergriff (82-583, $2.25)
High in the North Country, three beautiful women begin new lives in a world where nature is raw, men are rough... and love, when it comes, shines like a gold nugget. Tamsen, Arab and Em McCleod now find themselves in Russian Alaska, where power, money and human life are the playthings of a displaced, decadent aristocracy in this lusty novel ripe with love, passion, spirit and adventure.

DAUGHTERS OF THE FAR ISLANDS
by Aola Vandergriff (81-929, $2.50)
Hawaii seems like Paradise to Tamsen and Arab — but it is not. Beneath the beauty, like the hot lava bubbling in the volcano's crater, trouble seethes in Paradise. The daughters are destined to be caught in the turmoil between Americans who want annexation of the islands and native Hawaiians who want to keep their country. And in their own family, danger looms... and threatens to erupt and engulf them all.

SISTERS OF SORROW
by Aola Vandergriff (89-999, $1.95)
Between twins a fine wire is strung, transmitting the vibrations of terror and the dangers of death... When Shannon and Shelly went south to claim their joint inheritance — an old plantation called Sorrow, they discovered the family secret. Madness and murder waited here for the Sisters of Sorrow!

WYNDSPELLE
by Aola Vandergriff (89-703, $1.95)
The year is 1720. A stranger steals a kiss from a beautiful servant girl, and suddenly — she is accused of being a witch! She must flee — there is no time to lose. But where would she go? Only one house would accept her — that she knew with terrifying certainty: the haunted grisly spectre of evil perched on a sheer cliff where nobody visited voluntarily... the house called WYNDSPELLE!

WYNDSPELLE'S CHILD
by Aola Vandergriff (89-781, $1.95)
Megan came to Wyndspelle, the House of Secret Sorrows, from far-off Scotland to care for a haunted, invalid child with no will to remember, to speak or to love. Whisperers said that the little girl was possessed, that she had set the fire that killed her mother. Others said it was her father who had done the deed. Yet, in this desolate manor where no flowers bloom, Megan finds love blossoming in her heart for the two the world condemns — for the child and for the tormented master of Wyndspelle.

ROMANCE...ADVENTURE... DANGER...

SKARRA
by Henry V. M. Richardson (89-126, $1.95)

Highland lord of a large and noble clan of Scotland, SKARRA is a soldier of fortune, an eloquent scholar and a fiery lover whose fierceness at battle and tenderness at love blaze a legend across 17th century Europe — and through the hearts of two very different women.

LADY OF SKARRA
by Henry V. M. Richardson (81-493, $2.50)

Tatti is THE LADY OF SKARRA and her tumultuous story takes her sailing the high seas, bound unwillingly for the colonies. Strapped to the mast riding out the hurricane's fury. Her beauty, her spirit, her tenderness sweep the granddaughter of SKARRA into adventure and love!

A PASSIONATE GIRL
by Thomas Fleming (81-654, $2.50)

The author of the enormously successful LIBERTY TAVERN is back with this gutsy and adventurous novel of a young woman fighting in the battle for Ireland's freedom and persecuted for her passionate love of a man.

LIBERTY TAVERN
by Thomas Fleming (82-367, $2.25)

A rich, full-blooded saga of the American Revolution and its scorching effect on the men and women of LIBERTY TAVERN who lived by their wits, their fists and their love for the country they were helping to conceive.

LILLIE
by David Butler (82-775, $2.25)

This novel, upon which the stunning television series of the same name is based, takes Lillie Langtry's story from her girlhood, through the glamor and the triumphs, the scandals and the tragedies, to 1902 and Edward VII's accession to the throne.

A FORBIDDEN YEARNING
by Ann Gabhart (82-879, $2.25)

As pioneers, they challenged nature. As lovers, they defied the world. But Sarah believed she would find more. The slim volume of poetry she had left behind promised love, and she longed for it!

ROMANCE...ADVENTURE... DANGER...

THIS TOWERING PASSION
by Valerie Sherwood (81-486, $2.50)
500 pages of sweet romance and savage adventure set against the violent tapestry of Cromwellian England, with a magnificent heroine whose beauty and ingenuity captivates every man who sees her, from the king of the land to the dashing young rakehell whose destiny is love!

THIS LOVING TORMENT
by Valerie Sherwood (82-649, $2.50)
Born in poverty in the aftermath of the Great London Fire, Charity Woodstock grew up to set the men of three continents ablaze with passion! The bestselling sensation of the year, boasting 1.3 million copies in print after just one month, to make it the fastest-selling historical romance in Warner Books history!

THESE GOLDEN PLEASURES
by Valerie Sherwood (82-416, $2.25)
From the stately mansions of the east to the freezing hell of the Klondike, beautiful Rosanne Rossiter went after what she wanted — and got it all! By the author of the phenomenally successful THIS LOVING TORMENT.

LOVE'S TENDER FURY
by Jennifer Wilde (82-635, $2.25)
The turbulent story of an English beauty — sold at auction like a slave — who scandalized the New World by enslaving her masters. She would conquer them all — only if she could subdue the hot unruly passions of the heart! The 2 Million Copy Bestseller that brought fame to the author of DARE TO LOVE.

DARE TO LOVE
by Jennifer Wilde (81-826, $2.50)
Who dared to love Elena Lopez? She was the Queen of desire and the slave of passion, traveling the world — London, Paris, San Francisco — and taking love where she found it! Elena Lopez — the tantalizing, beautiful moth — dancing out of the shadows, warmed, lured and consumed by the heart's devouring flame.

LILIANE
by Annabel Erwin (79-941, $1.95)
The bestselling romantic novel of a beautiful, vulnerable woman torn between two brothers, played against the colorful background of plantation life in Colonial America.

AURIELLE
by Annabel Erwin (91-126, $2.50)
The tempestuous new historical romance 4 million Annabel Erwin fans have been waiting for. Join AURIELLE, the scullery maid with the pride of a Queen as she escapes to America to make her dreams of nobility come true.

STEP INTO THE PASSIONATE 17th CENTURY WITH A MAN FOR ALL SEASONS, McTAGGART, LAIRD OF SKARRA!

SKARRA by Henry V. M. Richardson (89-126, $1.95)

SKARRA IS A WARRIOR — tall, powerful, fearless — killing seventeen Cossacks singlehanded on the snowy plains. SKARRA IS A TEACHER — inspiring the brawling, wenching students at the University of Dorpat to ponder the meaning of life. SKARRA IS A LEADER — rallying the fierce Scots to battle the English and making peace with dignity. But above all SKARRA IS A LOVER — wooing the beautiful blonde Geness, the love of his life, and winning the noblewoman Lydia, who helped fulfil his dreams. SKARRA is "the kind of historical fiction we've not seen the likes of since *Anthony Adverse* — and it's long overdue."—*Hartford Courant*

WARNER BOOKS
P.O. Box 690
New York, N.Y. 10019

Please send me the books I have selected.

Enclose check or money order only, no cash please. Plus 50¢ per order and 10¢ per copy to cover postage and handling. N.Y. State and California residents add applicable sales tax.

Please allow 4 weeks for delivery.

_____ Please send me your free mail order catalog

Name_____

Address_____

City_____

State_____Zip_____